THE THEORY OF THE SOFA

A NOVEL

JESS SHAPIRO

"Stay out of small Italian sports cars,

avoid a major drug habit,

and keep your overhead down.

Don't marry and have children until you are ready for that.

Render unto Caesar what is Caesar's, but no more.

And always remember the path back to the well.

This is not investment banking;

it's music."

James Taylor

to students at the
Tanglewood Music Center
August 1998

ISBN: 979-8-9906920-5-3 (Paperback)
ISBN: 979-8-9906920-6-0 (Hardcover)

Cover and book design: Erin Papa, The Turning Mill

Printed in the USA

Something Clever Publishing

JessShapiro.com

. . . . .

TWO THUGS ON A THREE-DAY TRIP

Day 1, 1972, Brooklyn NY to Darren NH

They had a reputation for getting in, getting it done, and getting out with minimal collateral damage, an outcome highly valued by the people doing the hiring. The difference this time was the location. They were warned repeatedly about the harsh climate and terrain. When they were in the car, they voiced to each other what they were unwilling to say in front of their superiors.

"Whadda' they think, we're from Miami Beach? We see snow every goddamn winter."

"Did you see the stuff in the back of the car? You'd think they were sendin' us to Alaska."

When they passed Prospect Park on their way out of Brooklyn this late March morning the stark, sharply outlined branches of winter were softened by fuzzy buds, and strips of color peeked through the ground from spring blooms. Despite the early hour the paths were crowded with what was, in 1972, a growing fad. Some of the joggers wore hats or gloves to ward off the early morning chill, but almost all sported brightly colored t-shirts and shorts. A winter storm was not on the thugs' radar.

After they reached Hartford the highway became hilly, and they noticed patches of snow in shaded areas along the roadside.

"Oh no, we better break out all that gear they packed for us."

"We could climb Mount fuckin' Everest in that shit and still be warm and cozy."

By the time they turned off the Mass Pike and headed toward New Hampshire the landscape was mostly white. Only south-facing slopes in the median had brown spots showing through. Though the skies were mostly blue, flurries occasionally rose out of nowhere and blew across the road. The snow didn't stick to the driving surface, though in a few spots swirly wisps hovered above the pavement before being scattered by their vehicle. Their comments became less mocking, more practical.

"This coulda' been a bitch of a drive after dark."

"Ya' think the four-wheel drive still works on this baby?"

The Jeep Wagoneer was used for illegal, or immoral, forays through the sands of Rockaway Beach, Sheepshead Bay, and the abandoned fields of Idlewild surrounding JFK Airport. They exchanged opinions on whether handling a skid would be the same in snow as it was in sand, hypothetical discussions with no sense of urgency. They were relaxed enough to take the thick white wrapping paper off two Genoa salami, provolone, and roasted red pepper subs, pop a couple of cans of Rheingold Beer, and split a cigar-sized reefer of Jamaican.

The snowbanks on the side of the road were now brilliant white and terraced, snowplows having pushed back the upper portion to make room for more. The reassuring drone of the wheels on the still dry pavement, the warm interior of the car, the beer, the dope, and their full stomachs created a very pleasant mood. This felt more like a weekend vacation in the Catskills than a business trip. They weren't going to start working until tomorrow anyway, and had a safe place arranged for tonight where they could relax, catch some college basketball scores, check in with the bookies. Plus, it wasn't like they had to prepare for some formidable foe. Their mark was a hippie kid, and all they needed to do was make sure the local yokel didn't make it to a hearing about a piece of land their bosses wanted to buy. The driving took some concentration but wasn't dangerous. Until they missed the exit for Darren and approached Franconia Notch.

They were in a white-out, a term neither in their vocabulary nor their experience. The late afternoon sun created a milky backlight to the opaque scene beyond the windshield. The passenger opened his door slightly so he could see the road below, just able to make out the line separating their lane from the shoulder. He shouted steering directions to the driver in a last-ditch effort to keep moving without going off the road.

"A little right, yeah, more right, okay good, now I think - shit, I can't see the line no more."

"Then how the fuck do you expect me - I see something! Is that a truck or a sign?"

Closing his door and looking ahead, the passenger could make out a vague rectangular shape. Then, as if turning the focus knob on binoculars, the white-out was over. Snow was still falling at a remarkable rate, but the exit sign was easily readable, Route 112, Lincoln.

"That's not our exit," he said.

"I don't give a shit. I'm gettin' off this fuckin' road. You call our contact and hope to hell he knows where we are. Wait, what's - '112 East Closed Ahead' - are you shittin' me?! I'm still gettin' off!" He swerved around the sawhorse with the "Road Closed" sign and spun uncontrollably before skidding sideways into a snowbank that stretched across the exit ramp. The driver took a deep breath, relaxed his white-knuckled grip on the steering wheel, and asked, "How could a piece of property in this goddamned place be valuable enough for them to send us here?"

"I don't know," answered the passenger, "but you saw who was at the meeting this morning. Whatever this is about, it goes all the way to the top." He hunched over his seat back and grabbed a leather case about the size of a large purse. It was a bag phone, a new piece of technology boaters could use to connect to land lines. It was especially popular with smugglers, allowing them to talk directly to their contacts on shore without marine operators overhearing their conversation. The case contained a phone similar in design to military phones, a pouch for batteries, and assorted short cables and accessories. He toggled the power on, opened a folded piece of paper with a series of numbers on it and punched the first series into the phone. When he got the correct number of beeps in response he punched in the next series, waited, then got the recognizable dial tone.

The driver got out and assessed the situation. When he got back his partner was holding the handset, offering only an occasional "Uh-huh." He signed off with, "We'll call back."

"What'd ya' find out?"

"We missed our exit a ways back, he knows exactly where we are, says the road's open to the west, just not the east. If we can get around the sawhorses, we can make a left, cross under the highway, then get back on heading south."

"My side's not bad. Isn't there a shovel in the back?"

"Yeah."

"Let's see if we can dig out and get back on the highway."

The two men went to work, each shoveling furiously for a few minutes and then passing the shovel. The driver trudged through the snow on one of his shoveling breaks, located the end of the ramp and the road, which as their contact said was recently plowed and open to the west.

"Hey," the passenger called, "I think the tires are clear."

"Okay. I think there's a chance we can get through."

Gently feathering the clutch and gas pedal, rocking forward and back a few inches at a time, the driver turned the car bit by bit until it was facing back up the ramp. When they made it to the road and back on the highway the passenger reconnected with their contact.

"We're out, headin' south. The roads suck, it's snowing like crazy, the meeting's gonna' be cancelled. We're headin' back to Brooklyn." Silence. "Are you there?"

"Yes. I wouldn't do that."

"Yeah, well, you're sittin' in a warm dry house. We're driving five fuckin' miles an hour through a goddamn fuckin' blizzard. We're soaked and freezing from shoveling like fuckin' zombies in our fuckin' loafers and slacks. It's gonna' be a week before any of you hicks can go anywhere anyway. We'll come back then." Another silence. "Hello? Did you hear me?

"It's not as bad here as it is where you are."

"It's not snowing there?"

"Oh yeah, it's snowing. But you were approaching the Notch, and the weather there is different than even just a few miles away. Route 112 East is the Kancamagus Highway, that road is *always* closed in the winter."

"It's fuckin' spring."

"I'd better check in and call you back. You've got a few more exits before you need to decide. Keep the bag phone out." The contact signed off, and the phone went silent.

The two men drove quietly through the gathering darkness, their eyes fixed on the two cones of snow-filled light from their headlights for about fifteen minutes before the phone rang and the passenger answered. "Hello?"

"How youse guys doin'?"

"Vinny!?" The driver's head snapped right, wide eyes meeting the passenger's, who nodded in astonished acknowledgement.

"Yeah," said Vinny. "Look, you gotta' stay at the safe house tonight. The contact says everything's gonna' happen according to schedule, they're used to this kinda' weather up there. He'll call you back in a minute with new directions, the roads'll be fine." The phone went dead.

"It's a go," the passenger reported. "We're gonna' get new directions from the contact."

"Can we still handle him like he's just a contact?"

"Ya' mean because he talked to Vinny?"

"If Vinny's in that means his dad Vito is in, and they're Catrones. We were told the Masciarellis were handling this."

"They're all part of the same family."

"But they don't always agree, especially the two dads. If something blows up between them, we could get caught in the crossfire."

"True. But Vinny wasn't at the meeting this morning. I say we stay cool, let the story come to us. I think we treat this guy like a regular go-between, nothing more."

"Did Vinny say where he was calling from?"

"No. Could be home, could be here, could be anywhere."

The contact called back with new directions. True to his prediction the highway conditions were better, with one cleared lane each way. There was even some traffic, moving slowly but steadily, and though it was now dark, and snow was still falling, it was gentler, the visibility much better. When they got off the highway the local roads were plowed and passable. They were amazed to see lights on in stores, people moving about the sidewalks.

"Jesus, it's just another blizzard to these assholes."

"If this happened at home the city would be shut down for a week." They followed their instructions, made a left onto Mountain Road. A half mile up on the right side of the road they saw a flash-light bobbing up and down.

"I guess that's us." They were now on high alert. The casual night before an easy assignment was no longer in play because of Vinny Catrone's call.

CHAPTER ONE

· · · · ·

LENNY

1969, Manhattan

We Baby Boomers had a clear plan laid out for us. Pick a career, get the appropriate degree, and follow the yellow brick road to fame and fortune. I was good with numbers and baseball, so I picked a college with a good baseball program and majored in business. My athletic prowess made me a high school star, but there were a hundred guys at the University of Michigan as good as I was, and a few dozen who were better. My boyhood dream of playing for the Mets was obviously not in the cards. Plan B was grad school and an MBA, but I found myself spending more and more time hanging with a crowd of long-haired friends who talked peace, love, and civil disobedience. They were also having tons of fun with the holy trinity: sex, drugs, and rock n' roll.

Another boyhood dream of mine was to fly F-14's over air shows with their wings seemingly inches apart. Wandering aimlessly around campus when I was a freshman I came across the ROTC building, walked in, and took the Marine Aviation Officer Candidates test. I must have done okay because Captain A. C. Tuckweiler of the U.S. Marine Corps recruited me for years.

"We're flyin' Phantoms now kid, and we'd sure love to have ya' piloting these suckers."

By then I was flying marijuana and LSD, the only word I heard was "suckers," and the only thing I knew for sure was I didn't want to be a dead one. Extraordinary experiences may await, but doesn't it take extraordinary people to do extraordinary things? What if I was just plain ordinary?

During my junior year the Vietnam "situation" intensified (politicians were falling all over themselves trying to avoid the word "war"), draft boards were tightening their screws, and I needed to make a decision. Was I really a hippie? Was sneaking away to Canada an option? Could I really do that? On the other hand, could I really be a soldier in the jungle?

I wasn't facing this conscription conundrum alone. I was never alone. I was a Baby Boomer, and the weight of our numbers was so great everything we did was average. Luckily my friends had it all figured out.

"Be a teacher!"

"Inner cities need teachers!"

"They get deferred because they're so vital!"

"If they're so vital, how come they get paid like shit?" Despite my sound economic reasoning, they were indeed granting occupational deferments to teachers. Being a teacher seemed a reach, but the alternatives were off the wall. I doubted my ability to be an authentic hippie or a Marine pilot, and draft-dodging hoaxes were lame. Stories about friends getting rejected after feigning flamboyant homosexuality abounded but were unsubstantiated, as were *faux* psychos like Arlo Guthrie's litterer from *Alice's Restaurant*.

So I crammed in enough education courses, but still lacked the semester of student teaching necessary for certification. I had to find some way to amass the required hours of relevant experience under the supervision of a certified teacher. My local reputation as a star athlete was still worth something, and I got an offer to be Assistant Head Counselor at a summer baseball camp. I convinced one desperate principal in the Bronx that teaching kids to keep their eyes on the ball and bend their knees was "relevant experience," and since the Head Counselor was a certified teacher, this could qualify as student teaching. Maybe.

"No problem," I assured my parents daily, "I've got it totally under control." They began each day over buttered bagels and coffee, reading aloud the numbers of Vietnam dead.

"You better stay on top of that principal in the South Bronx, so you won't have to risk your life in the jungle." It had clearly been a while since my parents had set foot in the South Bronx.

"Speaking of risking my life," I segued, "I ran into Vinny Catrone yesterday."

My parents froze when I said the name. My father, on his way out, stopped his hand halfway to the doorknob. About twenty seconds passed in silence, my father staring at me, my mother avoiding eye contact with both of us by scanning every corner of their apartment.

> *Our apartment? Was this my home? The past four years I lived at college, and summers I worked at hotels in the Catskill Mountains. Whenever I came home, I slept in the den/guest bedroom. A "For Sale" sign went up in front of our real home in Westchester exactly one day after I graduated from high school. Two weeks later I got a postcard at the hotel where I was working with our new address on Third Avenue in Manhattan. Did my parents like suburbia? I don't think so!*

1950s–60s, Westchester

Vinny Catrone was the kid no one was allowed to play with.

He was tough, mean, and a head taller than everyone else. Vinny was always in trouble and couldn't have cared less. His father was a police officer in our town, which confused parents but came in real handy for Vinny. In Little League he was a local legend, a huge 12-year-old who could sling the ball up there at 70 mph with pinpoint accuracy. The adults wondered why, if he had such great control, he hit so many batters. I knew why. It was the only time his green eyes lit up with joy.

Everybody else's favorite player was Mickey Mantle or Willie Mays or Jackie Robinson. Vinny's favorite was Sal Maglie, a New York Giants pitcher nicknamed The Barber because of his propensity to throw right under the batter's chin, giving him a "close shave."

I was the only one able to catch Vinny, who got suspended about halfway through each season for hitting too many batters. Deprived of the opportunity to cause pain with a baseball he resorted to schoolyard beatings inflicted randomly on the male population, a practice we accepted into our high school years. By the time Vinny was pitching for the varsity I was the shortstop except when it was Vinny's turn to pitch. Then I would strap on the "tools of ignorance,"

> *A baseball euphemism for catcher's gear, suggesting you had to be pretty dumb to cover yourself in padding and a mask on a hot summer day, squat uncomfortably behind home plate and let the pitcher fire hardballs at you while the hitter swung a bat in front of your eyes. It was a tongue-in-cheek compliment instead of an insult because baseball players know catchers are usually the smartest players on the team, which is why more ex-catchers manage baseball teams than ex-players of any other position.*

switch to my catcher's mitt with a sponge inside for added protection against Catrone's fastball, now clocked in the low 90s, and become the catcher. Then one day Vinny disappeared.

He wasn't in school; his locker was open and empty. Coach provided no information, but it was clear Vinny was gone. I felt the proverbial weight of the world lifted from my shoulders. The responsibility of catching Vinny gave me a headache. He was a time bomb, his olive skin turning crimson if he thought the umpire miscalled a pitch, and I would have to ask for time, trot to the mound and try to calm him down enough to continue. I packed up my catcher's gear (for the last time!) and started home. It was a beautiful day in early May, Vinny was out of my life, and the cherry on top of the whipped cream sundae was Rosalie Corio, appearing as I turned a corner. Rosalie lived in a development of identical split levels adjacent to ours. We never called ours a "development," because *our* developer was clever enough to alternate three different house styles to give the appearance of individuality, bolstering his transparent ruse with curvy streets and creative landscaping. This enabled him to charge twice what a comparable house in Rosalie's monotonous development would cost, and we residents of Harbour Lakes - no lake, no harbor with or without the King's "u", no water of any kind - were appropriately smug about our ability to pay the difference.

Rosalie Corio was the first girl in town to have tits. I'm not talking about small mounds hinting of things to come, I'm talking about TITS. She was teased mercilessly in fifth and sixth grade ("Ros-a-lie, Ros-a-lie, with the milk, fact-or-y") until she began hunching her shoulders forward in an effort to minimize her protrusions. She was more an object of ridicule than desire because fifth and sixth grade boys didn't know the difference. This all changed in seventh grade. Our town had a Junior/Senior High School, one building for seventh through twelfth graders. There were separate wings, but Rosalie's twin peaks bridged the gap.

The older boys were not into making fun, and Rosalie's posture changed markedly. Shoulders back, prideful smile, she'd saunter through the halls as if she knew things we didn't. I saw less and less of her, since I was in College Prep, she was in Business, and she rarely walked home anymore. By the time we bumped into each other that spring day her metamorphosis was complete.

She was an absolute knockout, a tiny nose between high, wide cheekbones, eyes that were kind of gray-green-blue. She was wearing lime green culottes that covered her hips but not her thighs. A white blouse with a scoop neck allowed a small bubble of breast to peek over the top. I felt pressure in my BVDs, considered reaching into my equipment bag for my jock and cup, ducking behind a garage, and putting them on to avoid embarrassing myself. We were friends once because we were the best athletes in our crowd, but that was before girls were allowed to participate in Little League, or any organized sport. The only way she could taste competition was to challenge us on the playground, and I was the only one who gave her a run for her money. Come to think of it, she was teased regularly back then too, for being a tomboy. Wow. I never realized how confusing all this must have been for her.

We walked home and chatted about baseball and the warm weather. The road to her development appeared, she smiled, waved, and walked away. I took a few steps toward my house so she wouldn't sense my eyes on her, then stopped and stared at the rhythmic lime-green clenching as it receded.

The morning routine during my high school years consisted of numerous fatherly visits to my room, each one escalating in increments of agitation until the final ultimatum to get up or else! That next morning, I was up and out the first time Dad opened my door. My plan was to leave for school early and walk slowly, maximizing the window of opportunity for another encounter with Rosalie. I also needed a few extra minutes of preparation so I could look my best without appearing to have tried. I slowed before each corner, looked ahead and behind so I could arrange a casual meeting, then raced to the next corner in case she had already passed. By the time I turned onto the street a block from the high school I was exhausted. I was also twenty minutes early, so none of my friends were in the parking lot ogling the seniors' GTO's and 409's. I needed to kill a few minutes to regroup and went into Ida's Deli. Ida sold bagels, lox, pickled herring in sour cream, chopped liver, just about every Jewish delicacy known to man. She also had a small candy counter. My goal was a Devil Dog and a You-Hoo, a popular chocolate water drink. Between me and Ida's door, however, was Vinny Catrone.

Vinny took the top half of my shirt into his huge left fist, lifted me off the ground, and pinned me against Ida's storefront window. His right hand jumped twice, rat-a-tatting my head against the window and sending blood and chips of teeth spilling into my mouth and down my chin.

"Stay away from Rosalie," hissed Catrone. A glimmer of awareness must have appeared in my glassy eyes, because he got angrier and rat-a-tatted me again. The back of my head was exploding in pain from repeated encounters with the plate glass, the front of my face was gushing blood, snot, and tears, and Vinny wasn't finished. A knee to the groin added vomit to my mess, and an uppercut right punctuated my eighteen Vinny-free hours of elation with blackness.

I didn't see Vinny again for six years, until the afternoon before I reminded my parents of his existence. I was leading my group of ten-year-old New York Yankee wannabes to the mess hall for lunch, when who should I see strolling toward us.

"Long time no see," he said. Not long enough for my stomach, which started doing the Ida's Deli Flip-Flop. Physically I appeared to be Vinny's equal now, though I wouldn't have given a plugged nickel for my chances in a fight. Catrone's high school wardrobe consisted of faded navy-blue Police Athletic League T-shirts, frayed chinos, and ratty black Converse Chuck Taylor All-Stars. He now sported a silky white dress shirt open at the collar, cuffs unbuttoned and folded back once, black slacks, and sockless black loafers that looked expensive. He seemed a lot older and a tad less volatile. "Dja' hear 'bout the lottery?"

What was he talking about? I had also matured, and one manifestation of my newfound wisdom was to not immediately say what popped into my mind, but rather examine it for any unwanted side effects. I let three seconds pass in silence. "No," I uttered, safely and wisely.

"Prob'ly in the papers today or tomorrow," Catrone's eyes left mine, flitted down and around as he talked, "about the draft. You should read it."

What was with the sidelong glances? Catrone never talked *to* you, he talked *at* you. "I will," I said. Safe and wise.

Vinny's eyes came back up to mine as he nodded toward my ten-year-olds. "Any players in your group?" There appeared to be a trace of a smile, though I didn't have anything in my Catrone file to compare it to.

"None like you." Oh shit. His green eyes flickered for a moment and the background headache was back, like it never left. There was an awkward silence.

"I gotta' get going," he said. "I left somethin' up at the camp office for you to look at."

Catrone strode back up the path toward the camp office and I led my charges to lunch. I was a total basket case the rest of the afternoon, searching in vain for a connection between Vinny, the camp, and me, with whom he had no contact for six years. I did learn you can count on ten-year-olds more than you might think. None got lost or injured despite minimal supervision from their counselor. When we had loaded the day campers onto their buses, I rushed into the office to confront the camp owner.

Mr. Bernstein was a repulsive-looking man. Short and pudgy, slicked back greasy silver hair, bad skin, thick glasses, the man had been whacked with the ugly stick. He had some connection with the Sisters of the Presentation of Mary, upon whose pristine grounds the baseball camp was permitted to function. He also had a connection with an ex-Yankee of little note, whose local roots and brief Major League career made him a partner in the camp, which bore his name. His picture in the iconic pinstripe uniform was everywhere, on the stationary, the signs, the brochures. None of us had ever seen him in person.

Everything coming from Mr. Bernstein was beautiful, as if in defiance of its origin. Intelligent, with a gentle sense of humor, he treated his staff like fellow humans. The camp itself was exquisite, as were all the communiques emanating from his office. Instructions to counselors, weekly newsletters to the parents, even brief memos to campers were all finely crafted works of art, always appropriate, never pedantic. He must have spent hours lovingly cultivating each missive about decorum in the mess hall. He certainly wouldn't want to spend too much time with Mrs. Bernstein, who was the reincarnation of the Wicked Witch of the West.

I blurted, "How do you know Vinny?"

"Vinny?" he replied, puzzlement replaced with recognition. "Ah, Vincenzo. He supplies our sports equipment. Does a fine job, fine job," nodding in agreement with himself. "His prices are low, deliveries on time. He's a salesman all right…aggressive, and efficient."

"That's the way he pitched."

"He played ball? Oh, that's right, he told me you two used to be teammates. He left something for you, in fact," groping through a pile of papers, then offering an envelope, which I grabbed and took to the parking lot.

I sat in my parent's car and stared at the envelope with my name on the front. A logo was in the upper left-hand corner, a bouncing basketball over the words "Team Sports, Inc." Inside was a self-congratulatory history of the company, a promise of bigger and better things to come, and an invitation to set up an interview to become part of the "Team Sports sports team." It was signed by Vincenzo Catrone III, President, Team Sports Inc. The Third? Could there really have been two other Vinnys?

There was a hand-written ballpoint P.S. by the president himself, and I could make out the faint ruled pencil lines enabling him to write straight across the paper. "If the lottery works out and you don't hafta' teach, we could use a business major. V.C."

This was the era when each Christmas we waited for the new

Sean Connery/James Bond flick, the number one TV show was *The Man from U.N.C.L.E.*, the sitcom hit *Get Smart* was its spoof with Don Adams as Agent Maxwell Smart, and the entire nation was wondering if the Mafia, Cubans, Russians, or the CIA killed JFK. The "personal" letter from Team Sports Inc. seemed big-brotherly, and George Orwell's prediction for 1984 was only fifteen years away.

Was Catrone watching me? How did he know where I worked, what I majored in, that I needed to be a teacher? Suddenly there was a loud rapping on the window, and I jumped and prepared to swallow the suicide pill hidden in my tie pin so I wouldn't spill state secrets to some evil torturer.

The evil torturer turned out to be one of the counselors. "You OK?" he asked.

"Yeah," I lied, "just waiting for the air conditioning to kick in." The car had been running for ten minutes. You could hang meat in the fucking thing by now.

I drove back to the city, checking my rear view mirror every few seconds, half expecting a black Mercedes to pull alongside, half chiding myself for my rampant paranoia. I got under control before I got home, which was good because the garage attendant hated me big time. My parents only used the car infrequently for weekend trips out of the city. Dad tipped the guy every time he walked past the entrance, though the clown did nothing to deserve one. When I was home, however, the poor guy had to actually work. His only silver lining was that he got to ogle braless babes and get stoned on secondhand smoke.

The newspapers were piled neatly on the magazine rack in the den (that's my room, remember?). Mom paged through the paper each day, tsk-tsk-ing at exorbitant prices and uncomfortable headlines. Dad read the Sports and the Arts sections. The front page generally went untouched, as they preferred getting their daily dose of reality from NBC's Today Show.

There it was, front page below the fold ("Oh, *that's* why we didn't see it!"), a story on the soon-to-be instituted draft lottery system. They were going to randomly assign a number between 1 and 365 to birth dates. Each draft board would take all of its 1-A's whose date of birth matched with number one, then those matching number two and so on until they drafted their quota for the month. If your DOB corresponded to a high number, you could be pretty sure your board would reach its annual quota without you. If your birthday matched a low number, you were screwed. The article listed several local draft boards and how high they might go. Mine was in Yonkers, a suburban town just north of New York City, with a probable between 250 and 300.

"Ve-e-ery interesting," as Arte Johnson said weekly on Laugh-in. The next morning, I dropped the "Vinny Catrone" bomb on my parents.

My father's hand retreated from the doorknob. He made his way slowly back into the kitchen and sat at the table, my mother right behind. I could see it all coming back to him, eyes clouding and shoulders sagging. He was outraged six years before when Vinny cleaned my clock outside Ida's. A professional man, his revenge would come through the courts, and he confidently sued for $100,000 in addition to medical expenses. My broken jaw had to be rewired, I had a major concussion resulting in the loss of feeling in my fingers that lasted a few months, and one of my testicles was black, blue, and larger than a tennis ball, possibly rendering me impotent. Dad thought my potential baseball career was seriously curtailed by Vinny's beating. I had to miss the rest of the season, had no feeling in my talented hands, and the hordes of college scouts he envisioned lusting after me might become disenchanted. And what about the big bucks Major Leaguers earned? Didn't Don Drysdale and Sandy Koufax just sign for the (coincidental?) sum of $100,000 each?

> *Dad vastly overrated my ability, and I was ambivalent about his enthusiasm. I reveled in the fact that I was really good at something cool like baseball, but hated the fact that he co-opted MY playing and made it part of HIS life.*

My father, typically a laid back, live-and-let-live type of guy, declared rather publicly that this time, by God, he was *not* going to get shortchanged. But the judge offered a more grounded appraisal of my earning power as a hardball hero, allowing $7,500 in doctors' bills, mostly orthodontic, and a cool five thou for damages. Dad was crushed and had some very bad days dealing with the insult added to the injury. The oft-repeated solace was that while Vinny was a loser headed nowhere, destined to roam our hometown streets a derelict, I was going off to college to become a leader. Wait until I told Dad that Vincenzo Catrone III spent the last six years building a sporting goods empire in the tri-state area.

Vinny started with one decommissioned patrol car he commandeered from his father's precinct. He drove around to schools showing gym teachers his samples and quoting low prices. By the time he made his mind-blowing appearance in front of me and my ten-year-olds he employed 45 people, had a fleet of twelve logo-bedecked vans, and made frequent trips to the Orient to check on his suppliers. To this day I have an ultra-sharp vision of the *tableaux,* Dad at our royal blue formica kitchen table with pink and yellow boomerangs that they brought with them from Westchester, reading the draft article with Mom standing dutifully behind him.

"So," Dad asked, "What does this mean?"

"It's totally out of my control." Yesterday I told them "I have it totally under control." These were my two favorite comments and Dad automatically disbelieved both.

"Why was Catrone at camp?"

"He sells the camp equipment, saw me and asked what I was doing about the draft, told me 'bout the story in the paper." The scene in front of me kept switching between reality and *Leave It to Beaver*, and I blinked hard a couple of times to control the zoom lens in my brain. I really had to stop those 4 am bowls of Afghani hash. Mom walked over, hung her arms around my neck.

"You okay, sweetie?" She thought I was blinking back tears. Ruthless, I played it up.

"Yeah," adding in eye rubbing, "it sure would help if I got a high lottery number."

Dad wasn't buying it. "Low or high," he said, pushing back from the table, resuming the man of action role, striding towards the door, "you're calling that South Bronx principal today or the car is no longer at your disposal. Let's go Dear, or we'll *all* be late."

My mother kissed my cheek, gave me one of those "I'm on your side, but you know your father" looks, and followed him to the elevator.

CHAPTER TWO

STEVEN

1953, Brooklyn, NY

Steven Masciarelli's favorite toy was a small plastic deep-sea diver with a helmeted head screwed onto a hollow body that could be filled with baking soda. Placed carefully on the surface of the bath water with body plumb, the diver sank slowly to the bottom in an upright position. There was no room for error. The slightest lean of the toy, tremor in the release, or current in the tub and the hapless diver would spin unevenly and land prone. But on those occasions when the diver remained upright, he would bob on the bottom then magically rise to the surface. If Steven maintained his zen-like still-ness, the diver might return to the bottom and resurface once or even twice, something Steven attempted daily, sometimes for hours.

It was not Steven's only odd habit. If he brushed his elbow against a wall, he would spin around to brush his other elbow before continuing on his way. If he touched one finger with his thumb, he would immediately touch the other three then all four on the other hand with his other thumb. He *never* stepped on cracks in the side-walk. But it was the plastic diver that haunted Steven's childhood. Too young to distinguish cause and effect, he blamed the toy for his peculiar behavior.

It all began when Steven and his friends would stampede through the tunnel under his apartment building to the backyard. Steven held his breath pretending to be under water, attempting to make a round trip without breathing, then two and then three, trying to break the diver's record. When he innocently confided his game, they all joined for a bit but quickly tired of it and moved on. Only Steven persisted.

This was the beginning of Steven's separation from the crowd. His friends would make up games, rules changing whimsically as circumstances dictated. Steven hated that.

"We said there was no running allowed."

"So what, Masciarelli? We changed our minds."

"But we all agreed. That's not fair!"

"Too bad. If you don't like it, don't play."

There was pushback whenever he suggested games. Nobody else was willing to test themselves against his unattainable goals. Anybody could get through the tunnel once without taking a breath, some maybe twice. But to Steven it was all about what happened after he had gone as far as his little lungs and legs could take him, after he had beaten everybody else and they had all gone on to some other game. Then Steven could go against himself, tap into the resolve that allowed him to stay motionless in the tub while the toy diver went up and down.

Steven's self-image also went up and down as he progressed through elementary school. He wanted to be just another kid, free to goof around and mess up and giggle, free from the demands of the plastic diver. He recognized the look in his friends' eyes as he was talking, knew he was pushing them away by the very words he was speaking. Yet he couldn't stop himself. The frustration was so overwhelming at times that he would shake, tiny fists clenched by his side, tears burning his eyes.

On the other hand, Steven thought the self-discipline learned from watching the plastic diver made him special, enabling his academic and athletic successes. If only he could use the diver's example when needed and ignore it when it wasn't! As he advanced through grade school he strived to fit in more with his peers. It took all his concentration, but he was committed and succeeded to some degree. His success accelerated during fourth grade when the arrival of organized youth sports gave Steven a venue in which to excel. He was no longer the weirdo who measured and timed every physical endeavor. Now he was measured and timed by adults with whistles and clipboards, and Steven's results were off the charts. He brought his competitive nature out of the closet and used it to drive his popularity.

Plus, he decided to be funny. Steven spent the first half of fourth grade in awe of Barry Longo. Hardly a day would go by without the teacher assigning a classmate to escort Barry to the principal's office because of some outrageous remark. Fearless, Barry would exit with a mugging expression cast backward to elicit one more laugh from his classmates. Steven would silently chip in with additional quips, but he would never voice them out loud. Instead, he would re-run Barry's behavior silently to himself, inserting his own dry, sophisticated humor as if he was the straight man, the Dean Martin to Barry's Jerry Lewis. On one occasion, he got so absorbed in his replay of Barry's antics, so taken with his snappy *repartee*, that he laughed out loud.

"Care to share the joke, Mr. Masciarelli?" A trace of a smirk teased the teacher's lips. She milked her rhetorical question longer than necessary. Steven felt his classmate's stares, his eyes starting to moisten. He decided to take the leap.

"I was thinking it would have been really funny if I told Longo he was holding his book upside down." The classroom erupted in laughter!

"Is that so? Miss Bernstein, would you please escort our *really funny* Mr. Masciarelli to the principal's office?" Over time, it became easier and easier for Steven to voice his *bon mots*. His popularity soared. The only one who maintained disapproval was Gail Bernstein, the oh-so-perfect designated driver who guided him to the principal's office with increasing frequency.

Barry Longo and Steven were similar in many ways. Both were tall and lean, exuding a vibrant, shining health that hummed with athletic energy. The youngest of the six Longo children, Barry was often left on his own with no parental supervision or guidance. He looked like Dion DiMucci of Dion and the Belmonts, was the dream boyfriend of every girl in school, and every parent's nightmare. Steven had northern Italian bloodlines, and features that were fairer and finer. He was an only child with more parental supervision than he could bear. Not only were Mom and Pop involved in every aspect of his life, he also had to deal with relatives who were somehow endowed with parental powers. On the rare occasions Mom wasn't in their apartment when he arrived home from school, he'd drop his books and race outside to join his friends, only to hear Aunt Angela yell from her apartment window, "Where do you think you're going in your school clothes? Get back inside this instant and change!" If Steven was hanging on the corner with a crowd that included some alleged troublemakers, Uncle Eddie would magically appear.

"Yo, Steverino, how 'bout helpin' your favorite uncle unload somma' that crap that just came into the store." Uncle Eddie's grocery store never got "somma' that crap" when Steven was with his usual buddies. Add a few older kids from a different neighborhood and suddenly the store had an immaculate delivery.

Steven not only excelled in school, but realized he could do so with minimal effort. He devoted most of his mental energy to figuring out his peers and their place in his world. How were they different from him? What was their family's daily routine like? How about those mysterious neighborhoods that were beyond his allowable boundaries?

Brooklyn in the late forties and fifties was all about neighborhoods. The suburbs had not yet sucked the middle class out of town, families were starting to have spare money, the proud hangover from the war still lingering. Steven's sincere interest in his friends' lives made him likable, helping his effort to be one of the guys. His increasing dominance on the athletic fields, along with his engaging sense of humor, made him someone others began to admire. A steady stream of friends started dropping by after school to ask Steven to play stickball, basketball, two-hand touch. Steven learned how to control his competitiveness when playing against his neighborhood cronies, then really turn it on when the rivals were from another neighborhood. He got the concept of territory in the streets.

There were setbacks. In fifth grade the science curriculum included biology, and his teacher's favorite gimmick was to present an experiment or formula in such a way that the obvious answer was incorrect.

"If you cross an "Aa" with an "aa" (writing on the board in overly large letters), what are the chances you'll get an offspring with "A" behavior?" There were 3 lower case a's on the board and only one upper case A so he was sure someone would say "One out of four."

But Steven got it immediately and shouted out, "Fifty-fifty."

"Why do you think that?"

"The one with two small a's *has* to give a small a, and it's fifty-fifty for the one with each. Since the capital A trumps the small a, the odds for the A behavior will be even-money. It's like the x-y thing with boys and girls."

His teacher was pissed. That was the exact explanation he was going to awe the class with after someone shouted out the wrong answer. If he saw the slightest smirk on Steven's face, he might have lost it. But Steven had his own problems. He had inadvertently used gambling slang (even-money, trump, odds,) that should not have been part of a fifth-grader's vocabulary. Steven was familiar with those terms because they were used by the adults in his family, though he was told never to use them outside the home. It was common knowledge that the mafia ran gambling activities. The importance of never providing an opening for suspicion was hammered home daily. But he had slipped. He sat motionless, staring at the blackboard, holding his breath, hoping the teacher didn't notice. He could feel his eyes start to burn, his hands clench under the desk. The moment passed, and Steven's rising popularity got another boost. Showing up a pompous teacher without getting in trouble will do that. But what Steven learned from the incident was, despite all his efforts, the little trembling boy with clenched fists fighting back tears was still too close to the surface.

By the time Steven was in junior high, where students from a number of elementary schools mixed for the first time, his neighborhood friends were known as "Steven's Crowd." At first, Steven resisted being a leader. He had succeeded to a large degree at acting like one of the guys, and imagined he would get so adept at the charade he wouldn't have to act anymore. He would simply *become* one of the guys. But the increase in his popularity brought new pressures, and he wondered if his internal struggles would ever end. Then came the seismic shock of the four-letter words, "girl" and "gang."

The arrival of the teenage girl was a game changer. When did familiar words start having hidden meanings? Why did all the boys, including himself, change their behavior around them? How could they be a silly waste of time as well as the most important thing in the world?

Gangs were part of city life, though in junior high they were mostly just ethnic groups. The borders separating different neighborhoods were mimicked in the school halls, the outside recreation areas, and the cafeteria. The Puerto Ricans ate lunch at the same tables every day. If there weren't enough seats the late comers ate standing up. They never crossed the line and sat with, say, the Jewish kids.

These unwritten rules applied to everyone except the inimitable Barry Longo. Technically aligned with the Italians ("Steven's Crowd"), he was just as likely to be hanging in the schoolyard with the black kids, shooting hoops and singing *a cappella*. If you came across a group of Puerto Ricans in the hallway, you might find Longo playfully engaged as they teased each other's fashion choices.

But the shocker came one day in the cafeteria. Steven was sitting where he always sat, in the center of his group. Longo was in his usual spot on the perimeter, with easy access to all other traffic. Gail Bernstein walked by, and Steven saw Barry grab her arm. Steven expected an altercation, maybe even a slap. He thought he might have to intervene so no teachers would get involved. But Gail continued her journey through "international waters" toward the Jewish area, and Steven was shocked to see a big smile on her face and an over-the-shoulder wave to Barry.

This made no sense to Steven. It was one thing for Longo to mess around with the guys or flirt with girls, but this was the ultra-aloof Gail Bernstein that used to escort them disdainfully to the principal's office. While Longo was one of the few who could challenge

Steven athletically, Gail was one of the few who could do so academically. They occasionally worked together on projects, were frequently opposing "captains" on superficial competitions that were the newest trend in the quest to make learning fun. They enjoyed the competitions in a polite, civil spirit. While Steven was becoming increasingly aware of her physical attraction and looked forward to these opportunities, he received no indication the feeling was mutual. He wasn't even sure what that indication would look like.

A few couples were starting to appear in junior high. What that meant was not exactly clear, neither to observers nor participants. Steven was unsure of the rules of this new game, though both he and Barry Longo were described as "cute" by the girls. He and Barry Longo were also the best in what mattered most to young teens.

Steven's voice was changing, physical signs of puberty were showing up. Conversations among boys were increasingly about girls, filled with wildly incorrect information. Steven was excited but fearful about this new arena, wanting to join in while hoping things could return to the way they used to be. He stayed on the sidelines and observed, ignoring rumors he was liked by this or that girl.

The exchange he just witnessed sent his head spinning. What could Gail Bernstein and Barry Longo possibly have in common? It couldn't be anything academic. He and Gail resided on a different planet than Barry Longo in that regard. Yet Barry was way ahead of Steven socially, totally at ease with both sexes and all ethnic groups. Steven realized Barry Longo was a problem he might have to address. What if there *had* been an incident between Longo and Gail? What could Steven have done? Barry was part of his crowd, Steven was the acknowledged leader, yet Longo played by his own rules. If Steven tried to interest Gail in a romantic relationship, would Longo be his competition? How could he possibly win *that* battle? And if he lost Gail to Longo, what would happen to his *de facto* number one spot in the crowd? Would it become "Barry's Crowd?" Steven realized, now that it might be challenged, how much he liked being the leader of his crowd. And how much he liked Gail Bernstein.

Steven became a leader among his friends because of his athletic skills, sense of humor, intelligence, and relentless determination (the deep-sea diver!). The Barry/Gail incident in the cafeteria challenged his leadership. Physically equal, Steven had Barry beat in intelligence, at least the type measured in the classroom, but Longo was way ahead in personality.

He recalled a similar situation with the same antagonist in fourth grade. At that time, he had closed the gap by going public with his sense of humor and athletic prowess. Maybe it could be that simple. Looking around the cafeteria he realized many of the kids seated in his area were in that fourth-grade classroom when he made his break-out move. The time had come for another one. His gaze expanded to the entire cafeteria. He was respected by all, but was he liked by any? He needed an all-out blitz of dazzling likability.

Steven spent the second half of that day formulating a strategy. Being funny in fourth grade had required a terrifying leap of faith, and appearing less weird was still a fulltime job. Steven had been successful at both, but becoming more likable in junior high was trickier. In addition to a well thought out strategy, conquering the empire he contemplated in the junior high cafeteria would require time and patience. He had to play it right, or he would be dethroned. He rejected the "all-out blitz of dazzling likability" in favor of "Rome wasn't built in a day."

The junior high sports teams consisted of all ethnic groups, giving him plenty of chances to interact socially with the complete spectrum. But Steven couldn't just start sitting with the black kids at lunch or hanging with the Jews or Puerto Ricans in the halls and schoolyard. He needed to add subterfuge to his quick wit and athletic reputation. His first foray was an elaborate scheme involving those strengths, attempted just days after the Barry/Gail incident.

Base running drills were a daily regimen for the baseball team. Their squad had a lot of speed, and aggressive base running was a big part of their strategy. Longo and Steven were among a handful of players who could really fly, but James Washington, a black member of the track team who also had decent baseball skills, was far and away the fastest. For a few days in a row at practice Steven was purposely clumsy when trying to steal a base and was picked off a few times by the pitcher. He finally got what he wanted, a calling out from Coach.

"Christ, Masciarelli, you look like you're carryin' a goddamn piano!"

After practice Steven caught up with James Washington's group of black friends and started grumbling. As hoped, Washington offered some advice.

"Your first step has to be a crossover step." Steven watched while James demonstrated, pretending to lead off first base with his eyes on the pitcher. He smoothly pivoted on his right foot while crossing his left leg over his right leg. He was now facing the imaginary second base. "See?"

"But doesn't that make it too easy to get picked off?"

"No, 'cause look," said James, reassuming his ready stance, "you don't hafta' be leaning toward second base. You're balanced. If the pitcher makes his move towards the plate, you're off to second. If he tries to pick you off you crossover the other way," this time pivoting on his left foot and crossing his right leg over his left, leaving him facing back towards first base. "Your first step is always a crossover step. Try it."

Steven knew all about the crossover step. He had purposely discarded it a few days ago, and while Coach noticed the results, only Washington noticed the reason. Steven now haltingly went through it as if for the first time. His audience was not impressed.

"Yeah, well...that's the right idea, but you need to work on it some."

Steven smiled broadly. "Like teachin' a white boy how to bugaloo?"

Laughs all around, Steven getting a friendly poke and advice from the nearest. "You got any Little Eva at home? You need to practice The Locomotion."

"I'm on it. 'C'mon baby, do-o-o the locomotion'...wait'll you guys see me tomorrow!"

They continued laughing and kidding and dancing their way to the street. Five black kids and Steven, who apparently could still be funny and mix with any crowd. Just like Barry Longo.

The next day after practice Coach called the team together. "Okay, good practice today. Tomorrow's our first game. We gotta' take the extra base every chance we get. You think you can steal a base, take it. Masciarelli, much better today—that's what we need from you." Steven looked over to where Washington was standing and gave a subtle thumbs up sign, which Coach noticed. "You help him out, Washington?"

Steven piped up. "He sure did, Coach."

"Yeah, Coach, I taught him how to bugaloo."

"I don't know what the friggin' 'bungalow' is, but if it ain't illegal, keep doin' it. Let's go shower up and we'll give out the game uniforms."

The whole team cracked up at Coach's malapropism. The story of yesterday's demonstration, accompanied by altered lyrics of Little Eva's Locomotion, was passed around on the way back to the locker room. Giving out game uniforms, always a big moment, added to the camaraderie to which Masciarelli and Washington were now linked. When Coach asked for suggestions about who should be named captain, those two names were shouted out, and Coach instinctively made the right choice. "Great. We'll have co-captains."

Steven knew the reason his first attempt went so well was the foil he picked. James was a star on the track team, an intelligent, thoughtful student of the technique of running who was happy to help Steven, and one of the leaders of the Black contingent. He couldn't rush into his next attempt with just anybody or he'd make a fool of himself. But baseball was only one sport, and a junior high team at that. These same boys would be together five more years. Same with basketball. Same with football, and that squad had about 30 players. There was plenty of time to pick and choose the right people and the right moments. For now, he was co-captain with a black kid on a multiethnic team, which was a pretty good start. Rome wasn't built in a day.

The egalitarian spirit of athletics was not shared in social activities. High school dances were battlegrounds, and junior high dances were basic training. The boy-girl thing was too explosive for Steven to take on. He needed to learn more about the social scene and enter carefully, one girl at a time. At least now he knew who that girl was going to be.

Just as Steven spent his time at school and in the streets trying to piece together how his peers' lives might differ from his own, he did the same with the bits and pieces of the adult world increasingly coming his way at home. Steven was now privy to conversations that used to be tabled with a terse "we'll talk about this later" or spoken in Italian. He loved to ask Mom or Pop about their childhood and their parents, especially Mom's side of the family, which was filled with interesting characters. Pop's side was not.

Uncle Stefano, Pop's twin brother and only sibling, was killed in the war. Steven only saw Grandpa Masciarelli when Pop took him to the nursing home, obligatory visits replete with sadness and bad smells. Grandpa would grunt a gruff sound and point a shaky finger at a photograph of a woman in a fur coat and elaborate hat, to whom Steven had to say "Hello, Grandma." Another sound, less gruff, ended the conversation. Steven was six when he died and felt only relief that the visits were no longer necessary. Neither Masciarelli grandparent ever really existed in his life, the man no more animated than the sepia woman.

But Mom's family was prominently woven into his early childhood. Mom's half-sister Aunt Angela, Uncle Eddie, and their five children lived in the apartment house next door, and Mom's younger brother Vito, his wife Louise, and Steven's cousin Vinny lived in nearby Westchester. Steven's images of Mom's parents, *Nonno* and *Nonna* Catrone, were vivid, especially *Nonno*.

Toward the end of the migration of Italians to America that began in the late 1800s *Nonno* Catrone, his wife and baby girl (Aunt Angela) left their produce and shipping empire in Sicily and boarded the transatlantic boat. His wife became ill immediately and did not survive the crossing. Faced with the prospect of starting life in the new world as a single father with an infant girl, *Nonno* put grief aside and moved quickly. His traveling companions included family members hoping to ride his coattails to success. He convinced a second cousin to marry him with the ship's captain officiating. What was initially a business arrangement became a lifelong bond. They had two children together, Steven's mom Christina and her brother Vito, and witnessed the birth of numerous grandchildren.

The hastily arranged shipboard marriage brought together different parts of the same family in a confusing array of half-siblings, aunts and uncles by marriage, stepparents and in-laws that blurred traditional family lines. This was not uncommon among immigrants in those days. The uprooting of families who were together in the same town forever required jarring adjustments with drastic consequences. The survivors made it because of their indomitable will and ability to adjust quickly, which is also how they survived after arriving in America.

Steven was aware of the mafia. He watched Robert Stack and his "Untouchables" every week on TV, saw movies about Al Capone and the Valentine's Day massacre. He would root for the good guys like everyone else but was ambivalent about the gangsters. He sensed the resemblance between fictitious villains and real-life family members and hoped there would be a way to punish them just a little so they wouldn't have to go to jail or die in the end. The film that really hit home was *On the Waterfront*.

Every Saturday afternoon, Steven would join his older cousins and walk to the local movie theater for the double-feature matinee. *On the Waterfront* was based on a series of newspaper articles exposing widespread corruption, extortion, and racketeering on the waterfronts of Manhattan and Brooklyn. The series, entitled "Crime on the Waterfront" won the 1949 Pulitzer Prize for Local Reporting. A lot of tension permeated the family in Steven's early childhood, and it resurfaced when the movie came out in the mid-fifties. Steven's questioning of his parents about their family history became focused and incessant.

"Why do you and Aunt Angela have different moms?"

"Aunt Angela's mom died when she was a baby, then *Nonno* Catrone married *Nonna*, and they had me and Vito."

"How come we call Aunt Angela and Uncle Eddie 'aunt' and 'uncle,' but Vito and Louise are just Vito and Louise?"

Whenever Vito's name was mentioned, Pop would extricate himself from the conversation and, in short order, from the room. Mom would pretend not to notice.

"Vito and Louise are more casual."

"Why are they always late for family dinners?"

"They live farther away."

Sometimes, after Pop left the room, Steven pressed for more information.

"How come Vito and Louise moved away from Brooklyn?"

"Vito was recommended for a good job in Westchester."

"Isn't he just a cop like he was here?"

"He is a *policeman*," Mom pointedly editing out "just" and correcting his slang, "like he was here, but he thought Westchester would be a better place to raise Vinny."

"Better than Brooklyn?!?"

"I guess so."

"Is Louise ever gonna' come back?"

"Have you finished all your homework?"

That meant the conversation was over. Steven was sure there was more to his uncle and cousin's relocation and his aunt's disappearance. He remembered a steady stream of men coming to his apartment to speak privately to *Nonno* Catrone, Pop, and Uncle Eddie, followed immediately by Vito, Louise, and Vinny moving to a house in Westchester. Then Louise had a private audience with Mom and Aunt Angela, kissed Steven goodbye and never returned. Steven thought something major had occurred which somehow affected him and made it his mission to find out what it was.

. . . . .

CHAPTER THREE

JEAN

1963, Darren NH

Darren, New Hampshire sits on the fringe of the White Mountain National Forest, its only claim to fame the high school ski team. They won the state championship last year thanks to Jean Giroux, who swept first place in all three disciplines: Downhill, Ski Jumping, and Cross Country. With a win in today's Cross Country race Jean, now a senior, would do it again and Darren High School would have back-to-back state championships.

There was enough distance between Jean and his nearest competitor for him to feel like he was alone in the woods. The only sound was the rhythmic swoosh of his waxed skis. He was in a zone, his body functioning aerobically and powerfully, the mantra of left-leg-flex-and-push, right...ski...glide, right-leg-flex-and-push, left...ski...glide, propelling him through this long uphill stretch. Eyes focused on the trail ahead, he could see the spot where it leveled off.

From there the trail turned right and started winding downhill through the forest before opening into a clearing at the finish line. Jean neared the crest, not at all concerned about the final descent. It was steep with sharp turns and could be tricky in a close race, but he had a comfortable cushion thanks to his superior strength and technique on the uphills. He mentally rehearsed his smooth glide to the finish line, deciding to raise both hands and poles briefly in understated celebration of his remarkable accomplishment.

At the top of the rise, before the right turn down, there was a spot where the trees thinned and a racer could briefly see the finish line below. Jean risked a quick look, expecting a scene with which he was quite familiar. There would be a group of parent volunteers at the finish line with the coaches from each high school, standing around a table with trophies on it. A little way behind them would be parents, maybe a sibling or girlfriend, mittened hands stuffed under armpits, booted feet stomping and steamed breath rising, waiting to cheer the student athletes as they finished. Jean's dad would be in that group even though he was a volunteer and allowed to be in the group closer to the finish line. Armand Giroux preferred to share the moment with Jean's mom.

But Jean's quick glance showed everyone bunched into one group, all pointing up the hill. His parents weren't there, and the Police Chief's car was, with lights flashing. Now heading downhill, wracking his brain for an explanation, Jean realized he was going too fast. There was a sharp turn left and down, and he wasn't going to make it. His speed and confusion conspired against him, and he tumbled to the snow. He scrambled up quickly, collected his strewn poles, looked urgently back up the hill. Still no sign of anyone, though now he could hear them. Jean pushed off down the trail.

"Focus, focus, focus," he kept saying to himself, but he couldn't. Where could his parents be? He could feel his sweat turning icy and damp. He started shivering, felt lightheaded and wobbly. He went down again, regained his balance, teetering on the edge of disaster but hellbent on getting to the bottom as fast as he could. As he crossed the finish line Jean saw Chief Wiggins walking toward him, his expression a mixture of pain and compassion, and went limp. The chief grabbed him under his arm and helped him into the cruiser. Jean only heard fragments of the Chief's explanation, "heart attack," "ambulance," "your mom's gonna' meet you at the hospital." Then the waiting room, he and Mom staring at the double doors, eagerly waiting for a doctor sporting a relieved smile. Then the doctor, no smile, and Jean clutching Mom as she collapsed to her knees.

The morning after the race, Jean, his mother, brother, and sister gathered in the kitchen of their farmhouse. No one knew what to do or say. Jean shuffled to the refrigerator to get some orange juice. He felt like he was walking through waist high water with waders on. Mom was leaning her elbows on the counter for support, looking nowhere. Jean closed the refrigerator without taking anything out. His younger siblings cast nervous glances between Mom and Jean, desperate for some direction from one of them. If Aunt Yvette hadn't shown up toting a picnic basket, they might have stayed that way all day.

"I brought breakfast. I know you're not hungry, but you gotta' eat something." Aunt Yvette was an emergency room nurse, familiar with unexpected death and shocked survivors. She and Uncle Guy lived next door, so she was also familiar with her sister-in-law's kitchen. She scurried efficiently from cabinet to table, laying out dishes, napkins, and silverware while the onlookers watched helplessly. "I'm gonna' join you, if you don't mind. I took today off. You'll be getting well-wishers dropping by, and I thought you'd need some help." Aunt Yvette paused, smiled warmly, and added, "Looks like I was right."

The four Girouxs remained motionless. Aunt Yvette gently nudged the two youngest to the table. Then, turning to Jean and Mom, said, "Sit." She wisely served small portions, half a biscuit, a strip of bacon, one spoon of scrambled eggs, juice glasses half filled. "When we're finished you two should get dressed," she said, pointing at Jean and his mom. "I'll help the kids, then clean up here."

Jean was struck by Aunt Yvette's inference that he was no longer one of the kids. He grappled with that expectation as he and his family followed her instructions, and the doorbell began to ring. He forced himself to greet people and thank them, sat with Uncle Guy, Mom, and their Pastor as they discussed funeral arrangements and composed the obituary.

"You need to suggest where people should make donations," the Pastor said.

Mom did not agree. "I'm not asking people for money."

"It's not like that, Bonnie," explained Uncle Guy. "They're gonna' want to do something and will need suggestions, or else you'll be swimmin' in tuna casseroles." Uncle Guy was rewarded with a weak smile.

Friday became Saturday and Saturday became Sunday without any difference. Nighttime was the hardest for Jean, the questions going through his mind nonstop. How did he enter this strange new world? What was he supposed to do now? What was expected of him? The Guidance Counselor stopped by Sunday to ask if she could make an announcement at the funeral. She wanted to hold a memorial for Armand at the Winter Sports Awards Night in two weeks, honoring him for all he did to support youth athletics. The family nodded their approval. Monday was the funeral and Jean got through it in a daze. Tuesday, Mom went back to work and the kids returned to school. Family and friends continued to come by with food for the family, hugs for Mom, and advice for Jean.

"Stay strong, son, you're the man of the house now." Already taller than Dad was, his thick black beard requiring a daily shave, he looked like he could play the part. Jean nodded every time and said "I know" but the only thing he really knew was he had no idea what that meant. The most surprising thing was the physical pain. He had heard people described as "hurting" when they lost a loved one, but imagined it was a figure of speech. It was not. Jean's body actually ached, dull and constant, like he had fallen off a ladder. The next hurdle would be the upcoming awards night. It would be the family's first public appearance without Dad, and he would need to be strong.

When Jean came home from school one evening, Mom was sitting alone at the kitchen table. She looked up and said, "Hi, sweetie. Aunt Yvette took the kids to the playground for a few hours."

"Okay."

She held his gaze for a moment, shook her head slowly then looked down at the table. "I wish I could just stay at work. I hate coming home. Oh, I'm sorry, Jean, I didn't mean..."

"It's okay Mom, I know what you meant. I feel that way too. The school routine is comforting, and this place is just, it's so,...Dad."

Jean's family lived in the farmhouse where Dad and Uncle Guy were born and raised, sitting on over 40 acres of rolling hay fields and forest. Jean's grandfather was a Canadian machinist from Sherbrooke who was often asked to travel south to install and maintain machines in New Hampshire's textile mills. After he and his bride honeymooned at a hotel in New Hampshire's lakes region, she began accompanying him regularly. When the opportunity arose, they sold their land in Canada, purchased the farmhouse, and started a family. Jean's grandmother was stricken with influenza during one of the epidemics in the 1930's and died when Dad and Uncle Guy were in their teens. Jean's grandfather filled the gaping hole with passion for his property, which he instilled in his two sons, and eventually Jean.

When Uncle Guy married Aunt Yvette, they subdivided out a five-acre parcel, and the two brothers and their father built a small cape-style house for the newlyweds. By the time Mom and Dad got married, Jean's grandfather was no longer able to live on his own, so Jean's parents moved into the farmhouse and cared for him until his death when Jean was twelve. Dad's fingerprints were all over the house, figuratively and literally. Jean's bedroom used to be Dad's.

It wasn't just the house, it was the entire homestead. Everywhere Jean looked he saw his father. When Jean's cousins started arriving, the two brothers added dormers to Uncle Guy's attic for more bedrooms, and eventually a small wing for Aunt Yvette's younger brother Lee.

The barn, technically on Uncle Guy's parcel, was shared by both families. There was never an issue over which of the two families actually owned the barn or the large vegetable garden, whether each family did their fair share of work tending the animals, ate more or less of the eggs or bacon. Whichever house the cousins happened to be in at dinner time was where they ate. There were the usual childhood tiffs over toys and privileges, almost all solved without interference from the adults. The children thought this was normal because it was all they knew. They had no idea how much effort the four adults put into this lifestyle to make it seem natural, effort that was driven by respect for each other and the homestead they inherited.

Jean's Dad and Uncle Guy owned Giroux Brothers Plumbing. Jean was unaware of the different visions each had about their company until he started working for them during school vacations. Uncle Guy wanted to do industrial projects instead of the small home repairs that were the bread and butter of their business. Dad thought they were doing just fine. The subject never came up while the families did chores around the homestead, fished for trout in the streams and lakes, sledded or skied at the local mountains. But it was a daily issue at work.

Uncle Guy might say, "Yvette says they're adding on to the hospital. She could probably get us an in with the contractor."

Dad would answer, "Then we'd hafta' borrow money for new equipment and hire full-time help. What would we do when the job was done, fire the men and sell the equipment?"

"No, we'd get another industrial job."

Jean got used to the bickering, accepted it as background music like the big band and swing coming from the radio. The arguments each brother used to support his position were left unresolved, a dangling "Yeah, but..." signaling a return to pipe cutting or soldering.

The underlying disagreement caused Jean to reassess his impression of the two men. Before he was accepted into the work environment he viewed them as one item, "the two dads." Uncle Guy was the oldest, fastidious about his appearance, even managing to look well dressed in Carhartt overalls. Armand's frame was similar, a bit shorter, and recently included a beer belly hanging over his belt.

Uncle Guy's clothes, his cars, his predilection for eating in restaurants, all gave the impression he had more income than Armand, which was not the case. The brothers were equal partners. It was dawning on Jean that the disagreement over the business plan was because Uncle Guy wanted more than the trappings of the well-to-do. He wanted to be rich, or at least richer, while Dad couldn't care less.

Ironically it was Jean who began tilting the scale toward expansion. An excellent helper, he anticipated what was needed and assisted with some of the planning. He was excited about Uncle Guy's ideas and the prospect for larger, more complicated jobs. He took mechanical drawing classes, devoured his monthly editions of Popular Mechanics, and got involved in shop renovation projects at school. Jean talked his dad and uncle into building a refreshment stand and bathrooms at the high school athletic fields by designing them himself. Built by volunteers with money from the All-Sports Booster Club, the stand included a commercial kitchen and hook-ups to town water and sewer. This past summer, the Giroux brothers took a few jobs they normally would have passed on because of Jean's proclivity for design and knowledge of newer techniques and materials. Jean included his designs and photos of the finished projects with his applications to a half dozen universities. Along with his good grades, athletic prowess, and community service he was accepted at every one. He chose Rensselaer Polytechnic Institute.

Troy, New York was about as far away as China in Jean's mind, which made the choice exciting. RPI's reputation was dauntingly elite, which made the choice challenging. Growing up in Darren, New Hampshire, surrounded by family and familiarity, excitement and a challenge were exactly what Jean wanted.

But that dream was gone. Cruising through his final semester with Dad at every baseball game, gone. Working with Dad and Uncle Guy until his departure in August, gone. His plan to go to RPI and become the engineer behind the expansion of the family business, gone. Mom needed help with his younger siblings and the homestead. Uncle Guy had to hire someone full time. Wasn't it Jean's responsibility to be that full-time employee?

These were the thoughts rattling around Jean's mind during the athletic awards ceremony. He looked around the gymnasium as if seeing it for the first time. The pushed-back bleachers on each side of the gym were old and worn, had to be yanked with all your strength and a few well-placed kicks to be pulled out for basketball games. The folding chairs on the floor were mismatched, the stage had a pile of frayed tumbling mats on one side and janitor's equipment on the other. The pennants commemorating championship seasons looked thrown together by students in their Home Ec. class. Was this what he had felt so proud about? What a charade! How childish! How meaningless.

And then there was Marie. Jean and Marie were the town's number one high school sweethearts, but their relationship started way before that. Marie was halfway through first grade before her classmates heard her say anything. She spent her free time alone, drawing with pencil and crayons. Jean, who also liked to draw, often watched from a safe distance, and one day was transfixed by what he saw. Marie put her pencil point down near the lower left corner of her paper and, without stopping or lifting the pencil off the paper drew a slope up, the outline of a tree, level ground, the outline of a house with a chimney, more ground sloping down, and the outline of a dog whose tail ended at the lower right side of the paper.

Jean thought the pencil must be magic. "Can I try it?" Marie reluctantly handed him the pencil. "How do you make it work?"

"I just draw."

Jean didn't believe her. "Oh yeah? Draw a truck."

Marie turned the paper over, picked up another pencil and started a flat road, then the rear tires and bed of a pickup, rising to form the cab, then down to hood and finally the road. Jean stared at her in amazement and Marie giggled, her first interaction with her first friend. Their parents thought it was adorable and joked about being in-laws someday. By the time Jean and Marie were in high school and going steady they were babysitting Jean's younger brother and sister as practice for when they would have their own.

Marie was not at the championship race, her absence the result of a tiff that had been recurring since October 23rd. That was the day after President Kennedy's televised announcement revealed reconnaissance photos of Soviet missiles with nuclear warheads in Cuba. He demanded their removal, imposed a blockade of Navy warships to prevent delivery of more, and declared to the world that any attempt to run the blockade would be seen as an act of war.

Historians would deem the next three days as the closest the world has ever come to all out nuclear war. Angst spread across the nation. Less than two decades removed from Hiroshima and Nagasaki and one from the Korean conflict, the Greatest Generation didn't want to be tested again. Their children's school days were regularly interrupted by Civil Defense air raid drills during which they knelt under their desks or against a wall in the hallway for protection from nuclear debris. Just three years prior, the movie *On the Beach* graphically drove home how futile those measures would be against the force of the exploded atom.

After the missile crisis was diffused, life seemed to return to normal, but the global brinksmanship took a toll and national uneasiness lingered. The young lovers were experiencing their own brinksmanship, and flare-ups were more frequent. After a few years of post-pubescent petting Jean and Marie had reached a critical stage. Marie spent a few weekday evenings and most weekends in the barn, ostensibly helping Jean get his pickup ready for the road. Dad had paid $100 for the truck as a 16th birthday present for Jean at the annual State Highway Department auction of vehicles no longer worth maintaining.

"If you can get it to pass inspection, it's yours."

While Jean was adept at all things mechanical, Marie's "help" slowed the progress. Not that Jean minded the distraction. In fact, the evening after President Kennedy's disclosure of the crisis, after a day of hysterical rumors in school, Jean suggested that since the world may end tomorrow they might as well do the one thing they had yet to experience.

This was, in 1962, an outrageous suggestion, especially to a devout Catholic. *The Adventures of Ozzie and Harriet* and *Leave it to Beaver* were the weekly visitors to everyone's homes, exemplifying the ideal American family. Mary Tyler Moore and her TV husband had to be in widely separated twin beds when shown on *The Dick Van Dyke Show*.

While the hypocrisy inherent in these shows was being challenged by a new wave of entertainers, they were mostly confined to independent venues in larger cities. Small town America was still living in the 1950's. Young men could "sow their wild oats," while young women were expected to "save themselves" for the first night of their honeymoon. Exactly how these mutually exclusive expectations might be met was never really spelled out, other than vague references to women of questionable moral fiber.

Marie was definitely *not* one of those, and neither, really, was Jean. They were in the pickup bed and things were progressing to new and exciting areas when Marie whispered, "We've got to stop" and Jean offered his opinion on how to deal with the missile crisis. Marie pushed back and sat up. Jean didn't expect her to say, "Okay, sure, let's do it," and was ready to support his position.

"I mean, there's a very real chance we're all gonna' be gone tomorrow. Do you really wanna' die without ever experiencing the act of making love?"

"I don't give two shits what's gonna' happen or not happen if we die," Marie countered. "I care about what's gonna' happen if we *live*.

I'm way more worried about you leaving for RPI next September and blowing me off than I am about some missiles in Cuba."

Jean was stunned. He never gave any thought to how a long-distance relationship would work. He assumed things would always be the same between them and seeing each other would simply require a drive across Vermont instead of a drive across town. The silence grew, hung, and was punctuated by Marie.

"Right. I'm going home." Marie pushed off the truck, straightened her clothes and left. There had been disagreements before, puppy love spats they always got through. This, however, opened a whole new can of worms. It brought into focus the impending end of life as they knew it, and not just because of nuclear holocaust or sexual intercourse. The familiar routines, clear expectations, and attainable goals of high school were about to be replaced by the adult world. Marie planned to stay local after graduation, get a job, attend Plymouth State College part time with the goal of becoming an art teacher. There was already chatter among her friends about sharing an apartment. How did Jean fit into that picture?

Jean opted for an early acceptance request at RPI. He visited with his family during the summer, then again during the Columbus Day weekend with his mom after his request was granted. It was overwhelming, but Jean's goal was excitement and challenge, and he was either confident enough or oblivious enough to welcome both. The real eye-opening experience, to Marie's point, had been the girls. Many were from the New York metropolitan area, and they were a different species. Talk about excitement and challenge. Jean's plan to visit RPI again over spring break was the cause of the most recent flap, and the reason Marie avoided the race.

She was seated on Jean's left at the awards night, squeezing his hand during the touching speeches about Dad. On his right was Mom, and next to her his brother and sister. Was this his new family unit? Was Marie ready for this? Was Mom? Was he?

Jean had taken the "man of the house" advice to heart. He decided he was not going to RPI. Plymouth State College was an adjunct campus of the University of New Hampshire, and he could take the generic freshman requirements there. He would work for Uncle Guy full time and take courses at night, similar to Marie's plan. They would get married, though Jean had yet to inform Marie, and enter the adult world together. He would be "the man" of two houses.

Jean's proclamation of his ascension into adulthood, made just an hour before the awards night, did not go over well with Bonnie Gir-oux. And neither did Jean's decision not to play baseball in the spring and instead request daily early dismissal, enabling him to work more hours with Uncle Guy right away. And neither did his unilateral decision not to bother going to the awards night. Mom went ballistic. Eyes flashing, cheeks flushed, she let him have it.

"I'm still in charge here, young man. You are going tonight; the *entire family* is going tonight. We'll pay our respects and thank every-one else who does, too. How do you think Dad would feel about you not playing baseball? About tossing RPI into the trashcan?" Jean's head was spinning. Her words stung, but he also felt a tinge of relief. Mom was coming back, taking charge. Tears dampened her cheeks as she continued, softening her tone as she noticed his eyes welling up also. "Look, sweetie, you and I have to work together here. How about we table this discussion 'til the weekend? We'll go over these topics together. I promise to listen with an open mind, but you need to promise not to take any action until after we talk."

They hugged, and it was the first time either had witnessed the other cry since the hospital hallway. Jean hoarsely whispered, "I promise, Mom."

. . . . .

CHAPTER FOUR

LENNY

1969, Manhattan

Unaware until Vinny's tip sharpened my focus, I was amazed at the abundance of lottery talk. Draft dodging schemes were revisited for those receiving a low number, while bliss was envisioned for those who might draw a number in the 300s. Much of the discussion concerned the gray area numbers, 250-300.

I believe numbers from the government are always exaggerated to counteract the expected skepticism from the public. This coincides nicely with the Theory of the No-Win Spiral, the initial entry on my self-help list of Rules to Live a Better Life which I began in high school.

The NWS Theory states as one increasingly exaggerates the magnitude of a situation ("This is the tenth time I've come into your room to wake you up, it's quarter past nine, you've already missed first and second period, goddammmit!!!!!"), the recipient becomes more doubtful of the veracity of the claim ("Aw, the veins in Dad's neck aren't standing out, he's not purple and bug-eyed, I've prob'ly got a couple more warnings before I *really* have to get up."). To which the response is a further exaggerated claim, followed by deeper disbelief. Thus begins a spiral of ever-increasing distance between the two parties. The better alternative is to state the facts simply and truthfully.

"It's 7:14. What time do you need to leave?"

"Um, uh, 7:30."

"That leaves 16 minutes to shower, brush your teeth, get dressed, and pack your book bag. How can I help?"

My birth date corresponded to number 283. Do I push the South Bronx principal so I can get an occupational deferment, or do I have enough confidence in my NWS Theory to enter the lottery? There were two problems with the latter course of action. First, casualties were regularly shipped back to the States in body bags for closed coffin services because their remains resembled pasta in tomato sauce. Second, the draft boards had to supply fresh new bodies on a monthly basis. The first month the lottery was in effect our draft board went up to number 26 to fill its quota. I would have to sweat it out for an entire year, watching the red line in the poster board thermometer creep up toward 283.

Nevertheless, I decided to gamble on the NWS Theory. Dad was purple and bug-eyed, neck veins standing out. Our relationship was strained at that time in our lives because he knew little about the real me, I even less about the real him. We were flat characters in a bad movie, no flesh, no flash. Only our differences were obvious, only our shortcomings mattered.

So, I cast my fate with Vinny. The uneasy urgency which permeated my actions and inactions during the early part of the summer disappeared. I made, for better or worse, a decision concerning the rest of my life. Even my relationship with Dad settled into *detente*. I was looking for an apartment and a car, which took up whatever time my camp job and social life didn't. Mom and Dad had developed their own lifestyle during the four kidless college years, and my return home on a full-time basis clearly threw a wrench into their routine. As we bumped into each other less frequently, our confrontations decreased exponentially.

The camp job became easier as well, thanks to Vinny. I learned an important lesson while I was temporarily insane after his surprise visit. The more responsibility I gave my ten-year-olds the better they liked it, the better they behaved, and the easier my job became. Sounds like the makings of another Rule to Live a Better Life. I decided to see how much responsibility I could give them, which increased my opportunities to hang out with Sheila Siegel.

The Women's Lib Movement was spilling over into the sports world, and females were shooting down male bastions left and right. Little League caved early on, but that was baseball. In high school and college, females played softball and Mr. Bernstein, ever on the cutting edge, added girls' softball to his baseball camp. His program was revolutionary, and Girl's Head Counselor Sheila Siegel was softball's Che Guevara.

Slim, boyish, not pretty piece by piece, Sheila nonetheless exuded something that made her the object of every male's desire. In an era of outrageous behavior, she was the queen of outrage. Her dad was the orthodontist who repaired Vinny's damage. Her mom volunteered for B'nai B'rith, was president of the sisterhood at the temple, and had dinner on the table each night at 6:00 sharp, 5:30 on Fridays to allow time for the *B'ruchas* and the *Shabbas* candles. Sheila was editor of the school paper, superstar of the drama club, and lettered in three sports. Just another ho-hum Jewish overachiever.

While her 1947 year of birth placed her squarely in the Baby Boomer generation, her three older brothers were all born *before* World War Two. The youngest was eight years older than Sheila, the oldest a full fifteen years her senior. Sheila's father was born on a train as it rattled his family away from the *pogroms* in Russia on the way to Odessa and America. Blessed with considerable intellect and a social conscience to match, he got caught up in the union movement in the thirties, shed blood in the battle for workers' rights, and associated with members of America's Communist Party. Sheila Siegel, the baby girl treated more like a granddaughter, arrived on the scene with her fist raised in defiance.

Sheila ran with a wild crowd, a group of aspiring actors, writers, singers, dancers, and artists of all shapes and sizes who lived in Soho. She was picked up after camp each day by Carl, a huge Jimi Hendrix clone on a Triumph Motorcycle. She'd hop onto the bike in her white camp t-shirt and navy-blue shorts, squash those cute little breasts against the back of Carl's leather silver-studded open vest, hands on his bare chest. All the male counselors popped immediate woodies, readjusted, and drove home alone with their fantasies.

Sheila thought I had RP. A clever gimmick of hers was to initialize phrases,

> *A bunch of us would pull into an empty parking lot three hours before a concert, she'd point to a spot immediately and say, "FIFO." We'd take the spot even though the rest of the lot was still empty, then trudge toward the far away stage trying to decipher her code until she said, "First In, First Out." For some reason, probably chemically induced, we would explode into knee-buckling fits of laughter. It worked in reverse also. Some guy would walk into a diner with an oversized cowboy hat, one of us would remark, "Whoa, look at that big fucking hat," and Sheila would go, "Hmm, a BFH." We would laugh so hard we spit food and drink all over the table, soda pouring out our noses, and be told to leave.*

and in my case, the initials stood for "Radical Potential" which, according to her, I suppressed because I was too concerned with societal conventions to actually *become* a radical. She made it her mission to goad me into outlandish acts, which I went along with because I assumed she had enough propriety to stop short of public humiliation. I was wrong.

Meanwhile, Vinny showed up regularly to fill me in on my upcoming duties, which were to begin as soon as camp ended in mid-August. I was doing adult things, apartment hunting, buying business clothes, planning travel routes, buying a used car. I was also getting thrown out of diners for causing a scene and spitting my food all over the table. The dichotomy of my life was in full bloom, Catrone the personification of one side, Sheila Siegel the other. The importance of keeping them separate was driven home one afternoon about a week before camp ended. I gave my boys the privilege of drawing the baselines and batters' boxes without my supervision. This allowed me to meander over to Sheila's group, which was engaged in base running drills. She put an assistant counselor in charge, grabbed my hand and told me she needed help with an idea. We walked to an area of statuary, Madonna with child, Jesus and disciples, Mary by the manger.

"I want a juxtaposition of sanctity and perversity," she explained, dropping her backpack and extracting a camera, "like, you mooning next to Mary's face, or, uh, laying your cock in Jesus' hands." A casual request made while fiddling with the camera, just your basic walk in the woods with good old Sheil. I looked around, and though somewhat screened from view, we were far from secluded.

"Here?"

"This is where the statues are."

"No way! You're nuts."

"It's *your* nuts I'm interested in," a subtle change in tone, an easy slide into flirtation, "and I'm willing to pay for what I want." She came close and turned on the heat. "You lay your cock in Jesus' upturned hands, and I'll lick it 'til it leaks," the last five words husky, throaty, sexy beyond belief.

She reached for the waistband of my University of Michigan Athletic Department shorts, slid her fingers under my BVDs at the same time, and worked them both down together. Then she quickly straightened up and looked over my shoulder. I pulled up my shorts clumsily as I turned and faced Vinny.

"We gotta' talk," speaking to me, looking at her.

My shorts were roughly in the correct place, underwear balled up half in and half out, face flushed. Sheila exited stage left, stopping to pick up her backpack. Facing away from us, she bent stiff-legged in those skimpy camp shorts, a view both of us appreciated. It gave me a couple of seconds to collect my thoughts and my underwear. "What's up?"

"Those two favors you asked me for," his eyes on Sheila's turn, wave, and departure, "I gotta' problem with one of 'em."

When I agreed to join "the Team Sports sports team" I had two conditions. I didn't consider them favors, but apparently Catrone did. Camp ended on Friday, and he wanted me to start on Monday. But a bunch of us had tickets to a music festival in the Catskills (Three Days of Peace and Music, August 15, 16 and 17, 1969). I figured I'd need a day or two to recuperate and wanted to start on Wednesday. The other sticking point was my hair.

"What's the problem?"

"Hair's gotta go," said Catrone.

I thought I came off as rather middle-of-the-road, but to Catrone

I was a hairy hippy. When he showed me his employee handbook, he specifically noted the section on representing the image of the company. I had my principals, was not about to sell out for the almighty buck. But standing there with one hand in my pants I figured one out of two wasn't bad.

"And I can start Wednesday?"

"Yeah."

"Deal."

It was a long day. Up early and off to work, Vinny, Sheila, and my johnson hobnobbing with Jesus, sealing the deal on my job with Team Sports, Inc., then looking for a place to live. Later that night I was in the warehouse loft in Soho where Sheila and assorted friends lived. We were passing around a bong hose as Sheila and I regaled everyone with our apartment hunting adventure. She had decided we would be young newlyweds looking for our first place together, and continually squeezed my hand, called me honey, and gazed lovingly into my eyes. It was a very convincing Donna Reed, and the potential landlady sucked it up, inviting us to sit and have a cup. She was a talker with no one to talk to, and we found out more than we needed to know about the apartment, the neighborhood, and her ex-husband.

"Son of a bitch wanted me to move to Scottsdale, Arizona. Can ya' believe it? We flew all the way out there, and it was a goddamn desert! 'It's right outside Phoenix,' he says. Phoenix! Now there's a one-horse town if I ever saw one."

Her name was Beverly McClary, and her house was in Mueller, near where I grew up. Sprinkled throughout Westchester were a handful of towns that hadn't changed. Like boulders in a stream, the suburban flood flowed around them for one reason or another, and they remained islands of antiquity in a sea of split levels. Mueller was such a town, and her house shared Church Street with the church, a three-story wood frame apartment house, a fire station, and a Ma-and-Pa convenience store. Affluence was diverted along with the developers, and the rent for what used to be a mother-in-law apartment ("Son of a bitch went without me. At least he took his goddamn mother with him.") was reasonable. But Sheila Siegel was never reasonable.

"You should buy the whole fuckin' house!" Back in my parent's Oldsmobile, goodbye Donna Reed, we hardly knew ye. Sheila "grokked the vibrations" that Mrs. McClary was dying to go to Scottsdale and join the son-of-a-bitch husband and goddamn mother-in-law but couldn't admit she made a mistake. "Make her an offer and she'll be desert bound before the ink's dry."

So, we were passing around the idea along with the hash hose, and it was playing to good reviews. Think the hash had anything to do with that?

"A country retreat, like, an Ashram or something."

"A commune!"

"Is there a backyard?"

"We can have a garden, grow all natural foods."

"We can grow dope!"

I could tell I was among true artists and hippies because not one question or suggestion had anything to do with money. But the former business major was all over it. I knew it was advantageous economically because I paid attention during my amortization class and knew mortgages were a cheap way to use other people's money. The concepts of equity, tax allowances, and inflation vs. real estate values made sense to me, and the realization that I could use this esoteric knowledge to my advantage in the real world got my adrenaline pumping. I guess I wasn't a hippie. Or maybe I was. Or maybe I wasn't.

Four years ago, just before I left for Ann Arbor, my dad and I sat on the balcony of their new apartment and he waxed poetic about how his investment in our Harbour Lakes house paid off. He explained how wise he had been to bite off the larger mortgage payments and spend the next twenty-five years busting his behind until it was all his. We were sipping Chivas Regal. The drinking age in New York in those days was eighteen, and the shared scotch was an invitation to become a peer, to join him in conversations about "man stuff." I soaked it all in, the heightened awareness, the city at our feet, high finance. It was heady stuff, I was included, and I remembered every word.

The house could also be a social windfall. A sociogram began to sprout that summer, and each spoke brought something with it to support the rim. Sheila and her *artistes* were outrageous city people, already finished with the latest craze, at the heart of every revolutionary idea. Sheila's roommate at The New School, her best friend Bobbi, was married to William, who was a few years older, had marched in Selma, witnessed blood spilt close-up in the battle for civil rights, and envisioned a new world order. Bobbi was into the green revolution, back to the land and respect for mother earth. Carl, he of the Triumph motorcycle, was one of the aforementioned *artistes* sharing the Soho loft.

A few local counselors from camp, already a group when I showed up, hung out with us, as did some of my high school friends. That left me, unsure of my commitment to anything and not very adventuresome despite Sheila's prodding. What was my contribution? I could say I brought the different segments together, that I was the hub, but common sense told me I was the hub only because I drew the wheel.

Mrs. McLary's house, however, could be the hub, the cool place to hang. I had the money for a down payment, which ironically came from the Catrone family's settlement of our lawsuit. My toned-down appearance - my hair would grow back little by little so Vinny wouldn't notice, like Grecian Formula for Men - would help with the bank officers. The mortgage payments would be less than rent, even when I figured in maintenance, taxes, and insurance, which I did. Remember, I was a business major and anal-retentive. Now I had to sell the idea to the trustee of the fund.

"Makes some sense, I guess," underwhelmed my father, "but not if you're drafted."

I considered explaining The Theory of The No-Win Spiral and how it applied to government propaganda, but that was a part of my life I didn't share. "It'll take a month or two to get a lawyer and arrange financing with a bank, right?"

"At least."

"Well, in a few months we'll know more about the draft board's quota. We could make it a contingency of the sale. I could rent the apartment in the meantime, so if I get drafted she'd just hafta' rent it to someone else."

"Is the house for sale?"

"Not really. Sheila talked to the owner for a while and thinks she wants to sell."

"Sheila?"

Mom chimed in, "That's Ivan's daughter."

"Ivan Siegel? That's *his* little girl who comes here half naked?" Just the underneath half, Dad. "Figures. Ivan always had trouble deciding where to draw the line." They were both leaders in the American Dental Association, Dad agreeing with Ivan in principle most of the time, but always taking the more conventional, practical side to Dr. Siegel's idealism. Dad's favorite quote was "Idealism increases in direct proportion to one's distance from the problem." Their last disagreement concerned recognition of Red China by the U.N., a hot topic in the dental profession because of their use of acupuncture as an anesthetic.

"We're redoing the apartment," offered my mother, "you could take most of the furniture," nodding toward the royal blue formica kitchen table with pink and yellow boomerangs as an example. "I mean either way, either for an apartment *or* a house." Mom never climbed down from her traditional perch on the fence of every issue. "Whatever you boys decide."

"It makes sense on paper," Dad said, "but you don't have a snowball's chance in hell of it all working out."

I took that as a "Yes."

Sheila took a bus uptown each morning to my apartment, where I met her as I pulled out of our garage under the baleful glare of the garage attendant.

As soon as she was in the car Sheila asked, "What'd your dad say?"

"I think he'll go for it."

"How much we got?"

"I don't know," I knew to the exact penny, "it's been invested in a trust fund for six years, some of it I can get and some I can't."

"Pull in here!" I jerked the car toward the curb at a NO PARK-ING BUS STOP sign. "I'll just be a sec."

Sheila hopped out, ran past the people waiting for the uptown bus, fished some change from the ever-present backpack, and ducked into a phone booth. I kept my eyes on the rear-view mirror, specifically a bus a few blocks back waiting at a red light. This could get ugly. The potential bus riders were scowling at me, eyes going back and forth between me and the solid wall of traffic now advancing uptown, swept along by the timed green lights on Second Avenue. The bus was riding the wave like The Big Kahuna, the people were jostling for position, not sure how many would have to wait for the next bus, whether my illegally parked car was part of the equation. Sheila emerged from the phone booth and started hustling back, sized up the situation and slowed to a seductive stroll, beaming at the crowd, ignoring the wheezing of the air brakes and the blaring horns, timing her farewell middle finger salute and jumping in as I screeched away from the curb milliseconds in front of the bus and four lanes of honking yellow taxis.

New Yorkers get criticized for our attitude, but people just don't understand what happens when you squeeze ten million people onto an island about the size of a rural township that accommodates less than 10,000. Everything's a battle. It was 7:05 am when I victoriously took my place at the head of the rushing traffic. Good morning and have a nice day.

"I'll drop you at camp," Sheila informed me, "and head back to Mrs. McLary's house. I just told Bernstein I had a female problem and couldn't get in 'til lunch."

"You're goin' there by yourself?"

"I've got a plan," reclining her seat, closing her eyes, shutting me out. As I pulled into The Sisters of the Presentation of Mary she yawned, stretched, graced me with a smile, and slid over to the driver's seat. I watched her make an illegal U-turn, bounce over the curb, and head off in the wrong direction. I began rehearsing the story I would tell my parents about their damaged car, realizing with a sinking feeling she probably didn't have a driver's license.

My ten-year-olds did not want to be at camp anymore, and neither did I. We learned all we were going to learn, finished our inter-camp competition earlier in the week with a tough defeat. The remaining days of camp were anticlimactic and loosely planned. I was trying to come up with enough activities to keep the boys from killing each other before camp ended, but by lunch time I was losing. Sheila returned, car intact, bummed expression on her face.

"Do you have $30,000?"

"No."

"That's what I thought. Here." She tossed me the keys and hulked off toward the girls' section of the mess hall. I was stunned. Did she think that in order to buy a $30,000 house you had to actually have 30,000 dollar bills in your hand? Was it possible she could be so smart and be a total ignoramus when it came to finances, an idiot savant in reverse? Did this mean the sale price was $30,000? I had almost $10,000, and there was no real estate agent involved. The mortgage payments would be well under $200 a month. Sheila was paying that much for what amounted to a garage with a galley kitchen and a bunch of mattresses on the floor.

"Hey, wait, this is good news!"

She flipped me the bird without turning around or slowing.

All through lunch I kept standing and trying to get Sheila's attention, to no avail. My slick methods of manipulating ten-year-olds had deteriorated to unheeded threats of violent mutilation if they didn't stop hitting each other with their hot dog rolls. It was one of those clammy August soot baths New York City is famous for, and the temperature inside the mess hall had to be near 125 degrees.

After lunch we trooped to Rosary Hall, an ancient brownstone building with a few tiny windows way up high, to rehearse for the awards banquet which closed out the camp season. There was absolutely no air in the building. As far as I could tell it was designed to forewarn potential sinners what hell hath in store, an impression amplified by my boys, who had smuggled in bread sticks and sugar cubes which they used as bats and balls in a blatantly disrespectful game of pitch and hit. The program director droned on, my clothes were plastered to my body, the boys were making a scene. My perfect summer job was now a nightmare, but my spirits could not be dampened. The house was do-able!

The stage-struck director gave us a preview of his full speech, *bon mots* included. Even Mr. Bernstein was frazzled, trying to signal the fool to cut it short, eyeing the exit. But I had my mantra. The house was do-able, the house was do-able. The program director finally relinquished center stage, and we mercifully left the building alive. All campers were instructed to change into bathing suits and report to The Pond, a four-acre lake with the typical white square lollipop pier, for free swim. This gave me the opportunity to confront Sheila face to face.

"Look, this can work."

"Oh yeah, how?" I was encouraged by how much she wanted the house to happen, reading into it the possibility of something special between us. Besides, I had tolerated enough heat and attitude already today.

"Stop being a flaming asshole for two seconds and I'll tell you how. First *you* tell *me* what happened with Mrs. McLary."

Taken aback by my uncharacteristic aggressiveness, Sheila stared at me, then related her experience. She told Mrs. McLary her husband - that would be me - didn't want the apartment because it was too small. But she had fallen in love with the house, loved what Mrs. McLary did with the decor, it would be a perfect place to raise kids, and clinched it by tearfully spilling the beans ("I haven't even told my husband yet!") that she was pregnant. Now it was my turn to be taken aback. Even *pretend* fatherhood was tough to swallow.

"And she bought it?"

"Hook, line and sinker," distracted from her attitude by her acting success. "Seems her creepy husband keeps calling and asking her to sell the house and join him and dear old mom. She wants $30,000. That blew my mind totally, but I stayed in character, told her we'd call her later. Where can we get that much money?"

"The bank." Now she was not only skeptical, she was pissed. Bank was a four-letter word, the epitome of the establishment, evil enemy of liberated souls, the reason those wonderful experimental theaters closed down. I had kept my mind off the torture at Rosary Hall by composing my explanation of amortization, simplifying without condescending, my ulterior motive being to impress Sheila with my wisdom. I plowed through it, looked expectantly at Sheila, and realized I was the only one taken with the functional elegance of my words. She was looking at me with the same icy expression she laid upon Vinny during our fellatio interruptus.

"You're un-fucking believable. Why doncha' just borrow the bucks from that pig you're gonna' work for? The two of you'll prob'ly get along fine. I'm calling Carl for a ride home."

As far as Sheila was concerned being conversant in the language of Corporate America was not an asset, it was damnation. Consorting with a bank was repulsive, and suggesting it made me their agent. Vinny and I were the same, a pair of assholes belonging to some prehistoric generation. As William Bendix used to say every week, "What a revoltin' development."

Me and Vinny? I had been locked in a circular discussion with myself recently, trying to figure out who I was. But what about Vincenzo Catrone III? Where did he fit? There was no clue in Vinny's clothing. I never knew if he owned one Police Athletic League T-shirt or a dozen, one pair of chinos or five. The same could be said for the current white dress shirts and black slacks. Even his hair was nondescript. Afros were in. Somewhere ahead of me on the highway, Sheila's hot little body was hugging Carl who sported one the size of a basketball. But Catrone *always* had dark curly hair. Was he sporting an Afro or not? What music, if any, did he listen to? I didn't know if he drank, did drugs of any kind. He could be in a movie playing a good guy or bad guy, set in the past, present, or future. Vincenzo Catrone III was timeless. Like a shark, his design needed no evolution. Other species frantically searched for keys to survival at the breakneck speed of one change per millennium, while the shark swam around with its original equipment, mouth open in a patient, fearsome smile. That was Vinny Catrone, hold the smile.

I, on the other hand, was like the fruit fly. We did experiments with fruit flies in Advanced Biology during 12th grade and I came to the unscientific conclusion that a fruit fly's generation lasted about fifteen minutes. The fucking things evolved right before your eyes. Me too. I took faded jeans and sweatshirts to college because the older kids I knew hung out in Greenwich Village and said, "Like wow, man." I brought Dylan and bongos, only to find the cool folks at the University of Michigan listened to Motown and wore three-piece suits. No prob bro, I bought new clothes and albums, and took the Marine Aviation Officer Candidates test. My junior year we started smoking dope and playing Rubber Soul backward to hear secret messages from the Fab Four. Groovy, I can dig it. Me and the fruit fly, evolving at the speed of light.

I found it significant that both the shark's method and the fruit fly's, though at opposite ends of the spectrum, were successful. I took that as a sign to do what I do best. Nothing. I made it through rehearsal today, I'd make it through the real thing tomorrow. Half a day of camp, then off to the rock festival. The whole group was going, we'd get stoned, laugh, Sheila would forget about "the bank" and things would be fine. Mrs. McLary could wait a few days too, make her wonder, always a good negotiating ploy. I was right but had no clue the next three days would change us, define us, label us, and bond us together forever as card-carrying members of a new group, The Woodstock Generation.

. . . . .

CHAPTER FIVE

TWO THUGS ON A THREE-DAY TRIP

Day 1, 1972, Darren NH

Their contact motioned them to turn in, then backpeddled up the driveway. When he reached the back of a pickup truck he stopped and walked to the driver's side of the Jeep. "There's a plowed spot on the left," pointing over his shoulder, "next to my wife's car. Park there. We'll go the rest of the way in my pickup."

"You want us to take all *our* shit out of *our* car and put it into *your* truck to go up the driveway?"

"It's hard enough gettin' up, no way you're gettin' back down in that boat. Drive straight up to my truck then back down and into the spot so you're facing out. I'll help with your gear."

Once their stuff was transferred, the three men squeezed into the old F150 and started bouncing up the unpaved driveway. "Sorry 'bout the weather. We get a lot of these spring snowstorms up here. Another month or so, most of the snow will be gone. I'm Fred."

The driver said, "Joe," and the passenger followed with "Moe." Fred, thinking they were making a joke, took his eyes off the driveway for a second and looked to return a smile. There wasn't one. The rest of the ride was silent until they reached the house, when Moe, expecting some rural equivalent of the ratty apartments shared by low level mafiosos back home, let out an audible "Whoa!" Outdoor lighting illuminated massive stone walls that terraced the land back and up to a two-story colonial with a large front entrance, and a breezeway connected to a two-car garage, with dormers and another front door.

Fred said, "I was told you wanted privacy, didn't want to see anybody who might recognize you at the hearing. That other door goes to an apartment above the garage that I use as my home office."

Following Fred's lead they grabbed their bags, went inside and immediately up a stairway into a large room above the two-car garage. There was an apartment size fridge, small sink, and a coffee machine on a counter along one wall. Across from that was a desk with a phone and adding machine. A day bed and a trundle bed that pulled out from underneath were both made up. At the far end was a kitchen table with two chairs and an open door leading to a bathroom. The walls were bare except for a crucifix and two framed photos, one of Pope John XXIII and one of Pope Paul VI. The men dropped the bags in the middle of the carpeted floor. It was the first time they saw each other in the light. Fred, like his house, was not what they expected. He threw his ski parka, hat, and gloves on the dresser, rode the desk chair over to the kitchen table, motioned to the kitchen chairs and said, "I have some information for you, and some questions."

Fred looked to be about fifty, blonde hair mixing with gray, clean shaven. He was wearing a black turtleneck under a grey sweater buttoned to his chest, black slacks, and two-tone brown and black duck boots. If Joe and Moe were from New Hampshire they would have recognized him as a successful businessman or professional. But they were from Brooklyn and, because of Vinny's call, had no idea what to make of him.

"Let's start with the information you have for us," offered Moe.

"Right." Fred rode the chair to the desk, picked up a notepad and scooted back to the table. "First and foremost, the Planning Board didn't think the meeting room in Town Hall could accommodate all the people, so they moved the hearing to the High School gym. They also rigged up a closed-circuit TV in the cafeteria in case of overflow. They'll need it for Town Meeting next week anyway because they're expecting an overflow then too, for the same reason."

"Which is?"

Fred hesitated, then chose his words carefully. "I'm the largest real estate agent in the county, both in dollars and number of sales. My family's been in the business for four generations, and this is by far the biggest deal I can remember."

Moe asked, "Won't they just change the date because of the weather?"

"They can't because the result of this meeting will affect Town Meeting, which as I said is next week."

"What's Town Meeting?"

Fred's eyes went from one to the other, looking again for some sign of intended humor. Again, nothing. He realized for the first time these men had no idea how New Hampshire worked, nor did they care. Fred felt a trace of doubt about his carefully orchestrated presentation, staged to allow him to direct the discussion. It always worked when he was negotiating business deals. Politely tell people where to sit, casually lay out an agenda, scoot around the office on the desk chair. Create the illusion that while he was just one of the guys, he was the one running the show. But these men were different. Looking into their faces was like looking at Mount Rushmore. Along with that first trace of doubt came the first twinge of fear.

"Lookit Fred," Moe said, "Me and Joe have been up almost twenty-four hours, and we ain't done. So, here's what happens now.

You tell us about this hippie, where and when he intends to deliver the evidence we're supposed to destroy, maybe draw us a map. We'll cruise around town tomorrow and put together a plan. The other door at the bottom of the stairs goes into the garage?"

"Yes."

"Is that the only other way in here?"

"Yes."

"Leave it unlocked. Is there a door from the garage into your house?"

"Yes." Fred's stomach started feeling queazy. He pictured his wife asleep in their bedroom.

"You can lock that behind ya' when you go. Joe and me are gonna' search this office and the garage for hidden microphones, cameras, cassette recorders."

"There aren't any."

Moe's tone became condescending. "You're on our side, aren't you Fred?"

"Of course."

"But there's another side too, right Fred?"

"People around here don't know anything about that kind of stuff."

"You gotta' guy from their side feedin' you info?"

"Yes, but..."

"So how do ya' know *they* don't have a snitch?"

Fred had no answer. This conversation was going places Fred hadn't anticipated. Now *he* was the clueless rookie, *they* were the crafty veterans, and they were in charge.

CHAPTER SIX

STEVEN

1960, Brooklyn NY

Steven's three-part goal was to be respected as a leader by all ethnic groups, learn all his family's secrets, and be the boyfriend of the prettiest, smartest girl in Brooklyn by the time they strolled hand in hand through the doors of James Madison High School as freshmen. Goal number one was right on schedule. There were no class presidents in seventh or eighth grade, each grade electing six student representatives. In seventh grade there were enough voters from Steven's Crowd to nudge Steven into sixth place. In the eighth-grade elections he finished first, more than doubling his nearest competitor's vote total. The impressive showing was clearly due to Steven's efforts to expand his contact with groups other than his own.

He was edging closer to goal two. His dogged questioning of his parents about their lives before he was born yielded a small but steady supply of nuggets. Steven created a list of family members and entered additions and corrections whenever he learned something new about one of them. The Catrone side of the family filled a whole page, the Masciarelli side just Grandpa, Grandma, and Pop's twin brother Uncle Stefano, all dead.

"Pop, were you with Uncle Stefano when he died?"

"No. I was in the Navy; my brother was in the Marines."

"Were you both heroes?"

"They were *all* heroes," Mom chimed in.

"But Uncle Stefano got a medal, right Mom? Was that why I was named after him, not Pop?"

"You were named after him to honor his memory, and because he was a smart, kind, wonderful person, like you."

"How come Vito wasn't named after *Nonno*?"

At the mention of Vito, Pop got up and, as always, left the room. Mom answered, "Vito is just a nickname. Did you finish your book report yet?" Conversation over.

Goal number three was completely stalled. Steven had zero confidence or experience dealing with girls, and his chosen target was not exactly an entry level assignment. Gail Bernstein's public persona was unapproachable, a busy young lady with no time for silly young boys except, apparently, Barry Longo. After she smiled and waved at Longo in the cafeteria and sauntered off with Steven's eyes still on her, he realized she was not only pretty, but...sexy! What was that about? What exactly was he feeling? Was it normal or was he some perverted weirdo? He handled his confusion by switching his focus to winning over the male population, but that image of her backside was not going away.

It took every ounce of his self-control to avoid staring at Gail's breasts and hips. Whenever they talked, Steven was back in fourth grade, internally funny but unable to voice his cleverness. Steven acted and sounded like a robotic buffoon, the complete opposite of the suave Barry Longo. He kept telling himself he had time, would get better at the social game, but seventh grade turned into eighth grade, and he just got worse. He was running out of time. Gail did not spend last summer in Brooklyn, so it was probable she would be gone this summer also. Then Gail informed him she was accepted at Bronx Science.

Bronx High School of Science is one of three special high schools in New York City, the other two being Stuyvesant and Brooklyn Tech. Open to all New York City residents at no charge, admission is extremely competitive. Only the top performing students can apply, and nineteen out of twenty who apply don't make the cut. The alumni list reads like a Who's Who, with luminaries in every field. Unfortunately for Gail, the two closest, Stuyvesant in Manhattan and Brooklyn Tech in Brooklyn, did not accept females. Bronx Science began admitting girls nearly a quarter century before Stuyvesant in 1969 and Brooklyn Tech in 1970, by which time Ms. Bernstein was at Harvard attending women's lib sit-ins and antiwar demonstrations.

In order to attend Bronx Science, she would have to traverse the largest city in the world twice a day at rush hour using public transportation. She would touch four of the five boroughs and change trains in two of them.

"Are you going?" Steven was shocked.

"I think so. I'm not sure. It's a great opportunity, but it's pretty scary."

"I'll say." Steven wasn't sure if he should be positive or negative. They had been in classes together since first grade, but they certainly weren't close, and Steven wasted a year doing nothing to change that. He let the topic drift away, but thought, *"If she's not sure, there's still a chance. Next opportunity, I'm making my move."*

The next time he and Gail worked together they were part of a group of six working on an English project. Instead of a regular book report they were supposed to lead a panel style discussion on <u>Billy Budd, Foretopman</u>. The first time the group met only Gail and Steven had managed to slog through the first chapter. The other four gave up and were trying to get their parents to sign a petition protesting cruel and unusual punishment.

"It was a play on Broadway," said Steven. "I think it was an opera too. My parents said they saw it." The four petitioners were unimpressed, but Steven noticed a glimmer of appreciation from Gail. Here we go, thought Steven, and he dove in. "Maybe instead of a panel discussion we can put on a play."

"Us?!"

"Does anybody even know what a 'Foretopman' is?"

"A play's got to be easier to read than this shit," said Steven, undeterred because none of the negative outbursts were from Gail, "and we'll get some serious slack with our grade for trying something creative."

Gail said, "What's the alternative? Does anybody think we can actually lead a discussion on this book?"

"You're the only one who could." Steven said it with a big smile on his face and got a couple of chuckles. Not from Gail, but there *was* a trace of the Barry Longo smile. "How 'bout this? Gail and I find a copy of the play, go over it, and see if it's even possible." Turning to Gail, Steven tried his best to look earnest. "The library here, or maybe the Brooklyn Library. My mom could take us."

Gail was taken aback, unsure why the arrow was pointing at her. Steven tried to deflect the attention and turned toward the rest of the group.

"Or we could get a copy of the opera. I'm a baritone - can anybody else sing in Italian?"

"You sound more like a tenor to me," Gail said, "let's stick with the play. I'll ask Mr. Ward if we can go to the library during English tomorrow."

On their way to the library the next day, Gail asked, "So you're a big fan of opera?"

Keeping his eyes straight down the hallway to avoid Sexy-Gail-Distractions, Steven responded casually. "Not really. My mom and dad go sometimes. My grandmother was a famous dancer, and my uncle designed clothes for Broadway stars before he died in the war. A lotta' them buy clothes at my parents' store, so they're always going to plays and stuff." Pop told him Grandma Masciarelli danced professionally for a while, and Uncle Stefano worked with Pop at Grandpa Masciarelli's clothing store before the war. Steven was embellishing, but this was the first time their conversation was even remotely personal. He hoped his "cultured side" would set him apart from the rest of the crowd.

"My uncle's writing a play," Gail offered.

"Really? He's a writer? Hey, maybe he can write our play!" He was rewarded with out loud laughter, another first. "So that's a no?"

"Yeah," Gail, still smiling, gave him a reassuring pat on the shoulder, "but nice try. Let's see what this library's got for us." Steven's shoulder was tingling. First physical contact!

They did have to go to the Brooklyn Library. Steven's mother drove them, and stumbled a bit when Gail inquired about her famous dancing mother but recovered quickly.

"Oh, that was my husband's mother." So, she thought happily, Steven's pulling out all the stops to impress this pretty young girl. She helped them find the correct section of the library, then went to kill some time in the travel section. On the way home the kids were excited.

"We read the whole play Mom!"

"Well, we really just looked it over, Mrs. Masciarelli, but we got the idea. We hafta' go back and take some notes so we can shorten it."

"Well, I'm available to drive whenever."

Steven's hopes were soaring by the next visit to the library. He was feeling more at ease with Gail. They selected the passages necessary to make their greatly abridged version understandable to the class and got the librarian to photocopy them. Gail then took a bunch of different colored markers from her book bag and began hi-lighting, a different color for each of the six cast members. Steven was impressed.

"I get the colors for each of us, but why the extras?"

"Yellow is for parts we may have to cut if it's too long, purple is for parts we can add if it's too short. Pink is just some stuff that may be useful to me in other classes."

"No wonder you got into Bronx Science."

On their way home Steven's mother casually said, "Now that you two are going to be actors, would you like to go to a Broadway show? *West Side Story* is coming back for a return engagement, and your father and I missed it the first time. We'll get four tickets instead of two."

Steven was aghast. What was his mother doing? He stole a furtive glance at Gail, expecting the worst. But she was wide-eyed and bubbling, "Oh my gosh, Mrs. Masciarelli, that would be so cool! I'll ask my parents as soon as we get to my house! Oh, and I can pay for my ticket - I earned some money last summer at my uncle's camp." She looked at Steven, her face lit up and beaming, too excited by her good fortune to notice Steven's shock.

"That won't be necessary, dear. Your mother is welcome to call me if she has any questions. Steven, give Gail our number."

Steven couldn't give anybody anything. "I've got it, Mrs. Masciarelli. It's on the sheet Mr. Ward gave us when he formed the group."

On the way home from Gail's house Steven was silent. At first, he was mad at his Mom *(I can ask a girl out on a date without my mother's help!)* but quickly realized this was what he had been hoping for, a date with Gail Bernstein. Sure, they would be with his parents, but when you're thirteen that's still a date. Steven's preoccupied silence went from sulking to planning. His mother could almost hear his brain whirring, a "sound" which was becoming quite familiar.

Their group met, rehearsed the first two acts, and needed the third, necessitating another trip to the library. When they finished their notes, Gail sent him to the librarian for six copies.

"We only need five," said Steven. "You've got one."

"I'll keep the original in case someone loses theirs. I want one to keep, anyway."

Shaking his head at her thoroughness, Steven went to the desk and asked for six copies. While he was waiting, he noticed a basket containing Playbills from current shows. He found *West Side Story* and paged through it, noticing that Leonard Bernstein and Gail Bernstein had the same last name, wondering if they were related. They were not, but he did learn the story was based on Shakespeare's <u>Romeo and Juliet</u>. Back at the table he showed off his knowledge to enhance his reputation as a man of culture. Gail was skeptical.

"Do you even know what Romeo and Juliet is about?"

"A guy named Romeo and a girl named Juliet?" His reward was another episode of out loud laughter, another playful slap on the shoulder. Same shoulder, same tingle.

"They're in love but their parents forbid them to see each other because the families are from...different..." Gail slowed, looked at Steven, stopped. They held each other's eyes briefly before Gail gave her head a little shake and resumed hi-lighting. Steven felt his cheeks burning, saw hers reddening. The ride home was filled with awkward silence. But it was also filled with a tension that was equal parts painful and exhilarating.

The next couple of weeks in school were strange. They resumed their relationship based solely on schoolwork, but there were moments when sparks flew between them. Rehearsing, and then putting on the play in front of the class was an intimate experience for all six, but especially for Steven and Gail. Since there were only male roles the girls had to play them and there was some physical contact required. The other four members of the cast treated it for what it was, just horsing around with no sexual overtones, but Steven and Gail couldn't be so casual.

The looming date added to the feeling of uncharted waters, and the night at the theater did not disappoint. The language, tame compared to the street talk they were used to, was embarrassing with Steven's parents sitting next to them. The bodies of the dancers were shown off by the costuming and these were real, live, beautiful people in close proximity. Most of all, the theme of love between members of different backgrounds struck a chord that resonated with the two teenagers. From the minute they left the theater Steven conducted a conversation with himself about what would happen when he walked Gail to her door. They saw enough teen movies to know about that first goodnight kiss. Those "painful and exhilarating" silences were bordering on meltdown. Pulling up to Gail's house, however, revealed about a half dozen adults sitting on the large front stoop, two of whom rose and headed for the car. There wasn't going to be any opportunity for the much-anticipated kiss. A polite "Thanks" and "Good night," awkward little waves, and it was over.

The afterglow of the exciting night on Broadway did not last long. A few days later, Gail told Steven she had decided to attend Bronx Science in the fall. Unwilling to give up hope, Steven asked about her summer plans and got the disappointing news. She was going to stay at her aunt and uncle's house upstate and work in the office at their summer camp, like she did the previous summer. They spent a fair amount of time together during the last six weeks of school, Gail coming to baseball games to learn something about the sport because her uncle's camp specialized in baseball. She was very inquisitive, used the same methodical, organized approach she brought to academics, colored markers and all.

The summer was almost normal for Steven. He played ball, strengthened friendships within his group and continued making inroads with others, and went to the Brooklyn beaches. The beach scene was all about boyfriend/girlfriend maneuvering and reminded Steven of drawings in his science textbook depicting atoms with missing electrons seeking atoms with extra electrons so they could hook up and become stable molecules. Steven didn't feel like he had, or needed, any "free electrons." He was content to be one of the inert gases for the summer and took their noble objective to heart.

Gail wrote a couple letters from camp, telling him she had enjoyed learning the finer points of baseball, how they helped her understand why the camp did things a certain way, and how much she enjoyed their new friendship. He struggled with his responses, wanting to pour his heart out but unable to express himself in writing. He settled for baseball minutia and summer gossip. They planned to get together between the time camp ended and school began, but Gail got caught up in preparations for her Bronx adventure, and Steven was involved in two-a-days with the football team. He had an outside shot to be the starting quarterback for the varsity as a freshman and chased the dream with his typical compulsion.

The starting quarterback was a senior. He was what Steven aspired to be except he didn't have Steven's talent. Only someone who possessed Steven's world class athleticism (or like the coach, had witnessed it firsthand) could recognize the difference between the two levels of performance. Chris Como was an excellent athlete and a team leader, but he was not Steven.

Coach could tell Steven, and to a lesser degree Barry Longo, might be special. He told his wife every night at dinner how this was the break that could make his career. Already a successful high school coach, the next four years could catapult him into the collegiate ranks.

He decided the two freshmen would only play sporadically during their first year, learning from the capable and experienced upperclassmen ahead of them at their positions. But he was already dreaming up plays for the following year that could take advantage of Masciarelli's lightning quick feet and bazooka right arm, coupled with Longo's speed, strength and sure hands hauling in touchdown pass after touchdown pass.

Things did not go exactly as Coach planned. Steven's ability was off the charts, his maturity astounding for a freshman. Steven competed as hard as he could, from the second he entered the locker room to the second he left the building, intent on proving he was the best choice to play quarterback. His political savvy served him well. Chris Como was the team leader, his position as starting quarterback a given in the minds of every returning member of the team. As hard as Steven tried to show he was better, he had to also show respect for Como.

He also had to put up with the jealousy his ability elicited from

Chris Como's friends. Como was the recognized leader of the neighborhood Italians, the high school version of "Steven's Crowd." On the streets, away from Coach's control, there was even harsher backlash against the new hot shot. Initially Steven was able to turn the other cheek, but as the competition on the football field intensified so did the verbal abuse. On the streets and at the beach it became more than verbal, and Steven eventually had to fight back. Just one week away from the start of school the tension in the locker room had escalated, and Coach realized he had a problem.

Steven was wired pretty tightly by the time he arrived at the field Monday morning for the final week of practice sessions. He saw a group of seniors, including Como, hanging near the back door to the locker room. Steven thought about going around to the front entrance, but they noticed him and evading the issue was not an option. Jaw locked, fists clenched, Steven maintained his purposeful stride as he approached the building.

"Mornin,' Masciarelli." It was Como, pleasant smile on his face, speaking casually.

"Hey, one-six," was another friendly greeting referencing Steven's jersey number.

Como said, "One more week of these fuckin' two-a-days, huh?"

Steven managed a smile. "Yeah, the games are gonna' be a vacation compared to this."

As he made his way to his locker everything seemed normal. Then the group of seniors followed him inside and an apprehensive silence gripped the room, like when a hawk grabs a perch on a tree limb and all the ground animals disappear. But the seniors went to their lockers and started laying out their pads as they undressed, chatter continuing among them and gradually spreading throughout the room. Coach came out of his office, announced "10 minutes, on the 50-yard line" as he did every morning, then stopped by Steven's locker.

"We're gonna' try Como at running back, so you'll be takin' the snaps at QB," Coach said in his normal voice, neither keeping the news private nor making an announcement.

"Okay!!" said Steven, way louder than intended. He immediately looked to Como, concerned he might have sounded disrespectful. But Como smiled at his enthusiasm and kept pulling on his uniform as if nothing happened.

Steven was perplexed by the sudden change in attitude. He decided to pack that particular puzzle away in the back of his mind and concentrate on the task at hand. It would be midway through the season before he found out what had precipitated the attitude adjustment.

Steven certainly had enough to concentrate on during the final week of preparation. He was now the quarterback, but he was still just a freshman, and could feel the lack of confidence from his teammates in the huddle. The season opener didn't help. Steven made some great plays, but not with the consistency necessary to put points on the board. Time was running out and Madison's offense had yet to score. The defense was great, holding their opponents to one field goal. Madison had the ball deep in their own territory with only enough time for one or two more plays. When Coach sent in a running play, "Sweep right," Steven was surprised. They were seventy-five yards from the end zone, and Steven thought Coach would call a long pass, probably two in case the first didn't result in a touchdown. Apparently, Coach didn't believe he could pull it off. Dejected and angry, Steven considered changing the play on his own, but thought better of it and called "Sweep right." Everyone in the huddle was surprised as well, and hesitated. Steven fiercely called it again, added his own "and make it work, goddamn it!" He received the hike, pivoted, and handed off to Como.

When a sweep is diagrammed on the chalkboard the quarterback is supposed to hand the ball to a running back, then run along the line of scrimmage looking for someone to block. That rarely happens. By the time the quarterback finishes the hand off and starts running he is unlikely to catch up to the running back and make a block that matters. Coaches don't belabor the point since quarterbacks are chosen for skill rather than size and strength, and often feel blocking is better left to the big lugs on the line. A smooth handoff is all quarterbacks are concerned with, and they just halfheartedly go through the motions after that. But Steven, who never did anything halfheartedly, had the diagram in his head as the play began. Pivoting smoothly after the hand off, Steven ran full speed along the line of scrimmage and caught up to Como, who was nearing the sideline and still had no opening to turn up field. Finding that other gear so few have, Steven accelerated and hurled his 165-pound body at the three behemoths in Como's way. It was a perfectly executed block, and he and the first defender rolled into the second, creating an opening. Como turned the corner, raced seventy-five yards for the winning touchdown, and was swarmed by his teammates.

There was no longer any question of trust or doubt about Steven's leadership. James Madison won five of the next six games. The Monday after the team's only loss Steven got a note from Coach to see him ASAP in his office. He nervously replayed the loss in his mind, wondering if any of his mistakes caused their defeat.

Coach greeted him with, "You know Washington's gone?"

Steven knew Rondelle Washington, their big, fast receiver who was Steven's favorite target, missed the last two practices but wasn't aware of the details. Barry Longo was Washington's backup, and Steven felt confident he could fill in adequately for a few games.

"How long will he be out?"

"25 to life."

"Oh. That kind of gone."

"Yeah, that kind. The only reason he made it this long was because Como was constantly on him to stay straight. That's part of being the team leader, and that's what I need *you* to do."

Just last week Steven was shooting hoops in the schoolyard with James Washington when Rondelle walked over to them and gave James an envelope "for Mom." James was embarrassed and Steven astonished. James just waved his hand in a "don't go there" gesture, and they continued shooting baskets. Steven and James had become friends since the base running lessons back in seventh grade. James was aware Steven was using him to increase his popularity with the black kids but knew it could serve both their interests. Plus, they enjoyed each other's friendship. James never mentioned Rondelle, and there was no way (except the surname, common enough to be a coincidence) Steven would imagine they were brothers. James was slim, lithe, average height, while Rondelle was one large slab of muscle. Their attitudes were polar opposites also, James friendly and easy going, Rondelle surly, non-communicative, and wired for trouble.

"Uh, I mean, I could talk to him too, but..."

"No, no, I'm done with Washington. I'm talking about Longo. Academic warning slips are out, and he's failing three courses. He needs to score well on his midterm tests, or he'll be ineligible for the rest of the season. I'm looking for you to do some last-minute tutoring."

"Did Longo ask for help? Because if he doesn't want..."

"I'll handle Longo, just like I handled Como."

The light went on in Steven's head. "You talked to Como that Monday before our last week of practice."

"No, on Friday. I figured he'd need the whole weekend to handle the situation."

"What situation?"

"You." Coach had dropped by Como's house Friday around dinner time so he could talk to the whole family. He knew Chris' parents were hoping for a scholarship. Losing his starting job to a freshman was not going to look good. Coach sold it as a selfless move by Chris because the team really needed a running back. If Chris could ease the transition for Masciarelli and the team wound up having a successful season, Chris' stock would actually rise. Coach was not about to mention any of this to Masciarelli, nor disclose his final warning after Como agreed to switch positions. "You better handle your boys on the team, and on the streets, the kid's gonna' have a hard enough time as it is." All Coach wanted from Steven now was his agreement to help. "Does Longo wanna' play football?"

"Yeah, but I'm not sure he sees the connection between..."

"I'll spell it out for him. Do his parents care?"

"I don't think they even know he's playing. They never come to a game."

"Got it. So, you're agreeable?"

Steven hesitated. "I'll try to convince..."

"He'll come to you. Get back to class before *you* need tutoring. See ya' at practice."

True to Coach's word, Longo approached Steven after practice. "Hey one-six, Coach says you know a way to sneak me through mid-terms." Longo's genuine smile and eager eyes showed no doubt about his smart friend's ability to pull it off.

Steven returned the smile, and said, "No guarantees, Longo, but I'll give it a shot."

"Wanna' start now? Coach says we can use his office."

"I gotta' call my Mom, see if it's okay." As the two boys walked to Coach's office to use the phone, Steven realized Barry didn't have to do that because his parents never cared where he was or what he did. And James hadn't mentioned his brother once in the two years he and Steven had been friends, nor had Rondelle mentioned anything all season. Up to a certain point you assume everybody's family life is similar to yours. Steven just passed that point.

They spent almost an hour touching all three subjects, and Steven's assessment was simple. Drastic measures were required to get Barry's nose above water in time for midterms. Steven was most surprised about Spanish. He often overheard Longo speaking Spanish at conversational speeds, yet he labored through the simplest lessons in the textbook. Steven suspected reading might be the problem, but he was neither knowledgeable nor capable enough to help. Ninth grade English was all about reading comprehension, and Longo struggled just to get through the titles of the required books. As for Algebra, he was totally clueless.

"I've got some ideas," Steven said. "Do you mind if I talk to Coach about them?"

"I'm in your hands, *mi amigo*," Longo proudly showing off his bilingual abilities.

The next morning at homeroom Steven got permission to see Coach. "Does Barry have to pass all three midterms to stay on the team?"

"Two would probably do it for the football season."

"Then we have a chance. I don't think he can read."

"Then how could we have a chance?"

"I mean I don't think he can read well enough to learn what he needs to learn in time for the tests. But he speaks Spanish all the time with his Puerto Rican friends. Maybe you could ask his teacher if he can take some kind of oral test?"

Coach stared at Steven in disbelief for a couple of seconds, reached for a pad, said "O-o-kay" as he wrote himself a note. "You want me to ask his math teacher too?"

"No. Algebra's a lost cause."

"And English isn't? You said he can't read."

"He can read some. I've got that covered."

"How?" Steven didn't reply. "This ain't junior high, kid. We know about Cliff's Notes."

Steven had thought about Cliff's Notes, but doubted Barry had the stamina to get through the compilations of important facts that could be on the test. However, Uncle Eddie's market had rotating stands of comic books and the lower half featured Classics Illustrated Comics. These were comic book adaptations of literary classics, complete with comic book style illustrations, as well as snippets of original dialogue between the main characters. The test was on American Literature, and the list of titles were well represented on Uncle Eddie's stand. "We're not doing Cliff's Notes."

"Care to tell me what you *are* doing?"

"Wouldn't you have to tell Mrs. Silver?"

"Is this scheme gonna' get you in trouble?"

"No."

"Then I don't need to know. I hope to hell you know what you're doing, Masciarelli. We gotta' have somebody catching your passes or this season's over."

Steven did, as usual, know what he was doing. Longo failed the Algebra test miserably, but got 76% on the English test on *Moby Dick, The Call of the Wild*, and *The Adventures of Huckleberry Finn*, and a mind blowing 88% on the oral exam arranged by the Spanish teacher and the reading specialist. The C-plus in English and the B-plus in Spanish were enough to counteract the F in Algebra. Longo caught eight touchdown passes from Steven over the next three games, boosting their record to 7 and 1, setting up a borough championship matchup with their crosstown rival Tilden on Thanksgiving.

Steven hadn't heard anything from Gail since her final letter from camp three months ago. He called almost daily but there was never an answer. He walked over to her apartment house and pressed the button next to "Bernstein," but no one responded. None of their mutual acquaintances had heard from her since she started attending Bronx Science. A couple Jewish kids thought she moved to Long Island but weren't sure. He tried writing another letter even though she lived just a few blocks away. Nothing. He taped a note to the Bernstein mailbox in their apartment house lobby asking her to come to the big game. A few days later, he noticed it was gone, but there was no response. Gail Bernstein had disappeared.

CHAPTER SEVEN

JEAN

1963, Darren NH

"It was the best of times, it was the worst of times." Jean couldn't get Charles Dickens' opening sentence out of his head. It was like a song you hear in the morning and keep singing to yourself all day long. Jean juggled his "tale of two cities" constantly, comparing life at home to how it would've been if he went to RPI. He was guessing how things *might* have been in Troy, New York as opposed to knowing *exactly* how things were in Darren, New Hampshire. He and Mom agreed on a compromise plan following Dad's death that was working out perfectly and was a complete disaster.

They came up with the guiding principle to keep all options open. It became their shared slogan, said by one to the other with a serious smile whenever a decision loomed. They informed RPI of their family tragedy, and RPI changed Jean's acceptance to a transfer option the following September. He and Mom met with the Dean of Engineering at UNH, who renewed his acceptance and placed Jean at their Plymouth State College campus. They set up a schedule of evening classes so Jean could work with Uncle Guy. An RPI education, instead of being "tossed in the trashcan" as Mom said before the awards night, remained a future option. Meanwhile Jean would live at home, minimizing the disruption to his younger siblings and easing the burden on Mom. Marrying Marie was tabled indefinitely.

Marie was attentive and supportive following Armand's death, but would they have stayed together if Jean went away as originally planned? Jean felt a tinge of regret about the missed opportunity with the New Jersey/New York girls. What did that say about his commitment to Marie? Was Marie conflicted also, happy to keep Jean home but wistful about missing the chance to be a young single?

Jean finished his high school career as if Dad were still alive. Uncle Guy got Aunt Yvette's brother Lee to fill in ("About time he started doin' something for his rent!") until summer when Jean could start working full time. By June, all his classmates were over the shock of Armand Giroux's death and took part in graduation celebrations with the expected amount of teenage excess. Jean threw his cap in the air, smiled, patted a few backs. Later that afternoon he played in the finals as his team procured another "New Hampshire Class S Baseball Champions" banner for the gymnasium wall. Coach invited him to play in a summer tournament against teams from other states, but Jean declined because he'd be working full time.

The Monday after graduation was the first day of Jean's new life. He drove Dad's pickup with its customized cap accommodating plumbing supplies and met Uncle Guy at the end of his spur. Uncle Guy waved and pulled out with Jean following. Thirty minutes later, on his back in wet muck after pulling himself under a porch, Jean squinted up through spider webs so thick they were opaque. Dead bugs and other debris fell on his face. He worked his pocket flashlight out of his overalls, the underside of the decking only inches from his nose.

"Okay, Uncle Guy, I see the water pipe, seems okay. Hold on, I'll try and follow - ah, the pipe's split. A floor joist sagged down onto it. Hold it...unnh, I can push it up off the pipe...but it just sags down again. Must be rotted."

"Okay, c'mon out."

"Don't you want me to see if there's anything else going on under here?"

"No. Won't fuckin' matter. He's gonna' hafta' rebuild the whole fuckin' porch anyway. Just get the fuck outta' there."

Jean squirmed out, dusted himself off and looked over at Uncle Guy talking to the owner. He never heard his uncle swear before, and it sounded forced. Was Uncle Guy trying to make him feel like they were peers, two men working together instead of a father figure and a teenager? Then another thought popped into his head. This was exactly the kind of job Uncle Guy was hoping to phase out to make room for commercial jobs. Was he exaggerating his displeasure to emphasize the aggravating aspects? Did he choose this job as Jean's inauguration to justify not taking the next one?

The owner's wife had turned on the hose Saturday to water her garden and no water came out. She got her husband off the sofa during the Red Sox game. He squeezed the nozzle, went to the spigot, turned it off, then on, and squeezed the nozzle again.

"Don't you think I tried that?"

"It's gonna' rain tonight anyways, you won't need to water this weekend. I'll call the Giroux brothers Monday morning."

The "Giroux brothers" were now Jean and Uncle Guy. It was force of habit for the homeowner to use the term he had been using for decades. It was also force of habit for him to call Guy on his home phone when he got "leave a message" from the office at 5:00 a.m. Monday morning, after his wife let him have it because they now had no water in the entire house.

They used a dug well sited by dowsers, locals who supposedly could tell by the lay of the land where there might be an underground stream to tap. A common sight after a hot dry week in August was a homeowner bent over his well, cover off, checking his water level. Curtailing lawn watering and laundry loads might be necessary to keep the well going through a dry spell. If it continued long enough the well would go dry, and might take a day, or two, or three to refill.

The family had no water because the pipe leading to the spigot was broken by the sagging floor joist under the porch. Water had run out of the break all weekend, combining with normal usage to drain the well. As far as Uncle Guy was concerned, their work here was finished until the owner called a carpenter to remove the rotted porch so they could fix the pipe. This was when Dad would say, "We can tear the porch off and replace it ourselves."

Jean was flummoxed. He was quite capable of doing the handyman work. It was a way to turn a small job into a significant project. Their price for the porch demo and rebuild wouldn't be any more than someone else's. They could do it while the owners waited for their well to come back up, the customer would be pleased, and pleased customers were how their business was built. But that was not the kind of business Uncle Guy wanted. Jean's inclination was to volunteer to do the work like Dad would have, but he couldn't decide if Uncle Guy's salty language was an attempt to create a "one of the boys" atmosphere, whether he was just in a bad mood unrelated to work, or he had an ulterior motive. Less than an hour into the first day of his new career and he didn't know what to do.

Uncle Guy strode purposefully toward Jean, whispered "follow me to Armand's truck" without breaking stride, and Jean hustled to keep up as Uncle Guy kept talking softly. "He wants us to tear off the porch, fix the pipe, and rebuild the porch. I told him I didn't know when we could fit it in, we needed to check the schedule in Armand's truck. You get behind the wheel and we'll act like we're checking - we need to talk before I give him an answer."

The owner followed, anxious to be away from his wife's glare. Uncle Guy closed the door, took out a blank pad and hunched toward Jean "I know you and I can handle the demo and rebuild, but our next appointment is for a job I really want. I kept putting them off 'til you were available full time, and I wanna' be able to tell 'em we can start immediately. I'm gonna' tell this guy we'll try to reschedule some jobs and get back to him before lunch. He'll wait for our call 'cause he knows we'll do it right and be cheaper. You OK with that?"

"Sure. What's the other job?"

"We gotta' go past home on the way there. Drop off Armand's truck, and I'll tell you on the way. I'll go handle him."

Uncle Guy was upbeat laying out the day's plan, which Jean noticed contained no cursing. The plan came together so smoothly there had to be some forethought and planning. His uncle was too meticulous to schedule a job in one direction and then another that required backtracking, like this one, unless there was a reason.

Uncle Guy's "You OK with that?" wasn't really a question. However, Uncle Guy was willing to risk losing the new job by putting it on hold until Jean graduated, so it must include engineering, drawing, or planning. And Uncle Guy needed Jean for that.

Jean had one more thought. He had to make some time to finish his truck and get it on the road. This truck would always be "Armand's truck."

"Where we goin,' Uncle Guy?"

"Waterville Valley."

"What's there?"

"The Mt. Tecumseh Ski Area," Uncle Guy said with a big smile on his face. Uncle Guy was playing with him. Jean decided to be grumpy and didn't respond. Uncle Guy forged on.

"Didja' know they're gonna' build a town there?"

"Uh-huh." Waterville Valley *was* a town, but only had a couple dozen residents. It consisted of about 40,000 acres in the White Mountain National Forest, and included Mt. Tecumseh, one of New Hampshire's peaks over 4,000 feet in elevation. The smallest of the 48 to make the grade, Tecumseh snuck in at 4,003 feet. The Civilian Conservation Corps cut a ski trail during the depression, but it was never developed.

The entire Giroux clan would picnic there on weekends or when school was cancelled because of snow, showing up with sleds, skis, lunch boxes, and thermoses of hot soup. The older, skiing Girouxs would hike up carrying their skis, then swoop down and scare the younger ones. The ski coach at the Holderness School, an incongruously posh prep school nearby, would occasionally bring his team there to show them what "old school" skiing was like, and his childhood buddy was Jean's coach. Since Jean was always the reigning state champion at every level, the Holderness coach wanted him there as a motivating factor, and Jean's coach loved to have his local racer stick it to the rich kids. The two coaches were good friends who competed against each other as children and were not inclined to stop now that they were adults. Those training sessions were Jean's favorite times on skis.

The racers would hike up, toting their equipment a mile up to an old cabin, where they would change into ski gear. Jean was always sure to show the other racers a framed drawing of the trail hanging near the wood stove. It looked like a pirate treasure map, hand drawn, with the following description, written in cursive:

"Mount Tecumseh Ski Trail, WMNF. This trail ascends the E. slope of

The visitors were awestruck, feeling more like explorers in the wilderness than racers. They would line up in front of the cabin and stare down at the fallen branches scattered across the ungroomed, narrow trail, further cementing Jean's home field advantage. At the shout of "last one down is a horse's ass!" they would take off down the bumpy slope. The only contest in doubt was avoiding the dubious distinction of being last. The winner was a *fait d'accompli.*

Jean's ability was obvious at the Fun Race events the local mountains hosted for children. He was recruited as a five-year old by one of the local ski areas to be on their racing team and rose up through the various levels of competition until he was in his teens. Then he faced a decision.

In order to keep moving up the ladder he needed a certain number of top ten finishes. Jean's level was now "children 13 and over." The upper half of that range had the bodies of grown men. They also had more wins to their credit, earning them lower bib numbers, which meant they would go earlier in the race. By the time "Bib # 114, now in the start gate" was announced, the course was rutted, new snow was skied down to hard ice, and the proper line through the gates was pitted by the falls of the previous racers.

Jean didn't mind the competition. But he was being told he needed to train year-round and dedicate himself exclusively to downhill racing. Plus, if he continued in the Junior Olympics circuit he would be ineligible to ski for his high school team. Jean, 13 and in eighth grade, made his decision one frigid day in early March.

It was the last race of the season, and Jean needed another top ten finish to earn a spot the following year. The race was held at Cannon Mountain on one of the toughest trails, facing due north top to bottom, where the icy wind seemed to come directly from the North Pole. By the time Jean climbed into the starting gate the afternoon sun was low and ineffective. The times relayed up by the coaches and gatekeepers indicated he would need his best time ever to nudge himself in with the big boys. He shivered from negative wind chills and the mixture of adrenalin and fear. He pushed off, skated and poled a few strides to pick up speed, tucked into a crouch to maximize aerodynamics and pointed his skis downhill, eyes on the high side of the first gate.

For the next 1 minute and 14.63 seconds Jean hurtled down the steep, icy, rutted slope, knees absorbing shock after shock, thighs screaming, skis rattling and bouncing, muscling his way through turns with skis dangerously flat to minimize any braking effect. It was almost half a minute before Jean took his first breath, another minute before he sailed through the finish line, strained his aching ankles to dig his edges in, skidded to a stop, and collapsed on his backside. He turned, looked at the clock and thought he might have done it.

He saw Dad and his coach furiously paging through results. They had written each racer's time as they finished, adding it to the morning results to get the combined time for each racer. Whenever a DQ (Disqualified, usually for missing a gate) or a DNF (Did Not Finish, usually for a bad fall) was announced they drew a line through that racer's name. You needed to finish both races, the morning slalom and the afternoon downhill, to qualify. Adding Jean's times, paging back through their results, they shot their hands in the air as they turned toward Jean, running in the ungainly gait caused by their ski boots, screaming "You did it!! You did it!!"

There were still more racers to go, but none of them had a realistic chance of besting Jean's combined time. They watched and waited while the remaining racers made it down, or didn't. They celebrated, then rushed to the lodge to wait in line at the pay phone, relayed the good news to Mom, and got in the truck for the ride home.

"How do you feel, son?"

"Tired."

"Happy?" Jean didn't answer. The silence hung for a moment, then Dad asked, "You okay?"

"Yeah. I just don't know if I want to do this all over again next year."

Armand stole a quick glance at Jean, returned his eyes to the road. He didn't see tears but could feel them. "You don't *have* to, son. This just means you earned the right to."

"When you and coach told me I did it, I was...disappointed. I think I was hoping I wouldn't make it."

This time when Armand looked over, Jean was looking at him. His eyes were wet, his expression confused. Armand turned his eyes back to the road, reached out and patted Jean's thigh.

"You could just ski for the high school next year. I know you're a downhill superstar, but they do cross country and ski jumping too. That means you'll hafta' spend more time with me working on your technique." Armand turned to Jean again, flashing a big smile. Jean was audibly crying now but sported a matching smile.

"You listening?" Jean's reverie was broken by Uncle Guy poking him with his elbow.

"Huh? Oh yeah, sorry."

"Where ya' been?"

"I was just thinking how much fun we used to have at Tecumseh, you know, the family picnics and all."

"Yeah, well...yeah." Uncle Guy's shoulders slumped, and he shook his head slightly, as if telling himself 'No' about something. Jean was suddenly aware he wasn't the only one dealing with Armand Giroux's passing. Uncle Guy lost a brother, a best friend, a business partner who he worked with all day, every day. He was about to say something, to commiserate, to share, but Uncle Guy abruptly changed gears. "You'll see in a minute it doesn't look anything like it used to. And we have an important meeting, I'm counting on you chippin' in with the sales pitch, and you've been ignoring me the whole time I've been talking!" Uncle Guy's tone was good natured needling, and both men smiled.

"Not the whole time, Uncle Guy. I heard 'They're looking for plumbers, and it would be the biggest job we ever bid on.' That's about when I - whoa!" They had just turned off the road not far from where they used to park in a small, flat clearing near the base of Mt. Tecumseh. But the small flat clearing was no more. Large land-moving equipment was pushing, pulling, digging, and piling. Men walked between equipment and stacks of building supplies. Uncle Guy pulled to the side and stopped for a minute, giving Jean a moment to let the scene sink in. He flipped off the AC and opened the windows, and the roar was like a nor'easter except for the beeps of trucks backing up. "I thought this was still in the planning stage! I didn't know...did they get all the zoning permits and stuff from the

White Mountain National Forest already?"

"Not all. The WMNF never likes its land to be used for condos or private homes, but they got enough to build a ski area, base lodge, a cross-country area with its own little lodge, a town square with shops and restaurants, and condos, some adjacent to the ski trails."

"Wow." Jean was overwhelmed, and a bit conflicted. On one hand there was the destruction of the idyllic, unspoiled, winter wonderland he had always known. On the other there was the power of engineering and design, the promise of progress he could be a part of. "Why did you wait for me? I mean, it's big, but it's just plumbing."

"It's more. The investors want to build these all across New England, all across the nation. They'll be year-round resorts, with golf, hiking, and boating in the summer, restaurants, shops, even theaters. For us local contractors, this is a tryout. They're hiring three or four plumbing companies to work on this project, and the best one will become the company plumbers. Same for electricians, framers, roofers, everyone. When I met with the General Contractor, he started firing terms at me that I wasn't sure of, things I've heard you say. He knows the Giroux Brothers are reliable, but I wanted you there to show him we're also willing and able to do the new stuff. I want more than just being one of the crews for this job. I wanna' be the plumbers they pick to join the company, with a bright new engineer and his shiny new diploma as part of the package." Uncle Guy's enthusiasm was contagious, none of Jean's sentimental nostalgia slowing his runaway dream. "That's what I was saying while you were day dreaming. Now let's go in there and blow the GC away!"

Jean was caught up in the challenge and the confidence Uncle Guy had in him. The dream in front of him could happen! There was just a slight tug over the loss of how things used to be.

They did blow the general contractor away, Uncle Guy with his knowledge of local suppliers and regulations, Jean with his responses to questions about newer products and methods. There was one rough patch when Jean tried to interest the GC in modular buildings. Jean's youthful exuberance caused him to belabor the point longer than necessary. He kept going deeper into the advantages of the new building technique until warning glances from Uncle Guy brought him back to earth.

"Well," the GC said, "it's probably too late for that stuff in this phase, but we got plenty of phases to go. I like the way you think, kid. Okay, so," turning his attention back to Uncle Guy, "Your company will be roundin' out our team here. When can you get started?"

"Can you give us a couple days to tie up some loose ends? Maybe the end of this week or Monday? Hell, we don't mind working weekends, if someone will be here let's say Saturday."

"I fuckin' *live* here. Saturday's fine. You'll probably be the only plumbers 'til Monday, but you're a bit behind so it'll give ya' a chance to catch up." The GC stood, shook Guy's hand, turned to Jean and said, "Welcome to the big time, kid."

They walked back to Uncle Guy's truck without fanfare, acting like it was just another day at the office. Once inside they broke into grins and shoulder thumps.

"Sorry about your weekend."

"No problem, Uncle Guy. I'm here to work." Jean waited, but there was no comment about how he performed at the interview. Finally, he said, "Did I do something wrong with the modular stuff?"

"Yeah, but it wasn't your fault." Jean was crushed. "They were great ideas, but we didn't need 'em to get the job. We were gonna' get it based on our reputation. The GC will definitely pass your ideas along to the head honchos, but when he does you can be damn sure he'll present them as *his* ideas. We no longer own them, and we could have used them to our advantage. We're not really on the same team as the GC. That's how it is in the business world. You had no way of knowing that; it takes time and experience. That's what you need your pain in the ass Uncle Guy for. You keep doin' what you're good at Jean, plumbin' and thinkin' and being creative, and leave the dog-eat-dog stuff to me."

It was quite the first day of the rest of Jean's life. The ups and downs continued through the summer. Jean threw himself into work, which often required overtime and weekend days. Aunt Yvette's brother Lee was the third man in their crew, and the trio worked well together. Jean was taking courses at Plymouth State two nights a week and spent the other nights finishing his truck. It was exhausting and rewarding.

Just not quite as rewarding as he had hoped.

He and Marie fell back into their old routine. She was hired at a preschool beginning in September and was working at their summer camp while looking for an apartment to share with her cousin Nancy. She still came to the barn most nights when Jean was working on the truck, but there was a difference. There was no more kissing and petting, neither one capable of making the first move to bridge the gap that existed since Armand Giroux's death. An invisible elephant had been added to the barn's menagerie, and neither could boot it out of the barn.

They were together again, just not quite as together as he had hoped.

There were times when he did something special at work, times when he and Marie laughed together like they used to.

Just not quite as many as he had hoped.

Then he had one of those days. Jean's baseball coach called and said the tournament was underway and some of the players were away with their families. Could Jean help out?

Uncle Guy said he and Lee could get by without him for a day. There was a doubleheader against a team from New York, which represented the adventure he gave up, so he agreed. The New York team lived up to the hype, winning both ends of the doubleheader. So did their girlfriends in the bleachers. Between games Jean got a closer look and realized they were *not* their girlfriends but their mothers, made up, coiffed, exposing more skin than necessary. He had stared from across the field as they shifted their legs exposing thighs, bent over flashing cleavage, and they were the same age as his Mom!

When Jean got home there was a note from his mother. *"Aunt Yvette took the kids back-to-school shopping, will get them dinner. Yours is in the fridge. You and Marie should stay in the house to make sure they go to bed on time. I might be late."*

He read the note twice, the last sentence five times. Was she going on a date? He took a shower, ate, tried to concentrate on "Introduction to Heating /Cooling Systems" with no success. He was in the barn putting the finishing touches on his truck when Marie drove up. She was in a very upbeat frame of mind.

"Hey Smooch, truck looks great. Ready for inspection?"

Jean was too self-absorbed to notice the reemergence of her nickname for him, which had been dropped from use along with their smooching. "Just about."

"Your mom called and asked if we could get back inside to babysit later."

"Yeah, she left a note."

"She has a date! Isn't that wicked-cool?"

"Yeah. I hear Aunt Yvette's car." He turned and headed toward the house, noticing Marie's smile was fading fast. He couldn't really blame her.

Later, sitting side by side on the sofa watching TV, his brother and sister asleep, Marie put her hand on his chin and turned his face toward hers. "This isn't right, Jean."

"Sorry. I'm not in a great mood."

"I'm talking about us. Why do we keep doing this? Are you glad when I show up here?"

Jean turned back to the TV, not really seeing it. He swung his legs up, put his head on her lap, a favorite position of theirs. Marie unconsciously put her hand in his hair, stared unseeingly at the TV. Jean remembered his first daring move, on this sofa, in this position, when they were thirteen. Marie had clasped her hands behind her head, causing her top to ride up and expose her stomach. Since that was not one of the areas specifically forbidden, Jean impulsively turned and kissed her belly button. There was a sharp intake of breath from Marie, and she held his head there, gently rubbed his face against her bare skin. Then, for some reason (nervousness?) he reverted to childish humor and blew hard while rapidly shaking his head, making a loud "raspberry" sound. They both laughed (nervously) and it became their special trademark move, repeated whenever one of them exposed bare skin.

Now, half a dozen years later and totally out of context, Jean turned, lifted Marie's sweatshirt and, before she could react, planted a loud, wet, sloppy raspberry on her navel. Marie gave a loud "oooh," then started crying. Jean shifted up, caught a tear on her cheek with his tongue, licked another off her other cheek. Floodgates opened, one long, lusty kiss followed by another, urgency fueling the passion.

Bodies squirmed, clothing pushed up, buttocks squeezed under boxers and panties. They heard footsteps upstairs, then, "Mommy, David's scaring me!!!"

This was not the first time the couple's sexual explorations had been interrupted by Jean's brother and sister, and instead of ruining the mood it somehow amplified the special closeness of their relationship. Marie smiled, touched Jean's lips with her fingers, whispered "I got it," and walked upstairs. "Hey sweetie, your mom's not here. What's up?"

"David's scaring me."

"I am not! She's a liar!"

"Okay, here's what we're gonna' do..."

When she came back down, she said, "I guess I better get going, Smooch." She smiled broadly, walked over to Jean and gave him an extra-long kiss, including a full-length body press. She stepped back, pointed at Jean, said, "Remember that one," and left.

Jean was left alone to ponder the events of the day, including the uncomfortable fact that he was now waiting up for Mom to come home from her date after ogling moms all afternoon. The phrase popped into his head, "It was the best of times, it was the worst of times." It would become a long-term resident there.

CHAPTER EIGHT

LENNY

1969, Manhattan

The year began with the inauguration of Richard "I am not a crook" Nixon, signaling the decline of the most powerful office in the free world. With the departures of Lyndon Johnson and good do-bee Hubert H. Humphrey there was no longer any pretense our government existed to serve *us*. The line was clearly drawn in the sand; Nixon and Agnew on one side and anybody with a moral conscience on the other.

Radical groups were learning electronic guerrilla warfare, evidenced by their TV takeover of the 1968 Democratic National Convention in Richard Daley's Chicago. Our political and cultural leaders were getting assassinated regularly, our landmark cities were being burned down from the inside out. We were probably closer to a civil war at that point than at any time in the preceding hundred years.

In early summer, Neil Armstrong took his small step off the Eagle as the world took a giant leap in incredulous awe. People looked up at the moon and said, "There's a guy walking around up there!" One brushstroke of daring and ingenuity changed the map of the cosmos forever. Having your feet planted firmly on the ground did not necessarily mean the Earth, and the celestial explorers suffered new and puzzling psychoses, eerily portrayed in David Bowie's Space Oddity.

The local sports world turned upside down that year as well. In January, Joe Namath brashly guaranteed his lightly regarded New York Jets would upset the National Football League champion

Baltimore Colts in Super Bowl III. Namath had thumbed his nose at tradition when he cast his fate with the upstart American Football League, which most experts didn't think could survive, let alone be competitive with the established NFL. This opinion was affirmed when the NFL's Green Bay Packers easily manhandled the AFL representatives in the first two Super Bowls. The Baltimore Colts had just wrested the NFL title from the Packers, and it was a *fait d'accompli* Baltimore would easily swat aside New York.

The city of Miami hosted the big game in the Orange Bowl. Tired of hearing about the impending Baltimore rout, and never one to keep a low profile, Namath announced his Jets not only wouldn't get trounced, they would win, and he guaranteed it. The next day every sports section of every newspaper had a picture of him in a poolside lounge chair, foxy blonde on each side, cat-that-swallowed-the-canary grin on his face, under the trumpeting caption, "BROADWAY JOE GUARANTEES WIN!" Baltimore's defensive linemen couldn't believe this long-haired, loud-mouthed kid was setting himself up for such a beating. But Namath used their overzealousness like a karate master uses his opponent's momentum, showing them how the game was going to be played from then on. As a result of the Jets 16-7 victory, the entire sports landscape was altered.

The madness continued as The Miracle Mets, owners of the worst record in the history of baseball, went from the basement to the penthouse. Led by Tom Seaver and his dog Slider they won the World Series, proving Yogi Berra's all time Yogi-ism, "good pitching stops good hitting - and *vice versa.*"

The entertainment world was upside down as well. As Marshall McLuhan predicted with his clever pun, the media was becoming the message. We passed through to the other side of the looking glass, our lives now a reflection of our art. Outlaw rock stars became our gurus, lyrics that were gibberish to older generations became our watchwords. A show that invited the audience to perform, with cast members leading them through a series of sensitivity games, had been running for a while, plenty of straights willing to plunk down big bucks for an *avant garde* experience. Sheila's older brothers were appalled by *Hair*. "That's music? That's dancing? A bunch of hairy freaks running around naked?"

"Those hairy freaks are my friends, and if you can't deal with that, go fuck yourselves!"

And then there was Woodstock. For a nanosecond in history, we were truly our own nation, isolated from the rest of the world. Arlo Guthrie stood on the stage and proudly declared, "The New York Thruway's closed, man. Can you dig it? Ha! Lotsa' freaks!" Conservative (?) estimates put the number around 350,000. We knew something was up when we came to a dead stop outside Monticello, New York, still a dozen or so miles from the grounds.

We had departed Mr. Bernstein's baseball camp in a small caravan; Sheila, Bobbi, William and their merry band in the quintessential VW bus with Carl's Triumph strapped on the back ("Just in case we need it around the grounds") following my parents' overstuffed Oldsmobile. We cruised across the Tappan Zee Bridge, flew up the Thruway to the junction with The Quickway, and were joking about Sheila's "FIFO" method of parking because it was only 1:30 and the concert wasn't scheduled to begin until 7:00. The festival was originally going to be held in the artsy town of Woodstock until the town fathers grew nervous about hosting such a large-scale rock concert and rescinded the permit. At the last minute, the promoters found Max Yasgur's farm in the town of Bethel and the venue was changed, though the name never was.

William climbed on top of my parents' Oldsmobile and reported this was as close as we were going to get. The scene was mind-blowing. Cars stretched ahead for about a quarter mile, all stopped. At the head of the line, cars were pulling onto lawns to park, the road ahead clogged shoulder to shoulder with people. A few cars made u-turns and tried heading back, either faint hearts scared away or wise guys looking for a different way. We held a car top to car top conference. I was familiar with this area from my summers working at hotels and assured everyone there was no other way.

William jumped down and offered the family gawking at us $10 to park the two cars on their lawn. When they hesitated, he threw in the promise of a ride on Carl's motorcycle for their awestruck twelve-year-old when we came back Sunday afternoon. We pulled onto their lawn, grabbed our backpacks and sleeping bags, unstrapped the bike and set out on foot for the promised land, Carl scootering along astride his silent Triumph.

It took us more than six hours to cover the twelve miles, but as the saying goes, getting there was half the fun. Food, drink, drugs, and good vibes flitted atop the river of hippies like water bugs dancing on a babbling brook. It was past 8:00 by the time we reached the grounds, fences trampled, security breached, tickets superfluous. Fortunately, it was still light enough

> *Was there ever a better feel-good idea than Daylight*
> *Savings Time? How could the all-work no-play adults*
> *who ran the world come up with something whose sole*
> *purpose was to extend fun time? Sure, they said it was*
> *devised to help farmers keep up with the extra workload*
> *in the spring, but I always knew it was really put in*

place so fathers and sons could play catch after work. My father and I fashioned a couple bases, a pitcher's rubber, and a home plate from white vinyl flooring tiles left over when our basement was remodelled into a den. Every spring evening I would meet him in the driveway, the tiles in my hands, and he would ask, "Carl Erskine or Pee Wee Reese?" The first was a pitcher, the second a short-stop, and how I answered his question dictated which gloves and vinyl tiles we brought to the backyard. Both were Brooklyn Dodgers, my favorite team despite the fact we lived in Westchester, which was serious New York Yankee country. Rooting for the Yankees was like rooting for U.S. Steel. They seemed to win every year, pinstriped corporate execs going about their business efficiently. Yuck. The Dodgers were perennial losers nicknamed Da Bums, loaded with characters and panache. Squatting behind home plate with a catcher's mitt pretending to be Roy Campanella, or straddling first base impersonating Gil Hodges, my dad would make up scenarios which wound up with me, as either shortstop Reese or pitcher Erskine, winning the seventh game of the World Series. He kept the play-by-play going while stabbing at my errant throws or pitches, his voice foreboding as things looked bleak for Da Bums, then rising in excitement as the inevitable conclusion neared.

One of the most poignant moments of my life came much later when my own son met me with three gloves and a baseball after I had a particularly difficult day at work. The last thing I wanted to do was throw a baseball around, and I realized my father must have felt the same way sometimes. So I sucked it up, and asked my son, "Rick Burleson or Luis Tiant" and imitated Curt for us to pick our way over folks and stake claim to about 150 square feet of semi-dry ground with a long view of the distant stage and scaffolding. We assumed Joan Baez was the small dot providing the beautiful, quavering tones of *Joe Hill.* Thoroughly stoned from shared marijuana on the hike in, we nevertheless set about rolling joints, which we fired up and passed around our territory and to neighbors. Other drugs were arriving steadily. I believe our balance of trade was favorable.

The carefree stupor, the soft drizzle pierced by electric guitars, beautiful harmonies musical and otherwise, all contributed to an otherworldly aura which amplified our humanity. Had the weather held out it would have been the ultimate company picnic. But it didn't. The occasional drizzle turned steady and intensified, the mud became a quagmire, soft wafts of warm air morphed into chilly gusts, and by Saturday afternoon it was a contest between man and nature.

Our own hardy clan awoke shortly after dawn on Saturday knee deep in mud. The carefully planned precautions of the night before were all for naught. Food and drugs were soaked beyond recognition, let alone use. Sleeping bags were soggy and filthy, as were our clothes. But you know, Jimi Hendrix serenaded us with the Star-Spangled Banner, and smiles, claps on backs, and raised fists repelled the gloom as the weekend wore on. Efforts were under way nationwide - that's Woodstock Nationwide - to aid those in need. A tent became an infirmary, dealing mostly with D.T.'s, cold turkeys, and bad trips. Another tent was pooling and sharing edible food. Our stars were not just performing, they were instructing and inspiring, using the stage like a pulpit to disseminate information. Cursing the government (Gimme' an 'F', Gimme' a 'U'...) they *became* the government, warning us about bad drugs and ripoff artists, communicating like town criers of old, "Barbara, please meet your sister at the pink and white tent, she just had a baby."

Woodstock was a pulley in all of our lifelines, but it was a whole block and tackle rig for William. Akin to being born again, his passion was not for the Lord but the new world order. A chance encounter with a toothless freak of indeterminate age and his traveling commune known as The Hog Farm set William on a course which altered the lives of those in our group, and some we had yet to meet.

The Hog Farm claimed connection to the Merry Pranksters, Ken Kesey's busload of original hippies. Their very existence held out hope that a life could be lived outside the confines of the establishment. The Hoggers could be found stabilizing scaffolding, repairing sodden electronics, rebuilding food carts, supervising crowd control, always with positive energy, always knowing which way the Porta-Potties were, what happened to Ravi Shankar's helicopter, why the Rolling Stones weren't coming. They were allowed places we weren't, had been places we couldn't imagine. William, whose intellect and energy were awe inspiring, was himself awestruck.

These were high school dropouts, trouble with the law runaways, school of hard knocks survivors. They didn't have the support us *faux* hippies had, or the safety net of a system that would welcome them back if they got a haircut. Something in their nature made them misfits, and the system is never kind to misfits. Most get ugly in the face of such overwhelming opposition, but the Hog Farm got beautiful. And they got William.

Sunday came and went, along with a half million tired, wet, hungry, dirty, totally exhausted hippies. We spent Sunday night on the Hog Farm, an area towards the back of the empty concert grounds. There were a couple of psychedelic school busses, army surplus tents, pets, even some fencing. It looked remarkably non-transient, as if these were feudal farmers working the land of Squire Max Yasgur. It was clear they didn't arrive Friday night like the rest of us, and a lead pipe cinch they weren't leaving just yet. Monday, mid-morning, we bedraggled our way home, *sans* William.

"I'll be back in a coupla' days." He decided to stay to help the Hoggers with the monumental clean up.

"How will you get back to the city?"

I would spend the better part of the next decade with William, see him in ecstatic joy and gut-wrenching agony, but whenever I think of him now the expression I see is the smile on his face at that moment. The issue of a convenient car ride was so mundane compared to what was going on in William's head it didn't need a response. What made William special was there was no holier-than-thou *insouciance* in his smile. There were plenty of bogus hippies smoking dope and spouting peace and love - I could be president of *that* club - but William was the real deal. He believed in Karma, he believed the stars were intertwined with our destiny, he believed love could save the world. His smile didn't say "you're a fool for being so petty," it invited me to join him in not giving a shit about a car ride, and hinted in time, if I let myself, I wouldn't either. Two weeks later, William showed up bubbling over with excitement and he insisted the whole group get together to hear about his fortnight with the Hog Farm.

It was an eventful two weeks back in the real world also. My mom, ever the den mother, greeted our wasted, muddy masses with three six-foot long hero sandwiches and insisted both carloads "stay for some food after your *ordeal*." Sheila and I had danced around each other all weekend, succumbing to the spirit of Woodstock, backing off because of my association with banks and lawyers, a little testy, a little unsure. She seemed exceptionally physical with Carl, but Carl was a hugger and back-pounder without regard to race or gender, so it was hard to tell.

It was my mom who completed the thaw. She spent an inordinate amount of time in rollicking conversation with Sheila. What could they possibly have in common to talk and laugh about? Was Sheila just being polite? When the Soho troop was leaving, Sheila tore herself away from my mom and took her turn hugging me. There was a bit of a linger, a softness, sensual though not sexual. It was certainly more enjoyable than Carl's "Hey, man, (pound, pound) keep the faith (pound, pound, pound)." And then she squeezed my hand, looked me straight in the eye, and said, "We really should get back to Mrs. McLary about the house. I'll call you." Blew my fuckin' mind, I tell ya'.

Tuesday was mine, and I needed all of it. What would have happened if Vinny had insisted I start on Monday? I was in no shape to "uphold the image of the company." The first order of business was to pick up my newly purchased car from my long-time friend Ricky, who had to miss Woodstock because of an impending dope deal. Besides having connections in Morocco, Afghanistan, Panama, Mexico, and the Caribbean, Ricky was trying to establish himself in Colombia, where a potent strain of marijuana known appropriately as "Colombian" was becoming the rage. The first kilo from this new source was due in over the weekend, and Ricky needed to be available in case it showed up. It didn't, which was why my car was ready on time.

Ricky was one of those people who knew how things worked. If you casually commented, "Does the bass sound right on *Come Together?*" you would wake up the next morning and find Ricky cross-legged on the floor in his underwear, butter knife in one hand, spool of solder in the other, one tiny Phillips screwdriver by his side, and your entire stereo system in pieces. Before you could summon forth an angry reproach, he would lift one leg towards you, proffering the lit joint held between his toes. If you still tried to be stern one look at Ricky's face would do you in. His eyes disappeared when he smiled, which was just about always. When he laughed his whole face folded in on itself, presenting a formless quivering chuckle, leaving nothing at which to direct a reprimand. Resigned, you'd take the joint from between his toes and toke, while he took his Bic out and heated the tip of the tiny screwdriver so he could continue soldering. No matter where you went, no matter how long you were gone, when you returned the stereo would be back in its place and *Come Together* would be boomin' its bass.

My car was a 1967 Fiat 124 Spider convertible that was rear-ended when it was one week old and was never the same. Ricky knew the guy who owned it, a fellow dope dealer who was transporting a trunk full of hash when he noticed a cop car following him. Paranoid, eyes glued to the rear-view mirror, he suddenly realized there was a traffic light in front of him and slammed on the brakes. Unfortunately, the light was green, and the patrol car rammed him at 40 mph, throwing open the trunk. Somehow the car wound up in Ricky's garage, where he was fixing "a few problems." Originally it was Italian green, but I had it painted Plymouth Duster metal-flake purple. I needed something a little showy. My haircut made me look like the poster boy for the Young Republicans.

Bobbi, on her way back to Bethel to join her husband William and the Hoggers, dropped me and Sheila at Ricky's. We tooled around in my spiffy sports car, top down, while we rehearsed our lines for Mrs. McLary.

"Time for the break-up," declared my imaginary wife. "I mean, ya' got banks and lawyers involved," saying 'banks' and 'lawyers' in the same sentence was a struggle for Sheila, "and, like, we're not really married."

"We could get married, buy the house, then get divorced," was my self-serving offer of a plan. I didn't *say* we'd have to go on a honeymoon.

"Let's say we were never married but were ashamed to admit it, especially to my new friend and confidant Mrs. McLary. When my parents learned I was pregnant they disowned me. Your folks are willing to help us out. Thus, *you* are buying the house in *your* name with money from *your* parents. We're gonna' live together, have a beautiful baby, my parents'll relent, then we'll have a wedding and invite Mrs. McLary to be Matron of Honor."

Maybe she hadn't heard my suggestion over the backfiring exhaust. The Fiat was running rough, my eyes yo-yoing from the road to the temperature gauge, which was on a steady climb. I remembered Ricky telling me there was a small crack in a hose that couldn't be fixed, and I should check the water frequently in hot weather.

"I don't know, Sheila, I don't think I could pull that off. I mean, you're an actress. Maybe you can do this, but I can't."

"Whaddya' mean? You were great the first time."

"I didn't say shit. You talked the whole time."

I pulled over down the block from the house, figured I had about a minute left before the car exploded. Sheila put her hand over mine, resting on the wildly vibrating gear shift knob. She looked deep into my eyes, the second time in 12 hours. Okay, forget the honeymoon - how about just a wedding night?

"Listen to me Lenny. When we're all together at my place you're one way. When you're home for dinner with your parents you're another way. When you're teaching the campers how to play ball, when you talk with that asshole Vinny, each time you play a different role. That's acting, and we *all* do it *all* the time. Doing it for a living just means you can't be found out. Don't say too much. You know the story line. Pretend you're watching a movie and we're all in it. It'll be fine."

And it was, in large part because I was outside fussing with my small Italian sports car most of the time. When I finally came inside "the gals" had already been through the pregnancy and disowning part of the deal, and we were ready to get down to business. Sheila established such a comfortable flow Mrs. McLary had no clue. The frustrating part was she also had no clue about real estate values. My brilliant ploys to reduce the price to a more palatable $25,000 sailed right over her head. I brought up the fact that the surrounding hous-es were inexpensive, which depressed the value of her house, and she offered a blank stare and said, "I need to get $30,000."

"Um, yeah, well ya' see, this house isn't really in a development, and there's a three-story apartment house next door. Some families would find it less desirable."

"But I'll still get my $30,000, won't I?" Sheila was rolling her eyes and sending signals of exasperation. She couldn't believe I was risking this cool adventure for something stupid like money, but it was *my* money, earned at the expense of *my* jaw and *my* testicles at the hands of the man I now called boss. Plus, I was caught up in the contest of negotiation. I was an adult now, in the real world of dollars and cents, where Darwin's rules applied. There were not enough acorns for all the squirrels, only the swiftest, strongest, and most persistent would get their share, and I aimed to be one of them. I was not about to give away $5,000 to some woman with an IQ probably little more than half of mine. This was my first contest, and I was determined to come out on top.

Then I remembered The Law of Louie, one of my Rules to Live a Better Life. During the second half of our senior year in high school my friends and I played poker a few nights a week. Our parents protested but were easily placated because we'd all been accepted into the colleges of our choice. The stakes were nickel, dime, quarter with a two-raise limit, high enough for significant gains and losses without causing serious trouble.

On that evening we were playing at my house in Westchester, sitting around the blue formica table, and I was doing pretty well. I decided it was time to try a major bluff and waited for an opportunity. The winner of the previous hand got to choose the next game, and when he called "Mariah" I felt a tingle. Mariah is a version of seven-card stud where everybody is dealt two face down "hole" cards, then four face up, and a final hole card face down. The best poker hand splits the pot with whoever has the highest spade "in the hole." Since two players win, the two-raise limit was waived, and the pots were huge. The moment was nigh.

When my second face up card was the ace of diamonds, I immediately raised the limit and kept raising at every opportunity, giving the impression the ace was matched by one in the hole, which it wasn't. My last face up card was the ace of clubs, and I immediately pushed the betting to a new high. Everyone thought I must now have three aces, and most folded. The ace of spades was not among the 28 face up cards now showing, and since it was assumed I had an ace in the hole and was betting like a maniac, it seemed probable that I owned it and would win the entire pot. When I didn't even look at my final hole card before starting the last round of betting with the maximum amount, the others all declared themselves out. Except for Louie.

Louie was a terrible card player. We always assumed his money would be divvied up amongst the rest of us. Everyone gaped at him as he responded to my bet with "Your quarter and I'll raise ya' a quarter." Suddenly I was unsure. What could he possibly have? He had a pair of fours showing, probably had the ace of spades in the hole and was playing for a split. Louie was obviously not going to fold now, and all we'd be splitting was our own money. I called, and he turned over his third four, the four of spades. Frantically, I flipped my last card and looked again at my other two hole cards. None were spades. Louie's three fours beat my pair of aces, and his lowly four of spades was the highest (the only!) spade in the hole, giving him the entire pot. I was embarrassed and pissed at Louie. How could he be so stupid?

"Why did you stay in? Don't you remember when I started raising everyone?"

"No, why?"

"Why?! Didn't you notice the ace of spades wasn't up anywhere?"

A blank stare. He didn't keep track of the face-up cards around the table, didn't use that info to help determine what cards the other players might have in the hole. It was a level of skill he never contemplated, choosing to rely on dumb luck. And then Ricky, the best card player among us - I wasn't in complete agreement with that consensus - uttered a basic truism.

"If you have to explain a bluff, it ain't gonna' work."

The Law of Louie. If you have to explain a joke, it ain't gonna' be funny. If I had to explain to Mrs. McLary why her house was only worth $25,000, she wasn't going to believe me. Her blank stare and Louie's were exactly the same, and so were the results. I was fucked.

I paused, took a deep breath, and settled my gaze on Mrs. Mc-Lary. I saw a short, squat body swathed in a pink running suit with magenta trim, large square tinted spectacles, and dyed red hair glued into the latest Jackie O. hairdo. I'd been in enough close ballgames to recognize when that ficklest of all friends, Moe Mentum, was about to switch sides. And here I was, playing on her home field, the crowd of one definitely rooting for her. I realized it was time to accept the inevitable.

"If I give you $30,000, could I move into the apartment immediately and stay rent free until I close on the house?"

"Just you?" Oops. It's tough to act without a script. Sheila jumped in.

"You know how men are, Mrs. McLary. They all have trouble with that 'we' part of it. But it would be great if we could move into the apartment right away. Things are really hairy right now between me and my folks." A little downcast glance as she finished the sentence, eyes glistening with held back tears, face troubled with the enormity of her problems, the mood restored. Damn, she was good.

"Well, I s'pose you could help me pack stuff up. And watch the house if I gotta' go out to Scottsdale. Yeah, I guess that's okay." Looking at me she asked, "How fast can you get the money?"

"Do you have an attorney?"

"Yep. He was gonna' be my divorce lawyer. Now he can be my re-con-cil-i-ation lawyer." Spreading the word out in exultation, Mrs. McLary was aglow. The dull slug was metamorphosing, willing the distant Arizona sunshine and her husband's love into a cocoon, emerging animated, eyes lit, wings spread. I felt myself smiling, and for the first time could truly imagine someone falling in love with Mrs. McLary.

I guess the negotiations were over, and I guess I was 0 for 1, batting zero-zero-zero. What a lean, mean squirrel I turned out to be. Maybe I was looking ahead to the night when Sheila and I would have to move into the apartment together for appearance's sake and figured that was worth $5,000.

We exchanged lawyers' names, wrote up an informal agreement, and sauntered out to the street, Mrs. McLary holding a pitcher of water for my dehydrated Fiat. She looked at the car and back to me, her face ugly again, like she had just belched up a bit of a bad meal.

"Where's the baby gonna' sit?"

"Oh, Lenny's sellin' this puppy, Mrs. McLary. Wanna' buy it? You'd look great drivin' out to Arizona with the top down." They hugged, I let the hood slam down, and we were off. "Man, I hadda' pull you through that one. What is wrong with you anyway? Why can't you just re-fucking-lax? Uuunh! You're such a goddamn project!"

I decided the best response was to turn the radio up loud and discovered why Ricky never got to that water leak. It sounded like we were sitting inside a concert-quality speaker.

My new job was fine, familiar phrases and concepts validating my four years at the University of Michigan. The only bummer was Vinny. I imagined he would display a different persona in this environment; energetic, personable, urging his employees onward for the greater glory of Team Sports Inc. But he was the same old Vinny. No gushing pride in his accomplishments, no spark of creativity, no personality.

"There's the loading dock. Here's where the stuff is stored, over

there we apply logos. There's where we sort and pack, there's my
office. Yours'll be where those guys are workin'." I wanted to pinch
his ear and say "Yo, goombah, where's da' enthusiasm?" But I didn't.

Team Sports, Inc. was a nondescript blue-gray corrugated
aluminum warehouse with a couple of overmatched shrubs out front
trying vainly for a touch of warmth. Inside it was Hemingway's *Clean
Well-Lighted Place*, a place for everything and everything in its place.
You could literally stand in the center of the painted concrete floor,
and in one slow rotation see the entire show. Vinny's office was on
a catwalk across the front gable end of the building, behind a wall
of plate glass. You could see his desk and two chairs. At the base of
the metal steps leading to the catwalk was a receptionist's desk with
a small switchboard. Facing her desk were two chairs matching the
two in Vinny's office, magazines on a table between them. When you
clanged up the metal steps and walked along the catwalk you passed
El Presidente's office, then a door to the executive bathroom, and got
to the only untidy spot in the building where my office was under
construction. It too would be plate glass. To remind me of Ida's Deli
storefront window? Like I needed to be reminded.

I spent the mornings in the building, using a bridge table and
folding chair as a temporary office. Initially, I was in charge of payroll,
inventory, and accounts receivable and would possibly become involved
with sales. There was a shitload of systems I needed to become familiar
with, and I never looked up until noon, when Vincenzo Catrone III
would enter.

"Let's go," was his friendly invitation to join him. I would immediately drop what I was doing, and we would head out in one of
the vans, stop for a Big Mac, and hit the road. We'd each pay for our
own lunch. Once, I put down a five-dollar bill and said, "I've got this,

Vinny," and he silently fished out his buck forty-nine and put it next to my five-dollar bill.

We'd spend the afternoons calling on customers, Brooklyn one day, southern Connecticut another, Northern New Jersey the next. Everywhere we went we were greeted like long lost relatives, everyone delighted to see Vinny. They were rewarded for their effusiveness with Vinny's typical deadpan demeanor. What was the deal? I could understand if he had the slightest hint of personality, but his charisma was null and void. I recalled the day Vinny re-entered my life at the baseball camp. Even Mr. Bernstein, an astute judge of character, was lavish in his praise of Vincenzo.

I was confident in my opinions, formed during the "I know everything" teen years and refined during the "hope I know enough" college experience. Intelligence was the primary determinant in all cases, and I was blessed with an unusually high supply. My judgment was impeccable, and those who didn't agree with me simply needed to have it better explained to them.

So recent events were disconcerting. I was outbargained by Mrs. McLary and totally in the dark when it came to Vinny. Did I have to re-evaluate my criteria? Could slow, plodding thinkers be as smart as I was? Could people who were obviously not cool have some other valid way, a sort of anti-Tao? How could such an obvious moron like Vinny be smart enough to run a successful business? I had plenty of time to ponder these questions as we cruised from Yonkers to Montauk, Newark to New Haven. Conversation? Yeah, right. The radio was permanently tuned to a station that had recently changed from Top Forty to All News, though Vinny paid no attention. It went on when he started the car, off when he killed the engine. I figured it was preset there before the format change, and Vinny hadn't noticed yet.

CHAPTER NINE

STEVEN

1961, Brooklyn

Steven's parents, aunts, uncles, and cousins were there for the championship game. He allowed himself a couple of moments before the game to look through the crowd, hoping to see Gail's face. He recognized a few of her Jewish friends, stared intently around their area, but came up empty. Then the National Anthem blared over the PA system, and it was football time.

Tilden was also 6 and 1, sharing the best record in Brooklyn with James Madison. They defeated Madison in the same situation the previous year and were defending champions. Their style was simple - hand the ball to a big strong ballcarrier and have him follow the biggest blockers straight ahead. Madison, on the other hand, relied on finesse. Chris Como wasn't strong enough to run straight through heavy traffic, but was shifty and speedy, and Steven could throw the ball a mile and put it right into the hands of a streaking Barry Longo. But Tilden's grind-it-out approach ate up huge chunks of time, and by halftime Madison trailed 14-0. In the locker room Coach gave an impassioned speech extolling better execution and more effort, but the third quarter was more of the same. Tilden added a touchdown and was driving toward yet another, which would put the game out of reach.

During a time out Steven grabbed Coach's arm and said, "I've got an idea."

Coach had learned not to dismiss his freshman phenom's ideas. "Better gimme' it quick."

"We split Como out wide, I get the snap and immediately hit'm with a bullet. Now he's got the ball on the outside with room to run. If they shift someone out wide to help cover him, it'll free up Longo for some bombs downfield."

"That's like the Carpenter play we used to run; a lot of the guys will remember it. Rothstein, go in for Jefferson for a play, tell him I need to talk to him. Go!" When Jefferson came to the sideline Coach grabbed him by the helmet and put his face right up to Jefferson's face guard. "We need the ball back, now! Every play, you and Rodriguez are going to ignore everything else and go straight for the runner. The first one there is not, repeat NOT, going to tackle him. The first one there is going to go for the football, hit it, pull his arm, kick him in the balls, I don't give a flyin' fuck what you do, just get it out. The second one keeps his eyes glued on the football. If it comes out, he falls on it. If the first guy couldn't get it free then, and only then, does he go for the tackle. Got it?"

"Every play?"

"Every goddamn play! Go!!" Coach then turned to Steven. "We get the ball back, we're gonna' go Carpenter. Not just once, we're gonna' go two, three, four in a row, until they commit to stopping it. Tell Longo to dog it the first time or two, like he's just a decoy, then be ready."

Coach turned his attention back to the field, energized by the possibility, slim as it was, his kids could snatch the proverbial victory from the jaws of defeat. Two plays later, Rodriguez stripped the ball and Jefferson pounced on it. It was deep in their own territory, but it was their ball. The third quarter ended, twelve minutes left, three touchdowns behind.

Coach called his offense to the sideline as they were switching sides for the fourth quarter, laid out the plan as quickly as he could, and sent them out there with the warning not to give anything away. They were on their own eleven-yard line, eighty-nine yards from a touchdown. As they approached the line of scrimmage Como drifted inconspicuously towards the left sideline, then went in motion further to the left. Steven took the snap, stood tall and fired a strike to Como. He sprinted across midfield and wasn't tackled until he reached the Tilden forty-two-yard line. Steven had him line up on the right side next, sent him further in motion, and did the same thing. This time there were a couple of defenders, and more coming quickly, but Como still had enough room to deke and dart, break free down the right sideline, and make it to the end zone. The extra point was good, 21-7, one minute eight seconds off the clock, 10:52 left.

Suddenly everything was different. The Madison kids in the stands, with nothing to cheer about all afternoon, were screaming their lungs out. The cheerleaders who had been struggling to remain upbeat were running wildly up and down the sidelines, doing flips and tossing each other in the air. The marching band's drummer started a beat, the brass kicked in.

Tilden took the kickoff and resumed their game plan. But Madison's defense was flying around the field fearlessly, fueled by adrenalin and hope. After a few first downs and about five minutes Tilden stalled and had to punt. Madison took over on their 20, 5:23 left. Before Steven ran out on the field, he looked to Coach for instructions.

"Keep pounding the Carpenter. If they adjust to stop it, we'll run different plays but always from that formation."

Steven called it again, got the snap, straightened up and cocked his arm to throw to Como. As he did, he saw a Tilden lineman anticipating the path the pass would take. He pulled the ball down, swiveled and looked to the other side of the field for Longo. But Longo was casually jogging with his back to Steven. The defensive lineman was now leaping at Steven, who ducked under the impending hit and saw a sliver of daylight straight ahead. It was dangerous for a skinny freshman, but there was some running room in the center of the field. Steven burst through and scampered fifteen yards before being sandwiched between two converging defenders. First down at the 35. Steven called a timeout and slowly wobbled to the sideline.

Coach said, "What hurts?"

"Nothing. We still going with Carpenter?"

"Yeah. But let's hurry it up. Tell the team if it's a positive play, we're runnin' it again, without a huddle." Coach grabbed him by the shoulder pads. "You all right?"

"I'm fine." When Steven got back to the huddle, he slapped Longo on the helmet. "What the fuck, Longo?"

"You said I should dog it."

"You're supposed to FAKE doggin' it. Keep your fuckin' eyes on me and get open." Then to the team, "We're goin' Carpenter again, to the left. If they stop it, we'll huddle up for the next play. If we gain yardage, watch me. I'll wave you up to the line, no huddle, and we'll run it again. You linemen gotta' keep those Tilden assholes offa' me. Ready, break!"

Once again Steven stood tall, started his throwing motion to Como near the left sideline. There were now three defensive backs on Como. Steven looked right and there was Longo, still casually daw-dling along. But just at that moment he put it into gear and raced past his defenders, looking back over his left shoulder at Steven. Steven felt the rush coming from Tilden's linemen, waited as long as he could, and let it fly at the last second. He got swarmed under, worked his head out of the pile in time to see Longo twisting around. Steven gauged the distance perfectly, but the rush of the linemen caused him to throw it slightly offline, over Longo's wrong shoulder. Longo got his feet tangled trying to adjust, but as he was falling stuck those soft hands up and held onto the ball as he hit the ground. First down, under five minutes and counting.

Steven raced downfield waving his team to the line of scrimmage. He ran beside Como and said, "They got three guys on ya' now. Step right into them before you turn to me. I'll pump-fake it. If they bite on the fake, go long." When he faked to Como all three defenders leaped into the path of the expected pass, and Como blew right past them. Steven threw a long, arcing spiral out ahead of the racing Como. Everything unfolded as if in slow motion, Steven's eyes going from Como to ball to Como to ball to the spot where they needed to meet. The ball started its descent into the far-left corner of the end zone, Como still yards away. As he reached the goal line Como launched himself, arms outstretched, got his fingertips on the ball, pulled it into his body, hit the ground, rolled over twice and leaped up with the ball in his hands. The referee's arms shot up. Touchdown. Extra point good, 21-14, 3:22 left. Coach called his defensive leaders over to him.

"Okay, the last two times you stopped 'em, once by a fumble, once by denying 'em a first down. You gotta' do it one more time, and you gotta' do it now. You seniors, this is the last time you're gonna' be on the field for Madison, your last chance to be champions. Don't hold anything back, sell out completely to stop the run. We get the ball back, you know we'll score."

The next two minutes were the longest two minutes in Coach's career. He was jumping up and down to the beat of the drums, chewing gum at a million miles per hour. His sky-high defense stopped Tilden. Coach called Steven, Longo, and Como over to him. "First play we line up in Carpenter, but you two (pointing at Como and Steven) switch positions, Como at QB, Masciarelli split wide. Four-two gets the snap, steps back as if to throw, and runs the QB Draw, right up the middle. If it's not there, throw to one-six or eight-oh." Coach poked Longo in the chest, hard, right between the eight and the zero. "Be ready if he needs you. If we get the first down, line up quick, no huddle, Masciarelli back at QB. Got it?" Three helmets nodded.

The decibel level, already deafening, increased again as Tilden lined up to punt. High school fields are typically not enclosed by seats, just bleachers along the two sidelines. But in urban areas the fields are often surrounded by apartment buildings, as was the case here, giving a stadium audio effect. Everyone was screaming at the top of their lungs, the band was blaring, stamping feet were threatening to collapse the bleachers. Ball snapped to punter, kick fielded cleanly and returned nicely to the Madison 34-yard line, 66 yards from the tying touchdown.

Tilden overloaded to defend Como, then started screaming and pointing as they noticed the position switch. The crowd noise obliterated the warnings, there was a last second of confused panic, Como took the snap, stepped back as if to throw, then ran through a hole a streetcar could have rolled through. Forty yards later he was dragged down by a desperation, touchdown-saving tackle. First and ten at the Tilden 26-yard line, 34 seconds left on the clock.

Steven got his team in position without a huddle. He had already called the next two plays in the previous huddle, both Carpenters, first one to Como second one to Longo. Tilden's coach was screaming for a timeout, but in high school football timeouts must be called by a player on the field, and they were too discombobulated to see him frantically waving.

On the Madison sideline, Coach stopped jumping and was the picture of serenity. This happens sometimes in athletic contests at moments like this. The thunderous noise disappears as if someone pressed "mute" and the action slows down. Coach had done all he could to put his boys in position to win. Everything that happened from now on was out of his control. There was only one more decision he might have to make, and he had already decided which way he would go. Coach watched his team line up, saw Steven take the snap, turn toward Como, and drill the ball through the tightest opening. Coach was surprised because three defenders were there, but they had been burned a couple of times in a row by fakes and were reluctant to commit to Como. They were hesitant, not aggressive. Steven's laser got through to Como, who caught it and burst right through them. All three got their hands on him, but arm tackles were not going to cut it. Como was determined. This would be the last time he would carry the ball for James Madison High School. If he scored, he could go out a champion. His peripheral vision picked up Tilden's toughest tackler coming at him. Como braced for the collision, lowered his shoulder, and delivered a blow to the tackler with as much force as was being delivered to him. He stayed on his feet, the tackler hanging on to his thighs. Como dragged him the final five yards and fell into the end zone. Tilden 21, Madison 20, 8 seconds left.

Coach told his placekicker not to go in. Instead of kicking the extra point they would run a play for a 2-point conversion. If we don't make it, we lose, if we make it, we're champs. He sent the play in – sweep right, the same play that went for a touchdown in Steven's first game.

Steven called the play firmly but calmly, with confidence, not a trace of panic, adding, "Everyone just beat their man, we're champs. We're gonna' go on the first thing I say, maybe give us a split-second advantage."

Steven crouched under center, barked out "Ready" as if he would continue with "Set," but the ball was hiked and Steven turned, handed off to Como, and sprinted along the line looking for someone to block. No need. The offensive line swept as one, Como strung it along, then cut forward and ran into the end zone untouched. Madison 22, Tilden 21.

The clock doesn't run during extra point plays, so there were still eight seconds showing on the clock. It took the referees, coaches, and police almost 10 minutes to clear the field of wildly exuberant and fiercely frustrated fans and restore a semblance of order so Madison could kick off. Tilden tried multiple laterals and handoffs in a last-ditch attempt to pull off a miraculous kickoff return, but the ballcarrier was tackled and the game was officially over. The swarming back onto the field was anticlimactic, with only a few isolated dustups between the Tilden crowd and the Madison crowd. Before Steven sought out his family, he went looking for Chris Como, caught up with him talking to a small group of men wearing different colored baseball caps. Steven recognized a couple of hats, the blue and white "PSU" for Penn State, the navy with an orange "S" for Syracuse University, and realized the men were college recruiters. Not wanting to butt in he turned to go, but Como saw him and said, "Hey one-six, quite a game!"

"Sure was. I have a question. Would it be okay with you if I wore 42 next year?"

Como pulled off his jersey, said, "It'd be an honor, one-six," and handed it to Steven. A flash bulb popped, and that picture was on the front page of The Brooklyn Eagle the next day under the caption "Passing the Torch at James Madison HS."

There was a spattering of applause, and Steven was surprised to see a small group gathered, including his family, who apparently knew the Comos. Of course, that made sense. Chris was the leader of the high school Italians, and his family members were prominent in the Italian community. "Passing the torch" indeed, on a number of different levels. Steven got hugs from Mom and Pop, his mother's eyes teary with pride. Como shook hands with Steven's parents, and said to Steven, "We better get back to the locker room. Coach'll be countin' noses."

Steven nodded, then hesitated. A man who had been hanging back was walking over, smiling. He looked vaguely familiar, but Steven couldn't place him. Then, with a jolt, he realized it was Gail's father. "You go ahead, I got one more hand to shake. Hi, Mr. Bernstein."

"Great game, Steven." Steven looked past him for Gail, his disappointment obvious. Mom was watching the interaction closely, and chimed in.

"Gail couldn't make it. She's not feeling well."

"What's wrong?"

"She's had a tough couple months," Mr. Bernstein said, "some kind of stomach issue. They've been trying to find the right meds to treat it. She asked me to be her substitute fan."

"Can I come over to see her?"

"She's staying out on Long Island with her aunt and uncle. They live right near the specialist, who needs to monitor her condition. Mrs. Bernstein's staying there too, and I go out as much as I can."

Steven started to ask if he could visit her on Long Island, but a scuffle was breaking out next to them. There was loud profanity, some pushing. Steven was embarrassed to see Vito at the center of the disturbance.

"Ya' wanna' go, Vito?"

"Bring it on, asshole."

"You got a big fuckin' mouth for someone who pimps his wife, ya' know that?" More pushing and shoving, a few punches, then Vito opened a switchblade.

Steven started forward, but Pop grabbed his shoulder pads and redirected him toward the school, walking briskly alongside until they caught up with Como. Aunt Angela got in Vito's face and backed her younger brother away from further trouble. Uncle Eddie got the switchblade into his pocket and herded everyone away from the melee. No arrests, no casualties. But waiting outside for Steven to emerge from the locker room, Pop could barely control himself. It wasn't just Vito's behavior. It was the realization that the delicate transition from shielding Steven to educating him, a process only recently begun with after dinner talks, was not good enough. The pace had to be accelerated, and it had to be his foot on the gas pedal.

Mom was also nervous. She hooked arms with Gail's dad and casually but quickly guided him toward the parking lot, keeping the conversation going with small talk centered around Steven and the game. Gail's father certainly noticed the abrupt end of the celebration, but she just kept smiling and striding, prattling on about "the kids" and the game, hoping the photographer didn't also snap a shot of the fight for the City Editor's desk.

Steven decided to concentrate on schoolwork during the next few weeks. There was some slippage in his grades due to his preoccupation with football, responsibilities as class officer, and the distraction of Gail's disappearance. But his academic issues were nothing like Barry Longo's. Steven was concerned that one or two B's might break an eight-year unbroken string of A's. The oft-repeated warning in Pop's after dinner talks with Steven was "Now that you're in 9th grade everything goes on your transcript for college," and since Pop's expectations were Ivy League, anything but straight A's was unacceptable.

After the flareup in the parking lot, Pop's talks picked up in pace and presentation. The casual, offhand manner was replaced with more intense, regularly scheduled sessions. Steven was proud that Pop was entrusting the family store's future to him. His curiosity was piqued when Pop ventured into loopholes and ambiguities in the law.

"Most people steer clear of them. But others, like *Nonno*, Vito, Uncle Eddie, and me, like to take chances. It's way more profitable. We kind of straddle the line, hopping back and forth like your cheerleader friends jumping rope. It's risky 'cause the line moves sometimes and you may be on the wrong side of the law. Then the line settles, and it's safe for a while."

"Is it like that now?" Steven, intrigued but more than a little nervous, replayed scenes from *On the Waterfront*, Rod Steiger taking the fall, Marlon Brando getting pummeled, Eva Marie Saint crying.

"Yes," Pop smiled, "but you remember when *On the Waterfront* came out?" Steven almost jumped out of his skin. *Could Pop actually read my mind?!* "Nobody in our family was safe then. It happens from time to time. When you walk a tightrope, you have to be able to withstand sudden gusts of wind, learn how to steady yourself. It takes self-control and discipline, which, by the way, you have in spades."

Steven, wide-eyed, shuddered involuntarily. It seemed like a scary way to live. "How often do those shaky times happen?"

"Not very. If you have a good lawyer, you can anticipate trouble and avoid it entirely. That's why I think you should be a lawyer. But that's enough for now."

Pop always closed the conversation with a teaser, giving Steven time to let the information percolate. A few days after the idea of becoming a lawyer was mentioned, Steven wanted to know what he should do *tomorrow morning* to start the ball rolling.

"For now, let's make sure those grades stay at an Ivy League level."

Steven could see his future becoming more defined after each of Pop's talks. Then Pop ended one with, "Politicians make decisions that affect everyone."

"I wanna' be a lawyer, not a politician." The last few days Steven had been picturing himself brilliantly holding sway in a courtroom, *a la* Perry Mason on TV. His Della Street was Gail Bernstein.

"Many politicians *are* lawyers. Remember what I told you about laws changing and legal boundary lines shifting? Nobody takes advantage of that better than politicians. They have inside information on where the line is most likely to go. That information is valuable to businessmen, who fall all over each other trying to do favors for politicians to get that information before their competitors. And anyway, you're already a politician."

"You mean that dorky Student Council thing?"

"You think that's 'dorky?' You got more votes than all the other candidates combined."

"It's just in school, Pop. It's like being a hall monitor. Nobody gives you anything or wants to do big favors for you."

"Oh really? Rico's boy called in favors on your behalf before the first game, and the blacks and Puerto Ricans were happy to help him out. And Coach asked you to bail out that Longo kid. Don't you think that you being an elected officer helped Coach get the ear of the Spanish teacher?"

Steven was flabbergasted and angrily snapped, "How'd you know all that stuff?"

Pop ignored the attitude, felt no need to answer Steven's question. He was silent for a moment that stretched until it bordered on uncomfortable. Then, with perfect timing, a *non sequitur*: "Did you know they say the President has the second hardest job in America?"

"What's the hardest?"

"Being Mayor of New York City."

"I don't wanna' be President *or* Mayor."

"Tell me son, why do you want to be the leader of your group?"

Steven blushed. He remembered seeing Longo flirt with Gail. "I don't know."

"It's hard to be careful what you say and who you say it to. You wouldn't make that effort if you didn't want to. You must know why you do it." Steven's cheeks reddened even more. "It feels good to be in charge, doesn't it? To have the power to make things happen?"

"I guess."

"And maybe impress a girl?" Steven's cheeks couldn't get any redder. "Enough. I have some orders to go over before tomorrow morning, and I'm sure you have homework to do. We'll talk again soon." But Pop thought he might wait a bit before they sat down again. For the first time the tone of the conversation had become adversarial. His wife was trying to arrange a way Steven could visit that girl out on Long Island. That might change Steven's perspective.

CHAPTER TEN

TWO THUGS ON A THREE-DAY TRIP

Day 1, 1972, Darren NH

Fred's mind was racing, searching for something to change the direction of the meeting with Moe and Joe. He needed to regain the swagger he had when directing the city slickers up his driveway and into his truck, the confident mountain man who knew the ins and outs of navigating the winter woods, assuring them they'd be lost without him. But now it was he who was lost, no leverage left if he gave them the information they wanted. And what if he refused? Was his life in danger? Grasping for straws, Fred played the Vinny card.

"I backed out of this deal once before you know, because of Vinny." The effect was not as stunning as he hoped. No gasps of horror, no recoils of trepidation. But there was a slight skip of the needle, a perceptible pause in the program. Afraid to let it pass without taking advantage, Fred pressed on. "The first time I met Vinny was in Boston at a sporting goods trade show. The guy who contacted me about the land deal suggested it as a place to meet. I brought my brother-in-law Guy 'cause we're both involved in youth sports. If nothin' else, we figured we'd get some good deals on sports equipment. Plus, Guy's worked on huge projects, which this definitely is." Fred took a breath, tried to assess Joe and Moe. They were still unresponsive, but alert and paying attention, unlike when Fred was talking about Town Meeting. He was unsure where this path would lead, but as long as they listened, he would continue, hoping something might pop up to give him some traction. "At the Team Sports booth I went over to a tall, athletic looking kid. It was Vinny. The only other man behind the booth was standing by a wheelchair, I didn't even notice him at first, but it turns out *he* was the one I talked to on the phone, the one who arranged the meeting. He introduced himself and his son who was in the wheelchair. The son was very knowledgeable, real sharp, knew all the facts."

"Where ya' goin' with this, Fred?"

It was Joe this time and Fred was surprised. It was the first time he heard his voice since the monosyllabic introductions. While Moe's tone was condescending, Joe's seemed friendlier. Fred shifted his attention and remarks toward Joe. "The son laid out the deal and it sounded great. He pointed out there would be resistance from neigh-bors, and asked if we were willing to get involved in things that might wind up hurting them. Of course, we both assumed he meant financially, and said we were willing. But Vinny clarified that 'hurt' might mean 'physically hurt.' He sounded like he was…looking forward to that part of it. My brother-in-law and I were shocked. We said we couldn't be a part of anything like that and left."

"Okay. But here you are." No patronizing from Joe, just a friend trying to understand.

"Me and Guy couldn't believe we were so close to getting into something we thought only happened in the movies. That's all we talked about for weeks, how lucky we were. Then the young man who was in the wheelchair contacted Guy and said we misunderstood, and he'd like another chance to talk to us. He made a point of saying it would be just him and his dad."

"So, you came back in." Simple statement of fact from Joe.

"He assured us there would be no rough stuff, Vinny was just trying to judge our commitment and he could see how we might have misunderstood. He made it clear he was in charge. So yeah, we came back in. And since then, we haven't seen or heard from Vinny. There was resistance from neighbors, but I'm used to that in my business, and it was nothing we couldn't handle. Then we found out they were circulating some damaging information that could squash the deal, and I called and talked to the kid's dad. He didn't seem bothered, said he was sure nothing would come of it, but then my, um, informant told me it would *definitely* kill the deal. I called again and left a message for the dad, but Vinny called back and said he was sending two guys up here to handle it." Fred was winded. Once he got to the point about Vinny and the "rough stuff" he was afraid to take a breath. He was nervous talking about the "two guys" since he was staring right at them.

"Vinny didn't send us." This time it was Moe, his tone more thoughtful, more attentive.

"The dad sent you?"

"We're not here to answer questions," said Moe, "we're here to do a job. We get hired for certain jobs because we do them with the least amount of damage. This job is no different."

Fred was stumped into silence. Was Moe saying no one would get hurt? Not really. Was "the least amount of damage" acceptable? Would it be acceptable to his wife or her sister Yvette and husband Guy, who were related to the ones who might get hurt? It was Guy who insisted he get assurances there would be no physical violence. Moe's response fell short of that, but Fred was pretty sure it was all he would get. Where should he go now? What were his options? He looked at the framed popes on the wall, one then the other, for guidance. He got nothing. He looked at the two men, one then the other. Nothing.

"So," said Joe, "back to business. Where does this hippie with the incriminating papers live, and what's he look like?"

CHAPTER ELEVEN

JEAN AND MARIE

1963, Darren NH

· · JEAN · ·

At the end of the summer, when he needed to decide about the transfer to RPI, the decision was obvious. Giroux Plumbing and Heating, Inc. was pushing hard for the top spot in the conglomerate at Waterville Valley. He and Uncle Guy eliminated most of their small jobs and remodeled two barn stalls into an up-to date-office. They hired Marie's cousin Nancy and her boyfriend Nick, the area's first hippie couple. Nancy recently returned from a six-month sojourn to find herself, spending most of it in California with a group of hippies, and she and Marie rented an apartment together. Despite her eccentric appearance, Nancy did a great job as the company's bookkeeper/receptionist. Nick, sporting the first-in-the-area male ponytail, was a capable plumber, and Aunt Yvette's brother Lee filled in when needed.

Jean was finishing the courses available at Plymouth State, leaving work early two afternoons a week. He would have to drive to UNH's main campus in Durham three nights a week for the more advanced courses. It was a grind, but even the basic engineering courses were interesting and paying dividends at work, and the courses he was about to start looked even more exciting. Living at home was mostly okay, not perfect.

His close relationship with Mom was being tested, as both were in transition. Jean had one foot out of the nest and one in, a working adult who could take care of himself. He got along well with his brother and sister, the age difference eliminating sibling rivalry issues and putting him in the role of idol/advisor. Jean and Mom replaced Dad as representatives at family affairs.

Bonnie Giroux, a 40-year-old widow with one child in college and two in elementary school, had to reinvent herself. She was active and attractive, was often told how much she looked like Marlo Thomas. Jean was as mature as could be but Cindy and David, unable to discuss their loss on an adult level, enigmatic and inconsistent in their moods, were a challenge.

The closeness of the two Giroux families was invaluable. Bonnie's sister-in-law Yvette was one of seven children. In addition to Lee, she had another brother and four sisters and all but the other brother stayed local. Their families rallied around Bonnie and the kids. There was no shortage of babysitters, food preparers, handymen, house-keeping help. Yvette was close enough to tell Bonnie when she was wrong about something. She was the one who convinced Bonnie she had to take care of her own emotional wellbeing to properly take care of her children and set up Bonnie's first date the night Jean and Marie rekindled the spark on the sofa.

It wasn't really a date. A local company was having a summer picnic at the lake, and one of the men recently lost his wife to cancer. Everybody knew everybody in Darren, and he and Bonnie were casual friends. They kidded each other about being blind dates, though it was way too soon for either of them. When she walked into her living room to find Jean waiting up for her it was clear her son was in a snit about something.

"What's up, Jean?"

"Nothin'."

"C'mon, sweetie, something's bothering you. What is it?"

"It's just a little weird to be waiting up for you to come home from a date."

Bonnie was tempted to dismiss the surly attitude but knew this was a subject she would need to address. She decided the best approach was light and breezy.

"Wow, really? I never thought of it as a 'date.' His company had a picnic at the lake, and Aunt Yvette thought I could use a little socialization. But you know, I'm glad you brought the subject up because some day I might have a *real* date. I'm sure it will be confusing for me, and now I see it'll probably be confusing for you too." No response from Jean, but his surly expression mellowed to uncomfortable. "We don't hafta' talk about this now unless you want to, but we'll have to sometime. Your father was my one true love, I miss him terribly, just like you do. That will never change for either of us. But life goes on, and both of us'll need each other's support."

"I know that, Mom. But it's still weird."

"For me too. We all need to adjust, you and me, your brother and sister, Marie, everyone."

The mention of Marie and his younger siblings brought Jean back to the evening activities on the sofa and that long and passionate good night kiss. His mood brightened, and though unaware of why, Bonnie could feel the improvement. "Go upstairs and read engineering until it puts you to sleep. We'll deal with this 'weird' subject, and we'll figure it out, together."

Marie finished her first year as a teacher's assistant in the kindergarten room and was inching her way toward a teaching degree. She and Nancy shared an apartment in downtown Plymouth. It had one bedroom until Jean installed a door leading to the dining room, which became her bedroom. A small table with two chairs was all that fit in the kitchen, so when the four of them ate together they stood around the kitchen counter. This was a small price to pay for separate bedrooms, since all four were more interested in sex than food.

Nancy, despite growing up even further in the boondocks than Marie, was more worldly. She wore clothes that were groovy, was politically and sexually liberal and liberated. Nick had a ponytail, and his sideburns were long enough to stand out from the local crowd. He listened to "underground" radio stations like WBCN from Boston, and he smoked marijuana.

Nancy did also, but neither did when Jean was around. They were concerned that Jean, and by extension Guy, would fire them. She got Marie to try it when they were alone in the apartment. Marie was hesitant at first, scared because it was against the law. Also, she didn't like doing something she had to keep secret from Jean. But Marie was in the "eye-opening" phase of her life, and Nancy was the main eye-opener, frank about her sexuality, her disdain for organized religion and the establishment. The conversations they shared when stoned were soul searching, yet full of laughter so hearty it often drew tears. Marie grew comfortable enough to join in when Nick was there, and even considered turning Jean on so the four of them could share the experience. The stumbling blocks were the illegality and the work factor that deterred Nancy and Nick. The two girls discussed how to overcome those obstacles, and agreed the initial turn-on should occur when Marie and Jean were alone.

Marie was anxious to end the duplicity between her and Jean and had to admit she was aroused by Nancy's explicit accounts of the intense sex she and Nick had when they were stoned. Marie and Jean still hadn't "gone all the way" at that point, but they certainly came close. An opportunity arrived when Nancy's parents were invited to spend a week in Florida with friends and Nancy had to house-sit.

Their first night alone in the apartment was enough of an aphrodisiac without any marijuana. When they reached the usual stopping point Jean persisted, rubbing his penis around Marie's clitoris before she pulled away. But this time her cautionary comment was different.

"Do you have a condom?"

Jean rapidly rolled out of her bed, found his jeans, groped for his wallet, and came up empty. "Shit!"

"In your truck?"

"On my nightstand at home." Jean stopped carrying his wallet in his back pocket because he was frequently in tight spots at work, and it had fallen out on a few occasions. "Shit," he said again, then, "We can get some at a drug store."

Marie laughed at the thought of them scurrying around town in search of a condom. Every store clerk or pharmacist would recognize Jean, know what they were planning, and with whom. Even if successful it would be hard to replicate the mood. "Nancy has birth control pills."

"Here?" Jean was unaware of how they worked and wasn't quite ready to admit defeat.

Marie laughed again. "No, Smooch, not here. You need to take them every day. There's a clinic in Boston that'll give you a prescription without permission from your parents, and Nancy said she'd get me an appointment."

"Did you go?" Jean was still hoping.

"Not yet, but I will if you want me to." Marie tried not to show her nervousness.

Jean kissed her gently on the lips, smiled and said, "Call Nancy *right now* and start the ball rolling." He planted his lips on her navel and made their trademark raspberry sound. The next night was when Jean installed the door to the dining room.

The trip to Boston was quite an adventure for the two girls. Both had visited Boston with their families when they were younger, but Nancy was there more recently with Nick to see the Red Sox a few times, Boston Garden once to see the Bruins, as well as a half-dozen times to clubs to see local bands. And to cop marijuana. And to the clinic for birth control pills. This time, without Nick, Nancy would be the guide.

She was well schooled by Nick, and their plan was sound. Park in a lot near Harvard Square and take public transportation to Massachusetts General Hospital, which was near the doctor's office. They left early enough to allow time for unexpected delays, which occurred immediately. They were on the wrong side of the tracks boarding the train and headed away from Mass General. By the time they realized it their extra time allowance was gone, and Marie was frazzled. They saw a sign for "Charles Street Station, MGH," pushed their way on a train and collapsed into their seats.

"No big deal," said Nancy, noticing her cousin's exasperation, "we'd only have to wait if we got there early."

"I guess." Marie was nervous about the appointment, unsure how to act. The only reason she wanted birth control pills was to have sex with her boyfriend. Was that enough? Should she lie? Nancy reassured Marie about the people at the clinic.

"They're all women, even the doctor. She's like, our parents' age, but she's cool."

The office had the typical sliding glass window where Marie checked in. The walls were covered with information about birth control, parenting resources and childcare alternatives. There was a bulletin board crowded with notices covering the entire gamut of women's issues: single mom support groups, domestic violence, a safe home for runaways. There was a list of discussion groups ranging from women in the military to NOW meetings to equality in the workplace. Instead of feeling intimidated by a sterile doctor's office, Marie felt like a member of a sisterhood with noble ideals.

She took a seat. When her name was called, she stood up, handed the escort her paperwork, and followed her down a hallway.

"I'm Lisa, Marie," she said as she knocked on a door and a woman's voice said "Come in." Marie followed her to the doctor's desk, where Lisa deposited her paperwork, turned to Marie, smiled, and said, "I'll show you out when you're through."

The doctor was biting her lip as she wrote, looked up, flashed a smile, and said, "Just gotta' finish these notes. Grab a seat over there and I'll join you in a sec," pointing to two chairs.

Marie sat, looked around and settled her gaze on the doctor who, perhaps because of Nancy's suggestion, *did* remind her of her mother. After a minute or two she put the pen behind her ear, grabbed Marie's paperwork, pushed back from her desk, and sat beside Marie.

"All righty then," scanning the form, "Hi Marie, I'm Dr. Klusze-wski, known around here as Dr. K. Pleased to meet you," offering a hand to be shaken along with a smile. "Anything you were afraid to put in writing?"

Marie was taken aback by the question. Dr. K was, like all the other women working in the clinic, wearing jeans and clogs, though she was the only one wearing a blue scrubs top. Her brown and grey hair was pulled back loosely into a ponytail, half glasses riding low on her nose. She presented an inviting manner while still exuding professionalism. Marie wanted to like her.

"I don't think so."

"Okay. So, living with someone?"

"My cousin Nancy. She's the one who told me about the clinic."

"I meant a boyfriend."

Marie blushed and said, "No."

"Are you sexually active."

"Yes- oh, no..."

Dr. K.'s smile increased. "I guess you need to clarify that answer."

"Well, we do...things, but we've never...uh, not yet."

"Let me help you along here. Is sexual intercourse the next step in your relationship?"

Marie gave an audible sigh of relief, gasped out "Yes!" with such obvious gratitude Dr. K. responded with good-natured laughter. Marie's blush deepened.

"You're doing fine Marie. This isn't a test. I'm here to help, not hassle. What's the young man's name, and how long have you two been in a relationship?"

"Jean. Since first grade." Now it was Dr. K.'s turn to be taken aback. Marie, in an attempt to explain, added, "I'm Catholic."

"I guess you are!" This time they laughed together. "So was I. Is that a problem?"

Marie didn't miss the past tense. "Not really. I mean, I don't think so."

"Do you and Jean have plans for the future?"

"Oh, yes! We both go to school at night and work during the day. Jean's gonna' be an engineer, and I'm gonna' be a teacher."

"I meant as a couple."

"Oh, like marriage? Well, I guess we don't have a specific time frame... I mean, we've always been a couple."

"Why did you decide to room with Nancy instead of moving in with Jean?"

"He still lives at home. His father died a while ago."

"How long?"

"Just over a year."

"Okay. So, I have a few contacts in the Catholic church who understand the kinds of doubt or guilt you might feel about moving this relationship to the next level. Would you like me to arrange that?"

"Do I have to?"

"No, Marie, of course not. I offer that option in case you aren't sure about what you want to do, have concerns because of your religious training, or the death of your boyfriend's father may be confusing the issue for the two of you."

"I'm not confused. I'm sure." It was the most declarative statement Marie had made, blush gone, eyes unwavering, different posture. For the first time Dr. K. felt like she was dealing with a woman who knew what she was doing.

"Awesome." Dr. K. got up and grabbed a pad from her desk, wrote on it quickly, tore off the top sheet. "I see you've been keeping regular appointments with a gynecologist with no problems. Lisa will go over what you need to know about the pills. My number's on the script and the pill container. Do not, repeat, *do not* hesitate to call me with any questions or problems. They don't have to be medical. If the Catholic thing rears its head, if your boyfriend wants to talk to someone about his father's death, if your parents find out and pitch a hissy, anything. Lisa will give you her number, too, if you'd rather talk with someone your own age."

"I'm fine talking to you."

Dr. K. put her hand on Marie's shoulder and said, "I'm fine talking to you too, Marie.

They went over how the dispenser worked, how to monitor her menstrual cycle, what to expect from her next few periods, and what side effects to watch out for. Nancy was asleep with a magazine on her lap when Lisa showed Marie out, the result of their early morning departure. Marie nudged her.

"Huh? Oh, hey, how'd it go?"

Marie grinned, waved the prescription, and said, "Let's go find a drug store!"

"I've got that covered. The receptionist let me call Nick, and he said we should check out Harvard Square, find a drugstore, then get our car."

"I don't think so, Nancy. I mean, we already got lost once today."

"She gave me the name and address of a drugstore near the square," pointing at the receptionist. "She can call it in from here, it'll be waiting for us."

"I'm pretty played out."

"Trust me, my dear cousin, it's worth it. Harvard Square is the coolest, grooviest place in the whole fuckin' world."

Nancy pushed Marie toward the window, where the receptionist was smiling, holding out her hand for the prescription, and concurred. "She's right, cousin, it *is* the grooviest place in the whole fuckin' world."

She pressed a button on her phone. "I've got the pharmacist on the line." Marie gave her the script. She read a few numbers into the phone, spelled Marie's name, said "thank you," hung up, and gave back the script and the address of the pharmacy.

All Marie wanted to do was sit down somewhere and relax. But ten seconds after entering Harvard Square she was reenergized. Nancy grabbed her hand and led her through a slow 360. When they had left New Hampshire in the morning it was snowing, and a biting winter wind was blowing. The morning scramble to the T station was snow free but still cold and windy. It was afternoon by the time they made it to Harvard Square, wind now coming from the southwest, ushering in clouds and unseasonably warmer temperatures along with a fine drizzle. The sidewalks were filled with people congregating in front of a variety of "attractions." A trio, two guitars and a Conga drum, were entertaining a small group right in front of them. On the corner, a man was reciting The Lord's Prayer over and over. There was a group handing out pamphlets and singing "Give Peace A Chance." Every cause was being proselytized, as if the bulletin board from the clinic had sprung to life. Marie caught the odor of marijuana, looked wide-eyed at Nancy.

"Yeah, I smelled it too."

"Right out on the street?!"

"I guess the cops have more important things to do than bust some college kids for smoking weed." Nancy nodded her head toward two people who were obviously living on the street with all their possessions in trash bags, then pointed to a poster on a boarded-up bank window offering a reward for any information about who threw the destructive bricks. "You know the bookstore at Plymouth State? Picture that, then check *this* out."

They were standing in front of The Coop, a cooperative bookstore founded in 1882 by Harvard students. Going inside was akin
to entering another world. A cramped staircase at the back led up
and down through four floors of books, people, Harvard University
apparel, even food at the Coop Cafe. They each had a cup of clam
chowder standing up, then squeezed into an opening on a bench for
a dessert of hot chocolate. It was the people watching that made the
place amazing, thought Marie. She could have stayed there all day,
then suddenly remembered why they came to Boston in the first
place.

"My pills!" she blurted out. "We need to find that drug store.
What time is it?"

A man standing next to them said "Just after three." He had to
be a professor, a rim of longish white hair surrounding a bald pate,
tweed sport jacket with leather elbow patches, checked shirt open at
the collar, corduroy pants, worn briefcase. "Is it an emergency?"

"Huh?"

"Your pills. Do you need medical assistance?"

"Oh, no, thanks. Do you know where this pharmacy is?" Marie
handed him the address.

"Left out of the door, then first left, the third or fourth store on
your right."

The cousins reluctantly gathered themselves and departed. They
took one more lap around the square, found the drugstore and their
car. It was a quiet ride home, Nancy concentrating on whether or
not the light rain might change to snow or freeze as they made their
way north, Marie's mind going over the events of the day. When she
saw the "*Bienvenue*" sign the French-Canadian community puts on
highways entering New Hampshire with the iconic "Old Man in the

Mountain" profile, her thoughts drifted back to the time her family had driven to the top of Mount Washington. Marie was nearing driving age by that time and was curious about all things automotive. She asked her father about the signs on the steep, winding road back down the mountain warning drivers to "Control Speed with Engine - Save Brakes!"

"What does that mean, Dad?"

"They want you to use a lower gear to control your speed, instead of riding your brakes the whole way down."

"Why?"

"Your brake fluid could overheat and not work. The straightaway at the bottom empties onto Route 16, and cars have blasted right through the stop sign because they couldn't stop."

"Don't those emergency ramps for trucks work?"

"Yes. You steer your truck onto it and the soft surface and uphill slant slows you down. But there's no room for those here."

The road they were on was tight against a steep rock cliff on one side and a precipitous drop on the other. The guard rail did not inspire confidence.

"Has anybody ever gone over?"

"I don't think so. But there have been some nasty accidents on Route 16." Marie imagined herself driving an 18-wheeler, careening down a hill with no brakes, and her stomach became queasy, like on a Tilt-a-Whirl at a carnival. She felt the same way now. All her training by church and family delineated the straight and narrow road with repetitive warning signs. Underlying every warning was the theme of controlling one's urges, denying the baser instincts, holding oneself to a higher moral standard. What she was about to do was against so much of that on so many levels. She was breaking the rules for selfish reasons, to experience forbidden excitement. She didn't doubt she was ready to take the leap. What scared her was the image of the runaway truck ramp. Once she weighed anchor and unfurled the sails, how was she going to control her speed?

· · JEAN · ·

Jean's first time getting stoned was mostly a positive experience. Mild at first, not sure if he was high or not, paranoia putting him on edge. He caught a glimpse of a drawing he had been working on for school, got totally lost in the details for what seemed like hours before finally realizing he was high. He looked up and saw Marie staring at him with a broad grin on her face.

"How long..." His question was interrupted by her laughter. He joined in, and by the time they got their breath back, he tried to continue, "No, really how long have I..." and they went off again. Finally wiping tears off his cheeks, Jean managed a heartfelt "Wow."

"So, whaddya' think, Mr. Giroux?"

"Fun. But a little scary. I mean, did we actually say anything funny?"

"I don't think so. How are the drawings?"

"The drawings? The drawings! Oh man, that's right - but why was that so funny?"

"Because we're stoned, I guess. I was amused by how intent you were, knew what you were experiencing, and your expression when you realized you were stoned made me smile. If we weren't stoned, we probably wouldn't have been hysterically laughing, but I still would have chuckled, you would have smiled back, maybe kissed me."

"I could still do that." And he did. And the sensation was overwhelming. Jean let out a heartfelt "Wow" that sent them off on another laughing jag.

"Okay, Smooch," Marie said when they stopped, "let's remember, Dr. K. wants me to have two normal periods on the pill *before* we have sex. And anyway," serious now, looking directly through his eyes to his brain, transmitting such pure feeling that it was almost painful, "I think we should be straight the first time."

They both went silent for a while, soaking in the ambience of togetherness and Crosby, Stills, and Nash's "*Our House*." They settled on the beat-up sofa, held hands, listened to the entire album, both sides, without saying a word ("It was the best of times..."). When it was over, they stayed silent for a bit and then Jean said, "I'm not sure I could get stoned with Nick and Nancy."

"That's why I picked a time when they weren't here."

"I mean, they both work for me. I'm not sure I can be silly and goofy on Tuesday night, then tell Nancy to do something Wednesday morning. And Nick, I mean, I'm just not sure."

"No worries, Smooch. It'll happen, probably by accident, and be fine."

Jean wasn't so sure. There was already ambivalence in his own mind concerning his position at work, and it was becoming more and more of an issue ("...it was the worst of times"). His mother inherited everything Armand owned, half of the homestead and half the business. When Giroux Brothers Plumbing changed to Giroux Plumbing and Heating, Inc., he, Mom, and Uncle Guy went to the lawyer's office to set it up. Uncle Guy was the President, Mom Vice President, and Jean was Director of Research and Development. There was one share of stock, Mom and Uncle Guy each owning half. Jean was still a minor at the time and would be paid an hourly wage which Uncle Guy suggested. It was much more than Jean had been earning, and Uncle Guy raised it twice since without Jean asking. But that still wasn't as much as his father made, and the business had grown. Mom, whose position as vice president was nominal only, wasn't getting a paycheck. Did that mean Uncle Guy was taking more than half?

Jean hated thinking like that. It was antithetical to the fatherly role his uncle had assumed for the past two years, to the way the two families operated. As his twenty-first birthday approached, Jean hoped things might change. But it came and went, and nothing changed.

And speaking of change, what was he to make of this marijuana thing? He and Marie were more together than ever ("It was the best of times"). They had, in accordance with Marie's wish, been straight when they made love the first time, and the next few as well. When another alone opportunity at the apartment presented itself, they got stoned, took a shower together, and the ensuing sex was so intense all they could think about afterwards was how soon they could arrange another tryst without Nancy and Nick. Even putting aside sexual ecstasy he loved getting high with Marie, but there were problems to consider. You could go to jail for having marijuana on your person or in your home, and she lived with Nick and Nancy. Wasn't that risky?

Also, it was apparent that smoking marijuana was not just another way to get high. It represented a new attitude, a changing of societal mores. He was comfortable with the old way, unsure of his ability to handle the new way. Could smoking grass or not smoking grass become a wedge between him and Marie? Could he continue to employ Nick and Nancy while keeping his knowledge secret from Uncle Guy? Jean knew he wasn't just another employee, but was he really an *employer*? What exactly was his position at Giroux Plumbing and

Heating, Inc? He loved the work, was clearly good at it, anxious to earn his degree and throw himself full bore into the future of the company. Uncle Guy was full of praise for his ideas, but lately was more interested in the business end of things and didn't seem to care if they were selling plumbing or women's shoes ("…it was the worst of times").

. . . . .

CHAPTER TWELVE

LENNY

1969, Mueller, NY

My apartment was detached from the main house in what used to be a two-car garage. A wall had been erected between the two halves of the garage, the half on the right remaining as it was. The left garage door was replaced with a front door and window, the inside remodeled into a kitchen with a nifty spiral staircase that cleverly concealed the plumbing for a full bathroom in the attic. A couple of dormers increased the attic floor space to accommodate the bathroom and a great room/sleeping loft paneled with recycled barn board. An antique wood burning parlor stove was the cozy finishing touch to a very groovy room. The apartment could not have been more different than the main house, nor could there be a less likely owner of that apartment than Beverly McLary. I was ready to rent it on first sight, but Sheila was determined to expand my horizons...and my debt.

We planned to move me in over the weekend, when Carl, Ricky, his girlfriend Marlene, and a couple of counselors from camp could help. When we described my potential apartment to Sheila's entourage in Soho on the day we saw it, Ricky and Marlene were inspired to start a new business. Upstate New York was full of falling-down barns, and decorators in the city were hot for the trendy barn board. Ricky's dad was an insurance agent who was aware of lawsuits resulting from decrepit barns toppling on children. The two entrepreneurs planned to use that data to scare owners into letting them safely dismantle their barns in exchange for the barn board. They purchased an old Daily News delivery truck, army green with that cool retro visor over the windshield, to transport the boards. Business was slow, so it was available for moving furniture, which was abundant because my parents' redecorating was under way.

We moved all my stuff up to Mueller, stacked everything but a few chairs and the sofa bed from my parents' apartment neatly in the garage awaiting transfer to the main house upon Mrs. McLary's departure. All that was left was for me to figure out how to segue from a group of good buddies to me and Sheila alone with a whole night and nothing but the sofa bed in front of us. The pizza was eaten, the six packs drained, doobies smoked, energy depleted. The moment was nigh, and I hadn't done shit about arranging my night in heaven. I kept waiting for a lead-in I could capitalize on. A few times I started but swallowed my words. She was such a hardass.

"Let's split," said Carl, and I glumly watched Sheila stretch, reach for her backpack and flannel shirt. I think she hesitated and gave me a weird look, but I was too stoned to be sure.

"Hello? Hello up there. Anybody home?"

Sheila yelled, "Sure. C'mon up, Mrs. McLary," pointed frantically to ashtrays, roaches, a baggie with some buds, and dashed to the top of the stairway. We stashed and hid and tried to look normal. "Need a hand, Mrs. McLary?"

"I always hated these damn steps. No, no, I'm all right. And I told you kids, it's Bev - I'm not *that* old, for chrissakes!" Rising through the circular opening, she appeared in stages. Dyed red immovable dome of hair, large square glasses, powder blue running suit with lavender piping. J.C. Penny must have had a closeout on pastel running suits. She looked around and paused. All seven of us had the exact same thought. Does she know? Can she smell the marijuana, see how bloodshot our eyes are, know why we're acting goofy? This was the worst part of smoking dope. When we were straight, we knew that anyone recognizing the effects of marijuana must have smoked some themselves, in which case they wouldn't care. But when we were stoned, that rationale went up in smoke. Was my new landlady going to kick me out, void the sale, call the police? Sheila rescued us from the paranoid silence.

"Not too bad for one day, huh Bev? We're really beat," hoping to explain our stupor.

"Because ya' had too mucha' that." Seven pairs of eyes followed her finger, seven pairs of lungs held their breath, and seven nervous giggles erupted when we realized she was pointing at the empty beer cans. That was legal. "Who owns the Daily News truck?" The writing had been painted over, but the shape was still recognizable to any New Yorker.

"I do," said Ricky, raising his hand like a fifth grader accused of passing notes. Carl and I started to giggle at Ricky's absurd expression, turning away from each other in order to swallow the hysterical laughter sure to come if one of us lost control.

"I gotta' business proposition for you, if ya' promise to lay off the beer." Dumbfounded silence. "Wanna' drive to Phoenix?"

"In that truck?" asked Ricky. "I don't think it's ever gone over 40 miles an hour."

"Well, Mayflower wants a goddamn grand to move my stuff. I'll give ya' 400 bucks, throw in another 100 for gas and we can all make out."

The two counselors, out of work since camp ended, looked at each other. "I'm into it, man, we could use the bucks."

"I'm in! Phoenix or bust!" We all laughed now, relieved it was finally appropriate.

"Here's the deal," explained Mrs. McLary, "I fly out'a here Wednesday. My lawyer says he won't need me 'til the closing when he'll need me *and* my husband, so I think we'll drive back. Leave my goddamn mother-in-law out there and make it a fun trip. Sweetie," looking at Sheila, "when you two honeymooners wake up come over and help me go through my stuff. We should be able to get it all packed tomorrow. Monday you boys bring that truck, load it, and I'll give ya' half the money and directions to our place in Scottsdale."

Wow. Beverly McLary, takin' charge. After she left, I looked at Sheila. A touch of color remained in her cheeks from the "honeymooners" remark. She didn't look at me, didn't join the spirited conversation about the trip to Arizona.

"We'll plan a route that keeps off the highways. We'll be fine."

"Sure we will."

"You brothers need a motorcycle escort?" Carl was all smiles as well.

"Absolutely. We'll be sure to go through all those redneck areas. Jimi Hendrix on a fuckin' Triumph. Should I paint a target on your back?"

"I got news for you, bro, you ain't makin' it through no redneck areas with those got-damn bell bottoms and wild hair. You gonna' need someone like me to cover yo' white ass. But we got rehearsals startin' Monday AM, don't we baby?"

"I'll be there." Sheila's eyes were flashing, cheeks spotting again. Baby? Is that what he called her? Carl was sauntering toward me, and I stood, wondering if this was going to be a confrontation. But it was just another hug from the big guy.

"Cool place, man," (pound, pound), "keep the faith." (pound, pound, pound). He made his right hand into a gun and shot Sheila. "Monday, AM."

Only the slightest nod acknowledged Carl, Sheila's face locked into an icy expression, the upbeat road trip vibes clashing with the impenetrable force field of the offended young lady. Legs, torsos, then heads disappeared down the circular stairs, the front door opened and shut, silence set in. Sheila pulled her flannel shirt tight against that hint of summer passing, the chill of an August night following a hot summer day. Man, did she look small and defenseless, like a little sister teased by her brother and his friends. She was huddled in an incongruous gold crushed velvet armchair from my parents' apartment. In motion she was clearly an athlete, swift and strong, but in the oversized chair she looked frail. About 5'4", she couldn't have weighed much over a hundred pounds, her short dark hair cut like a boy's. The phrase about eyes being the window to one's soul was written about Sheila Siegel. They were dark brown, too big for her face, and lit from within. She was wearing a white camp t-shirt with navy-blue trim and pinstripes, "Head Counselor" covering one bra-less breast, the interlocked NY over the other, gray flannel shirt acting like a coat of armor. Her faded jeans were worn through in spots, flowery embroidery covering the largest holes and hemming the bell bottoms. Seeing her sitting there pissed and vulnerable, my heart ached, physically ached, like the hot pang that shoots across the top of your stomach when you're hungry and smell a pot roast cooking.

> *If you're wondering about that romantic image, remember the two recent pulleys in the lifeline of this relationship were my mom and Mrs. McLary, both from the Pot Roast Generation.*

I imagined myself standing, walking behind her, putting my hands on her shoulders, kneading until she relaxed and joined me on the sofa. But I couldn't move. The excitement of moving day, the angst about the impending evening with Sheila, the last-minute explosion of Mrs. McLary's Arizona bombshell, the electric *tete-a-tete* between Carl and Sheila with me as the excluded third party, magnified by alcohol and cannabis, all combined to render me immobile.

Unexpected and unsolicited, a new Rule to Live a Better Life crystallized in my brain under a flashing neon "Theory of the Sofa." When sitting on a sofa with some job to do, whether it's putting the empty pizza boxes and beer cans into a garbage bag or standing up to hug your sweetheart, 95% of the work is simply getting off the sofa. Once you're up and moving, the job's as good as done. This theory, as metaphysical as it sounds, is factually substantiated by the basic building blocks of physics. Newton's laws about inertia tell us that while a body in motion tends to stay in motion, a body at rest tends to stay at rest. And the laws governing solids, liquids, and gasses tell us that while a calorie is the amount of energy needed to raise the temperature of one gram of water one degree Celsius, that 100th degree, the one that boils the water, requires *extra* calories to liberate those molecules and change their state from liquid to gas.

I cranked my dial a couple of notches higher and broke free from the sofa's gravitational pull. As theorized, once up and heading in the proper direction I coasted effortlessly to my goal and began kneading. Sheila followed my envisioned script, burrowing in hard and soft on the sofa. But my analytical mind couldn't let go, and I blurted out, "What's with you and Carl?"

She slowly extricated her arms, sighed, held her flannel shirt open, turned and pressed her thinly clad body against mine, knee to shoulder. "So, you wanna' talk about Carl now?"

"Your body can't remember pain" was my high school baseball coach's favorite saying. When I was a senior and a star, I had the temerity to question his wisdom.

"How come then, Coach," I offered, "when a hard ground ball catches me on an in-between hop and is headed for my groin, my body flinches? What exactly is it trying to avoid?"

Most of us knew more about baseball than our coach, which wasn't saying much because he didn't know shit about baseball. He was our gym teacher, and also coached three other sports he didn't know shit about. His name was unpronounceable, a Slavic conglomeration of consonants that pressed "y" into duty as a sometimes vowel. He was known simply as "Coach" when he was within earshot, "Nanook" when he wasn't. His family settled in Northern Wisconsin, close enough to the border to add some Native Inuit genes to his appearance, accounting for his nickname. How he wound up in Westchester threatening upper middle-class adolescents was hard to say, but he definitely found a home. In high school a good athlete usually played two or three sports, so odds were you would have Nanook for a coach in at least one of them. If not you were worthless in his eyes, and he was not above letting you know. His favorite method of intimidation was to take the school-issued white towel, roll it diagonally into a whip, and with a quick backhand snap raise a welt across the buttocks of anyone who didn't "listen up," "hustle up," or "shower up," which was basically all he ever said in gym class.

His vocabulary increased slightly when he was coaching

Whether he was right or not about the body remembering pain, I knew for sure that Sunday morning in my new apartment that the body certainly remembered pleasure. The sleep sofa had been the sight of many fantasies during the four years it lived in my parents' den. All it took was moving it 20 miles north to turn them into reality. I was awakened by a gargling sound that turned out to be just that, followed by the emergence from the bathroom of Sheila Siegel, resplendent in crumpled t-shirt and nothing else. And then, Coach, it all came back to me, my body remembering every fiery touch, synapses crackling, nerve endings alive, replaying the sensation of her bony hips digging into me, her surprisingly strong legs milking me, her hardened nipples brushing mine, the bumpy aureole that was just about all of her breast under my tongue. I was lying on my back under a sheet, which was beginning to resemble a tent. Sheila looked past the rise, locked onto my half-opened, pleasure-glazed eyes, and stood, hands on hips, wry disapproving expression on that memorable face. I didn't know if I was about to get a lecture, a frozen dismissal, or a blow job. As it turned out I got all three before we made it to the main house to help Mrs. McLary pack.

The lecture was all about how our relationship did not change last night, nor would it. We were friends, did some really fun stuff together, including on *rare* occasions (her emphasis, not mine) sex.

Five Sheila-less workdays loomed, but we had a big party planned for the weekend. William was coming back, and according to Bobbi what he had to say would blow all our minds. It was unlikely the counselors would make it back from Scottsdale. They were behind schedule despite bringing along an enormous supply of pink footballs, those delightful 15-milligram Dexadrine pills of the aforementioned shape and color which got most of us through college. When they asked Ricky for more speed in the truck that was his response.

Mrs. McLary left on Wednesday. I was slowly moving out of the apartment and into the main house, preparing for my welcome William/housewarming bash. I was apprehensive about dealing with Sheila and Carl in a group situation, but figured they would be so consumed with their new show nothing else would matter. Theater people are like that, a self-absorbed tunnel vision defining their lives. Plus, I was really looking forward to William's report on life with the Hoggers. For some reason, perhaps the soul stirring look he gave me when we left the Hog Farm, I felt he would direct his report to me, that I was somehow second in command. This was totally unfounded since I was merely a fringe player, but that was before I had (drum roll, please) the house. We would be meeting in *my* house, sitting on *my* furniture, eating *my* food as we caballed. Exactly what we were going to cabal about was beyond me, but it gave me something cool to imagine while Vinny and I drove the highways and byways of the tri-state area in silence.

Bobbi was settling in as the First Lady of our group, Sheila was her best friend, and Sheila and I were an item now, weren't we? The four of us would sit around and plan stuff, wouldn't we? The rest of the group would listen and say, "Far out, man," wouldn't they?

Bobbi was a fierce proponent of equal rights, her eyes flashing at any slight of womanhood. Her diligence redefined nitpicking but, like the old cabinetmakers used to say, you need something rough to make something smooth. Bobbi's abrasiveness was necessary to sand away millenniums of male chauvinism. It's easy to think she didn't need to be so caustic, but that's how the collective consciousness is raised, the same way it's lowered, by repetition. The insidious effect of daily references to bimbos, dumb blondes, niggers, polacks, kikes, all add up, stick to our souls like many coats of ugly paint covering a beautiful antique. It takes painstaking care and untiring effort to sandpaper away prejudice, and I admired Bobbi for taking it upon herself to lead the way.

Bobbi was tall and narrow, with large breasts that swung free under a never-ending parade of homemade shifts. Madras, tie-dye, paisley, all scoop necked, all mid-calf, all with large armholes through which you could see, were you immature enough to peek, most of her breast. A gifted photographer - it was under her tutelage Sheila tried to capture sanctity and perversity - with numerous collegiate awards and no way to turn them into income, she used her fine eye and interest in theater to design sets, props and costumes for Off-Broadway productions. She had a mental toughness, a sense of purpose she could transfer to any task, menial or monumental. She had a fanatical respect for fairness, whether she was the beneficiary or the donor. And most of all she had William, whose counsel she needed and heeded, articulated beautifully by Sir Paul in *Let It Be*.

Friday night arrived, the harbinger of many clannish gatherings at my house. William could hardly contain himself. He tried, with some small talk about my house, the new show, Ricky's reclamation of my car. As usual there were bottles of the popular Mateus, joints of all types and sizes, and an occasional exotic drug thrown in like peyote buttons, psychedelic mushrooms or, on this particular night, mescaline. Sometimes I wonder how we all survived such intense abuse. Then I remember some of us didn't.

These gatherings followed a bell curve. Starting slowly, letting go of the work week, social dynamic and drugs meshing, soaring angelic choral sopranos aah-aah- aahing behind Jagger's guttural _You Can't Always Get What You Want_, ("PLAY IT LOUD" it said, right on the album cover. Is that cool or what?), then my favorite part, the leveling off at the top. The way up was exciting but there was a dangerous edge. Because of the absence of quality control in the drugs we ingested we never really knew just how high we would get, and once the active ingredient was swallowed there was no getting off the bus. I constantly assessed how high I was, anxiously awaiting those first signs that the peak had arrived, and I had survived the trip. Still high as a kite, some semblance of control returning, an intense feeling of wellbeing would take over. My mind had been bent but not broken, and the long, easy coast downhill beckoned. I guess that's why by the following weekend I would be willing to take the giddy ride again. Of course, _not_ knowing was the part Sheila liked best, which succinctly summed up the difference between us.

During the mellowing time William started to speak. A few of us were in the kitchen when he began relating his experience with the Hoggers, and little by little the crowd grew. A few people came giggling in, went to the refrigerator for munchies or a drink, were drawn in by the tale and sat on the floor, backs against the cabinets. I was at the kitchen table, which had followed me from Westchester to Manhattan to Mueller, entranced by the realization _it was happening_, the first installment of weekly episodes in the soap opera of our little group.

"So anyway," William was saying, "we decided we should leave for Boston the next morning, where a major hippie summit was goin' down. This was gonna' be like the back rooms at a political convention. The platform had to be acceptable to all groups and the Hog Farm needed to be heard. Policy would get hammered out and groups would have to compromise, like when The Big Four met to divide up Europe, ya' know what I mean?"

William had a great voice. Not a singing voice, a speaking voice. He did hilarious impressions of ranting DJs on Top Forty AM stations ("SCOTT MUNI HERE, WELCOMING YOU TO SCOTLAND'S YARD!!!") who suddenly got hip, modulated their tones and joined the groovy FM stations ("good evening. this is scott muni, inviting you to join us as we explore the newest trends in music here on double u en ee double u eff em..."), alternating the styles mid-sentence until our cheeks ached. When recounting a story his mellifluous tones gave the impression you were listening to a performance, or Laurence Olivier lecturing on the intricacies of a Shakespearian plot. Ever the school-teacher, William stuffed too many analogies into every description, painting a picture, looking for a flicker of understanding, plunging into another even more detailed analogy ("ya' know what I mean, ya-knowwhatImean?"). True to his beautific soul he never assumed you were too dense to get it, instead accepting the blame for not doing a good enough job explaining.

"We hadn't even started talking about what we were gonna' do in Wyoming," he said. "I mean, that's what the Wyoming Project was supposed to be about, ya' know what I mean?"

"I don't see the problem." I was looking to solidify my imagined role as first lieutenant but had been so distracted I hadn't a clue what the Wyoming Project was. I was going to have to try and bluff my way in and hope The Law of Louie didn't bite me in the ass. "Let's tick off the main goals of the Project." Jump in here, William, c'mon…

"Okay, there are less than 100,000 registered voters in the state of Wyoming. There were a half a million freaks at Woodstock, and we were just the tip of the iceberg."

Bingo. "So we all move to Wyoming…"

"Elect the governor, mayors, legislators, legalize marijuana, outlaw guns, protect the environment, limit development…"

"Like a hippie homeland."

"An H.H.," chimed in Sheila, adding some levity to the lecture.

"So how did it finally come down?"

"It fell apart. It was, like, a clash of cultures. I mean, to Leary's group, doin' acid was a religious experience, something you planned and prepared for. Find some idyllic spot, retreat for a weekend with a small group of friends, drop acid and contemplate the universe. But the California crowd didn't give a shit about all that stuff. They'd drop a tab of Purple Owsley while ridin' a bus to work in downtown L.A. just for the fuck of it."

I tried to imagine tripping with Vinny, involuntarily shuddered. William picked up on it.

"I know, man, but you need to understand the Hoggers. These guys were stoned, drunk, and trippin' in high school, ya' know what I mean? The Boston crowd was kinda' proud of bein' outlaws, but the Hoggers were 'No Laws'."

"N.L.'s." Sheila was on a roll. I often wondered why we found the initializing funny. Whenever we tried it on someone outside of our *coterie*, we were met with blank stares instead of rollicking laughter. I came up with a mini-theory, the Theory of Cumulative Humor. Some things, like cuts from The Firesign Theater or Cheech & Chong albums, were funny all by themselves. Others needed to build up to a reaction. The standup comedians of the Bob Hope/Henny Youngman era understood this, firing ten one-liners a minute at you, none of which were individually very funny. But they wore you down, starting with a groan, eliciting a smile around joke #8, a chuckle by joke #15, and tears of laughter by #30.

"Actually," William continued, "we would have been just fine if it wasn't for the Chicago-Berkeley crowd. I mean, those folks were goddamn guerrilla warriors. They had machine guns in the trunks of their cars! They wanted to rob all the banks, raid all the corporations that exploited the masses, blow up the Pentagon. They thought we were a bunch of candy-assed liberals. I mean, that's what the right-wingers call us! It's like politics is a circle, not a straight line, and by the time you get as far away as possible you're back around to where you started, ya' know what I mean? I mean, if these guys were in charge of Wyoming I wouldn't want to stay there. They'd probably want to invade Montana or something, yaknowwhatimean? A few of us suggested the project needed a little more reflection and direction. Someone's family owned a farm in New Hampshire, and we decided to head up there for a few days to clear our heads and re-focus our energy."

"This place was incredible." Bobbi took the handoff and ran with it. "This girl, Nancy, she grew up in New Hampshire and her family owns this farm, right? But they were up in Canada at their fishing camp, so Nancy said we could all crash there. Un-fucking-believable. Huge hay fields with incredible stone walls framed by white birch trees and humongous pines. Just getting there was a trip. At first it kinda' looked like the Catskills, but then we all took a ride through this pass..."

"Notch," corrected William.

"Yeah, Franconia Notch, which was *really* like a *pass*," Bobbi didn't appreciate William's editorial assistance, "that cut through these mountains and when you came out on the other side you were in a different world. In Boston it was summer but up there the trees were turning color and it was freezing at night. We hiked this trail up into the mountains to a place called Bridal Veil Falls, which was a campground with these incredible falls and a natural pool, and it snowed! I mean, it was August, right? And these people we met at the campground were far out, forest ranger types, straight and crewcut but cool, right? They were part of this club, the Adirondack Mountain Club..."

"Appalachian." A gentle insertion by Editor William, blithely ignored by Bubbling Bobbi.

"...that was tryin' to link up all these hikes into one humongous trail that you could take all the way from Canada to New Orleans." The accuracy of Bobbi's geography was inversely proportional to its distance from Queens Boulevard. But her ebullience was irresistible, her descriptions captivating, the flora of the White Mountains being brought to us in living color by the photographer's eye. Tiny blue flowers peeking through mossy carpet, newly emerging colors in the leaves, an icy mountain stream turning into a pool in front of 75-foot waterfalls, rode the artist's back all the way to Westchester.

As taken as she was with the hiking trail into the White Moun-tains, her first love was the farm. "The farmhouse rambled on and on. The original house was simple, like a Monopoly hotel only white. Then there were a couple zig-zag additions, and the last one connected the house to this classic red barn with white trim. But the stone walls did it man, they were really outa' sight. There was no cement, or mortar, or whatever, holding the stones. They were just carefully placed and fitted and went on forever, rolling with the lay of the land. And you know why they built stone walls?"

Actually, I did. It was part of a course on the changing economy following the Civil War, but I wasn't about to steal Bobbi's thunder.

"They put their plow in the ground, right? And the horse, or oxen or something pulls it and it hits a rock. So, they stop and dig it up and push it to the side of the field. And then, 'cause they're in rocky New England, they hit another rock. And another, right? And tote *those* off to the side of the field. Soon they've got humongous piles of stones around the edge of the field, and then somehow, they turn from farmers into artists and build these beautiful stone walls. There were old photographs in the farmhouse, and one showed two guys rolling a boulder up a plank to its place on top of a stone wall, with their team of horses standing nearby hitched to a plow. I mean, they must have been plowing and hit this boulder, then spent half the day getting it off the field and onto the wall. New Hampshire's almost all woods now, but back then it was mostly cleared pasture with stone walls crisscrossing the entire fucking state!"

"It's even heavier than that." I couldn't hold back any longer. Everyone was in the kitchen now, and we had all been transported to a different time and place by William's eloquence and Bobbi's artistic enthusiasm shaping our own drug-induced images. "Before the Europeans came, New England was 85% forest, 15% pasture. They cleared woodlands for farms and pastures until by the Civil War those percentages were reversed. Mills sprang up to process wool from the sheep, boosting the Industrial Revolution. But the environment favored trees, not grasses, and it took constant effort to keep the fields cleared. When the Civil War began, most of the young men went to fight and there wasn't enough manpower to attend to the fields, so the forests started coming back. When the war ended, and these guys were in Missouri or somewhere, they'd put a plow in the ground and go all day without hitting one rock. They figured they were better off staying out there, and the Westward Movement was underway. Today the percentages are all the way back to how they were before the Europeans showed up. I was part of this baseball thing where the best high school players from New York, New Jersey, and New England went up to New Hampshire for this tournament. Behind the outfield fence was woods and when someone hit one out, we had to hop the fence and retrieve the ball. I remember asking a couple of locals why they built stone walls through the woods. They cracked up, slapped their knees, the whole bit. 'They didn't build 'em *through* the woods, they were there *before* the woods.' Man, did I feel stupid, the clueless city slicker." Quiet settled over the kitchen, each of us lost in our own *reverie*.

"So," I continued, "is the Wyoming Project dead?" The kitchen breathed a sigh, and everyone returned to earth. "I mean, it's still a good idea, isn't it? What do we need, fifty thousand and one freaks to take over the state?"

"Oh no, it's way less than that." William had been looking at me during our moment (minute? hour?) of silent reflection, as if he anticipated my question. "All 100,000 registered voters never vote, and there are blocs and splinter groups and things like that. It's like, according to our politicians, one and one don't really equal two."

"You had politicians there?" Sheila was incredulous. They were worse than bankers.

"Well, I guess they were ex-politicians who got frustrated trying to make things happen within the system. They know their shit, let me tell ya'. They think 30,000 like-minded folks would do it."

They continued their saga like a team of sports broadcasters, William the dulcet toned play-by-play man reporting the facts, Bobbi the ebullient ex-jock filling in the color.

"So," William was saying, "Nancy from New Hampshire is friends with this couple, David and Julie…"

"Get real!" Sheila might accept bankers, lawyers, and politicians, but she couldn't buy the heirs to the Republican throne.

"I know, right? Everyone calls them 'The Ikes,' but they sure don't have anything in common with *that* David and Julie. David's Mexican."

Bobbi's turn. "His real name is Diego Martinez, like his dad, but they changed it to David Martin to avoid getting busted by immigration cops. Nancy met them at a concert in San Francisco when she was bummin' around out there."

William took the floor. "Julie's, like, Miss California Surfer, ya' know what I mean? Long blonde hair, big blue eyes, killer bod…"

"OK, William, she's pretty. That's not the point."

"She's way more than pretty." William would not be swayed. "I mean, she wore old ratty tee shirts and cutoffs like everyone else, but hers look like some Italian tailor designed them for her, ya' know what I mean?" William's hands were in front of his chest, hefting imaginary breasts.

"We're not here to talk about tits, William," Bobbi softened her remark with a big smile and exaggerated rolling of her eyes. This Julie must really be something for her beauty to interrupt William and Bobbi's purposefulness. And it was dawning on me this recitation by William and Bobbi Lipson was indeed purposeful. Not just a casual retelling of adventures, it was taking on the quality of a meeting. Rapt attention was being paid, to the point where someone asked if we should be writing stuff down for those who couldn't be here.

"Right. But these are not your everyday tits…"

"William! So, they're at this free concert in a park by the Golden Gate Bridge, right? And somebody passes them a doob, and they start talkin', and it's this girl Nancy from New Hampshire. Before you know it, the three of 'em are sitting on this psychedelic bus headin' up the California coast with the Hog Farm."

"Actually, the Hog Farm was heading to Oregon," - William was always correct, never vague—"to where Ken Kesey was writing a book about rivers and loggers. But David, Julie, and Nancy got off at this groovy little artist's town, Mendocino, 'cause Nancy knew some friends from back home who were living nearby.

Now Bobbi paints us a picture of the Mendocino commune. "There's this narrow strip of woods nobody owns, called pygmy forest 'cause the trees are only about twelve or fifteen feet tall, and a bunch of freaks built homemade cabins and sheds connected by paths. I mean, it's like a little village in the woods."

"These folks are trying to organize themselves into some kind of a unit," said William, "like the thirteen colonies trying to organize into a nation, yaknowwhatimean?"

"Wait. Whaddya' mean, nobody owns the woods?" This was a difficult concept for a business major to grasp.

"Nobody owns 'em," was Bobbi's explanation.

"Everything is owned by somebody. Who has the title, the deed? Do they have permission to be there?"

"They're there, that's all." Bobbi was getting defensive. She didn't want to get bogged down in details, and Sheila was sending me those signals of exasperation I saw during my negotiations with Mrs. McLary.

"Actually, I was skeptical myself." Sir William to the rescue. Was I his number one lieutenant, or what? "That's one reason we didn't want to make a long-term commitment."

"Commitment? To what?" Sheila sprouted a visible energy field - I guess I was still tripping - that shimmered and jangled around her body. Her's was the only movement, everything else in the entire universe stood stock still in anticipation.

"Shit, William, you blew the surprise!" Bobbi glared at me, clearly annoyed that my obsession with economic banalities had interfered with their dramatic presentation.

"I wasn't talking about THAT surprise," William blurted out, then stopped short.

Everyone's eyes went back and forth from Bobbi to William, who were staring at each other with the same strange expression. Bobbi blushed, tried to look angry but couldn't quite pull it off, and William's smile and gentle hug overcame her peevishness.

Sheila got it first, shouting, "You're pregnant!" She catapulted out of her chair and hugged Bobbi, who was now beaming ear to ear. Everybody except me joined in an exuberant and joyful group hug, excitedly demanding info about due date, boy or girl, names. I managed a smile, a pat on the shoulder, and best wishes. I was still focused on the other surprise, and as soon as possible redirected the conversation back to "nobody's land." William was relieved to change the subject.

"Nancy reunited with David and Julie at Woodstock and said a bunch of us should go out there and join the commune."

"A bunch? How many is a bunch?" Sheila was our mouthpiece, the one among us with a psychic critical mass large enough to over-come our astonishment.

"Oh, I don't know, whoever wants to, I guess. Bobbi and I decided we're going. They could use some help getting their shit together. Nancy got excited when I said I was a teacher 'cause about a dozen families have kids. They've been talking about setting up some sort of alternative school, and I could help with that. Bobbi would like to do more photography, and they're trying to form some sort of craft association, see if they can generate some income to buy the stuff they can't grow or make. Mendocino has a bunch of art galleries and craft shops."

"Also, a couple theater groups and summer stock playhouses." Bobbi was looking at Sheila when she said this, and the invitation was clear. Everyone went silent, ruminating, digesting, trying to fit themselves into the picture. My mind was racing ahead. The mundane money matters Bobbi and Sheila found so distasteful were my forte. I figured the group out west was more like Bobbi and Sheila and would need someone to handle the finances. I pictured Sheila and I, CFO in charge of big bucks, gamboling in the woods, enjoying our stature as second family in the New World Order. Probably not wearing any clothes.

I blurted, "How, um, uh, when…"

"Nancy, her boyfriend Nick, David and Julie are headin' back out there shortly," said William. "They're up in New Hampshire now. Nancy's trying to talk her cousin Marie, and maybe Marie's boyfriend Jean into going too. Bobbi and I asked them all to come down, maybe next weekend, to give us some details. There's about five or six of them from New Hampshire, so Nancy wants to find out how many can join the group in Mendocino. She doesn't think it'll be a problem, there's plenty of room in the woods, you know what I mean? We were thinkin' of going out in June, hanging there for the summer, seein' what's up, how we fit in. I figured those who wanna' go could chip in, buy an old school bus cheap. Ricky, you could help with the automotive stuff, and we could pull all the seats out and use it to live in for the summer. I was wondering if we could park the bus here when we get it, work on it weekends, use this place as kind of a staging area. If it works out in California and we decide to stay, maybe some more of us could come out. If we do make a long-term commitment to this thing, we're gonna' need to settle some of the legal and financial issues you brought up, so maybe you could come out with the next wave, help set up the business end of things, yaknowwhatimean?"

"The next wave?" My expression must have changed markedly because William was obviously taken aback.

"I didn't think *you'd* wanna' go with us. Some of us can take the summer, and if it doesn't work out, we'd just come back and resume our lives here. But you'd hafta' make a decision sight unseen. I mean, you don't get summers off anymore."

Poof. 'You don't get summers off anymore.' I could feel the sympathetic eyes on me, mumbled some sort of weak "Oh yeah, no big deal" disclaimer, but I was devastated by the implications. That simple sentence was a life sentence, five days on, two days off, forever. The conversation whirled on without me. Remodeling the bus, having an opportunity to live the life, walk the walk, be a real honest to goodness hippie, all the good vibes, all were for *them*, not *me*. I was short of breath, felt bands tighten across my chest. Was I going to throw up? Pass out? Die? Was this how it happened, a bad trip turned fatal? I tried to will my diaphragm to drop a little so my lungs could expand, and fresh air could rush in to fill the void. I tried to concentrate on those cute little bicuspid valves, one-waying the blood through my heart. They say High Dalai Lamas reach such a pure state of concentration they can take control of their involuntary nervous system. I better get there, stat.

CHAPTER THIRTEEN

· · · · ·

STEVEN AND GAIL

1962, Hewlett Harbor, NY

· · GAIL · ·

The week after the Thanksgiving football game, Gail's mother told her that Steven's mom had arranged a Saturday visit to Long Island so Steven could see her. The two moms got to know each other the previous spring when their children studied together for the 9th Grade Regents exams. The New York State Board of Regents creates standardized high school final exams covering the entire year of a specific subject. Steven and Gail were finishing eighth grade but were eligible to take the ninth-grade exams because of their academic record. If they scored well enough, they could "test out" of a subject and take the tenth-grade level course in ninth grade. They met regularly, as they both had lofty ambitions. These study dates were also when Steven explained the finer points of baseball to Gail, in preparation for her summer at her uncle's baseball camp.

The moms made it clear they were taking the time to chauffeur the kids around so they could study for the Regents, not "spend time gabbing, gossiping, or doing *something else* you shouldn't be doing." The "something else" the parents meant was the same "something else" that dominated Gail's thoughts. There were opportunities when she felt Steven was about to make a move, but he never did. And then she was gone, to the baseball summer camp and Bronx High School of Science.

Gail was nervous about the upcoming visit. She wasn't sure why he wanted to come see her. Her mom said he was just being a good friend, but their relationship was more complicated than that, at least to her. How much should she share about her health? Would he say something about her appearance? She decided the best approach would be to let him choose the dance, then follow his lead. But when her mother and Steven's mother left to do some shopping her aunt ushered them into the den and they were alone. Gail was never good at following, so she abandoned her plan, immediately asked him to promise not to tell anyone what he was about to hear, and dove in full bore.

"Not just promise, but swear to God, or the Pope, or whoever Catholics swear to." When Steven smiled at that remark, Gail let him have it. "This is no joke, Steven. I need to talk to someone. I thought I could trust you. If my parents find out, I'll never get to go back home."

So, Steven solemnly swore to God *and* the Pope. Gail's voice was just above a whisper, but she spit the words out with venom, pacing back and forth as she spoke. "There's nothing wrong with my stomach, it's all in my head. There was so much schoolwork I forgot to eat, lost weight, then started eating and couldn't stop. I got all mixed up, couldn't figure out when to eat and when not to, kept gaining weight and losing weight. I got so weak I had to go to the hospital. I'm not seeing a stomach specialist, I'm seeing a psychiatrist. My parents are telling everyone it's a stomach specialist because they're too embarrassed to admit their perfect little daughter is crazy." She collapsed back into her chair. "There, I said it."

They looked at each other silently for a bit, looked around the den, back at each other, the ceiling, the floor. Finally, Gail said, "My dad said you were great at the game." Steven smiled and shrugged.

Uncomfortable with the silence, Gail got up and began pacing. Steven watched with an uncertain smile on his face. "Stop looking at my ugly body. I'm so fucking fat." Realizing what she said, Gail put her hand to her mouth, widened her eyes, looked at the door-way and then back at Steven, and giggled. They both laughed, and the tension eased. They spent the rest of the time talking about the Brooklyn crowd, Steven's football exploits, what James Madison was like. When they heard the car pull into the driveway, Gail grabbed Steven's hand and whispered "I need a friend Steven. I haven't talked to a kid my age in months." Steven nodded his head.

"Hey kids, we're back!"

"Hi Mom," Steven said.

"Hi dear. Help Gail's mom with her packages, then we should go. The traffic's bad already, and it's only gonna' get worse."

After they left, Gail was so mad at herself she stomped up to her room, sat on her bed, held her head in her hands, then threw herself down on the bed. She heard Mom come up the stairs.

"You okay, sweetie?"

"No. I'm such an idiot, I ruined everything, I scared him, he's never coming back, and I really want him to, and...and..."

Mom smiled, put her hand over Gail's mouth, her finger on her own lips, and softly said, "Shush baby, take a breath. You don't know..."

"You're wrong, I know what I did, and it was so stupid."

"Let me finish, sweetheart. You *don't* know yet that this boy is the one for you, and if he is, one misstep is not going to scare him away. You don't need boyfriend problems on top of what you're going through right now. You should talk to Dr. Lieberman about it at your next session, ask her what she thinks."

Gail did, and her shrink agreed with her mother. Gail was suspicious, wanted to confront her mother and demand to know if she had talked to the doctor first but, before she had a chance, Steven's mom called and asked if it was okay for him to visit again.

It was a damp, gray Sunday afternoon the day Steven came. Her uncle was home to chaperon, so her aunt went shopping with the two moms. Gail and Steven were waved into the living room instead of the den so Uncle Murray could watch football without any distractions. While the den had been warm and welcoming, the living room was formal and foreboding, and Steven was obviously uncomfortable. Gail was sure this was her only chance to make up for the disaster of the previous visit and she tried to relax the atmosphere by sprawling comfortably on one end of a huge sofa and throwing her feet up on the coffee table. Steven sat stiffly at the other end, feet firmly planted on the plush carpet. He couldn't imagine putting his feet on the ornate table, whose glass surface was covered with delicate chintz and be-jeweled ashtrays, tiny boxes, and vases filled with fresh cut flowers. Undeterred, Gail nonchalantly nudged a few of them with her feet, grabbed a pillow and beamed a radiant smile across the expanse of sofa.

"I can't believe you came out here after I was so obnoxious."

"You weren't obnoxious."

"Yeah right. I was sure I'd never see you again."

"I'm not that easy to ditch."

"That's a good thing! Wait, did you think I was trying to ditch you? I wasn't, honest."

"Then *that's* a good thing too."

"I really miss my house, my school crowd, our...friendship. I want to be back in Brooklyn so bad."

"What has to happen for you to come back?"

"It's hard to say. The doctor says I'm doing better, but she also says I make it too hard on myself. I know when I start thinking wrong, know when I'm getting myself into trouble with food, but I can't always stop myself." Gail was looking down at her hands now, folded on her stomach. The room became silent enough for them to hear the muffled TV through the closed door to the den. They sat that way for a minute or two, then Gail's uncle let out a loud "Shit! Goddamit! Shit, shit, shit!" Gail smiled, made the "crazy" sign by spinning her finger around her ear and pointing to the den.

"Is he the uncle with the baseball camp?"

"No, that's Uncle Ralph, my dad's brother. He's awesome! This is Uncle Murray, who married my mom's sister. There's no way I could ever spend the summer with…"

Right on cue Uncle Murray came out of the den, crossed the living room on his way to the kitchen. "I'm grabbin' a beer and a snack," then looking directly at Steven, "anything I can get ya', son?"

Neither of the teens missed the pointed exclusion of Gail. Steven said, "No thank you, sir." Gail bit her lip, then stuck her tongue out at her uncle's back as he passed into the kitchen. Steven smiled, amused by the switch from troubled teen with adult problems to a child with a kindergarten retort. Then a thought came to him as he replayed Gail's description about knowing when she was "thinking wrong but wasn't able to stop herself." That's exactly how he felt when he used to explain intricate games to his friends on the playground. He could relate! He might be able to help. Steven moved closer, and they were almost touching.

"Steven! Why are you looking at me like that?"

"I know how you feel. I've felt like that too when you know

you're getting yourself in trouble and can't stop."

Uncle Murray passed back towards the den, noticed their proximity to each other. "You two okay?"

"Oh, Uncle Murray, look. The rain stopped and the sun's coming out. Would it be okay if we went for a walk on the bike path?"

"I don't know. Can I trust you two to keep your hands off each other?"

"Uncle Murray!"

"Don't you like football, son? I'm watchin' a playoff game."

"I don't really follow the pros, but I play high school football."

"You play? For Hewlett Harbor?"

"Uncle Murray, this is *Steven*, from *Brooklyn*, remember? He's my *friend*."

"Don't get your panties in a bunch little girl."

"Unc-le Mur-ray!!!"

"Okay, I got it, he's your friend Steven from…hold on a minute. You're not that kid from Madison, Steven Mala…Masa…?"

"Masciarelli."

"Holy shit, kid, you don't 'play' football, you're a star!"

"Please Uncle Murray…"

"Hold on a minute Gail, this is business. Has anyone talked to you yet about your future?"

"I'm just a freshman."

"Don't be coy with me kid, I know the rules. It's what I do. It's what pays for all this," Uncle Murray spread his hands wide, "and it's just the tip of the iceberg. In the next few years, it's gonna' get big, BIG, **BIG**."

"Well, *I'm* going for a walk. Wanna' come Steven?" Steven immediately jumped up and looked for his jacket. "It's in the hall closet, I'll get it. We'll be back soon, Uncle Murray."

"Fine. But if the ladies aren't back by the time you return from your little walk, this young man and I need to talk. It's business!"

Gail powered through the kitchen into a porch with jalousie windows. It was large enough for a sitting area with wicker love seats around a wicker coffee table, a separate area with a round, golden oak clawfoot dining table and four spindle back chairs. The table was completely set with expensive looking dishes, cloth napkins in silver rings, and the same cut flowers that were on the coffee table in the living room. One of the jalousie windows was a door which Gail opened and strode through without closing it or looking back. Steven closed the door and hustled after her, across a fieldstone patio, past a grill and stone fireplace under a portico, and caught up in time to open a gate in a stockade fence.

"He's such a jerk! I hate him!" They followed a narrow dirt trail through brush for a few feet, then came to a wide, paved path. Gail hesitated, turned right, and resumed her aggressive pace.

After a bit of silent walking Steven asked, "Is that a park on our left?"

"No. Up ahead we'll enter a park. This is just some rich guy's property."

"Your uncle seems like a rich guy."

"I know. What a house, huh? He's such a jerk about that, too. He's just a jerk about everything!" The manicured landscaping continued on the left. On the right was a succession of different fences separated from the path by overgrown brush, occasionally interrupted by narrow paths similar to the one Steven and Gail took outside Uncle Murray's fence. "See, the people who own the houses on that side of the path," said Gail, pointing toward the fenced side, "are rich and have houses like Uncle Murray's. But the people on this side," pointing to her left, "where my Uncle Murray *really* wants to live, are so-o-o rich they don't have houses, they have estates." They continued along in silence, passed a sign saying they were entering a town park, the only change being that beautifully maintained land was now on both sides of the path. "It's so pretty here, so peaceful. The first few times my shrink came to talk to me we walked here. The trees still had all their leaves, and they were turning colors. It was really beautiful."

"It's pretty nice now, too."

Gail stopped abruptly, faced Steven, hand on her cocked hip. "What did you mean on the sofa when you said you know how I feel? Were you just trying to kiss me or feel me up?"

"Honestly Gail, I was just trying to tell you, as a friend, that I've felt that way also. I was only trying to say maybe I could help you, just as a friend, at *that* particular moment."

"Just as a friend at that particular moment?"

"Yeah."

"But not all moments?"

"No." If this were a Frankie Avalon/Annette Funicello beach movie Steven would pull her close and kiss her, and "Bobby Socks to Stockings" would start playing in the background. But this was not a movie, they were not actors, and there was no script feeding Steven clever lines. "*This is the time,*" thought Steven. He had chosen the intellectual route to her heart because it was where he had an advantage over all other suitors. It was time to abandon that ship and be Barry Longo. But he hesitated too long, and Gail's patience wore out.

"We'd better be getting back," Gail said softly.

Steven nodded. "Is this path a loop?"

"Yeah, but it's real long, like three miles, I think. I know you're a super jock and all, but I was out'a breath when we stopped."

"You were moving at a pretty fast pace. Do you always walk that fast?"

"Only when I'm pissed," she said, reaching out her hand. "Let's go."

"Were you pissed at me?" Steven unconsciously took her hand as they started back.

"No. Maybe. I don't know." She laughed at herself, and he joined in.

"Do you like to walk? Or run?"

"Definitely not run. You're the athlete, I'm the genius. Walking's not bad, but I don't think I could walk the whole loop. Not now, anyway, not with this fat body."

"I bet you could." Steven's tone was different, and Gail gave him a sideways glance to assess the change.

"Maybe I could. Why?"

"Because you don't need any special talent to walk or run. Especially when nobody's trying to tackle you or tag you out. It's just you."

He was trying to make a point, but she was done guessing. "Yeah, so? What are you getting at?"

"What I was trying to say in the living room is I've had times when there were things I didn't like about myself, things I needed to change. I know you're the one with all the different colored markers and study tricks, but I have tricks too. I pick one small part of what I want to change, maybe not even the most important part, and make up a game I can play against myself to help me change it."

"What if you don't win the game?"

"I don't let that happen. I start with something small, something I know I can win. It helps me move on to a little bigger thing. I take it very slow, always picking something I can control all by myself."

"Like running." Gail connected the dots. "Except I don't know if it's something I can do."

"Then don't. You gotta' *know* you can win the game. Make your goal to walk the loop without stopping. If it's three miles, it should take an hour."

"I'm not sure I could walk for an hour without stopping."

"Make it an easier game. Walk for fifteen minutes, turn around and go back. That's half an hour. The next day, walk for twenty minutes before you turn around. That's forty minutes. Each day add a few more 'til you can do thirty each way, then you can walk the whole loop."

"Okay, so I'm walking the whole loop. Whoop-dee-do. How does that get me back to Brooklyn?"

"You can't think about that. That's too hard a game."

"So, what does it get me?"

"A win. Once you're walking the loop without stopping, you've won that game. Next game is *running* the whole loop without stopping. Try and run just a little bit. Remember the spot where you went back to a walk. Next day, run a little more and remember *that* spot. You don't have to do more each day, but never do less. The trick is not to go too far too fast. Even a few steps more running is progress. Soon you'll be running the loop, and that's a game you *never* thought you could win."

They walked the rest of the way lost in thought, Gail digesting what Steven said, Steven wondering if he insulted her. When they got to Uncle Murray's gate, they both realized they had been holding hands. They quickly dropped hands, looked at each other and giggled. Gail shook her head.

"What?" Steven asked.

"You're as weird as I am!" They rejoined hands, exaggerating the swing like little kids, laughing as they sashayed into the backyard.

"Perfect timing!" It was Steven's mom, looking out the jalousie door. "We just got back, and we've gotta' get going, or we'll sit in traffic for an hour. Don't even take off your jacket!"

· · **STEVEN** · ·

Steven didn't want the emotional high to end, though he was relieved to avoid the business talk with Uncle Murray. He and Gail exchanged an enthusiastic goodbye, and he was already planning his next visit, how he was *not* going to miss another chance for a kiss. But the holiday season got in the way. Gail's family celebrated Hanukah, which came the week before Christmas that year, then Christmas and New Year's. Mom tried a few times in January, but the timing didn't seem to work. The next few times Steven asked her to arrange a visit she seemed evasive. When he asked her again one night at dinner, Pop answered.

"I think you'd better not count on going out there again." Steven looked at Mom for an explanation, but Mom looked at Pop to continue. "Her parents don't want you to see her anymore," he said. Steven was stunned. Again, he looked to his mother.

"We don't know that for a fact," she said. "It may be her uncle that has a problem, it may not have anything to do with you."

"He wanted to talk to me last time," said Steven, "but we had to leave quickly and didn't have a chance."

That got Pop's interest. "Did he say why he wanted to talk to you?"

"He knew about my playing football, said he wanted to talk 'business' with me."

Pop shook his head, a rueful smile on his face. "Yeah, well... I don't think that's the problem. Whether it's her parents, her uncle, or all of them, they don't want you around their little girl because they don't think you're good enough for her."

"What do you mean? I do everything I'm supposed to. I've never done anything wrong!"

"Again," Mom said, "we don't know what the reason is."

"Well, we gotta' find out Mom. I'll ask Gail. I'll talk to her parents, I'll even talk to her uncle." Steven was confident that, as always, he could fix what needed to be fixed.

"It's not you, son," Pop explained, "it's all of us. It's *Nonno*, may he rest in peace, Uncle Eddie, Vito, our family. Her uncle probably did some digging to find out more about you because he wants to be your agent and saw the connection. He just assumes we're all gangsters. Unfortunately, this is something you're going to have to get used to. It's part of what I've been talking to you about after dinner, part of what makes us different. You can't argue with people who think they know everything. You just have to be stronger than they are."

"I don't wanna' be stronger, I wanna' see Gail!"

Pop stood up. "I know, son, but you're gonna' have to forget about her and move on. I'm sorry," he added as he left the room.

"What happened, Mom? I don't understand. Who told you I can't see Gail?"

"Nobody told me. But each time I called Mrs. Bernstein she sounded more and more like she didn't want to talk to me. The last time she suggested I stop calling for a while."

"But that's not fair! How can I explain if I can't talk to them?" For the first time in a few years Steven felt his eyes moisten, heard his voice start to crack.

"Sometimes these things just pass. You can't force them, Stevie," Mom said soothingly. "Let's just wait a few weeks, and I'll try again.

Maybe it's something about Gail's health."

"But Pop said…"

"I know. But let's just wait a couple of weeks to be sure." Steven's mother didn't like contradicting her husband, but Steven was standing now and clearly fighting to control himself. He caught her implication, seized on the shred of hope, and sat back down.

"Does it have to be a couple weeks?"

Mom smiled, came over and kissed him on the forehead. "It may take less time; it may take more. This is the kind of thing a woman knows better than a man. I'll call again when I think it's appropriate. One thing I know for sure, it'll come quicker if you don't think about it all the time. You certainly have enough things to concentrate on. Isn't there a tournament soon?"

Mom's ploy to divert Steven paid immediate dividends. "Next weekend," Steven said. "I'm going downstairs for a while." He went into his room, grabbed his official NBA basketball and headed for the elevator.

Occasionally a group of high schools arranged an unofficial tournament on a weekend, mostly to give the subs a chance to play. This one was a three-day affair because school was closed on Monday for President Lincoln's birthday, and it included girls' teams and some special events. Steven was playing a new position and was anxious to play in a game that didn't count so he could experiment. He and Barry Longo had always been the tallest players on the team and played either center or forward, but in high school there were older kids who were taller, and Steven was shifted to guard. Longo wasn't on the team. Lately, he was absent from school more than he was present.

Now that Steven was no longer stationed near the basket, he was working on shooting jump shots from the perimeter. The coach wanted him to release the ball at the apex of his jump, allowing Steven to exploit his height advantage over the smaller guards defending him. The tunnel beneath his apartment house where he first pushed his physical limits had an arched ceiling. Lightbulbs hung in a line down the center of the arch, about nine feet from the floor. Every night after dinner Steven stood under a light and tried over and over to jump high enough to touch the protective cage. Once he could, he tried jumping with a basketball in his hands. Steven used an official NBA basketball, which was a half-inch larger in circumference than the high school basketball, because it made the high school ball seem easier to handle. He progressed to being able to jump with the NBA ball in two hands and touch it to the light. His next challenge was to jump in front of the light and try to "hang" there for a split second while moving the ball to his right hand so he could shoot.

The tournament was held at a large community facility. There was more down time than Steven expected. Watching a girls' game and bored, he remembered seeing a small auxiliary gym down the hall, took a ball out of the team bag and went down the hall to practice his jump shot.

A tall girl in a basketball uniform walked in while he was shooting. "Steven?"

"Yes?"

"Hi. I'm a friend of Gail's, from Bronx Science."

"What? But that's not - she's not - you're not..."

Amused by Steven's confusion, she let him stammer a bit before explaining. "I transferred back to Midwood so I could play basketball. When Gail heard both our schools were gonna' play in the tournament she asked me to give you this." She was holding an envelope in her hand. Steven stared at it for a few seconds, reached for it and let the ball he had been cradling on his hip drop and bounce away.

"Oh, sorry, uh..." Steven took the envelope, saw a heart drawn on the front in bright red marker, and looked at the girl.

"My address is on the envelope. If you want to respond, mail it to me and I'll get it to Gail." She walked toward the door, stooped to pick up the ball, and in one motion whipped a behind-the-back pass at Steven. He snared it and hugged it to his chest without dropping the envelope. "Nice catch. Better hurry, Romeo, Valentine's Day is the day after tomorrow."

As she opened the door, Steven regained enough composure to yell, "Hey! Thanks, um..."

"Irene. If Tilden loses their game, we'll be back here tomorrow for the finals."

Steven set the ball down, sat cross-legged on the floor and opened the envelope. The card inside was written in six different marker colors. "I ran the whole loop! Love, Gail." Steven sat there a few minutes reading and re-reading the message. He got up and took a few shots but was no longer into it. He placed the card back in the envelope, tucked it into the elastic waistband of his shorts, picked up the ball and walked back to the main gym. He watched the girls' semifinal game, found himself rooting for the team that was playing against Tilden so Irene's team could be in the finals. Then, Madison's boys played their last game of the day. They already clinched a spot in the finals, so Coach played all the subs, even some JV players. Steven went in for a few minutes but let a pass from his teammate go sailing by and Coach took him out.

The game finally ended, and they packed up and got on the bus. Steven grabbed a seat towards the back and sat by himself. Coach joined him.

"Something wrong, Masciarelli?" Steven shook his head. Coach waited for a response that was more Steven-like, then, when none came, nodded, and went back to his seat at the front of the bus. "Good luck trying to understand teenagers," he said to the bus driver.

They made a couple stops to drop off players who lived out of walking distance from Madison. The next to last stop was near Gail's apartment house. Steven saw a Hallmark store on the corner and impulsively grabbed his bag and hustled towards the door.

"This ain't your stop, Masciarelli."

"I know, Coach. I wanna' grab a Valentine card for my Mom. I can walk home from here. It's just as quick as getting off at school and walking home."

Steven hustled into the store and went to the Valentine section, scanning the headings: Wife, Husband, Mom, etc. He found Romantic but it was too flowery. The Humorous cards were embarrassingly sexy. He was stumped. Then he saw the "Blank" designation and found a card with a red heart on the front and nothing inside. Perfect. He could say anything. Now he just had to figure out what he wanted to write.

Steven bought the card and stood outside the store, unsure of what to do next. He found himself walking towards Gail's apartment house, stopped across the street from her building and stared at the third-floor windows. Her apartment was 3A, so he figured it would be on that floor in one of the corners, and arbitrarily focused on the corner to his left. Steven felt weird, like this was not really happening. Since Irene walked into the gym, his world had bounced sideways.

The February afternoon turned chilly, he shivered involuntarily, zipped his jacket, and turned up the collar. He was in a TV show playing a private detective, Paul Drake tailing a suspect for Perry Mason, a cigarette dangling from his lips.

Steven shivered again and returned to reality. He was not Paul Drake, just a boy who needed to get home before dark. He hustled back to the Hallmark store and bought a flowery Valentine for Mom. If he was going to get involved in subterfuge, he would need her help.

CHAPTER FOURTEEN

· · · · ·

JEAN

1970, Darren NH

On Thursday morning they were stopped outside the gate by the general contractor Tony standing next to his truck. A few other trucks were there and a group of men were with Tony. Uncle Guy stopped and Jean rolled down his window.

Uncle Guy yelled across Jean, "What's up?"

"The heads of the project wanna' see both of you at the office before you go to our trailer. They're gonna' tell you that me and all my subs have been fired, that you should pack up your stuff and be gone by the end of work today."

"Are you shittin' me?!"

"Unfortunately not, Guy. There's been a misunderstanding. Listen to what they say, then come back here and we'll all decide what we're gonna' do."

"I Iop out here Jean," said Uncle Guy, "and wait for Nick and Lee. They're just a few minutes behind us."

"You both should hear what they have to say," Tony suggested. "I'll flag down your boys. They drivin' that white step van?"

"Yeah, thanks." He put the truck in gear and drove onto the site.

Jean was sure he had done something wrong, was somehow to blame for this. But how? Could it be related to marijuana? He glanced at Uncle Guy for a clue, but he looked like he was also trying to figure it out. "Did I do something wrong, Uncle Guy?"

"You? Why would you think that?"

"Tony wanted me to come with you, but not Lee or Nick."

Uncle Guy shook his head. "No son, this is one of those times when you and I get singled out. We're management and they're not. We're just caught in the crossfire of some bullshit. It's gotta' be about Tony, not us."

They were greeted by three men seated behind a table, and a fourth, in suit and tie, standing alongside them. He directed Jean and Uncle Guy to a couple of chairs and got right to the point.

"Tony Donato has been linked to some questionable business practices on a previous project. He may or may not have been the one responsible for those practices, but he definitely had knowledge of them."

"Have you asked him about it?" Uncle Guy was not intimidated by either the news or the scene. Jean was struck silent by both.

"We have."

"Did he admit to 'questionable business practices'?"

"I can't discuss what was said between us and Mr. Donato. I can tell you there is no evidence of any wrongdoing on *this* project. Nor is there any indication Giroux Plumbing and Heating, or any of your employees had knowledge of the past wrongdoings."

Jean found his voice. "But you're firing us anyway?"

"Actually, we can't fire you, because you don't work for us. You work for Mr. Donato. The General Contractor hired you…"

"Yeah, yeah, we get it," said Uncle Guy, "but that just makes it worse. Tony won't have the resources to give any of us severance pay or repay us for the supplies we bought for this job."

"I can't speak for Mr. Donato, and have no knowledge about how he handles his subs. Giroux Plumbing and Heating's work has been exemplary. If you use us as a reference for future jobs, that, and only that, is what we will say. But we're a partnership of public and private entities here, which requires a high standard of accountability. Now that Mr. Donato's past is known to us, we have to sever all connections to Mr. Donato. Unfortunately, that includes his subs. We need all of you to vacate the trailer by the end of business today."

"You gonna' hire a new GC?" Uncle Guy asked.

"As soon as we can."

"Will that GC be able to hire us?

"Our new general contractor will have full responsibility for hiring subcontractors, and will be able to hire whoever he, or she, finds acceptable. The new general contractor *will* be made aware of our need to disassociate ourselves from the previous GC."

"So that's a 'No.' Let's go Jean, we're done here."

Back in the truck Jean asked, "Whaddya' think Tony did?"

"Could be nothing, could be almost anything."

"I guess we'll find out from Tony."

"Don't be so sure. That guy wearing the suit and doing the talking is a lawyer. Once they're involved, anything you hear from *either* side is nothin' but bullshit."

They pulled off the road, parked behind Nick's white step van. Tony wasn't visible as Jean and Uncle Guy approached the crowd and greeted Lee and Nick. One of the other subs came over and said, "While Tony was waitin' for you two, Gerry asked him about his last job, wonderin' if they were buildin' anything else near here. Gerry kept pushin', so Tony's in his truck talkin' to his boss."

"On a CB?"

"Nah, he said he has, like, a maritime phone for boats. He called it a bag phone."

Tony hopped out and addressed his subs. "They had a big project ready to go in this area but it fell through, and they put me on this project. They've found another property, but it's landlocked. They need abutters to give them road access. He said it could be any day."

"Or not at all." Uncle Guy wasn't into hypotheticals.

"That's always the case, Guy," acknowledged Tony, "but they're gonna' build it somewhere. They got a pile of dough invested in start-up already. Like I said, I was gonna' start hiring subs for them before the seller pulled out at the last minute. They said I should just hang loose; it could be a go any time."

Jean could see Uncle Guy edging toward his truck. He had listened to enough wishful thinking and was ready to move on. But Gerry stopped him.

"Hey Guy, isn't your brother a big shot real estate broker? Maybe he's got a property these guys could use."

"My brother died, Gerry. You mean my brother-*in-law*, Fred. Even if he had one, they wouldn't be hiring any plumbers or roofers for a while. We're heading to the trailer to pack up, then we'll try to wake up some of our old customers."

Walking back to their trucks, Lee said, "Fred does have some huge properties up for sale, Guy. And he's been havin' me clean up the Stinson property behind ours." Lee did odd jobs for Fred to supplement his part time plumbing income.

"Stinson's kids are selling?"

They had reached their trucks. Lee shrugged his shoulders. "I don't think it's officially on the market, but that wouldn't stop Fred. They don't call him 'Fast Freddy' for nothin'."

"Let's go pack up. We can talk more back at the shop while we're unloading."

Jean's shock had morphed to outrage at the injustice of the situation. He was sullen as he packed the gear and supplies, didn't join in the bitching from the subs as they gathered their stuff. Jean and Uncle Guy used the barn on their property for storage and only brought what they needed for a day or two, so they were the first to finish. Jean, Nick, and Lee went out to wait for Uncle Guy, who was handling the goodbyes and the condolences. Tony stood outside the trailer, giving everyone a chance to clear out before he went in to clean out his desk. When Uncle Guy came out and started walking toward them, Tony joined him.

"Just between you and me, and no one else, the reason the last job fell through was because some two-bit politician lost his spot on the Zoning Board to the guy we bought the land from. He was so pissed he said the money we paid the guy was a bribe to change the zoning." They reached Jean, Nick, and Lee. "I can't promise anything, but my bosses feel responsible, and they're gonna' try and come up with some severance pay for me. Anything I get I'll split with the subs. I'll give you the money, if there is any, and let you distribute it."

"They'd appreciate that."

"Yeah, well, like I said, no promises. If I'm ever workin' in this area again, you guys are the first subs I hire. Maybe your brother in law comes up with something and we have a chance to work together again. And," he said, turning toward Jean, "I didn't forget about some of those great ideas you had. Maybe we'll get a chance to use 'em."

Jean's silence continued during the ride home. He had a hard time accepting they were sent packing because of something someone else *might* have done. "I can't believe this is happening. And we don't even know why."

"It ain't the end of the world, Jean, we'll be okay. Tony said the money they paid for the property was considered a bribe to get approvals. He whispered it to me while we were walking to my truck. He doesn't want anyone else to know."

Jean digested the information for a couple of minutes, then asked, "If he did call you, would you work for him again?"

"I'd think about it. Tony's easy to work for, no drama, realistic demands. You don't have anyone to compare him to, but that's rare among GCs. Your dad and I worked for some large construction companies. The GCs were terrible. They gave the best jobs to their favorites and wanted a kickback to put you in that group. They didn't know half as much as we did about plumbing, so their demands were unrealistic. That's why we started our own company. If this worked out like I thought, we probably would be hired directly next time to be THE plumbing contractor. It certainly looked like that was gonna' happen."

"Until they found out Tony bribed somebody."

"We don't know that."

"But if he did, he got a lot of people fired, including himself."

"Yeah, well, chalk it up to experience. It's not like it was a losing proposition. We made good bucks, got our feet wet in a new area, got a crew together that works well…"

"What's gonna' happen to Nick? And Nancy…we won't need an office person anymore."

"Don't go singin' the blues yet, young man. There's work out there, and we know how to get it and do it. This job was starting to wind down anyway, and I've already been thinking about what's next. I've got a few ideas. You kids were gonna' go see those new friends of Nancy's in New York this weekend. Go, have some fun, and I'll make some calls. Make it a long weekend if you all can and come back ready to work. Good old Uncle Guy will have something by then."

It was neither Uncle Guy's optimism nor Tony's compliments that elevated Jean's mood, though he knew both were justified. Giroux Plumbing did really good work and Uncle Guy had a lot of connections. Jean was pleasantly surprised that Tony remembered his ideas. But it was the prospect of a long weekend in New York that put some life back into his voice.

"I guess you're right, Uncle Guy. We are a pretty good team."

They had planned to leave for New York Friday night after work and drive back Sunday night. Back at the barn, Jean quietly told Lee and Nick that if they busted their humps packing, they might be able to get tomorrow off. Nick let Nancy know, and she came out of the office and helped. By three-thirty, everything was cleaned and packed away. Uncle Guy gave them Friday and Monday off and assured them everything would work out fine.

Jean hung around the office, waiting for a callback from Marie about Friday and Monday. He was surprised how much he was looking forward to visiting "the commune" again. Marie had been effusive describing her first weekend with Nick and Nancy and David and Julie, imploring Jean to join them the next time they went down.

"You gotta' see these guys, Smooch, they're so cool! I mean, they're wild and crazy, but way smart, and they have incredible plans. They're just so much fun to talk to!"

The more Marie raved about the place the more suspicious Jean became. Eventually, Marie's enthusiasm and persistence won him over and he agreed to join them. He had expected to find holes in their plans, expose them as clueless hippies looking for any excuse to get stoned. But, despite himself, he was impressed with William.

Marie said he was the leader of the group, and Jean could see why. They spent less than two days on Jean's first trip down, arriving late Friday night and leaving Sunday afternoon, but William seemed to take a special interest in Jean, who felt he had found a kindred soul.

Another surprise was Nancy. Jean had never seen her like this. Comfortable leading discussions, verbally sparring with the know-it-all New Yorkers, rarely backing down.

Jean was aware his perceptions may have been clouded since he smoked more marijuana during that day and a half than he normally would in a month. He now smoked regularly with Marie, though not as often as she, and until that weekend in Mueller avoided getting high with Nick and Nancy. Marie was right about that also, saying it would just happen sometime and be fine. It did, and it was.

When Uncle Guy said the job was "winding down anyway" he was right. The remaining work could be handled on automatic pilot. Jean's mind strayed and replayed that first New York weekend. He'd settle on a deep discussion with William, a tear-producing bout of laughter with Marie and others or zoning out on music with closed eyes then opening them and locking eyes with someone smiling knowingly like they had just shared a mind-altering experience. Which, Jean supposed, they had. The next trip came during a busy time at work, and just Marie, Nancy, David and Julie went. Now Jean was going back, and they might have an extra day or two. With his contrary attitude behind him and his mind free to wander during work, Jean came up with a few reasons it could be even better this time.

His Civil Engineering courses included city planning, which dealt with infrastructure, environmental concerns, and societal ramifications. He had ideas galore, but stayed out of the discussions about the utopian village Nancy and the New Yorkers were hoping to create in Mendocino. Their plans were just that...*their* plans. There was no way he could leave his responsibilities toward his family and the business. He had made that decision when he opted out of RPI five years previously. There were *more* reasons to stay now, not *less*. He and Marie were nearing their collegiate degrees, and marriage was an accepted topic for discussion. New Hampshire was their home. They were sensible enough to realize they might want or need to relocate, maybe to a different part of the state or another part of New England, but never California. Jean asked Marie about that after her last visit.

"Have you ever thought about going out there with them?"

"No - well, I have thought about it, but not seriously. Certainly not without you."

"Well, that's encouraging!"

"How about you?"

"I guess if you were dying to go, of course I'd consider it. But I'd try to talk you out of it. It sounds exciting and scary. But I'm excited about our future here, and we can make that happen without the scary part."

Jean imagined a different role the next time he went back to New York. Why shouldn't he take part in the Mendocino discussions? He could offer suggestions, help with the bus remodel, get involved as a friend. He saw himself imparting his knowledge without sounding like a know-it-all. There were already enough of those in that crew! Most of his daydreams during work were about him sharing his vision and practical knowledge. Most, but not all.

Jean thought he noticed something during the two nights he and Marie slept in New York. The owner of the house shared his room with the most outrageous member of the crew, Sheila. But the next night another couple went up there with them. Jean couldn't be sure whether he was just imagining things because of the large amounts of marijuana, but he sensed sexual undertones. There were also occasional visits to the guest house by more than a single couple at a time that had the same suggestive aura. Jean was aware of the "free love" philosophy, which conjured up images of hippies on LSD having wild orgies in the woods.

But these people were his age, had jobs, some were married. Could his suspicions still be correct? Jean and Marie had recently seen *Bob and Carol and Ted and Alice*, a groundbreaking mainstream movie about open marriages. Unsure whether he would face ridicule as a country bumpkin or outrage as a pervert for suggesting such a thing, Jean kept it to himself. He was unsure how Marie would react. Would she think he was pushing them to take part? Was he?

Marie called back, disappointed. She couldn't get Friday off, but she did get Monday. "If it's slow, like it is sometimes on Friday afternoons, I may be able to get out early. Maybe three-thirty or four?"

"Great. We'll all be ready by then, and we'll go whenever you can."

"How's everyone doing there? Was it terrible?"

"It was, but I'm over it. I'll tell you all about it tonight. I'll grab a couple grinders and a Greek salad and meet you later at your place."

Jean walked outside and was surprised to see Uncle Guy and Lee still hanging around. As he was walking over to them, a pickup pulled into the yard and Jean recognized Uncle Fred. Not technically Jean's uncle, Fred had married Aunt Yvette's sister, and he and his wife often participated in family affairs. They were very supportive after Armand's death.

"Hey, Uncle Fred, long time no see."

"Well, hello there, young Mr. Giroux. Why didn't you guys tell me Jean was gonna' be here? I would've brought over that pair of skis

I've been telling him about."

Uncle Guy and Lee were looking at Jean like he just stepped off a flying saucer. "We thought you went home," said Uncle Guy. "Where ya' been?"

"In the office, waiting for Marie's call. What's up?"

"Lee thought we should, uh, follow up on Gerry's suggestion and, maybe, see if Fred had any properties floating around that might suit Tony's bosses."

"Now?"

Uncle Fred picked up on the awkward undertone and jumped in. "Lee's working on a couple of pieces of raw land for me this weekend, and I thought I'd swing by here to get some details, then maybe take your Uncle Guy to see a few tomorrow or Saturday. Wanna' come?"

"I'm going away for the weekend. Is this about Stinson's property?" Some open mouths, but no words. "I heard Lee mention it when we were leaving the job site. Is it really for sale?"

Uncle Fred, the supreme smooth talker, gave Jean a broad wink and said, "Well, Jean, that depends on who's asking. To anybody but us, the answer is 'absolutely not for sale.' But the kids wanna' sell, and, apparently, they have the family's approval."

"But it's not big enough for a project like the one we work... *worked*...on."

Uncle Guy said, "Probably not. But one idea I was thinking about as our next step was a small subdivision. We'd be the developer and contractor, sub out what we didn't want to do."

"But Uncle Guy..."

"I know, I know. I just started thinking about it, and there are more questions than answers. I was gonna' look at the property tomorrow with Fred, then go over it with you when you got back. If you stop here tomorrow morning before you hit the road, I can tell you what I've been thinking, and we can get serious after the weekend."

"Marie can't leave 'til the afternoon. I can go with you to the Stinson's in the morning."

"Okay. Why don't you meet me here at 7:00, you and I can talk, and we'll meet Fred at the Stinson's at 8:30."

"You know the logging road just past their driveway? Let's meet there," said Uncle Fred.

"I'll be there too," said Lee. "Some trees I hadda' cut down are laying across the road about a quarter mile in. I was gonna' clean 'em up tomorrow."

"Great," said Uncle Fred with a broad smile. "A family business meeting at 8:30, a quarter mile up the logging road. Better bring snowshoes, there's still snow in the woods and the terrain's a bit rough." Uncle Fred's hand hadn't left the open door of his truck, and he hopped back in, gave a cheery "See ya' tomorrow" and U-turned out of the yard.

Jean said, "I'm gonna' pack for the weekend," and walked over to his house. He was anxious to get away from the awkward conversation with Uncle Guy. There were others recently and the common denominator was Lee. He rubbed Jean the wrong way lately, acting like he was above Jean, more a peer of Uncle Guy. Jean and Lee *were* different generations. Lee was Aunt Yvette's brother and Jean her nephew. But Yvette was the first of eight children and Lee the last, while Jean was Armand and Bonnie's oldest. The actual age difference was only four years. Lately, working together created scenes like the one that just took place.

Lee assumed he was part of the decision-making process when he really wasn't. He found ways to insinuate himself into issues that didn't concern him, like the meeting tomorrow. Lee was the one who brought up Stinson's property in the first place, a property that conveniently had a pile of felled trees waiting for him to clean up. How did Uncle Fred get here so quickly with background information when they all just got fired this morning? Had any of this been pre-planned by Lee or Uncle Fred? Uncle Guy excluded Lee from the early morning meeting with Jean, but Lee was ready with an 'I'll be there anyway' for the ensuing 'family business meeting.' Giroux Plumbing and Heating was indeed a family business, but neither Lee nor Uncle Fred was a Giroux, or, for that matter, a plumber. This was exactly the kind of thing that amplified Jean's uneasiness about his position in the company. When Tony separated them into management and non-management this morning it wasn't the first time he had done so. Did Lee really not get it, or did he just ignore it and keep plugging away at his own agenda?

What also bothered him was Lee's behavior during Jean's first visit to New York. Lee tried unsuccessfully to attach himself to William and a few of the older members of the group. He also tried to act like he was an experienced marijuana smoker but took very small tokes and blew the smoke out immediately, like you do with a cigarette. He declined stronger hallucinogens using inappropriate excuses, trying to make it seem like he was an old pro at tripping and just wasn't in the mood, in stark contrast to Jean and Marie's honest "we're new at this and too scared to try anything that strong."

Jean was positive Lee had never tripped. He was also pretty sure Lee's mini tokes weren't getting him stoned, and noticed he was consuming a large amount of alcohol in an effort to get buzzed. As a result, Lee made a complete ass of himself fawning over Nancy's friend Julie, though to be fair Jean could appreciate the attraction.

Lee eventually went so far out of bounds that her boyfriend objected, and the owner of the house had to intervene. Jean apologized for his friend's behavior, and thanked Lenny for informing Lee he was acting like an asshole.

Anxious to redirect his train of thought from Lee to the upcoming weekend, Jean called Marie and asked if he should pick something up for Nancy and Nick.

"No, they're staying at David and Julie's tonight. They'll all come down here tomorrow afternoon to pick us up."

So, they would be alone tonight. He called Darren House of Pizza, ordered a large meatball grinder, a small cheesesteak, and a Greek salad. He left a note for Mom saying he was having dinner with Marie and didn't know when he'd be home. Both he and Mom knew that meant he'd probably be sleeping there, but neither was inclined to be more specific. Jean went through a mental checklist of what he packed, completing his shift of focus from Lee to the weekend and reminding himself to ask Marie about possible sexual shenanigans. He smiled, thinking if Marie got upset, he *would* be sleeping at home tonight. He started thinking about ways to gently work it into the conversation. He shouldn't have bothered.

"Yeah, you're right. There's some swinging going on."

"Swinging?"

"Swinging. You know, switching partners."

Embarrassed by his naivety, Jean needed more details. "Do they go into separate rooms to do it, or just climb all over themselves in one bed?" Marie giggled. Jean was encouraged. "Do they watch each other? Do it next to each other? Keep the lights on? Does one naked man ever rub against the other?" Marie was now cracking up. Jean was emboldened and pressed on. "Are they with the other guy's partner for the whole night, or do they switch back and forth? Do they do it simultaneously? Does somebody say, 'ready, set, go' and then they start?"

"Stop it, Jean, so I can tell you what I think." Jean made a zipping motion in front of his smile, and Marie said, "It's just about sex. Nobody's cheating on anybody, nobody's looking to fall in love with anybody. They're just having sex for fun."

"Would you do it?"

"I don't think so. I guess I'd think about it if another couple asked us. Meanwhile, nobody's asking, so I guess we'll just have to do it by ourselves." Which they immediately did.

When Jean got to the office Friday morning, Uncle Guy was seated at a drafting table with a town property map under a sliding rule, an empty chair next to him. "Morning. Have a seat."

"Whatcha' got?"

"Here's our property. This rectangle is the section we subdivided out for my house, and here's the Stinson property," waving his hand over each section as he named them, "and this here's the logging road where we're meeting Lee and Fred. Are you familiar with it?

"Yup. Dad and I cross-country skied there." Uncle Guy never liked talking about how things used to be with Armand, and Jean respected that. But Jean was beginning to appreciate the memories, so he pushed on, maybe because he thought Uncle Guy felt bad about yesterday afternoon's awkward conversation. "When I started racing cross country Dad coached me there. Mom would ski with David, and Cindy used a pair of those short, wide, plastic skis. We'd joke that Mom and David skied ten times further than us because they were always circling back for Cindy. David hated that arrangement. He wanted to ski with the big boys too. I'd tell him, 'You'll get your chance', but then…"

Jean's voice tailed off. Uncle Guy stood, walked over to the window, and looked out. The two stalls they converted into their office had screens and storm windows jerry-rigged onto the outside, but the old windows, the kind that slide between the inner and outer walls of a barn, were still there. Uncle Guy played with the one he was looking through, sliding it open, then closed. Jean continued, "So, why are we lookin' at this property with Uncle Fred and Lee?"

Uncle Guy turned around quickly with a startled expression, as if Jean just entered the room. "You sounded just like your dad," Uncle Guy said softly. "That's what he would have said, and how he would've said it." He gave Jean a wistful smile and turned back to the desk. "You don't like the idea of developing Stinson's land?"

"It's not that I don't like it. Yesterday, when Tony said his company might nail down a property soon, you warned Gerry that it could take months before they get approvals and start hiring people. Wouldn't it take that long for us? What would we do in the meantime?"

"I've got a few leads for immediate work. But if this is a good idea for the future, and if it takes time, then we should start the ball rolling now."

"And how do we do that?"

"First, we walk the property and see if our future engineer sees any problems. Does your degree include surveying?"

"It will when I get it in June. Do we have topos?"

"What are topos?"

"Topographical maps. They show elevations, steepness of slopes, soil types, wetlands."

"Can't we use this? It has all the metes and bounds."

"Some of the lots might be too close to a stream, or wetlands, or on a steep grade. Topos have all those details."

"For these specific properties?"

"For every square foot of land in the U.S. of A."

"Really? How do we get 'em?"

"Just ask. They're from the USGS." Jean saw Uncle Guy's expression and added, "United States Geological Survey."

"How much?"

"I don't know. The school gets 'em for nothing. I can check and see if we have one for this area, and if not, order it." Jean grabbed a notepad and pen. "What's Stinson's lot number?"

"Uh, let's see, it looks like '37,' and ours…"

"Ours? Why would we need ours?"

"Because look here. Our original property is 38-1, and my five-acre rectangle is 38-2. We can subdivide the farmhouse onto another five-acre rectangle for you, call it 38-3, and still have more than thirty acres left to develop."

"You want to develop our land?" Jean was shocked.

"Not now. But someday your mom may want to, and you may, too. It's two-acre zoning, so fifteen building lots."

"Not really. Some of that land can't be built on, and we'll have to build a road. We'd be lucky to get ten."

"Either way, it's something you're gonna' have to think about. There's a lot of money sitting in that land."

It was Jean's turn to stand up, walk over to the windows. At this time yesterday morning they were pulling up to the Waterville Valley site, thinking it was going to be just another Thursday at work. Because someone he hardly knew may have done something illegal everything in his life changed. It was like the moment he looked down to the finish line of the cross-country race and didn't see his parents.

"Are Lee and Uncle Fred involved in this?" Jean was surprised he voiced the thought out loud, and it sounded adversarial. He turned around to see if Uncle Guy was offended.

"It's not their land." Uncle Guy didn't look bothered. "Have you and your mother talked about this?" Now there *was* an edge to Uncle Guy's tone. He and Aunt Yvette took exception to Mom's recent behavior. She reentered the dating game with a vengeance. There weren't many new bachelors in town, and the retreads she associated with rarely met their approval. There was a rumor she was seen at a bar with one of Lee's friends, closer in age to Jean than to Armand. Aunt Yvette's family was being called upon more often to watch David and Cindy. Jean tried to take up the slack, but he was working full time, going to school at night, and recently added the New York contingent to their social life. Jean felt guilty enough to broach the subject.

"I don't have to go to New York this weekend. I can stay home with David and Cindy."

"I'm not talking about babysitting, Jean. I'm talking about land. You need to have a sit-down with your mother and go over all the options. They're good, don't get me wrong, but it's not my place to interpret Armand's wishes. Once the two of you have a clear under-standing what you want, I'll be glad to offer my advice. Right now, my advice is let's put all this bullshit aside and take a look at the Stinson property as a future option for the Girouxs. And let's keep our minds open to every potential problem and every potential windfall."

There was still, as Uncle Fred had warned, snow in the woods, and snowshoes were necessary. The logging road, wide and mostly free of vegetation, was a road in name only. Steep rises were immediately followed by sharp dips, the road was often canted to the left or right and crossed seasonal streams. It was not passable in a car or pickup.

The Stinsons maintained it so their tractors could haul out firewood, which they sold. They also logged lumber-grade trees and milled them at their sawmill on the property.

The going was slow. It was past noon when they reached a gate with a sign that read "Entering White Mountain National Forest, Motor Vehicles Prohibited." This marked the end of the Stinson property. The logging road made a right turn in front of the gate. On the other side a narrower trail continued, which was where Armand used to take Jean cross country skiing.

The four men turned right and followed the road. It flattened out at a staging area filled with logging equipment covered by tarps, past the quiet sawmill. Spring in this part of New Hampshire was referred to as "mud season" due to melting snow and swollen rivers and streams. Heavy equipment would have to wait before navigating logging roads. They continued a short distance to the Stinson's farm. Lee's van was parked in front of the farmhouse where Uncle Fred picked him up this morning. They piled in and drove back, in ten minutes, to the logging road where they had met five hours ago. It was almost two when Jean and Uncle Guy returned to the barn where Nick, Nancy, David, Julie, and Marie sat outside on some benches.

"You guys been waiting long?" asked Jean.

"Just long enough to eat lunch. I saved you some pizza, Smooch. There's plenty here if you wanna' join us, Uncle Guy," Marie offered.

"None for me sweetie, thanks. Jean, grab a slice and let's look at the town maps while it's still fresh in our minds."

When they were in the office Uncle Guy said, "So, what'd you think of the land?"

Jean said, "First, it's huge. What'd the map say, 200 acres?"

Uncle Guy searched with his finger for the details. "195, plus or minus."

"Second, it's rough. Putting in roads would be necessary for a subdivision, and expensive. Do you want to tackle something that big? Is there a market for that many homes in this area?"

"Right now, those answers would be "No" and "No." But it'll only get more expensive in the future, and *now* is when it may go on the market."

"Are you thinking it's something that Tony's bosses would be interested in?"

"It crossed my mind."

"Did he tell you what their project is?"

"No, but it's probably some kind of resort like Waterville Valley."

"Well, it sure is raw, but it's a beautiful location. I'd need to see the topos for exact elevations and sight lines, but I'm guessing there are views of the Presidential Range, especially with some selective clearing of trees. It would be perfect for a resort, except..." Jean hesitated, staring at the map.

"Except what?"

"The town will want at least one extra entrance for a resort that size, maybe another for service vehicles. The Stinson property's road frontage won't be enough. The only other boundaries are with the National Forest land and the back of our property. Remember Tony saying the deal that fell through was landlocked? This may have the same problem."

"Okay. We'll leave those details to the lawyers if it gets that far. I say we get those topos and see what we think."

"I'll call school right now and order them."

"Oh, and..."

"I know, I know. You want the topos for our property also."

Uncle Guy grinned and said, "You really do sound just like your dad. Call the school, then get goin'. It's supposed to snow, and I want you far enough south before dark so it'll be rain."

Jean returned the grin. "Now *you* sound like my dad." He had been in his element during the walk through the woods, his formal education providing the whys and wherefores to his lifetime of experience. All questions were directed to him by the other three men, and he had all the answers. Uncle Guy was obviously impressed and let him lead the discussion in the office. And the best part was next. Jean was going to offer his opinions about land use to the New Yorkers as they planned their Mendocino adventure, his plumbing skills to the remodel of their school bus. He was looking forward to laughs, great music, stimulating talk, maybe even some sexual experimentation. It promised to be an extended weekend of drugs, sex, and rock and roll.

Growing up, Jean was respected by peers and elders alike. He was a considerate friend, did well in school and on the athletic fields, gave back to his community, was always respectful to adults. But ever since Dad died there was a sense of things being half a bubble off level. The "best of times, worst of times" theme was a constant drag preventing him from moving on. Now seven years after Dad's death, a new equilibrium was being established. It wasn't a matter of getting over the loss of his father, but rather accepting the fact there would always be a hole, a burden he would have to carry. The relevant task was figuring out how to carry it more comfortably.

Small victories gradually picked up momentum, turning into a year-long series of events that restored Jean's confidence. They began the morning after Tony and the crew were fired by Waterville Valley (...it was the worst of times) when Jean and Uncle Guy met Lee and Uncle Fred at the pile of felled trees on the Stinson property, followed

by a successful unveiling of the new Jean Giroux during the weekend
at the commune (it was the best of times…).

CHAPTER FIFTEEN

LENNY

1970, Mueller NY

I guess Sheila and I wound up sleeping together, one of those asexual times she predicted. The drizzly dawn found us both still fully clothed on the sofa, my feet on the coffee table,

> *a euphemism for some concrete blocks and a couple of 2 by 10's. I also had a "wall unit," which was three tiers of the same configuration housing stereo components, books and a TV.*

her head on my lap. She dozed off - or passed out - around 2:30am. I couldn't sleep. My mind just wouldn't shut off. I tried to bore myself to sleep by alphabetizing the inventory at the Team Sports warehouse. I went over all the trades I would make if I owned the Mets. My mind was still yo-yoing from the unexpected turn of events. Like the little rubber ball on the elastic string, I soared higher and higher, only to have the "next wave" and the "summer bummer" snap me back to a painful reunion with the paddle. Why was everything in my life like that? Why did skipping along with Rosalie Corio's sun-bleached thigh fuzz end with Vinny's right fist? Why did this euphoric evening end with such a personal crash? If only I could anticipate the apex of the rubber ball's arc away from the paddle, I could do something about the return smack. But that elastic string was attached to the paddle as surely as it was to the ball, kinetic and potential energy inversely related, yin and yanging as long as they both shall live.

Roscoe, the all-night DJ on WNEW-FM, was playing George Harrison's "I, Me, Mine," and it seemed he had selected it just for me. I was destined for a lonely life as a selfish recluse, never again to enjoy the camaraderie I had come so close to being a part of just a few short hours ago. I was sure everyone noticed my sullen silence amidst the upbeat excitement about the new adventure. They had every right to characterize my pouting as the epitome of sour grapes. And my status as first lieutenant? What a joke! I wasn't even on the team. I didn't make the cut. I *always* made the cut, goddammit.

On the other hand, they were planning to use my house, weren't they? This year-round job, this albatross, paid for the house, didn't it? The mortgage came due *even during the summer.* Apparently, it was going to be up to me to pay the rent, utilities, probably supply the food and drink more than not. I would then be eligible for the *next wave.* By then they'd probably screw the whole thing up, be in debt up to their ears, get arrested for trespassing, probably get Julie's Mexican boyfriend deported.

"Mark Lane, son of Morris Lipshutz." I hadn't thought of him in a few years. Like Julie's boyfriend David Martin, Mark Lipshutz changed his name. He was our pledge father, the *liaison* between the brothers and pledges, the only brother we were allowed to address without the "Sir," the one we could whine to about unfair treatment at the hands of the loutish brotherhood we were trying our hardest to join. A junior when I was a freshman pledge, a senior and chapter president when I was a sophomore young turk leading the best pledge class ever, Mark and I spent a fair amount of time in esoteric conversations about the role of fraternities in the changing campus lifestyle of the late sixties. He was a communications major, did sports reports for the college radio station and play-by-play for some of the lower profile sports. He hated the way his name sounded on the radio (lip shits) and took the stage name Mark Lane for its phonetic simplicity. After the brothers heard it, he was forevermore introduced as "Mark Lane, son of Morris Lipshutz."

We were gearing up for Spring Fling, an annual rite of drunkenness and debauchery. Each year, the Inter-Fraternity Council paired sororities and fraternities randomly and we made floats, put on skits, sold food, all for charity. Angst abounded as we awaited the pairings, but every year the cool frats were matched with the cool sororities, and the dweebs with the dweebs (*"What a co-inky-dink!"* Moe, Larry, and Curly). Another co-inky-dink was the timely reawakening of the planet, the appearance of green grass and flowers complemented by bare legs and midriffs, the birds echoing in conjunction with the staccato motorcycle rat-a-tats off the brick buildings, romances blossoming with the flora. The shared effort of stuffing dyed tissue paper into chicken wire frames provided the seed, watered by purple passions (grain alcohol and grape juice) and endless kegs of beer.

I had a great idea for our skit, a take-off on Sergeant Pepper's Lonely Hearts Club Band. It was the 20th anniversary of Spring Fling, instituted to brighten the spirits of the war-weary, and the words lent themselves to inspired rewriting:

It was twenty years ago today, Zeta Beta Tau'd the band to play.
They've been going in and out of style, but they're guaranteed to raise a smile.
So let me introduce you to, the one and only ZBTs,
And Zeta Beta Tau's Lonely Hearts Club Ba-and!

I wanted a drummer atop scaffolding, foot-booming his bass

drum in total darkness to open the show, then electric guitars joining as a single spot illuminated Carleen DiBruzzi, the sweetest and purest of all sorority sweethearts, belting out the raunchy rewritten classic. The brotherhood did not agree.

The arrival of marijuana and psychedelic rock n' roll precipitated the inevitable backlash from those who liked things just the way they were. The upperclassmen had paid their dues and risen to the top of this specific culture. They had no use for a counterculture. Still young enough to ridicule their out-of-date parents, they were in no mood to be out of date themselves. Creative brilliance was beaten back in favor of blatantly obvious double *entendres* and sophomoric pratfalls. Man, was I pissed. I sulked and skulked, derided and decided not to find anything they said or did the least bit humorous. Mark Lane, son of Morris Lipshutz, set me straight.

"This Spring Fling shit is really drivin' you nuts."

"It's total bullshit, man."

"You know, you really ought to go somewhere else that weekend.

"Huh?"

"You know, a road trip or something. How about that girl you met from Northwestern? You could visit her maybe." We were standing in the downstairs hallway between the dining room, which was a mini version of a school cafeteria, and our Chapter Room, with a couple of sofas, old easy chairs, and a TV. "I just think it's gonna' be tough on you. Everywhere you look there'll be reminders your idea lost. Everybody else will be partying and celebrating and having fun."

"What are you trying to say?"

"I'm saying that in a democracy the majority wins."

"Even if the majority's wrong?"

Mark nodded toward the Chapter Room, and we went in and sat.

He said, "I heard something this morning on public radio."

"Is that considered homework for you communication majors?"

"Someone said that when JFK hosted a dinner for Nobel Prize winners, it was the greatest amount of intellect assembled in the White House since Thomas Jefferson was there alone." He paused for effect, took out a box of Callard & Bowser butterscotch sucking candies, unwrapped one and popped it in his mouth. Expertly tucking it to one side, he continued without a trace of interference with his enunciation. "Jefferson and the boys who wrote the Constitution never said anything about the majority being right. They just said the majority wins."

"And being right is irrelevant?"

"Absolutely. And…" a shit-eating grin on his face, "irrelevant never forgets."

I got up, walked out the back door to the blacktopped parking lot, stopping along the way to pluck a basketball out of the bin of assorted sports paraphernalia by the door. I dribbled out to the basket and started shooting. A couple of guys came out, then a few more. Soon we had three teams of three, two playing one waiting, winner stays on the court. We played for almost three hours before the game broke up. I was bent over, hands on my knees. My team finished with a streak of five consecutive wins, and I was totally gassed. And I knew Mark was right. Either I get into the bogus skit, do my best to make it no worse than all the preceding bogus skits, or I might as well go to Chicago to see that girl. What about the weekends leading up to Spring Fling, or immediately following? Should I go away then also? I didn't like the girl from Northwestern *that* much.

It was as simple as the business principle of cost versus benefit. The benefit was always having guys around to shoot hoops, to get some pizza, to primp and preen and make fun of before a big date. The cost was you needed to occasionally subordinate your personal wishes to those of the group. Fraternal living was communal in many ways, another example of William's observation that the political continuum is more a circle than a straight line.

I sat on my sofa, left side rendered numb from hip to toes by Sheila's head. My eyes were on fire, background headache beginning to burgeon to the fore, stomach queasy from questionable foods eaten too late, sharp crick across my neck and shoulders. I needed something to help me change my direction, and it came courtesy of the only plural heading in my collection of Rules to Live a Better Life, the Copernicus Memorial Theories.

I recalled how, walking back into the fraternity house with the basketball under my arm and reconciliation on my mind, I tried to reconstruct what the brothers must have said to Mark to have him talk to me. Then it dawned on me. They didn't say anything to him. There was no meeting aimed at getting the prodigal son back into the flock. Nobody even noticed I was missing. Mark just thought I was acting like an asshole and told me so. Nobody ever notices you as much as you think. We are not, as we learned from Copernicus, the center of the universe. Perhaps nobody noticed my anti-Mendocino petulance. Sheila still chose my lap to lay her head on, didn't she? All-seeing, all-knowing William was as complimentary as ever after his minimal reaction to my reaction, wasn't he?

The Copernicus Memorial Theories consist of those rare pearls of wisdom we learned in class that actually apply to the real world. The prime example, of course, is that we aren't the center of the universe. Another example is the formula describing simple machines: Output equals Input, minus Friction. This could also apply to things like fraternity meetings about Spring Fling, or friends planning a cross-country adventure. There may be a lot I still didn't know, but one thing I *did* know was I did *not* want to be the friction.

I eased myself slowly out from under Sheila, supporting her head with my hands and then repositioning it carefully on the couch. I dead legged to the stairs, pins and needles replacing numbness, rotating my neck to relieve the crick. I needed to go upstairs, stretch out in my own bed, catch a few hours' sleep. By mid-afternoon, I'd be back in the thick of things, talking about the bus and the trip, and my brief counterproductive episode would be history. I found my bed occupied, however, and an astonished double take confirmed its occupants were Carl and Andre. A child protege whose future greatness as a figure skater in his native Hungary was already assured by age 8, Andre's dream was derailed by the failed 1956 revolution. His family escaped to the USA, where Andre's skating and ballet training eventually led to his current career as a Broadway dancer living in Sheila's apartment. Thin, wiry, effeminate, it was no surprise to find him in bed with another male. But Carl! As Popeye liked to say, "Dat's all I can takes, and I cain't takes no more!"

Stumbling back down the stairs I arranged some cushions on the coffee table for my legs, slipped my lap back under Sheila's head and tried to let sleep overtake my ravaged mind. A few cognizant thoughts waged the losing battle with bizarre dream-like hallucinations as I flitted between wakefulness, dreaming, and still tripping. I remember thinking it would help my status as a member in good standing to be partnered with Sheila. This melted into George Harrison in a fuchsia tutu and matching lipstick shouting "I, Me, Mine" in my ear. George turned into a bowlegged cowboy in a 1930's black and white western, wearing chaps and a ridiculous Tom Mix Stetson, strumming his guitar. Wait, that's no Beatle, that's my father! A cartoon sunset was on the fake backdrop behind Dad, who brandished his staff at me and proclaimed, "Ivan begat Sheila, whose head resteth just two thin layers of cloth from your future issue!" His staff turned into a baseball bat, Dad became Vinny in a New York Yankees uniform nonchalantly fungo-ing the heads of Hog Farm members into the New Hampshire forest as cognizance conceded the contest and the trip finally ended.

The dawn drizzle deteriorated into full-on rain by noon. I found Ricky in the half of the garage that was still a garage, replacing my water hose. I heard some stirring from upstairs in the apartment, but I was not about to go up there and check it out. Who knew what I might find? I was still a little shaky, still slightly altered.

"Here, hold these." Ricky handed me four little black rubber things. I stared at them as if they might hold the secrets of the universe.

"What are they?"

"Suppressors."

Oh. Political? Medical? "What do they suppress?"

"Electromagnetic waves." Ricky's eyes did their disappearing act as he chortled his response. How could he always be so cheerful?

"Un-huh," I responded without conviction. "Gotta' suppress those old EMWs, I suppose."

"I took your car for a spin this morning -"

"Really? While you were tripping?"

"- to get the engine hot enough for the hose to leak, and I noticed some static on the radio. I must have amped the radio up so much it's picking up your spark plugs firing."

"I hadn't noticed."

"You gotta' crank the volume up pretty loud and have the engine red-lined. It was pretty cool. I could hear that I hadn't advanced the timing enough for high speeds."

My incredulous indignation was interrupted by the opening and slamming of the apartment door as Sheila made a quick u-turn into the open garage, her flannel shirt protecting her head.

"Yucch! You oughta' make a connecting door from the kitchen into here."

"Can't," said Ricky without looking up from the engine. "Refrigerator, sink, stove," his arm reaching up and pointing in succession along the dividing wall, succinctly illustrating the lack of room between the appliances on the other side. "Let me have one of those black beauties, willya?"

I complied, then turned to Sheila. "Where is everybody?"

"Ricky and Marlene are upstairs," shaking and folding her shirt. "I *thought* I left this shirt up there last weekend. It's really empty since we moved into the main house. We need some furniture, you know? Make it like a guest cottage." Now isn't that Vanderbilty? And who would be the Lord and Lady of the manor? "I'm not sure where everybody else is. William and Bobbi went out looking for something after Andy called."

"Andy called?" He was one of the two counselors moving Mrs. McLary's furniture.

"Suppressor number two, please," interrupted Ricky. "Yeah, they're in Wheeling, West Virginia. They wanted me to diagnose an engine problem for them."

"Over the phone?"

"Yeah, well, it's a pretty distinctive sound. They were obviously low on oil and the valves were tapping. Suppressor number three, please?"

"They gonna' be okay?"

"They should make it home. The final suppressor - oh, and you got another call. Bobbi took it. Some of their friends from New Hampshire are trying to get here. That's where they went, to find 'em and guide 'em in. Guess we gotta' have another party tonight."

We did have another party that night, and so it began. Over the next two years our numbers swelled to almost two dozen, though the entire ensemble was rarely in attendance at one time. The regulars were those who spent more time at my house than their own. Some even moved in, though it was always viewed as temporary, and mostly was.

We came from disparate groups. Sheila and Carl's *artistes* over-lapped with William and Bobbi's revolutionaries due to the friendship of the two women. A few camp counselors had a group of friends who fit in with me and my high school buddies like Louie, Ricky, and Marlene. There were a couple of curious Mueller locals from my softball team that I wasn't afraid to expose to the craziness. There was nobody from work. The dichotomy defining my life was becoming more defined, not less. I accepted my fate, working by rote Monday through Friday, 50 weeks a year - including summers - and living for the weekends.

We were joined on that inaugural weekend by what would become known as the New Hampshire Five. They followed William and Bobbi back from a gas station located in the median of the Hutchinson River Parkway, from which they had placed the collect call. I was explaining the importance of keeping a written account of extrava-gances like collect calls when William and Bobbi pulled in, followed by a capped pickup crammed with people. It took me a while to realize there were five of them, because I couldn't tear my eyes away from Julie. William had nailed her description, exaggerating neither her beauty nor her bra size. She looked like a blonde Wonder Woman, nearly my height, sex-goddess body, curly mass of wheat-colored hair spilling onto her shoulders and halfway down her back. I knew such women existed because I saw them in movies, Marilyn Monroe, Sophia Loren, Ann Margret. But this real, live creature was in my backyard in a T-shirt and cut-offs (wow), smiling (wow) at me. I hated David Martin *nee* Diego Martinez already.

Sheila snapped her flannel shirt at my butt, *a la* Nanook with his gym towel. I broke out of my Julie trance, jumped in to help unload their stuff.

"Where do you want 'em?" asked William. "They brought sleeping bags and camping stuff."

Bobbi shook her head. "They can't camp out in the rain, William. They can use the upstairs apartment, spread their bags on the floor."

"That's cool," said one of the New Hampshire girls, who then turned to me. "I'm Nancy. That's my boyfriend Nick, and," pointing as she rotated, "Marie, David, and you've already, um, kinda, met Julie."

"Leave the stupid car alone, Ricky," said Sheila, "and grab some stuff. You two also," pointing at William and me then re-entering the apartment kitchen, the Lady of the Manor leading her guests to the guest house. The Lord of the Manor scrambled and shoved in a failed attempt to be the one directly under Julie and her cut-offs as they ascended the circular staircase.

Though it was a little strange to have an influx of a whole new group, there was no hint of awkwardness Saturday evening. People showed up, drank, smoked, munched, and chewed some peyote buttons supplied by David and Julie. Nancy, David, and Julie brought instant creds because they were the only ones who actually had seen the promised land, owned by nobody. And Nancy drove the pickup - how could you not love a girl driving a pickup with a snowplow rig?

The rest of us basked in the reflected glory of William, who obviously impressed them during his visit to Nancy's farm in New Hampshire. Nancy chaired the meeting, William and Bobbi slipping into the roles of co-hosts. That left me with no role, but I was okay with that, my newly adopted mellow attitude courtesy of the Copernicus Memorial Theories.

As the mescaline kicked in, I began seeing them as a five-piece rock band, with Nancy the lead singer, Nick and David on guitars, Marie and Julie singing back-up. The words they were "singing" described the communal village in Mendocino, the people there, the soon-to-be bus that would take us there and the beautiful life we all would lead. I would frequently lose track of their lyrics as my mind wandered off on side trips, but the experience shared by all in the former house of Beverly McLary was transcendent.

I was a believer. This year or next, first team or second-stringer, I was all in. We were shooting the moon, and my new house was the launching pad. Our weekend get-togethers were work parties, and despite our binges of excess we made progress. A rhythm was established as members of the clan juxtaposed short-term, real-life concerns with the long-term goal of an idyllic life in Mendocino. A school bus was purchased and towed to my backyard, where the retro-fitting and repairing took place under Ricky and Nick's supervision. Ricky and Marlene moved into the guest house but kept a section of the upstairs floor clear for weekend guests.

Sheila had a nominal room of her own in the main house. She still kept the loft in Soho, which she shared in some sort of loose arrange-ment with Carl, Andre, and a few others. She occasionally slept in her room, more often in mine. I was getting comfortable with the noncommittal fluidity of our relationship. My fantasy of us becoming the number two power couple in the hierarchy went the same way as me becoming a Hall of Fame shortstop for the New York Mets. The free love lifestyle of our groovy group and the arrival of additional women had a lot to do with my uncharacteristic willingness to go with the flow.

The hallmark of the liberated woman - or man - was being comfortable with your own body, rising above the embarrassment of public nakedness recently on prominent display in rain-swollen ponds and puddles at Woodstock, and being mature enough to appreciate the beauty of the human body while restraining your lewd and lascivious instincts. The proud parade of unclothed body parts diligently kept under wraps during and after my pubescent years were a challenge my evolution couldn't quite overcome. I was mostly content to window shop, willing to settle for discreet voyeurism. My occasional, intensely satisfying trysts with the ever imaginative and energetic Sheila Siegel were enough to keep my libido in check.

Julie was the number one mannequin in the window, as well as the toughest hurdle in my effort to maintain my mature outlook. In addition to Julie's remarkable beauty, brief glimpses of her passing vagina seemed to reveal an absence of pubic hair. Unsure if her white-blonde hair was simply creating a clean-shaven illusion, I was on the horns of a dilemma. I was neither cool enough to blatantly stare between her legs at close range, nor liberated enough to ask her to hold still and spread her legs so I could get a closer look and some tactile verification.

Julie wasn't the only female who cast puritanism to the winds, and as the communal feeling settled in over the next couple of months, I began to take it for granted. As the mystery faded so did my prurience. We were brothers and sisters in a new-order family, and love need not always equate with lust.

As Friday nights approached people would start appearing at the house. Some peripheral, not committed to the Mendocino undertaking, coming for the party and to offer occasional assistance. The New Hampshire Five, under the guidance of their lead singer Nancy, were regulars. Shared peyote cemented my rock band analogy and my clever name for them stuck, though two were from California and their numbers fluctuated from three to seven. Sometimes Nick or Marie couldn't make it because of work, sometimes Marie's boyfriend Jean joined them. Lee, a relative of Jean's who was also a plumber/ handy man, showed up infrequently. The NH Five were Ricky and Marlene's most frequent guests. My initial impressions of them ranged from "a glimmer of truth" to "dead wrong."

Nancy was a rural version of Bobbi. She had an agenda she aggressively pursued for the good and welfare of us all and had specific skills and knowledge us city slickers didn't. Plus, she was a good time girl, always looking for ways to have fun, always willing to put in the effort to make the fun happen.

Nick was hard to figure. He seemed perpetually preoccupied with something else, as if he was a brooding author, artist, or musician. But he was a plumber. Can you be a brooding plumber? I kept waiting for him to surprise me with a collection of unfinished paintings or Act One of a partially written three-act play. But there were no surprises from Nick.

David and Julie couldn't even be considered as individuals. They were "The Ikes," a teasing reference to that other current couple, David and Julie Eisenhower *nee* Nixon. You rarely saw one without the other and all they ever said when they were was "Hey, do you know where David/Julie is?"

Marie was a mystery, the quintessential fifth wheel, seemingly unsure of why she was in the group at all. She tried so hard not to be objectionable she was invisible, except when her boyfriend Jean came with them. Suddenly vibrant and engaging, her personality burgeoned forth. Instead of nondescript she was subtly understated, her plain face becoming pretty in its simplicity. Her body, undetectable beneath formless attire, pushed against the same old clothes in all the right places with renewed enthusiasm. Like a planet, she needed a star's light to reflect.

Marie's boyfriend Jean could easily be a small town William. He was a couple of years older, like William, and very socially responsible. He didn't like to talk as much as William did, often restricting his comments to a two-word, well-placed opinion. "Not necessarily." "Useful information." "Not bad." He was, like William, one of those people who just seemed to know more than the rest of us without appearing superior.

As the weekends went by and the hours we spent together added up, my caricature snapshots began to develop like photos in a darkroom, magically filling in until they were sharp and detailed portraits. We became an extended family, united in a cause, accepting of idiosyncrasies, enjoying each other's individuality. There were occasional flareups and bickering, usually caused by male prideful posturing or female silent suffering. These infrequent incidents were often fallout from the free-love lifestyle, which turned out to be not entirely free.

But the shared goal, abundant laughter, profound conversations, and overall good times prevailed, especially as summer neared and the trip west approached liftoff.

CHAPTER SIXTEEN

STEVEN

1963, Brooklyn

Steven agonized over the wording of the Valentine's Day card he would send through Irene. He wanted to match her message of "Love, Gail" but wasn't sure if she meant "Love" as just a figure of speech. He wanted to match her enthusiasm for running the whole loop but wasn't sure if he should encourage her to "win another game" more relevant to her goal of returning to Brooklyn. He filled a few pieces of scrap paper before settling on "Happy Valentine's Day. I knew you could do it!" He signed it "Luv, S." and was pleased with the casual tone.

Over the next few months, their secret correspondence continued with the logistical help of Irene and Mom. The letters grew longer, more personal, and more exciting. They were partners in a forbidden activity. Gail's efforts to normalize her health and return to Brooklyn led to discussions about teenage anxieties they were both experiencing. Their separation provided enough protection to write things Steven could never say in person. While he couldn't rival her smooth prose, his stilted style was honest and heartfelt, and apparently pleasing enough to Gail. There were hints about the future direction of their relationship, how geographic proximity would speed the transition from friends to boyfriend/girlfriend. All signs pointed to Gail's return by the start of their sophomore year. She could not go to her Uncle Ralph's house for the summer to work at the camp and filled her time by writing more frequently. Emboldened by the safety of long-distance correspondence, they started writing about imagined scenarios where they might be alone. Gail's flowery descriptions read like a teen romance novel.

We walked hand-in-hand along Brighton Beach as the sun began to set over the sea. We couldn't bear the thought of our enchanted day coming to an end. We walked to a spot where the dunes shielded us from the prying eyes of our peers. We stopped, and you turned to me. Your face was framed by the fiery sunset, the waves pounding behind you.

"We're alone," you said in a soft, husky whisper. And then, finally, you pulled me close and we kissed.

What happens next?

Love, Gail.

Steven had no expectations of being able to write, so there was no self-consciousness about the quality of his response. As far as the content went, it was clear that realism was not a factor.

We laid down on the sand. We kissed again. I moved on top of you. We rolled around and soon you were on top of me.

You said, "I've got sand in my bathing suit."

I said, "Take it off. No one can see us."

You said, "Don't you have sand in yours too?"

I said, "Let's find out!" I stood up and pulled off my suit. Then you stood up. You were wearing a bikini, and pulled off the bottoms, then turned around.

"Untie my top," you said. I did and it dropped to the sand. You turned around and faced me naked.

What happens next?

Luv, S.

Each letter pushed the scenes toward, and eventually through, having sexual intercourse. The one thing Steven was unwilling to share was how, before he fell asleep, he would reread the letters, picture the scenes, and masturbate. He didn't know if, let alone how, girls masturbated. That possibility was so erotic the result was often a second masturbation. Then in August he got the ultimate good-news, bad-news letter. It was short and combative, like the confrontation on their winter walk.

I'm moving home next week. I'll be back at Madison, but I'm not allowed to be your girlfriend. I think Uncle Murray is the reason my parents said this. Is your family really in the Mafia? Do they have people killed, turn girls into whores? What does that make you?

No "Love, Gail" this time. Steven was furious. He balled up the letter and threw it in the waste basket. He took it out, smoothed it, reread it. At the back of his closet were boxes of old comic books, magazines, and athletic award certificates. Gail's letters were divided among the boxes so they would be harder for Mom to spot. He took them out to throw down the incinerator chute in the hallway, but instead returned the boxes to the closet, sat on his bed holding the letter.

"Steven?"

"Yeah?"

"Are you okay?"

"No."

"Can I come in?"

Steven hesitated then said, "Sure."

Mom walked to his headboard and grabbed the tissue box, sat beside him on the bed. He handed her Gail's letter. Before looking at it she dabbed his eyes and handed him the box. Steven was unaware he had been crying.

Mom read the letter and said, "I'm sorry, Stevie."

"Pop was right all along. It's all over, and there's nothing I can do about it."

"Maybe she can just be a friend, not a girlfriend."

"She thinks I kill people, make girls be prostitutes."

"She's angry, like you are. Those words, those thoughts, they're not hers. She knows what you're really like, and it's none of those things."

"I thought Uncle Murray liked me. He wanted to talk to me, I told you that, remember?"

"I remember."

"And anyway, she's gonna' be living in Brooklyn with her real parents, not in Uncle Murray's house. I just don't understand."

"Listen to me Steven. You're a very smart boy. If there's something you can't understand, it's because you don't have all the facts at your disposal. Wait a few days. Wait until neither of you are angry anymore. Then write Gail and ask her to explain."

"I don't know how to write that."

"You will in a couple days."

It took Steven more than a couple of days. First, he confronted Pop at the next after-dinner talk. Steven went to his room, came back with Gail's letter and laid it on the table.

Pop glanced at it and said, "Mom told me."

"How should I answer her?"

"I wouldn't answer at all. She's asking if members of your family are murderers and pimps. The people who told her that don't know what they're talking about."

"The guy on the field after we won the Thanksgiving game called

Vito a pimp, said he pimped for Louise. Then Vito pulled out a knife."

Pop couldn't help but be impressed. Steven was clearly afraid, voice cracking with anxiety. But he didn't back down, instead surprising Pop with relevant facts. Pop took a moment, then answered in the same tone he used to deliver his lectures. "If somebody ran out of our store with an armful of clothes I would call the police, they would find the thief, arrest him, and give us back our clothes. But if he stole stuff I wasn't allowed to sell, like liquor, I couldn't call the police because they'd arrest *me* for selling alcohol without a license."

"Does our store sell illegal stuff?"

"Remember I told you *Nonno*, Uncle Eddie, and I like to take chances with some things that might cross the line from legal to illegal?"

"Like cheerleaders jumping rope."

He's throwing my own words back at me. That kid remembers everything. "The store never takes that kind of chance. But we might pay a politician for information we could use when dealing with banks, or insurance companies, or the stock market. If that information gets stolen, we can't go to the police because we shouldn't have had it."

"So, who *can* you go to?"

"Nobody. That's why we put up with the stories about the mafia hurting anybody who takes something from us. Vito is very good at acting tough. People are afraid of him and will usually just go elsewhere."

"Has Vito ever murdered anyone?"

"Not that I know of. But every time he flashes a knife at someone, he lets everyone think he might. That's enough to make them leave us alone." Steven was silent for a bit. Pop was aware these talks were about to go where he wasn't prepared to go yet. "Let's skip tonight's talk, and maybe a few more. You've got plenty to think about." He got up, gave Steven a pat on the shoulder, and left the kitchen.

Summer was almost over when Steven finally responded to Gail's letter. He filled three pages of scrap paper before coming up with one acceptable paragraph.

Dear Gail,

I'm sorry it took me so long to write back. The football team has been practicing for almost a week, and school will start in two weeks. Just because we can't be going steady doesn't mean we can't talk to each other. If you don't want to write to me anymore, maybe we can meet somewhere at school to talk. We could even just be friends. I would really like you to explain why things have to be this way.

    Steven

Dearest Steven;

    I am so, so happy that you wrote back. After I put that last letter in our box I regretted it. I ran back out, but it was already gone. I thought you were too, just like the first time you came to see me at Uncle Murray and Aunt Rose's house, when I told you about my illness. I was sure I drove you away. But like you said, you're hard to ditch. Now we have new issues I thought would drive you away, and once again you're willing to stick with me.

    Of course we can talk at school. I'm not sure if we can be just friends, as you put it. It will be hard, after all we've shared, to look at each other and not think of the lovers in our letters. But we can try. My shrink says I shouldn't start a real romance now anyway, with all that's going on in my life, but I'd love to keep our friendship alive.

    You don't have to write to me through Irene anymore. We'll see each other in the halls of James Madison soon. Who knows, maybe someday those letters will come true!

    Your friend,

    Gail

Steven was not sure what to make of it the first time through, and like all her letters he read it more than once. He tried to convince himself it meant their relationship could return to how it was before she left for Bronx Science, but it wasn't that simple. The sex thing was out in the open, even though they still hadn't even kissed. They were sixteen now and knew a few peers who "went all the way." So had the characters in their letters, in explicit detail, and there was no doubt who those characters represented. Steven had exercised supreme self-control to keep their relationship platonic. But how could he look at her now, in person, and not think of the scenarios in the letters? How could he not picture himself masturbating to the images of them making love, especially since she dangled the carrot of them coming true someday?

And there was the Mafia reference. Gail hadn't responded to his request to explain other than to say, "we have new issues." What was that conversation going to be like?

Steven decided to take a wait and see approach. He repositioned Gail to the back burner and threw himself into the two-a-days, so focused on football that the first day of school snuck up on him. When he walked into his first period class and came face to face with Gail, he was unprepared. He hadn't updated his image of her in nine months, and the shock was obvious.

"Really Steven? It's still me." Gail smirked, shook her head, and took a seat.

That certainly wasn't the way he wanted to start this new phase of their relationship. He thought he could feel Gail's eyes on him, but she was one row over and a few behind. He managed a few surreptitious glances over his shoulder, but she was either staring at the blackboard or writing in her notebook. He kept replaying their brief meeting, trying to assess the damage. He needed a do-over. When the bell rang Gail blew right past him into the hallway. Steven realized he hadn't paid any attention to the teacher, wasn't even sure what class he just sat through. He grabbed his books and hustled out, his long strides pulling him alongside Gail.

"I need to borrow your notes."

Gail stopped, hugging her books with her arms crossed in front of her, and glared at him. "Did you forget what I looked like? Did you not recognize me?"

"I was surprised."

"Surprised? We're the only two sophomores in the class. How could it be a surprise?"

"I'm sorry. I guess my mind was elsewhere."

"Yeah, well, so are your fuckin' notes." Gail turned and huffed away. Steven caught up with her again and walked alongside, but kept his mouth shut. He knew they were going to be in many of the same classes. James Madison used the "Track" system, and all their classes were A-Track. He and Gail were the only sophomores taking some eleventh-grade classes, so scheduling options were limited, and he would have plenty of opportunities to regain his composure and get a fresh start.

They were together in another class before lunch, and though Gail avoided sitting next to him, they did walk together through the halls. Silently. In the cafeteria she sat with her Jewish friends. Steven saw her leave midway through lunch, stood to follow, then decided against it. She could be going to the girls' room or her locker, and he'd feel stupid standing in the hallway with nowhere to go. When she returned, she walked straight to him, dropped a small pile of papers in front of him and said, "First period notes," then continued to her table.

"At least she didn't say 'first period fuckin' notes," Steven thought. That was the paradox of the new Gail. The last time he heard her say "fuck" it slipped out and, afraid an adult may have heard, she giggled like a little girl with her hand in the cookie jar. This time she spit it out then stomped off like a hard-ass. After abruptly accusing him of trying to steal a kiss and a feel on the sofa, she held his hand as they sashayed into her backyard like two characters from The Wizard of Oz. She wrote flowery fantasies about making love to him, then called him a hitman and a pimp, before hinting the fantasies may come true. There was an unpredictable, sharper edge to her now, a protective facade she never needed until she crashed at Bronx Science.

Steven could see past this because he knew the Gail who had no weaknesses, needed no protection. But as he gathered his books and prepared to share another silent walk through the halls, a different possibility caused him to pause. Maybe this is what adults mean when they talk about true love, how two people in love communicate without even talking. Maybe this means he and Gail are in love, the real, true, rest of your life love. Gail was waiting at the cafeteria doors, which added a few watts to his moonstruck, goofy smile.

"Thanks," he said, holding up the notes. Gail stared, puzzled at his odd expression, which increased his smile even more. "Really Gail? Did you forget what I looked like? Did you not recognize me?"

So the first day back turned into a stalemate, a hint of what their high school relationship would become. Steven's biggest fear, dealing with the fantasy lovers, never materialized. Romance was off the table due to parental (and doctor's) orders, so they morphed into something more like a sibling relationship. They were supportive, helping each other through the ups and downs of growing up, even teasing each other about their occasional romances.

"C'mon Steven, Gina Stanzo? She's just trying to add you to her collection, looking for another notch on her belt."

"She has a very nice belt."

"That is so disgusting!"

"You brought it up."

Steven could take it as well as dish it out. When he dished, he was careful to use a lighthearted manner with a smile on his face. Sometimes it worked perfectly, like a jump shot that touches nothing but net. Other times it was like trying to dribble a football.

"I hear Howie's in trouble again."

"That's because he thinks outside the box."

"You better hope he stays outside the *Juvie* box."

"You're the one who should worry about being dragged into Juvenile Court. You'd meet your entire family in jail!" Glare, turn, stomp off in a huff.

Howie was a senior, a year ahead of them when he started dating Gail. He was the first top student with outspoken disdain for the establishment, and school authorities had not yet devised a plan for disciplining someone like him. Howie took advantage of their clumsy efforts by pushing the limits of free speech and enjoyed embarrassing them. He became a lightning rod for the growing Vietnam protest movement. Steven thought he was a foolish blowhard who loved to hear himself speak. Gail, fully into that young adult phase of wanting to cure the ills of the world, was infatuated.

Steven and Gail's politics were diverging, though Steven was not interested in ideology. He leaned to the right simply because that's where his blueprint for success was clearly defined. He was Ivy League acceptable, a local legend athletically, heir to a successful family business.

Gail, on the other hand, was *all* about ideology. She was captivated by the prospect of change, intoxicated with the potential power of the people. "You conveniently forget that our founding fathers were revolutionaries. Thomas Jefferson wanted a revolution every ten years!"

"Well, we do change our leader every *four* years, without upsetting any apple carts."

"But they're all the same! We *need* to upset apple carts!"

The only place their views overlapped was the awareness that the police force was not necessarily their friend, and, in some cases, their enemy. The business enterprise Steven was preparing to lead was on the fringe of legality, often standing squarely on the wrong side of the law. A fragile coexistence with the police was maintained by mutual acceptance of unspoken compromises. Steven was appalled by protesters yelling "pigs" at the police, concerned, and even frightened, by their willingness to skewer sacred cows.

Hey, hey, LBJ! How many kids did you kill today?

"He is our President, you know."

"He may be yours. He's not mine."

"Is Eugene McCarthy yours?"

"Maybe. I'm not so sure we need a President."

Their choice of colleges echoed their differences. Gail almost followed Howie to Columbia, the increasingly radical east coast cousin of UC Berkeley. But she realized Steven was right about Howie's self-aggrandizement and opted for Harvard, no slouch when it came to political activism. Steven's choice was Dartmouth, which was eighth out of the eight Ivies in political activism. His choice was based on pragmatism, not politics. He had numerous offers of athletic scholarships from universities with big time programs, but they all wanted him to choose between football and baseball. Dartmouth was willing to allow him to play both.

Steven obsessively filled every minute of his days with productive activities so he'd have no time to obsess about anything else. He was a freshman at an elite university, away from home for the first time in his life, in the demanding major of pre-law, and participating in two sports. He also signed up for two clubs, International Law and Writing Poetry. An upperclassman in his dorm advised him to get a jump on law school by joining some clubs to pad his resume, and Steven thought he might be interested in international law. He also heard writing was an important skill and was going to sign up for a seminar on expository writing. The same upperclassman talked him out of it.

"Sign up for Writing Poetry."

"Why?"

"You'll be the only male in the group. It's awesome, man."

There was only one other male in the class of twenty-five, and it turned out to be a great experience. Poetry was one of the rare things in which Steven had absolutely zero ability, and the weekly meetings didn't change that. But he did meet a lot of coeds, enjoyed the readings, and learned enough to slip snippets of humanity into his otherwise dry essays and practice briefs, separating him from the crowd.

He also became friends with the other male in the group. Ronnie had accepted being gay but kept it to himself. Emboldened by the recent Stonewall riots and weary of juggling two lives, he confided in Steven that he was thinking about going public. Steven could relate because a large part of his life was off limits to everyone except family.

"That's one of the steepest prices you'll have to pay," Pop would warn him repeatedly during his high school lectures.

"Why do you always say that?"

"Because it's hard to go through life without a best friend. That's why you need to fall in love with a woman who can be your wife *and* your best friend."

Steven thought he had that covered with Gail, though as things currently stood that seemed unlikely. They maintained their sibling-like relationship with occasional phone calls, each sitting on a chair in the dorm or frat house hallway, ignoring friends' impatience as they tied up the house phone for what seemed liked hours. They got together a few times during their first year of college when their breaks coincided, meeting for lunch or a beer.

Those occurrences became less frequent, as did Gail's visits home. Her radical political views caused friction with her parents, and family get-togethers deteriorated into shouting matches. She didn't come home at all the summer between her freshman and sophomore years, opting to stay at her Uncle Ralph's house and work in the office of his summer camp. When she went back to school she became increasingly involved in antiwar and women's rights protests. She was clearly recognizable in a Boston Globe photograph of students being stuffed into paddy wagons following the student occupation of University Hall. The students were demanding the end of ROTC programs and were nonviolent until the administration called in city and state police, whose unprecedented use of mace and billy clubs sparked nationwide attention. Her parents were notified, and Uncle Murray thought she had been brainwashed by some cult. He wanted to mount a secret res- cue operation, resulting in the most bizarre phone call of Steven's life.

"Steven? This is Murray Bennett, Gail's uncle." Uncle Murray also contacted Steven during his senior year in high school, asking to be his agent. Steven politely informed him he wouldn't need an agent because he was not entering baseball's amateur draft, but Uncle Murray tried to talk him into changing his mind. Steven thought, *"How could I be forbidden to see Gail yet allowed to be your client?"* He held his tongue, managed to end that conversation before losing his temper, and was hoping to do the same now. He assumed this phone call was a result of his recent selection to play in the Cape Cod Summer League. He was wrong. "We need your help with Gail. She's in serious trouble and won't let us help."

Steven and Gail had one of their long phone conversations just a few days ago, and Gail hadn't mentioned anything about trouble. It was one of their best calls in months. Tired of Gail's strident proselytizing that dominated their dialogue, his calls were now being made more out of obligation than friendship. But Gail was very upbeat this time, and neither had wanted the conversation to end. She was particularly excited about Roberta Gibb, the first woman to run the Boston Marathon. Women were prohibited, so Ms. Gibb put her brother's Bermuda shorts and hooded sweatshirt over her bathing suit, hid in the bushes near the starting line, and jumped into the crowd of male racers. Her amateurish disguise didn't fool anyone, and the men around her immediately realized what was happening. She expected to be harassed, but the racers were supportive and said they'd make sure she could continue. Relieved and overheated, she discarded the sweatshirt. News spread that a female was running, and by the time she raced past women-only Wellesley College students lined the course and screamed encouragement.

Gail had taken to running ever since Steven urged her to run the loop near Uncle Murray's home, and regularly ran six or seven miles along the Cambridge side of the Charles River. She vowed to run in the next Boston Marathon, legally or not. Gail got emotional when she told Steven how important he had been to her recovery.

Steven, ever the encouraging friend, said, "You need to start training now if you're serious about it. I'm available for advice."

"I'm gonna' hold you to that, Masciarelli!" They promised to talk again in a few days. "You're the best thing that ever happened to me, Steven. I miss you."

And now Uncle Murray wanted his help kidnapping her.

CHAPTER SEVENTEEN

JEAN

1970, Darren NH

When Jean and the crew returned from their long weekend in New York, there was an interview at the hospital to do plumbing and HVAC for an addition. It was similar to the job Armand and Guy had argued about before Armand died. The director was very impressed with their presentation, local reputation, and Jean's knowledge of new materials and systems. They were asked back for another meeting, then awarded the job. A few months later it was a similar scenario at Plymouth State College, though this time it was Jean, not Aunt Yvette, who had the connection. His first professor was now a department head on the expansion committee. Jean introduced him to Uncle Guy, which led to an interview to become the plumbing and HVAC contractor for new student housing, classrooms, and teaching labs. The school was anticipating zoning issues and knew Jean was about to become a Civil Engineer. That combination of qualifications was the clincher, and the committee unanimously awarded them the job. The business and Jean's role in it were becoming exactly what he envisioned.

Jean's theory about his advisory role at the commune also played out as hoped. His advice was well received, his technical expertise greatly appreciated. Whenever work or family obligations prevented him from joining the crew, Marie would tease him upon her return.

"They're bummed when we show up without you. They don't give a shit about me. It's like, why even bother to come without the almighty Jean?"

Things were also looking up for Jean's mom. Some of her friends rented condos in Florida for school vacations and she visited a few times. She brought Jean's brother and sister during the Winter Break, which spanned the last weekend in February and the first weekend in March. David was a junior in high school and, like Jean, an excellent athlete. A story caught his eye on the sports page of the local paper, and he excitedly called out, "Mom, c'mere! It says the high school baseball team is off to a promising start after last year's disappointing season."

"That's nice."

"It's not nice, Mom, it's unbelievable. Their record last year was 14 and 34."

"That's terrible."

"Mom, that means they played 48 games! We try and squeeze in 16 after the snow melts, usually only get 12 or 13. It says they won three out of their first four games. They're already playing baseball!"

Bonnie was impressed. They had taken a bus to Logan Airport because leaving their car in an uncovered lot this time of year could result in it being buried in snow upon their return. She said, "They're not playing in Darren, that's for sure."

"Boy, I wish we lived here!"

Bonnie just smiled and gave him a consoling pat on the shoulder, but the thought had crossed her mind also. It was one reason she had brought the kids with her. The friends she was visiting planned on retiring here in a few years and had children the same age as David and Cindy. The kids were having a ball, outside all day at the pool and playground. The timing for an immediate move would work for Cindy. She'd be entering high school next year if they stayed in New

Hampshire and would have to make new friends either way. But David had a nice core of friends centered around athletics, and Bonnie had concerns about his adjustment. His comment about wishing they could live here was encouraging.

Bonnie had her own reasons. Recent changes were liberating when she expected them to be depressing. Transferring Armand's half of the business to Jean made her feel proud, not sad. Yvette and Guy were now a lesser a part of her life, as was the familial obligation which had played such a large role in her daily routine. She found that change refreshing.

The subdivision of the property brought simplification instead of remorse. The new subdivision, closely monitored by Jean, had a five-acre lot for each of the two Giroux houses, side by side on the road. That left a thirty-three-acre tract of land behind them. On Jean's suggestion, the surveyors included a strip two hundred feet wide between the two houses as part of the new back parcel. This was important because the back of their land bordered the Stinson property, and the two Giroux house lots took up all the frontage on the road. The strip between the houses allowed them to build a road for possible development later.

Changes at Bonnie's work provided further impetus for a move. A large national bank purchased the bank where Bonnie was the branch manager. They were offering attractive packages to those who agreed to relocate. Bonnie's current visit was in a suburb of Naples, and Bonnie noticed at least half a dozen branch offices.

There was no mortgage on the house in Darren. Jean and Marie were already openly living together. If they moved into the house and paid her what they were currently paying in rent, that would cover taxes and insurance with a little left over to offset the rent on a condo in the Naples area. It would give her and her two youngest a way to test the waters without diving into a permanent commitment. She would no longer be defined as Armand's widow. It would be a fresh start for her, and just might benefit all her children. On the plane ride home Bonnie formulated a plan. She decided not to say anything to her kids right away. She would make preliminary inquiries at the bank, then have a family meeting to gauge their reactions.

When they returned to the farmhouse late Sunday night there was a message on the answering machine to call Jean right away no matter how late they got home.

"Hello?"

"Oh, hi, Marie. Sorry to call so late, but Jean left a message. Is everything all right?"

"Everything's fine, Mrs. Giroux. Here's Jean."

"Hi, Mom, welcome home."

"Marie sounded funny, Jean. What's wrong?"

"Nothing's wrong. She sounded funny because I cornered her mom and dad after church today and quietly asked for permission to marry their daughter and they said yes."

"Oh my God!!"

"Then, I told Marie I had to show her something in the barn, drove over to our place, walked to where my pickup used to be when we worked on it, and proposed."

"Oh my God!!"

"And she said 'Yes.' We're getting married, Mom."

"Oh my God!! Oh, I'm so happy for you, son! Oh my God - put Marie on the phone!"

This time Marie was her usual bubbly self. "Hi, Mrs. Giroux, sorry I was abrupt, but Jean wanted to be the one to tell you."

"Oh, sweetheart, I am so, so happy for you, I - oh, I'm crying."

"Me too!"

"Is there a date?"

"We have some ideas but wanted to get you and my parents together to talk. We're thinking outdoors, maybe at Cathedral of the Pines."

"Oh my God."

Marie started laughing and said, "Your son says you gotta' stop shouting 'Oh my God,' he says he could probably hear you without the phone."

"You put that little stinker on the phone this instant!"

"Hi Mom. Pretty cool, huh?"

"Very cool son, very cool. I'm so excited, I don't know how I'm going to sleep."

"Take a deep breath and have a glass of wine. I'll call you at work tomorrow when you have your calendar in front of you and we'll make plans. Marie wants to know a good night for us all to get together."

"Any night. Call her folks, wake 'em up, and we can talk right now!"

"Let's just stick with you looking at your calendar tomorrow."

"Good idea. I'm so happy for you two. I love you, son."

Jean could hear tears; knew she was thinking about Armand. "I love you too, Mom."

The next time they went down to New York, their news received hearty congratulations until Marie added the disclaimer. "The place we want to have the wedding is booked up until the fall, and you guys will all be in Mendocino."

"We'll just have to come back," Bobbi assured her.

William was not so sure. "That's a long roundtrip, Bobbi."

"Our plan is to spend the summer checking it out, then decide if it's what we really want. It'll make packing easier if we know we're coming back in three months and can reload."

Jean appreciated the support. Marie always downplayed her role with the group, sticking with the 'I'm only here because of Jean' theme, though she and Bobbi connected over their mutual interest in art. Marie gave Bobbi a watercolor she had painted based on one of Bobbi's photographs from her first visit to Nancy's farm, and helped her with the psychedelic design for the school bus. During one weekend visit, Sheila organized a "girls' day in the city" that included several art museums, Fifth Avenue window shopping, and hanging in Greenwich Village. It was Marie's first time in Manhattan, and she came back totally energized.

That's what Jean liked best about their relationship with the commune. He and Marie were exposed to things most New Hampshire folks were not. It wasn't just the counterculture politics or the drugs. People who lived in New York had an air of confidence, a "bring it on, baby!" attitude that permeated everything they said and did. Jean understood it was why New Yorkers were usually viewed as assholes in New Hampshire. But when you get even a small taste of a place where everything imaginable is available day or night and ten million people all want it now, you began to see why that hard edge is necessary.

Jean tried to work a little bit of that edge into his understated Yankee demeanor. It gave him an advantage in business negotiations. It enabled him to stand up to Uncle Guy when there were differences of opinion, though they often wound up agreeing. One exception was the impending sale of the back parcel. Tony's bosses were interested in the Stinson property, and Uncle Fred was in the process of securing an option to purchase. The sticking point, as Jean had predicted, was the need for another entrance. This could be solved if the Giroux back parcel, with its approved road access between the two Giroux homes, was part of the deal. The offer from the developers was very enticing, but Jean objected.

"I don't want to live with supply trucks rumbling through my front yard all day."

"You're overstating that," Uncle Guy responded. "it'll just be an occasional delivery."

"Yeah, like whenever our children are kicking around a soccer ball."

"With the amount they're offering you could pay someone to kick the ball back whenever it went near the road."

Jean countered, "We could get two times as much if it was sub-divided into lots, and five times as much if we built houses on those lots. Then the only people using the road would be the homeowners, and they would be way more careful than a trucker with a deadline to meet."

This argument bore a striking resemblance to those between Jean's dad and Uncle Guy, the two men continuing to solder and cut pipes while they argued. They handled this issue the same way. The topic was tabled as life, and plumbing, went on.

CHAPTER EIGHTEEN

LENNY

spring 1971, Mueller, NY

Work was a drag, Monday through Friday, nine to five. My duties settled into mind-numbing routine, future responsibility never materializing. Team Sports, Inc. was, like Vincenzo Catrone III, stuck in a time warp. Goods came in and were shipped out, money came in and went out, people got paid. Nobody ever got fired and, except for me, nobody ever got hired. I was stuck in junior high detention, forced to do simple arithmetic for all eternity. Unless I quit. And that was all I thought about. Though I hadn't voiced it to the Mueller crew, I decided to take the leap to Mendocino, job be damned. Filling neat little numbers into spreadsheet boxes with my sharpened #2 pencil, I whiled away the hours dreaming of an endgame strategy.

It stood to reason that leaving would be as cut and dried as my job. I would give two weeks' notice, collect one final paycheck, and leave the rat race for good. Simple. Except I would be giving my notice to Vinny, who took "simple" to such an extreme it went all the way around the loop and back to "complicated." In defiance of the Karmic belief that people who anticipate problems encounter more than their fair share, I anticipated a problem. Krishna may be powerful, but this was *Vinny*.

So, I increasingly found myself staring through the glass wall of my office over the heads of the employees busily traversing the ground floor of Team Sports, Inc. while I imagined Vinny's reaction to my resignation speech. Until one Friday morning when it all became moot.

Vinny came into my office, dropped two packets on my desk, pointed to one and said, "You need to sign."

The lack of explanation was typical. The request for my signature was unusual, though not unique. I replaced my pencil with a Bic, flipped through the pages looking for a signature request, then slowed down as I realized I was looking at an IRS form.

"Vinny, I can't..."

His huge hand slammed down on the form, closed it quickly and, keeping his hand firmly on the form thumbed to the last page. "Just sign here."

"It says 'Tax Preparer.' I'm not qualified to sign this, Vinny. You need..."

"I need you to sign, here."

"See, under that line, it says 'CPA.' I'm not a CPA, and here it asks for my certification number..."

"That's what this is for," pointing to the other packet, "just sign now, we'll put in the number next week."

The cover page was a reminder that this year's CPA exam was scheduled for the following Wednesday, Thursday, and Friday at Yonkers Raceway. Stunned, all I could manage was a stammering "Um, there's no way..."

"Don't worry about the registration deadlines," Vinny interrupted, self-satisfied smirk on his face, "I got someone in the registration office. You're all set."

"No, I'm not all set!" I was done walking on eggshells with Vinny. "The CPA exam has four parts, and it's almost impossible to pass all four the first time you take the test. If you pass at least two parts you just need to retake the parts you *didn't* pass, otherwise, you gotta' take the whole fucking thing again. Oh, and they're only offered twice a year, so even if by some fucking miracle I passed two fucking parts it would be fucking November before I could try again with the other two."

I paused to catch my breath and assess Vinny's reaction to my tirade. He was smoldering, like he used to when I trotted out to the mound to calm him down. Only this time it was me, not the umpire, causing the problem. I decided to push on in a more moderate tone.

"Ya' know, Vinny, I think I'm not really the right guy for this job. You have people downstairs who could handle the basic bookkeeping, and I don't have the qualifications to do the other part of the job. I would totally understand if you want to go that route. I could stay for a week or so and bring the new people up to speed."

"You can't."

"Whaddya' mean?"

"I saw you slow down and read the numbers."

"I slowed down when I realized it was an IRS form."

"There's things you saw you can't know about if you're leaving."

"I don't know anything except it's an IRS form and I'm not qualified to sign it."

Vinny glanced at the glass front wall of my office, then we locked eyes. I wondered if the wall was as strong as Ida's Deli storefront window. I wondered if the hallway on the other side was narrow enough for me to sail over the railing to the concrete floor below. I would need more than a visit to Sheila's dad for new braces.

But there was something unusual in Vinny's menacing visage, an unrecognizable spice altering a familiar food. Could it be embarrassment? Almost, but not quite. Vinny knew he fucked up by letting me see some very large numbers and was furious *at himself.* That was it-the same scary fury but divided now between the two of us. Maybe that was all I needed.

"Why don't I get my stuff into some boxes? I'll take 'em home tonight and come back Monday morning with whatever I need to help the person who's taking my place."

"Sign those papers now or you're leaving now, taking nothing outa' this office and never comin' back."

"If that's what you want. You'll send me my last check?"

"Oh, I'll send you something." Vinny cast another glance at the glass wall. "A reminder."

"Of what?"

"Of what would happen if word gets out about the IRS form." Vinny grabbed the two packets of paper, turned, and left without looking back.

MLK's words leapt into my head, *Free at last, free at last, thank God almighty, I'm free at last.* But I was also scared. It had been eight years since Vinny confronted me in front of Ida's and hammered home his order to never see Rosalie again. It had been two years since he reappeared at the summer camp and rerouted my future. I was prepared for my departure, but not the threat of retaliation, especially the open-ended, unnamed, ominous sword of Damocles.

I had a lot to digest on my drive back to Mueller. If I told everyone the way it went down they'd all be waiting for the sword to fall. If I tried to relate it in an offhand, lighthearted manner, wouldn't they see through my artifice?

Or I could keep the details to myself, use this opportunity to announce I quit. "My heart and soul are with the group going to Mendocino, and goddammit, my body is going too!" I needed direction and guidance and received it from my catalog of Rules to Live a

Better Life. The Copernicus Memorial Theories had proven prophetic many times, from my Spring Fling peevishness to my recent snit upon my exclusion from the first wave to Mendocino. No one noticed my truculence then, so maybe no one would notice my paranoia now. I gathered my mental forces and pulled into my driveway.

All hail Copernicus! The completion of the bus and the excitement of its upcoming maiden voyage took center stage, and I was just another cast member. The remodeled bus was becoming less an RV, more a motorized comfort station. All the seats but the driver's and the first two rows were removed. Windows on both sides of the back third were removed, and storage cabinets for clothes, sleeping bags, tents and tools replaced them. The rest of the windows remained. The floor was covered in cork squares to provide cushioning for sleeping bags in inclement weather. The middle third had secondhand kitchen appliances along one side, courtesy of Jean, and a fold down counter along the other. The rear third had a bathroom with a toilet, sink, stall shower, apartment size washer/dryer, also courtesy of Jean. The back wall of the bus was torched out, edges ground smooth, and remounted on mammoth hinges just above the rear bumper so it opened from the top, out and down, forming a ramp. There was just enough room for a compact car, or Carl's motorcycle, to drive up the ramp and squeeze in. The original rear door had to be removed and replaced with sheet metal so the ramp would be functional, but that still left the doors in the front and middle.

It was an ingenious design. PVC waste and supply pipes were revolutionizing the plumbing industry, so Jean and Nick could teach us unskilled laborers how to apply the glue and connect the pipes. They and Ricky handled the joints requiring solder and packing, all torching and welding, as well as installation of tanks under the floor for fresh water and waste.

Marlene's father was a retired World War II Naval officer, and she and her dad were always tinkering with their sailboat. There was an assortment of mismatched cabinetry in their basement, the seafaring kind that won't swing open or allow contents to shift with the rolling seas. They were in need of attention, but Marlene was adept with a chisel and a plane, and Ricky picked up some rough carpentry skills during their occasional tear-down of a barn. The rest of us did the lugging and the lifting and the cleanup.

There was a spectacular psychedelic design for the exterior Bobbi and Marie planned, but as her due date neared William was constantly admonishing her to take it easy.

"Don't lift that!" "Here, honey, let me help." "No need to run!"

We all expected her to bite his head off at the suggestion she was somehow restricted by pregnancy, but Bobbi exhibited none of the moody spells and irrational demands that were supposed to accompany gestation. The quintessential Earth Mother, she sensed William was in uncharted waters and might need some motherly handling. We unanimously agreed with William's suggestion to delay the outside paint job until *after* we arrived in Mendocino. Carl, always aware of PP (prejudice potential), made it purposeful. "Some of those areas we'll be driving through, going incognito is a good thing."

So, the outside was basic school bus, with patches of rustproof primer wherever bare sheet metal was exposed. Ricky, of course, was in charge of getting it in proper running condition. William requested everybody's attendance the weekend after I "quit" my job, so we could set a departure date and finalize plans. The baby was due in a few weeks, and William hoped we could leave as soon as possible after that.

Friday evening, we all piled into the bus. Ricky was the last one on and raised his hands for silence. He was wearing a formal tux jacket with tails over his jeans and t-shirt. He said, "Test run," ceremoniously flipped back the tails and swung himself into the driver's seat, rotated the handle pulling the doors shut, held the key up for effect, inched it toward the ignition, and turned it. The sucker purred like a kitten. We laughed, applauded, woo-wooed. Ricky said, "Here we go!' and we were off. We tooled around town, and at every stop sign or traffic light Ricky showed off another feature.

"Windshield wipers," (applause) "and washer fluid!" (wild applause)

"The horn!" (applause)

"Music!" (standing ovation drowned out by concert quality music)

Ricky turned onto a highway onramp, then pulled all the way to the right and stopped. He put the bus in neutral, set the parking brake, turned off the music, and held up a two-foot-long black rubber strap with a loop on one end. He securely lashed the other end to the post next to the driver's seat, leaving the looped end hanging.

"There is one problem. At highway speeds, the gearshift lever pops out of fifth gear." Ricky began an incomprehensible description of the problem, but the blaring horns of irate motorists who had to veer around us became so insistent he feared it might escalate into violence. He cut his dissertation short, vaulted back into his seat, released the parking brake, jammed the bus into first gear and hauled ass back onto the ramp. We all stared at the gearshift stick intently as Ricky gradually worked his way up to fourth, then, at about 50 mph, fifth. He eased the bus up to 60 and settled into an uneventful cruise for about three minutes. Then the stick popped out of fifth into neutral and the bus started to lose speed. Ricky double clutched and down shifted to fourth, then back up to fifth. Without turning around or taking his eyes off the road, one hand on the steering wheel, he reached for the rubber strap, stretched the looped end as far as it would go, and deftly fit the loop over the gearshift knob so it could not pop out again (and the crowd goes wild!).

The next night there was a full house at the Mueller branch of the Mendocino commune. It was nitty-gritty time, the only thing still uncertain about our departure being the delivery of William and Bobbi's baby. The due date was now less than two weeks away, so our goal for the night was to finalize what we could prior to the birth. They planned a natural childbirth, the mother and the fetus were in excellent condition, and Bobbi mentioned at least five times every day how peasant women used to squat down in the field, pop out a baby, and continue harvesting. Ricky set the over-under on the number of days between birth and departure at 10, and the betting was heavy on the under.

William began the night waxing poetic about cosmic timing and how the stars were aligning with our voyage.

I was having a hard time diving in, focusing instead on my kitchen table with its pink and yellow boomerang outlines floating on a royal blue field, formica frozen forever until a tab of LSD set them free. William's rap about the stars and our destiny was background music, my brain tripping lightly over complicated syncopations. The boomerang outlines started dancing to a lofty guitar solo, then glowed at their ends like planetarium illustrations, faint lines connecting bright stars forming constellations. William was steady and distant, then brought it home to my sign, and the Ram was right there on the cosmic table looking up at me.

"Aries is a fire sign," he said, then again, "Fire!"

I tore my eyes away from the tabletop heavens, stared at William.

He looked rattled. I heard other people yelling "Fire!" and that's the precise moment all our lives changed direction.

A smokey odor was suddenly prevalent. Did somebody drop a joint on the carpet? Maybe something was burning in the kitchen? People were standing, looking around, starting left or right then stopping, looking at each other, not knowing what to do. Then we all froze. There was an unidentifiable noise in the background. We strained to hear it better, and then, in unison, we all knew what it was. The crackling of flames.

"Everybody out!" Sheila shouted as she moved quickly from room to room, yelling again up the stairs, "Fire! Everybody outside!"

William and Marie were teachers and knew we needed a meeting place to account for everyone. "Meet across the street! Everybody meet across the street!"

We all joined in the chorus, putting all our energy into the ferocity and frequency of our warnings. It was our only productive outlet until Sheila out-decibelled us all. "STOP! Everybody's yelling 'get out' but nobody's getting out. So shut the fuck up, and calmly but quickly get your asses across the street. I'll be the last one out. When you see me, the house will be empty. Remember, quick but calm!"

We all power-walked to the door and began an orderly exit. As soon as we got outside, we saw where the noise was coming from. The three-story apartment house next door was engulfed in fire. The leaping flames, acrid smoke, and roaring noise stunned us motionless, creating a bottleneck at the door.

"Keep moving, keep moving! Across the street!" Bobbi, who was pushed out of the house first by William, jabbed us out of our stupor one by one with a shoulder slap and elbow push toward the street. My house was not yet on fire, but sparks from next door were coming perilously close. Mueller had an all-volunteer fire department, and the firehouse was just down the block. I figured somebody would be on duty and started sprinting there, but then the loudest, most blood-curdling scream I ever heard came from above.

"MY BABY!"

There was a woman surrounded by flames in a second-floor window clutching an infant. I ran back, stopped a few feet away from the heat of the building. The window was only six feet above my head. I reached up as high as I could.

"Here! Here! Throw me the baby! C'mon, throw me the baby!"

And she did. The throw was a little short and to my left, but I lunged, my shortstop reactions and soft hands made the grab and cushioned the baby as I rolled to the ground. Jean had run over. I handed the baby to him, scrambled to my feet and looked up at the window. It was blocked by the mother, who decided to follow her baby and was accelerating toward me at 32 ft. per second per second. No slick shortstop moves this time. I was just the pillow, and I didn't have to move an inch. I guess I did my job, because I was flattened, and the mom was okay. She kneed me in the crotch and stepped on my face as she scrambled wildly toward Jean and the baby. I pulled my groggy self upright. I didn't see any blood or feel any pain, but my head was ringing loudly. No, it wasn't - it was four short blasts of the siren atop the firehouse, followed by a three-second pause, then repeated, which was the alert code for volunteers to get to the firehouse.

I looked down the block and a fire engine was coming out. Other emergency vehicles were arriving. Volunteer firemen were pouring out of cars, some going into the building, some keeping us away from the flames. They started hosing down the apartment house and swinging ladders into position. Another fire engine screeched in, adding its hoses and waterpower to the fight. Two ambulances arrived, as did more vehicles carrying more volunteers. The flames were dying down. The situation seemed under control, but I noticed a large cloud of sparks bouncing off the bus. I grabbed the arm of the nearest fireman and pointed. Then I saw Bobbi trotting/waddling toward the bus. So did William.

"Bobbi! Get away from there!" She waved him away and stepped into the bus. Just because she was pregnant didn't mean she was incapable of moving the bus. William tore after her, was tackled by a fireman while two more raced toward the bus lugging a hose. "She's pregnant!" screamed William.

Bobbi started it up and began backing away from the sparks, but another cloud descended on the bus and the rear end exploded. Two more fireman carrying a stretcher between them were just reaching the front half of the bus. Within seconds - the longest of my life- they came back out with Bobbi on the stretcher and ran toward the ambulance. Another loud "pop" and the entire bus was a ball of fire.

"Where are you taking her?!" William's heart-wrenching wail was not acknowledged by the firemen, but Bobbi raised an arm and flashed the peace sign. It was the last time we saw her alive. That image is tattooed on my brain, over a fancy script signature on a scroll.

Vinny

CHAPTER NINETEEN

STEVEN AND GAIL

1969, New England

· · STEVEN · ·

"I talked to her on the phone the other day," Steven told Uncle Murray, "and she sounded fine."

"That's because she's been brainwashed by a cult. Did you see her picture in the newspaper, being arrested? She looked like a doped-up zombie for chrissakes. We gotta' sneak up on her, get her out of there, get her home where she belongs. We're very, very concerned about her, Masciarelli. Aren't you?"

"Like I said Mr. Bennett, I just talked to her, and she sounded fine."

"Going to jail may be fine in your family, but it's not in ours!"

Steven struggled to stay civil. "Again, Mr. Bennett, she sounded fine, didn't mention anything about jail."

"She was on the front page of the goddamn Boston Globe! Going to jail! Look kid, I don't mean to yell at ya' but we need your help. She won't talk to me or her parents. We know she, uh, always uh, liked you. We know you two get together, talk to each other and all that. Her parents are at their wits' end. If we could just meet her somewhere in Boston, I'm sure we could talk some sense into her. Could you help us arrange that?"

"Arrange?"

"She won't agree to see us. Maybe if she thought she was gonna' see *you*...”

“I’m not gonna’ lie to her Mr. Bennett.”

“Are you able to get a message to her?”

“We talk all the time. I don’t have to get a message to her.”

“Could you at least tell her how concerned we are? That her mother doesn’t do anything but cry day and night?”

“I’ll tell her about your call the next time we speak.”

“As soon we hang up?”

“It’s not convenient for me right now.”

“You’re not fuckin’ with me, are ya’ kid?”

“I don’t fuck with people, Mr. Bennett.” Steven’s implied message went right over Uncle Murray’s head.

“Take my number. We’re all counting on ya’, kid.”

Steven called Gail a few days later, and she thought it was hilarious. “Can you believe what a fascist pig that asshole is?”

“Actually, I can. But not your parents.”

“Yeah, Uncle Murray and Aunt Rose have Mom all confused. Hey, maybe we could kidnap my mother.”

“Excellent idea. I told you my ROTC classes would come in handy.” They shared a lot of laughs about staging the capture. It was the second great phone call in a row, and they both milked it for all it was worth.

“I’ll call my dad as soon as we hang up. He’ll handle Mom.”

“Make sure he lets Uncle Murray know I called. I don’t want him to think any less of me than he already does.”

“Why would you waste one solitary second thinking about that douche bag?”

“Because he connects me to you.” It just slipped out. There was a long silence. He couldn’t take it back, so he changed course. “People

I know who run marathons say you need to be able to run half the distance on a daily basis."

"Brilliant advice, Masciarelli. You can be my coach." Another silence. Neither wanted the conversation to end on this awkward note. Gail took the plunge. "I like being connected to you too, Steven, even if it takes my Uncle Murray to make it happen."

"We play Harvard next Saturday, then we're taking a bus to Providence because we play Brown Sunday. I'll probably have some time to kill."

"Great! I'll come watch the superstar in person. Maybe I'll start a demonstration protesting the lack of women on the team, attract a crowd, get the police involved..."

"Did you actually get booked and locked up?"

"Yes, but I don't wanna' talk about it. It was the most degrading, disgusting display of power run amok. It was..."

"I thought you didn't want to talk about it."

"You are so smart Mr. Masciarelli. Tell me again why I had to escort you to the principal's office almost every day?"

"Because I bribed Mrs. Demeter so I could spend quality alone time with you."

"Ah yes. I remember those high-quality walks."

"I'll see you Saturday."

"It's a date."

And just like that Steven was back in junior high. What did she mean, 'It's a date'? Was she just casually using the expression, or was she suggesting this would be different than two friends meeting? It was like when she signed the Valentine's card 'Love, Gail' and it took him half a day and three pieces of scrap paper to come up with 'Luv, S.' If she meant a *date* date, it would be their first since *West Side Story*.

He was a total basket case the second he replaced the receiver, the Rolling Stones *19th Nervous Breakdown* serenading him to his room.

College baseball in the late sixties was not a spectator sport. Thousands of students packed state of the art gymnasiums for basketball, and 100,000 rabid fans routinely filled mammoth stadiums for football. Baseball games were casually watched by maybe a hundred spectators on bleachers at no cost. The team rode the bus to Cambridge wearing their uniforms, clothes for the weekend road trip packed away. They padded across the parking lot in socks, spikes tied together and slung over their shoulders. Steven scanned the bleachers looking for Gail but came up empty. He smiled as he recalled doing the same thing five years ago at the championship game against Tilden. How could he possibly be in the same situation now? When his team's practice time was over, he spotted Gail walking toward the fence that separated the bleachers from the field and stopped on his way into the dugout, leaned over the fence and gave her a hug, then trotted to the dugout, smile still on his face.

"Someone special?" It was his coach, with a smile of his own.

"Oh, no, just a friend who goes to Harvard."

"Uh-huh. Didn't look that way. Mind on the game kid, the coach of your Cape League team is gonna' stop by. He wants to see you play, meet you after."

That was all the motivation Steven needed. For the next two hours his focus was almost complete, allowing himself only an occasional quick glance to make sure Gail hadn't left. After the final out, a sinking line drive he charged full speed, dove for, and snagged just before it hit the ground, Steven met his current and future coaches by the third base foul line.

His coach said, "This is Cap Giovanni, Steven."

"Nice to meet you, Mr. Giovanni."

"You too, Steven. My players call me Cap. Helluva catch to end the game."

"Thanks." Steven looked over to Gail and flashed five fingers twice.

Cap said, "I won't keep ya' long."

"Oh, no problem, she's just a friend."

His coach chimed in, "That's what he keeps tellin' himself," and the two men laughed.

"Anyway," said Cap, holding out a folder, "this here's the contact info for your host family, and the basics about what's expected of ya'. Did you play any positions besides centerfield before college?"

"I pitched."

"Yeah, I figured that when I saw your throw from the gap nail that guy at third."

"And played some shortstop. I'll be happy to play wherever you put me."

"We'll figure that out when we get the whole team on the field. I'll let you go. I just like to see you guys in person when it's possible."

"Pleasure meeting you, Cap. I'm really looking forward to competing at the next level."

Coach said, "The bus'll be leavin' in about 45 minutes. That'll give you some time with your, ahem, 'friend'."

Steven turned to Cap and said, "Coach'll be riding me about my friend the whole way to Providence." All three laughed, then Steven walked over to join Gail.

· · GAIL · ·

Gail was standing with some friends when the Dartmouth bus arrived and decided to hang back for a bit. She watched from afar as

Steven took batting practice, swinging so hard with his entire body she was amazed he could keep his balance. He shagged fly balls in centerfield, her runner's eye noting his easy speed and powerful stride. When he received a throw, he relayed it to a teammate so quickly it looked like he just redirected the ball without ever catching it. She was too far away to see Steven's facial expression, but his body was clearly smiling. When his team started to head toward their dugout, she left her friends and walked down to the fence separating the spectators from the field. He stopped on his way to the dugout, leaned over the fence and gave her a friendly hug. It wasn't enough.

It was never enough when it came to Steven. He always stopped talking just before he said something romantic, shortened his touch before it could mean something. He was always there for her, just not the way she wanted. She sensed his lack of interest in her phone calls lately and was ready to tell him not to call anymore. Then she decided instead to make one more concerted effort to force the issue, and the phone conversations got better, more personal, bordering on romantic. To be honest, he never crossed *that* line without her prodding. The only time he ever did were those high school letters about them having sex. Even then her subtle flirtations eluded him until she got so graphic, he couldn't miss the message. At that time, it was just enough of a reward to keep her trying. and she wasn't ready to quit this time.

"You look cute in your uniform."

"Yeah, that's why we wear 'em. Harvard is going on a road trip too, so they decided to shorten the game to seven innings. We should have time then. Hope you don't get too bored."

"I brought a book. And like I said, you look cute in your uniform."

His smile was warm and sincere, exactly like when they reclasped their hands and sashayed into Uncle Murray's backyard. It was still not enough, and it was all she would get until the game was over. When he flashed "10 minutes" and continued to the dugout it only strengthened her resolve to give this opportunity all she had.

"Who were those two guys?"

"The one in the baseball uniform was the Dartmouth coach. The other was the coach of the Falmouth team I'll be playing for."

"So, you just play baseball all summer?"

"Not really. I live with a host family, and they arrange a summer job for me. I work every day and play baseball every night."

"Doesn't sound like much of a summer vacation."

"It's not. The Cape Cod League is a college all-star league. A lot of the players go on to a professional career. It's a great opportunity. How's it been going with your family?"

"Oh, it'll be fine. I talked to my dad, and he smoothed things over. Wanna' get a cup of iced coffee or something?" They walked over to the concession stand, sat on the grass, sipped, and had a donut. "I'm thinking of changing my major to pre-law, so they're thrilled that I'm joining the establishment again."

"Wow. That's quite a change."

"It's all your fault." Gail put down her cup, reclined on her elbows. "The establishment still sucks, but I'm knocking my head against the wall and not making much of a difference. I think I can accomplish more by challenging the system from within, like you did by being an officer in high school." For the past month Gail had been heaping compliment after compliment on Steven every time they talked, emphasizing how much he meant to her in their younger days. She had one more card to play. *Here goes, sink or swim.* "Have you ever been to the Cape?"

"No."

"It's beautiful. A lot of Boston folks vacation there. Did you say Falmouth?"

"Yup. The Falmouth Commodores, defending champions of the Cape Cod League."

"A grad assistant who's helping me change my major is interning with a law firm this summer on the Vineyard. He says they're looking for some gofers who think they may be interested in law."

"What's the Vineyard?"

"Shit, Masciarelli, don't you conservative yahoos at Dartmouth have any fun? Martha's Vineyard is an island off Cape Cod. It's like Fire Island or the Hamptons, but with a social conscience."

"I don't have much time to thumb through resort brochures."

"It's not a resort, it's an island. Didn't you read about Ted Kennedy and Mary Jo Kopechne?" Steven's expression was blank, but Gail was undeterred. "There's no bridge or tunnel to Martha's Vineyard, you gotta' take a ferry to get there. I've gone a couple of times. It's really cool. The ferry leaves from Falmouth."

Steven realized she was taking a circuitous route to arrange another get together. Sensing a rare bargaining advantage, he decided not to make it easy for her. He stretched on one elbow, face close to hers, flashed a smile and said, "Yeah, so?"

"So-o-o, if I sign on for one of those gofer positions, we'll be a short ferry ride from each other." Gail's expression was apprehensive, Steven's a shit-eating grin.

"I have an idea," he said with a playful smirk, "why don't we try and see each other over the summer?"

"You know, Masciarelli, sometimes I wonder why I even bother... oh, I think one of your coaches is coming to get you."

Steven held her eyes with his for a couple more seconds. Feeling rakish after the *tete-a-tete*, he stood, helped her up, kissed her cheek and said, "Let me know about your summer job on, uh..."

"The Vineyard."

"Yeah. The Vineyard."

Gail waved when she spotted him among the crowd exiting the ferry. She noticed the same cocky smile he sported in Cambridge after the baseball game. "*So,*" she thought, "*looks like this is going to be a contest.*" But she was prepared for the challenge, wearing a bikini top, cut-off dungaree shorts, and flip-flops. Advantage, Ms. Bernstein. They hugged, enough bare skin between them to fluster Steven. Game, Ms. Bernstein.

"You've been running," Steven blurted.

"What makes you think that?"

"You feel, uh, look, uh... I thought you were the genius and I was the athlete."

"Let's run a few miles and see." Set, Ms. Bernstein. Gail's smile was now so big it was audible. They walked along a line of parked cars until she stopped by an old Willys jeep with no top and held up the keys. Steven just stared at her, befuddled. "You look a little lost, Masciarelli. Hop in, I'll drive." Game, Set, Match, Ms. Bernstein.

Gail pointed out the gingerbread houses on the right and the sailboats on the left. Steven was unresponsive at first, still a bit flum-moxed, but the beauty of their surroundings took hold and Steven tuned in. The gingerbread houses were followed by huge gingerbread inns, then gave way to a lake on the right. The water on the left went all the way to the horizon, their narrow road the only thing separating the two bodies of water.

Steven said, "You don't usually see a lake right next to the ocean."

"It's actually connected to the ocean. This bridge we're coming to goes over an inlet. There's another one after that where we cross into Edgartown, and a bunch of kids will probably be jumping off the railing right next to a sign that says, 'No Jumping from Bridge'."

"The waves are really small," Steven said.

"Well, geology isn't my thing, but the brunch we're going to is at the Chappaquiddick Beach Club where the waves are small like these. But a short bike ride away is Wasque Beach where the waves are humongous. We'll go there after the brunch if you want."

"Aren't you supposed to wait a half hour after eating before you go in the ocean?"

Gail laughed, said, "Yes, Miss Emily Post, you are. The bike ride will take care of that."

Steven got the feeling he was being led through a well-planned itinerary. *"You know Gail and her colored markers,"* he warned himself. *"She always has a plan."*

Inching down Edgartown's Main Street in traffic Gail pointed out the stately homes and the Old Whaling Church. Instead of horn honking from impatient drivers there were courteous waves directing pedestrians to cross in front or vehicles to enter from a side street. She cut through a parking lot and wiggled along a succession of narrow side streets lined with meticulously maintained homes. Not a speck of dirt marred the sparkling white clapboard homes with shiny black shutters, or those with brilliant white trim and grey weathered cedar shakes. It was one picture postcard scene after the other, roses spilling over picket fences, weedless lawns outlined by rhododendrons, azaleas, blue hydrangeas, and hollies.

They stopped again behind a line of cars, and this time Gail turned off the engine. Steven looked around for someplace that might be hosting a brunch, but all he saw were more homes.

"We're waiting for the Chappy ferry," Gail explained. "They want you to turn off your engine while you're in line."

"Another ferry?"

"More like a raft with a motor. It only takes three or four cars at a time." Gail grabbed the top of the windshield and stood, shaded her eyes, and said, "We've got a couple of minutes. C'mon, I'll show you." Steven thought it was weird to leave the car in the middle of the street but didn't say anything. Gail seemed to have an explanation ready each time he questioned something.

There was one arm of a railroad crossing gate in the down position. The ferry had just left, carrying four cars, a couple of bikes, and a half dozen people. Another was leaving from the other side of the harbor, only a couple hundred feet away, coming toward them with a similar load. To their right Edgartown Harbor was filled with boats swaying on their moorings, and off to the left the entrance to the harbor was marked by the Edgartown lighthouse.

They watched the ferry approach, reverse engines, and dock. The connecting ramp was locked in place, the railroad arm raised, and cars started off. When Steven heard the line behind him start their engines he exclaimed, "Our car!"

"No problem," Gail said calmly. "We're not gonna' make it on this trip anyway."

Steven resolved not to ask any more questions or show surprise at anything he saw. He was following Gail down the rabbit hole and had no choice but to put himself in her hands. Literally. Gail grabbed his hand as they sauntered back to the car, like their sashay into Uncle Murray's backyard.

The Chappaquiddick Beach Club was located on a crescent of

sandy beach just down the road from where the ferry deposited them. You could look back across the harbor at Edgartown's impressive waterfront homes, or straight across to the southern shore of Cape Cod. Sailboats were moored offshore, and more were further out under full sail. The Sunday brunch, usually reserved for senior partners, included all company lawyers, legal aides, interns, and office personnel. They were celebrating the successful conclusion of a case that had kept them working around the clock for the past few weeks.

Gail kicked off her flip-flops and shorts and pointed Steven toward a row of changing cabanas with the iconic red, white, and blue striped tops. When Steven emerged, Gail popped out of the water and waved. He jogged to the shore and dove in.

A few hours later, the party started winding down and most of the younger folks were grouped around an empty buffet table. Gail had introduced Steven as a "a friend who's also interested in becoming a lawyer" but she underestimated the breadth and depth of Red Sox fans. His name was familiar to many of the men and even some women. He had been drafted by the Red Sox when he graduated from high school but opted to go to college instead, and a surprising number still followed his exploits at Dartmouth and the Cape League. He was treated like a celebrity, which was *not* what Gail had in mind. The intern who recommended Gail for the job pressed Steven on the details of playing in the Cape League. His name was Hal, and he wanted to specialize in the newly emerging area of sports law. His idol was Marvin Miller, the Executive Director of the Major League Baseball Players Association, who was organizing the players to demand rights the owners were unwilling to grant. Hal kept peppering Steven with questions and throwing out historical facts about the United Steelworkers Union when it was under Miller's direction. All other conversations had stopped, Steven was feeling uneasy, and Gail was bored.

"Hey Hal," she interrupted, "did you bring your bike here?"

"Yeah."

"Could you get a ride home if Steven borrowed it? He wants to see some big waves, and I thought we'd take a ride to Wasque."

"Oh. Yeah, I guess. The riptide is wicked though, better stay near Swan Pond."

Hal's bike was new, with multiple speeds, nubby tires, and shock absorbing springs. Gail was riding an old Schwinn girl's bike, no crossbar, no gears, wicker basket loosely attached to the handlebars with a couple of beach towels bouncing inside. Gail was miffed at being ignored during the party and set a daunting pace. The scent of competition was in the air. The final half mile was on an unpaved road, some areas packed down and rutted, some soft and sandy. This was more challenging for Gail's bike, and Steven made enough gains to almost catch up. But Gail was determined, and her long-distance running stamina won out. She was glistening with sweat, and Steven was winded.

"Care for a dip?"

"Absolutely," Steven replied. "What did Hal mean about the pond and the riptide?"

"I'll show you." They carried their towels through a path over the grassy dunes and came face to face with the ocean. A couple was walking along the beach between the dunes and the water, their dog running back and forth around them. "See where the waves are break-ing out there? That used to be the far end of a pond before the sides were eroded. It still is at low tide." Steven could make out the barely submerged sides Gail was alluding to. "It'll shield us from the riptide."

The waves on either side were crashing onto the shore and rushing rapidly back out to sea. The water directly in front of them was rising and falling without the fury. Steven followed Gail in. They swam, floated, splashed, dunked, laughed, and lazed. The couple and their dog returned, waved, and said "Enjoy the evening," then left over the path Gail and Steven had used.

They spread the towels and sat side by side, clutching their knees. To their right the sun was setting, off to their left a half moon hung low in the dusk. It was a long time before they spoke, content just to be a part of the magnificent scene.

"Nice place, huh, Masciarelli? I think I have some sand in my bathing suit."

Steven looked puzzled by the incongruous remark, then his eyes got wide as he remembered the sexy letters from Long Island. Gail's smile was toned down, but the heat was way up. Steven leaned in and they kissed. They had shared friendly pecks on the cheek before, but this was the real deal. They didn't rush it, maybe because they had waited so long, maybe because they knew where they were headed, maybe because they were in the Martha's Vineyard time warp. They smoothed the towels carefully, put their bathing suits and flip-flops on the corners, settled back in, and resumed kissing. It went slowly and steadily from there, no part of their naked bodies ignored. It wasn't the first time for either of them, but it was the first time the connection was intense on every level. When they were done, they lay side by side, silently watching the light fade from the sky. Steven took her hand in his and kissed it.

"I don't know if this is on your mind or not," Gail said softly, "but I'm on the pill."

"My mind is totally useless right now."

"I hope everything isn't useless." Gail reached down and playfully bounced his testicles, then stroked his resurgent penis. This time the sex was uncontrolled, rolling around in the sand, ignoring the sharp shells, yelling, pulling, pounding, and scratching, like two sex-starved teens in the back of a car by the side of the road.

· · STEVEN · ·

On the ferry back to the mainland Steven had forty-five minutes to digest the events of the previous twenty hours. Socializing at the company beach party reaffirmed his career choice to become a lawyer. These were the people he would one day associate with professionally. From the youngest who were his age, to the oldest who were Pop's age, they exuded an air of confidence. Steven, confident in his own abilities, felt like he belonged. And Gail! He tried to keep a lid on his excitement, but he kept remembering Pop's advice about marrying a woman who could also be his best friend. Did he have a chance to finally check that box?

The euphoric weekends continued through the rest of the summer and carried over when both returned to their respective colleges. Steven couldn't imagine how life could be any better. He had cemented his baseball future with a spectacular season in the Cape League, reenergized his focus on law, and was head over heels in love. He remembered another tidbit from Pop: "It's a funny thing about girls, son. You chase 'em and chase 'em until *they* catch *you*."

The drive between Hanover and Cambridge became almost a weekly event, shared equally. Gail was adamant about equality of the sexes, wasn't about to shirk any of the responsibilities that came with the territory. She officially changed her major to prelaw, establishing a satisfying purpose to her life, and she, too, was in love.

Steven's Writing Poetry friend rented a cabin at Burke Mountain to share the Christmas break with his partner, but at the last minute decided instead to go home and come clean to his parents about his sexuality. Steven gladly agreed to pay the rental fee, and he and Gail enjoyed the winter beauty of Vermont's Northeast Kingdom. They skied, tried snowshoeing and cross-country skiing, and made love two or three times a day. It was a blissful preview of what life together could be like. Gail concentrated on finding a Spring Break *redux*. Timeshare resorts were beginning to sprout, and she found one offering a free week in Sedona if you agreed to attend a sales presentation. Once again, they immersed themselves in honeymoon-paced sex and a spectacular landscape foreign to two kids from Brooklyn. But reality infiltrated Eden.

Masquerading as a young married couple shopping for a time-share brought the future into the present. Gail's vision included the two of them working together to change the world for the better, like Steven's earlier fantasies of Perry Mason and Della Street. And just as unrealistic.

There was increased harping from Gail about Steven's family business. "You've got to avoid the illegal stuff. We both know there's some of that going on. It just can't involve you."

"I don't do anything illegal."

"Your family does."

"No, they don't."

Unable to come up with a middle ground solution, Steven stopped responding. They would silently sulk for a while before getting back into their vacation mode. Their political disagreements were more animated.

"Like him or not, you still need to respect the President of the

United States."

"Not when he bombs women and children in a country we have no business being in."

"Protecting our interests and defeating our enemies *is* our business."

"But we're making enemies faster than we can kill 'em. Is that a sustainable policy?"

"So, we should all join hands and sing *Kumbaya?*

By the time the week in Sedona ended both were relieved to put a little separation between themselves. They planned to repeat their seminal summer, Steven returning to the Cape League and Gail re-upping with the law firm on Martha's Vineyard. But increased vitriol from Gail and silent stoicism from Steven pointed toward an impending explosion. In what amounted to an ultimatum, Gail threatened to spend the summer in the DC area with a more activist law firm unless Steven distanced himself from the family business. Steven was unwilling to do so, and hoped she was bluffing. She was not, and the ensuing breakup was not amicable.

"You can find someone else to fuck, maybe one of your Italian whores like Gina Sanzo!"

Steven handled the heartbreak in his customary manner, moving their relationship to the back burner and concentrating on baseball for the rest of the summer. The couple tried to resolve their differences, recapturing the glow for short periods of time before it blew up again. The final straw was Steven's decision to enlist in the Marines after college.

A few weeks before Steven was due to fly to Fort Bragg, he began to notice a change in Pop. Their after-dinner talks during high school had become long sessions whenever he was home from college, eventually morphing into regularly scheduled weekend business meetings. Steven was obviously being groomed to succeed Pop, and there was a lot to learn. But lately they had stopped. Pop seemed to be distancing himself from Steven, leaving the room whenever the conversation turned to business like he used to when Vito's name was mentioned. When Pop informed Steven he wouldn't join Mom and him on the flight to Fort Bragg, Steven was concerned enough to ask Mom what was up.

"It's complicated," Mom said. "You need to know some things we never told you. We'll get some alone time on the flight."

"We're alone right now."

"Practice your patience, dear. It's a long sad story, but it has a happy ending."

CHAPTER TWENTY

TWO THUGS ON A THREE-DAY TRIP

Day 2, 1972, Darren NH

The day started smoothly for Moe and Joe. Their first chore was to case the high school. The two-story brick building sat directly on the street, a small staff parking lot in front and a larger one alongside. Behind the side parking lot were athletic fields, now covered in snow, stretching back to a forest. They pulled out the town map Fred gave them showing nothing behind the school but the forest. A few trips up and down side streets confirmed the only access was from the street in front of the school.

"Nothing here," summed up Moe.

"Yeah. Let's go check out were he'd be comin' from."

By the time they arrived at the driveway leading to the commune there was no reason to enter and risk being seen. There were a half-dozen stretches, secluded and steep with sharp curves, on the road between the high school and the commune perfect for staging an accident.

Satisfied, the two men drove back into town and stopped at a Cumberland Farms where they had noticed an outside phone booth. Brooklyn did not want their number connected with Joe and Moe's bag phone.

"I think we've got it worked out. You said you had a guy near here willing to do a couple months' time for DWI?"

"Yes. He can be there in a couple hours. When do you want him?"

"Before dark. Does he have any experience causing accidents?"

"He'll be fine. His name's Barry Longo, he'll call the bag phone in ten minutes. Keep it available."

Joe said, "Get the bag phone out and turn it on. I'll grab some lunch to take back to our room, and we'll come up with a plan."

"Did they say the guy had experience?"

"All they said was 'His name is Barry Longo' and 'He'll be fine.'"

"I hope they're right."

Moe set up the phone while Joe went next door to Darren House of Pizza and bought some grinders and a couple of slices. The call came on the way back to Fred's. Moe gave Barry directions to Cumberland Farms, told him to call when he got close, and they went upstairs to work on the plan.

"What is this stuff?" Moe was holding a soft, doughy triangle with some red sauce and cheese on it.

"I know what it ain't. It ain't pizza." They tried the grinders and shook their heads. "Doesn't anything got a crust in this goddamn town? It's white bread for Chrissakes."

There was a knock on the door from the garage. Joe put his finger to his lips and walked downstairs. They figured it was Fred, but caution was a way of life for them, and they took nothing for granted.

It was Fred, clearly upset. All he could do when Joe opened the door was point his finger upstairs and repeatedly whisper, "We've got a problem! We've got a problem!"

CHAPTER TWENTY-ONE

LENNY AND JEAN

1971, Mueller NY

· · **LENNY** · ·

They saved the baby. This gave a huge morale boost to our devastated crew, but my morale was impossible to boost. I was responsible for Bobbi's death. My action had caused Vinny's reaction, my decision to keep it to myself had put my friends in harm's way, resulting in Bobbi being burned to death. End of story. End of everything. Our commune in Mendocino, my house full of friends, any chance of ever being happy. I couldn't concentrate on anything except my complicity in the crime, couldn't climb out of the mental abyss I had fallen into, couldn't see how anyone could help me because *they didn't know.* They didn't know about the cooked books I refused to sign; they didn't know about the threat. And they didn't know Vinny.

My grip on reality was tenuous and I couldn't gain a foothold. I saw my friends through the wrong end of binoculars, comforting each other and embracing William, too small to touch, too distant to hear. The aftermath of the fire was a mixture of paranoia, fear, and hopelessness unlike anything I experienced before or since. I'd sit on my bed staring at the closet for hours because my clothes were in disarray, and I didn't have the energy to organize them.

I went back over my Rules to Live a Better Life but couldn't muster a flicker of inspiration. I tried every drug, but all they did was just amplify my predicament. I even tried downers, which I never liked, because I heard drugs sometimes had the opposite effect in extreme conditions and realized my dysfunction was extreme. They didn't work either. I can't remember whether this black period lasted days or weeks, but I *can* remember I was depressed enough to entertain suicide. Isolation was the obstacle no drug could overcome. Everything I loved was centered around my friends, the camaraderie we enjoyed, the dreams we shared. I couldn't interact with my friends because I was afraid I'd blurt out my secret and everyone would turn on me. "You knew this could happen? You could've prevented this disaster. You killed her!" I pictured them pointing fingers, judging me unworthy of their friendship.

But in the end, their friendship rescued me. Not Wise William nor Sexy Sheila, not Cool-Cat Carl nor Julie the Jewel. It was Modest Marie and Just Jean. And the new girl, Gallant Gail.

· · JEAN · ·

The one thing Jean had trouble handling with the New Yorkers was being stoned in public. Whenever something unexpected required that he and Marie to go out in public while stoned he questioned their ability to do so. Were they too high to act appropriately? Could they handle an emergency? One time they waited at a red light for what seemed like an unusually long time.

"Something's wrong," Jean said. "The light must be busted. I'm going through it."

"It just seems that way 'cause we're stoned. Let's wait." They sat in silence, afraid to go through the intersection.

"It's definitely stuck." Jean couldn't wait any longer, but just as he took his foot off the brake the light turned green. They stared at each other for a second, mouths open, then sped through the intersection.

Whenever he mentioned his concern to people who got high, he always received the same response. "If it's something important you straighten up immediately and you handle it. It's not like getting drunk. Did you ever see someone start a fight because they were stoned?"

No, he hadn't, but the uncertainty remained, though not as much for Marie and certainly not for the New Yorkers. They'd all be high as a kite, up all night listening to music, then jump into a car and drive to the Throgs Neck Bridge to watch the sun rise over Long Island Sound. Jean would get nervous, feeling that they had been gone for too long and that something bad had happened.

The night of the fire Jean thought to himself, "*This is it. This is a real emergency situation and we're all stoned.*" And as predicted, he no longer felt stoned. Everyone filed out of the house in an orderly fashion and went to the designated meeting place. Lenny was a hero, making split-second decisions in a life and death situation, risking his own to save a mother and her child. Jean received and handed the baby to its mother calmly. Jean thought, "*They were right, we handled everything perfectly.*" Then Bobbi, the only one *not* stoned in deference to her pregnancy, waddled over to the bus and once again his life was blasted off course by a tragic event, way worse than getting fired at Waterville Valley, more immediate than his father's death. Once again, he was lost, didn't know what to do, or what would come next.

Jean and Marie returned to Mueller the weekend after the fire to see how William and the baby were doing and drove William to the hospital the following morning. The little boy was holding his own, the prognosis positive. William couldn't commit to a name, so the basinet was still labeled "Lipson, Boy."

Lipson Boy was the focal point of whatever positive energy the commune could muster, his improving condition the only topic with a hint of happiness. Jean knew Marie was especially fond of Bobbi. During the week at home, he tried to come up with something to ease her grief. On the drive back to New York he had an idea he thought might work, help the commune, and make things easier for his family. He broached the subject as they sat in the hospital hallway.

"What if we move up our wedding date?"

"Why?"

"I just think we all could use something to celebrate."

Marie looked down the hall to where William was staring through the window at the premies. Then she said, "Cathedral of the Pines doesn't have any earlier dates available."

"I know. I thought maybe we could have it at our place, kind of outdoors and in the barn. That way we could do it as soon as possible. My mom could get settled in Florida before the school year starts, so David and Cindy wouldn't have to arrive in the middle of a term."

Marie squeezed Jean's hand and closed her eyes. "You've thought this all out?"

"I thought of it on the drive down. I wanted to let it percolate a bit before suggesting it. It's just an idea, I mean, we don't have to -"

"It's a beautiful idea, Smooch." Marie returned her gaze to William. "We need to ask William what he thinks. It may be too soon for him to celebrate anything."

"I didn't think of that. Yeah, maybe it's not such a good idea. I was trying to do something to make you, make everybody, I don't know…"

"We just need to include William in that conversation."

"Of course, you're right. You just get smarter and braver. I love you so much."

Marie smiled and said, "You're just trying to flatter me into being the one who asks him."

Jean laughed out loud, and William turned to them, waved them over to take a look at the baby again. He stood between them, left arm around Marie, right arm around Jean. "I just can't stop looking at him, ya' know what I mean?"

"Hey guys, whatcha' lookin' at?" It was Sheila, coming off the elevator and smiling at her own rhetorical question. Sheila was one of Jean's least favorite people in the commune. He found her abrasive, often flat out rude, and totally self-absorbed. He admired her energy, knew she was one of the reasons everyone made it out of the house during the fire. He just didn't find her likable. He also didn't find her trick of initializing everything funny. "Why, it's LB. And isn't he just too cute. LB is TC." Then she smiled at Jean and gave Marie a hug. "And how are my New Hampshire friends doing?"

Marie looked briefly at Jean and raised her eyebrows. Jean gave a quick nod and Marie said, "Actually we'd like to run something by you guys. Jean thought if we moved our wedding date up it might lift everyone's spirits a little. We'd have it at Jean's family farm as soon as we can. There's plenty of room, not necessarily indoors, but there's a barn."

"Wait," William said, "is that the farm we stayed at with the Hoggers after Woodstock? Bobbi loved that farm, said she wanted to live there." William's eyes filled up, Sheila moved closer and hugged him.

Jean softly said, "That was Nancy's farm. Our place is nearby, also in Darren."

"Oh yeah, right." He looked at Marie. "You painted that from one of Bobbi's photos. She hung it over our bed." William paused, then said, "Darren? That's the name of the town?"

"Sure is," said Marie, "good old Darren, New Hampshire."

"That's what I should name our son. Bobbi would like that."

Sheila said, "I was kinda' hopin' LB would stick. Maybe two middle initials?"

"We could spell it out," said Jean. "Like, e-l-b-y."

William made it official. "I like it. Darren Elby Lipson. *I love it.*"

They all looked back at the baby, silently assimilating the moment. Finally, Sheila said, "So the group's gonna' go somewhere after all. It's so thoughtful of you two to do this."

"William?" Jean needed affirmation from William, not Sheila.

"Absolutely. I mean, I'm not in a party mood right now, you know what I mean? But life's gonna' go on, and me and Darren, we gotta' go on too, yaknowwhatImean? I know you're doing it mostly for me, but it'll also keep the crew together a little while longer."

"I'm gonna' head back to Lenny's to spread the news," Sheila said. "He's been a real asshole lately, and now we've got a road trip to plan! I gotta' give that guy a swift kick in the butt." She glanced at her watch. "Maybe I'll try an MBJ."

Jean and Marie looked to William for clarification as Sheila hustled toward the elevator. William said, "Beats me. Oh, I got it, Morning Blow Job."

CHAPTER TWENTY-TWO

STEVEN AND MOM

1970, in the air between Brooklyn and Ft. Bragg

MOM

The plane had leveled off at its cruising altitude. She knew it was time for Steven to learn the history behind the strained relationship between Vito and Pop, the truth about the deaths of Uncle Stefano and Grandma Masciarelli, and the tragic effects it had on both families. She knew first-hand that war changes soldiers in many ways, and felt it was important for him to hear it from his mother now, before their relationship changed.

"I found the family tree you made," Mom said, "when I was packing your stuff. Very impressive. You had a lot of comments about my side of the family, not so much about your father's."

"I think I started it after I saw *On the Waterfront*."

"That was *not* the movie your cousins said they were going to see. It dealt with things you were too young to understand. We were concerned you would get the wrong idea about what your father really did. It's why Pop started those after dinner talks, and why he began with just the clothing store before expanding to the neighborhood businesses involving Uncle Eddie, Vito, and your grandfathers."

"I just wanted to understand all I could about our family. I knew what happened, but not always *why*."

"That's because we withheld the *why*. You didn't need it to know then, but you do now." Mom nervously licked her lips. "I can start with answers to any questions you have."

"I guess I'd like to know how it all got started."

Mom smiled, raised her eyebrows, and nodded. "Good idea. Let's start with the Masciarellis, since you only had three entries on your list for Pop's side of the family. You know Grandma and Grandpa Masciarelli came to America from Milan?"

"Of course."

"But not why they came?"

"Same reason as everybody else, for a better life."

"Not really. Milan was a very stylish city then, just like now. Grandpa worked in his father's high-end clothing store, and Grandma was a model for the top designers. They were a beautiful couple poised to inherit a profitable business, but Grandpa wanted to do something on his own. He convinced his father to send him to America to see if there was some way to expand their market. When he saw the garment district, he traded his return trip for a one-way crossing and wired Grandma to join him. They settled in Brooklyn and opened a store in Manhattan."

"The same store we own now?"

"Yes. When Grandpa got too sick to run it, he passed it on to Pop, as Pop will to you."

"What did Grandpa die from?"

"That's part of what we kept from you, and I'll get there. For now, let's just say a broken heart caused by Grandma's death. When the Stock Market crashed, their store stopped making money, and they had teenage twins, Pop and Uncle Stefano. Grandpa's parents never came to America but had connections here and found laborer's work for Grandpa. Grandma helped out by taking advantage of her good looks and dancing skills to find occasional work in shows and night clubs. Grandpa Masciarelli got a job in a warehouse owned by *Nonno*

Catrone. All the kids lived in the same neighborhood, Aunt Angela, Uncle Eddie, me, Vito, and the Masciarelli twins."

"This neighborhood?"

"Yes. The neighborhood was protected by *Nonno* Catrone and Uncle Eddie's father, another Sicilian."

"Protected?"

"Many of the immigrants only spoke Italian and were ignorant about how the system worked. They had no connections for jobs, were suspicious of the police, and were easy victims for wise guys. That's what the mafia did before prohibition, help local businesses get started, keep competing mafia families from intruding. When Uncle Eddie married Aunt Angela the two families were officially united and took control of the neighborhood. Meanwhile your two grandfathers became friends. *Nonno* Catrone always had his eyes on the future of the organization. Uncle Eddie would do fine taking over for *his* father, but he worried about my brother Vito's temper.

Grandpa Masciarelli was different from the rest of the men hanging around the front stoops discussing the issues of the day, often disagreeing with *all* of them. He was soft spoken and polite, but never backed down from his opinions. *Nonno* Catrone was surrounded by men who wouldn't dare disagree with him and was smart enough to see the value of a differing opinion, especially when delivered in such an elegant package. Grandpa Masciarelli was the man he hired for the present, but he also thought your father would make Uncle Eddie's life with Vito more tolerable in the future. Whenever the families got together, the chemistry between me and Pop was obvious. Fortunately for *Nonno* Catrone's plans, our puppy love matured into the real thing."

"So, Vito was always a handful?"

Mom smiled at her son's diplomacy. "Worse. He became your *father's* handful."

"How?"

"That all happened after the war. Pop and Uncle Stefano were in their mid-twenties when the war started. By this time Grandpa Masciarelli had reopened the store. He was also becoming the confidant, advisor, and partner in a number of projects with *Nonno* Catrone. The twins had taken over the daily chores of operating the clothing store, but Pop and Uncle Eddie were also dipping their toes into the neighborhood enterprises. They, along with Vito, were now the likely successors, just as *Nonno* hoped."

"Not Uncle Stefano?"

"No. Uncle Stefano wanted no part of that. He was totally into the clothing store, enamored with the world of fashion. Most of his friends came from Grandma Masciarelli's world of dancers and entertainers. His artistic creations impressed Grandma's crowd, widening the store's market to include up-and-coming entertainers as well as some *bona fide* stars. Uncle Stefano's, um, love interests were not, uh, restricted by gender, which was no problem with his crowd, but a major concern for his father.

"Uncle Stefano's lifestyle and that of his friends and lovers represented a risk to Grandpa Masciarelli. Both boys enlisted, Pop in the Navy and Uncle Stefano in the Marines, but Grandma and Grandpa Masciarelli were not in agreement on the matter of Uncle Stefano's enlistment. Grandpa felt he needed some toughening up and the Marines was the place to accomplish it. Grandma loved both her twins, but Uncle Stefano was her soul mate, artistic, beautiful physically and emotionally needy. The thought of him in the Marines frightened her.

"Pop was in the Pacific when the news came about Uncle Stefano's death in France. Grandpa blamed himself, and Grandma agreed. She let him have it, full force. He took the constant berating because, with Uncle Stefano gone and Pop still overseas she was all he had, and he was all she had. As destructive as their life together became, at least it was a life together. Unfortunately her demons were worse than we thought.

"One morning, less than a month after we learned of Uncle Stefano's death and just two days before Pop was due to arrive home, she took the gun they kept in the nightstand, put it in her robe pocket, and walked into the bathroom. The official police report listed her death as an accidental shooting, citing the fact that she was found on the toilet wearing her robe and her wounds were in the abdomen near the pocket. That was the family's explanation, and what everyone, including you, has always been told. But that's not what happened.

"Grandpa was awakened by Grandma yelling obscenities in the bathroom. He was unaware she had the gun. Her voice alternated between exaggerated male voices, baby talk, and her own frantic screeching. Frightened, he started toward the bathroom and heard the gunshot. She was slumped over the toilet, back to him, as if she had been urinating like a man and fallen forward. Blood and flesh were everywhere. Whatever her hallucinations, they led her to put the barrel of the gun to her vagina and pull the trigger."

Mom's eyes were locked on Steven's, looking for signs this might be more than he could handle. When she got to Grandma pulling the trigger, Steven's eyes widened, and he recoiled as if he had been shot.

Steven started to say something, then stopped. He was following the story intently, felt like he was in the bathroom with his grandparents. After some thought he said, "And now Pop's worried he's doing the same thing with me."

Mom stiffened, held up her hand and said, "That's only partially true. You're not Uncle Stefano, I'm not Grandma, and *their* circumstances were totally different. When Pop was on his way home from the Pacific the family got together and decided all Pop needed to know was that his mother accidentally died. The only people who knew the full truth were me and Grandpa, Aunt Angela and Uncle Eddie, and *Nonno* and *Nonna* Catrone. And Vito."

"Why Vito and not Louise?"

"They hadn't met yet. Vito met Louise at a V-Day parade. He was hugged and kissed by a stranger with green eyes, flaming red hair, and a temperament to match. The kiss turned into a two-day drinking binge, then a "victory tour" across the country and back that took more than four months and included a trip to Las Vegas to get married. When Vito arrived home with his new bride the reception was, let's say, *less* than friendly. We maintained the pretense of acceptance only because Louise was pregnant." Mom took a breath. She was reliving it as she was telling it, and it was harder than she thought. "Maybe we should take a break."

Steven smiled and said, "I'm okay, but if you need to take a second…"

"No, I'd need way more than a second." She continued, "Pop, though shaken to the core, was able to carry on. Grandpa was not. He needed help, but was too stubborn to ask. To be fair, that type of help wasn't as available as it is now. Pop tried to engage him in conversation, ask his advice about the store, make him feel needed. He got nothing. Pop was trying to run the store by himself and, with Uncle Eddie, fill the void created by Grandpa's withdrawal. When I started helping out in the store and we were together all day, I couldn't live the lie any longer. One night I told him I had been hiding something from him. As soon as I mentioned Grandma he said, 'Oh, that. I know.' I didn't believe him and asked what he knew. He said, 'I know how she killed herself.' I was shocked, and very, very, angry." Mom stopped, closed her eyes, and replayed that night for the thousandth time.

"Do you know what I've been going through trying to protect you? How hard this has been for me? I loved Stefano like a brother, closer to him than I am to my older sister. I absolutely idolized your mother; thought she was the bee's knees. How could you have not been aware of that?! How could you let me go on thinking…when did you find out!?"

"Vito started teasing me the day after I got home. Still does, every chance he can. It gets pretty vulgar. I'm sorry Christina. I thought you were just embarrassed to talk about it because it was so, I mean, you're a girl and…I thought you knew I knew. I didn't want to make you talk about it, didn't want you to have to go through it again."

They were silent for a bit, neither one knowing what to say. "We both made a mistake, Gino. You know how strong you are? Well, I'm that strong too. That's how we earned each other's love. Neither of us need protecting. All we'll ever need from each other is the truth."

Mom opened her eyes. She looked at Steven, who had been respectfully patient, took a breath, and continued. "Vito threatened a power grab, trying to take advantage of Grandpa Masciarelli's absence. Pop's battles with Vito at work were all-consuming. What got us through was the strength of our relationship. We spent all day at the store together, talked about business at home. Pop had another business, of course, which was off limits to wives. When he left the store to take care of other interests, I played the game of Mafia wife, not pressing for details. I knew where he was going, and I knew where he *wasn't* going. He wasn't running around with a Tommy Gun shooting up speakeasies. He wasn't running a pack of prostitutes. He was meeting with union leadership and management groups, bank officers and politicians, higher-ups in the Mafia. It's true the subjects they discussed were buying loyalty from lobbyists, trying to influence union officials, and cheating the IRS. But most people thought those kinds of things were acceptable. In our neighborhood, Pop was a respected businessman."

"Why cheat the IRS?"

"One lesson learned from the prohibition bonanza was you needed a way to report your income or the IRS would bust you, like it did Al Capone. Those who had legitimate businesses, like *Nonno's* produce and shipping empire, Uncle Eddie's grocery stores, and the clothing store, had built-in fronts. Grandpa Masciarelli was very good at developing systems to stockpile "clean" money which they then lent to other Mafia families. Under Pop's leadership they became, like, a bank for the other families."

"Pop never did the other stuff?" Steven's family was the reason he and Gail's romance ended badly, and he needed to know the extent of their illegal activities.

"*Nonno* Catrone, Grandpa Masciarelli, and Uncle Eddie's father always flew under the radar, supervising the small-time rackets, keeping the neighborhood protected, and spending their time, money, and influence on labor unions and money laundering. Their goal was to stay out of the way of all the noise created by the more notorious families. It was difficult at times, but *Nonno's* wealth allowed them to remain relatively independent. When *Nonno* needed help to keep Grandma Masciarelli's suicide private he knew who to go to, expressed gratitude when the deal was done, and offered to repay the people responsible. The *Don* said, 'Your partner lost his wife and son. The boy was a hero.

I'm happy to handle this, and you owe me nothing.' But it wasn't so easy ten years later when Vito almost went to jail."

"For what?"

"*On the Waterfront* was based on a newspaper investigation of corruption on the waterfronts in New York. That investigation accidentally uncovered a prostitution ring on Vito's beat. There was evidence my younger brother not only looked the other way but was pocketing significant cash for his lack of vigilance. Vito broke everybody's rules - the city's, the Mafia's, the NYPD's, even the Feds. Making it go away was complicated. Louise was involved and had to be dealt with, and the arrangements had to include a totally different police force. Uncle Eddie and Pop were mostly silent as *Nonno* laid out the facts to the *Don*. Pop almost lost his life that night."

"What! How?"

"I guess there was no proof Vito was responsible, but all *Nonno* could get was a promise to 'look into things.' *Nonno* sat silent for quite some time, making no move to get up. Finally, the *Don* broke the silence. Turns out his daughter had married a guy just out of law school who was interested in Labor Law. Pop reached for a pen, and all the *Don's* men reached for their guns. He ignored them, pulled out the pen and the store business card, wrote his home number on the back, told the *Don* he should tell Pop what his son-in-law wanted, and he'd make it happen. Pop slid the card across the table, looked the *Don* straight in the eyes and smiled pleasantly.

"There was another long silence and Pop waited patiently, aware that the periods of silence were as important as what was said. They were neither a pretense nor a bluff, just a reflection of an Old World way of life. There was no outside interference, everything else could wait while all possible ramifications were pondered. Finally, *Nonno*

Catrone, Uncle Eddie, Pop, and the *Don* arranged a deal that kept Vito out of jail. He was transferred to a small-town police force in Westchester. Louise was charged with prostitution to explain the cash, not a large leap in our opinion. She was in short order convicted, put on probation, and had the judgement vacated. A cash settlement was made to Louise, and Aunt Angela and I greased the skids out of town. Vito *was* named after *Nonno*, as I told you, but none of the family members felt he earned the right to use his father's name as his own. The prostitution episode was the latest in a long line of misdeeds confirming that skepticism. Vito thought he was unjustly criticized and had the oversized ego to name your cousin after himself and *Nonno* - Vincenzo Catrone III."

Steven took a minute to digest the saga. The Masciarellis had come to life, the grumpy old man in the nursing home and the woman in the faded photograph now flesh and blood, *his* flesh and blood. He imagined Grandma, a roaring twenties flapper doing the Charleston, jaunty *chapeau* with a satin bow, sequined short dress, long beads swaying as her knees crisscrossed her arms while her legs kicked out to the side. And Grandpa, the smooth love interest, escorting her to speakeasies that only he had access to. Pop and Uncle Stefano, typical twins, one thoughtful and reserved, the other the opposite. And Uncle Stefano gay! Or at least bisexual. Mom skirted *those* details.

Also, the Catrone family was now illuminated in a different light. The three generations of Vincenzo Catrones, *Nonno*, Vito, and his cousin Vinny, the friendship between *Nonno* and Grandpa bringing the two families together, Mom and Pop the fulcrum that cemented the connection. And why Louise was never accepted as a family member.

"So that's why they moved to Westchester," Steven said, "and why Louise never came back. The stranger this story becomes, the more it makes sense!"

Mom laughed, and said, "It gets stranger! The postwar economy was great for legitimate business, not so much for the not so legitimate. People still wanted things that were illegal, but the logistics were more complicated. We cornered the produce market, with *Nonno* running the shipping and wholesale and Uncle Eddie's family running the retail operations. Pop ran our store and the "bank." Vito supplemented his income by smuggling drugs and wanted to move up to the big-time families. *Nonno* didn't think the time was right for a move. When he passed away, leaving Uncle Eddie, Vito and Pop, Vito pushed harder. Meetings frequently threatened to blow up, and Pop was caught in the middle.

"And now, like you said, he's going through the same experience that derailed Grandpa, *except* there was no disagreement between Pop and I, and you are much more grounded than your uncle was. When the draft board picked your number, a decision had to be made and you opted to serve your country. You *could* have had another option. Pop and Uncle Eddie were diligent about maintaining the connections made by *Nonno* and their fathers. Favors could've been cashed in to fix the problem with the local draft board, but as I said, this was a tough time for Pop, Uncle Eddie, and Vito to agree on anything.

"Uncle Eddie wanted to go legit and pull the produce/shipping business out of the organization. He knew pulling out would seriously hamper Vito, who needed a legitimate business big enough to launder large dollar amounts from his smuggling schemes. The tension was heading towards a boiling point, and the three men were running out of ideas to save the organization. Pop had been touting Las Vegas since the early fifties but they didn't have enough money then. However, by the mid 1960s there were discussions about legalizing Las Vegas style casinos in Atlantic City to revitalizing tourism on the Jersey Shore. Also, the Catskill Mountain resorts were well within reach of New York City and the Mafia's influence. While smaller hotels were going out of business, the larger resorts still attracted big name entertainers, reinforcing the comparison to Las Vegas. And New Hampshire was a favorite summer getaway for the Boston and Providence Mafia. In the White Mountain region, large tracts of inexpensive land were available and, like Nevada, New Hampshire has no state income tax. The three men agreed to dedicate their money and influence to exploring those three locations. If they could get in on the ground floor and one of those three came to fruition, they would own a legitimate money machine able to support all the enterprises they could imagine. The future of the neighborhood organization which endured from the turn of the century would be assured. If not, it would cease to exist. Pop believed there would be another Las Vegas, and it was up to him to make sure his organization was a major player right from the start."

STEVEN

Steven was now able to fill in the blanks that frustrated him while growing up. He also seized on Mom's description of Uncle Eddie wanting to "go legit" and pull the produce/shipping business out of the organization. Pop's talks now included his vision of a casino large enough to launder money from Vito and Vinny's drug smuggling, enabling Uncle Eddie to pull the produce conglomerate out. He and Pop would have the clout and the money to wrest control from Vito and Vinny. That was Pop's dream.

But now Steven could have his own dream. He could never be entirely honest with Gail when he denied illegal family activities. If the casino became a reality, Steven and Pop could run the casino legally. They wouldn't need Vito and Vinny's drug money, or dirty money of any kind. After a few years, the books would be cleared from previous connections with the Catrones, and Steven would be freed from the consequences of living a double life. There would be nothing to keep secret from Gail.

319

CHAPTER TWENTY-THREE

LENNY

1971, Mueller NY

Someone was knocking on the door and calling my name. I didn't recognize the voice, didn't feel like seeing anybody. Whoever the asshole was wouldn't stop so I shuffled to the door.

It was a woman holding a briefcase and nursing a tentative smile. "Lenny?"

My first thought was *"She's an FBI agent and I'm going to be charged as an accomplice in the murder of Bobbi Lipson."* I almost blurted out a confession.

"You probably don't remember me. I'm Gail, I worked at my uncle's baseball camp when you were Head Councilor there. I'd like to come in and talk to you but, uh, maybe you should put some clothes on first?"

I looked down and realized I was in my tighty-whiteys, no shirt, no shoes, no socks. I looked at her again to see if I could place her. She was wearing a navy-blue blazer with thin white chalkline pinstripes over a white blouse and perfectly pressed jeans. I didn't quite stack up sartorially. *I am such a loser!*

"C'mon in, have a seat," waving vaguely toward the kitchen, "I'll be right back." I went upstairs and stared hopelessly at my closet. I snatched the first pair of jeans my hand touched, did the same with a pile of t-shirts. I didn't go to the trouble of putting on socks or shoes. She was sitting in William's traditional seat at the formica table, so I decided I didn't like her. "Sorry I'm, uh, going through a bit of a tough time right now. I don't remember you."

"I understand. I worked in the office, rarely made it down to the ballfields. I wanted to..."

"Hey Lenny." Sheila breezed in through the back door. "Good to see ya' up and about." She stopped, look quizzically at Gail, then said, "I know you from somewhere."

"Yes, you do. My Uncle Ralph runs the baseball camp."

"Gail, right?"

"Yes." Gail stood up, extended her hand and a professional smile. "Gail Bernstein. And you're the girls' softball Head Councilor, Sheila, uh..."

"Siegel. Sorry, I didn't mean to interrupt you guys."

"No problem," Gail assured her. "Are you two, um..."

"Oh no, we're just friends."

Apparently I didn't need to participate in the conversation. I was about to excuse myself and go back to bed, but Gail said, "In that case, Sheila, I need to speak to Lenny alone."

"That's cool." Sheila looked at me. "Anyone else around? I got some good news. Jean and Marie are moving up their wedding date, and we're all invited."

"I thought they *were* married."

"No, Lenny, they were *going* to get married *after* we left for Mendocino, but thought we could use something to celebrate, thought it might cheer us up." Sheila shifted to Gail and added, "Don't let him go back into hibernation when you're done. He needs cheering up, big time." And Sheila was out the door, leaving behind an awkward silence.

I still had nothing to say, and this person sitting in William's chair was clearly not happy about being put in charge of my rehab by Dr. Siegel. She opened her briefcase and took out a pad and a set of assorted felt tipped pens. She managed to work up half a smile—her mouth was not really involved - and said, "So, you're the owner of this property?"

"Yes."

"And you have a mortgage?"

"Yes." I decided to give her one more question before asking her to leave and going back upstairs.

"Well, that means you have insurance that covers the damages from the fire. Have you filed a claim yet?"

"You're trying to sell me insurance?"

She snorted a short laugh. "Of course not. The bank wouldn't have given you a mortgage if you didn't have insurance. I'm an attorney."

"And I'm an accountant with a degree in business from the esteemed University of Michigan. I know more than you ever will about how mortgages work. I'm just struggling right now, and I don't appreciate you laughing at me in my own house sitting at my kitchen table in William's chair one week after his wife was, was..." I was standing now, gripping the edge of the table so tightly my wrists cramped. I looked down and saw splotches of water on the table. Realizing they were my tears, I collapsed back into my chair and bawled like a baby. I dried my eyes, looked across the table. Her expression was equal parts astonishment and pity, which I interpreted as "How fast can I get my ass out of here?"

But she didn't move, instead calmly asked, "Do you know a man named Vinny Catrone?"

It was the first time since the night of the fire that I allowed his name into my thoughts. It got through my defenses because it was a sneak attack, and the shock jumpstarted my brain. Theories bubbled up where a moment ago there was only stagnation, as if someone added carbonation to a glass of flat Ginger Ale. The only thing me, Sheila, and this attorney had in common was Mr. Bernstein's baseball camp and some connection to Vinny. Was this a conspiracy? Were Sheila and the attorney just pretending their meeting here was a coincidence? God knows Sheila can act! How much do they know about me and Vinny? What did she say her name was?

"Look, uh..."

"Gail."

"Right. So, Gail, what are you doing here?"

"My law firm asked me to investigate a fire that may have been started by a man named Vinny Catrone. There was a salesman by that name who sold sporting goods to the camp. When I looked through the reports of the fire I recognized your name, and it seemed odd that you two were somehow connected."

My brain was up and running now. I thought she might be dangling a lifeline that could pull me out of my abyss but wasn't sure how to grab it. I felt the need to confide in somebody who was not part of our group, and she was a lawyer. You can always trust a lawyer, right?

"So, Gail, let me ask you something. Don't you have to keep things I say to you confidential?"

"Only if you're my client."

"Do you have a client?"

"No. My firm just asked me to see what I could find out about the fire."

It was fun communicating with someone, figuring out what to say and how to say it. I was feeling better word by word, though she was tough to read. But I could taste the relief of unloading my burden, and she was sitting right there in William's chair.

"Would you like to be my lawyer?"

She thought for a few seconds, her expression reverting to that half smile. "The confidentiality laws are meant to protect the attorney as well as the client. How about you tell me a little, I'll tell you a little, and if something makes either of us nervous, we'll stop."

"I used to work for Vinny." That was easy. It was something my friends already knew, and I could feel the monkey crouching, getting ready to jump off my back.

"In what capacity?"

"Bookkeeper."

She changed to a blue-tipped pen, wrote it down, looked at another sheet and asked, "Would that be for Team Sports, Inc.?"

"Yes."

"And you no longer work for that company?"

"Correct."

"How come?"

Ah. Therein lies the rub, as another doomed man once said. I needed to choose my words carefully because I needed to hang onto that dangling lifeline. Gail uncovered some different colored pens while awaiting my response. "He asked me to do something I didn't want to do."

"Which was?"

I started slowly, withholding specifics. She was the consummate listener, the dam broke, and it all came out. Vinny throwing baseballs at ten-year-olds, beating up kids in the playground, knocking me out because I walked home with Rosalie Corio. His shocking appearance at Mr. Bernstein's camp, the job offer, draft dilemma and disappointing drudgery of a job going nowhere, then the confrontation over the IRS forms. Through it all Gail listened attentively, switched pens from one color to another, jotted notes and offered encouragement. I was just getting into the dynamics of our group, how I - and my house and bus - fit in when William, Jean, and Marie returned from the hospital. I was unsure how to introduce Gail, but she did it herself.

"Hi, I'm Gail. I was bringing good news about insurance reimbursing Lenny for damages caused by the fire, but I was unaware of how tragic the fire was and the enormity of your loss. I am so sorry. My good news seems so trivial now."

William said, "No, no, we need good news here, trivial or not. We just got some from Jean and Marie," pointing to them as he spoke, "who are getting married sooner than we thought, and we'll do our best to celebrate when the time comes. I'm glad Lenny can get some money back."

Sheila came in and heard the last few words from William. "*I'm glad Lenny's still awake.*" Turning to Gail she said, "Nice job pulling his head out of his ass." She rewarded me with a smile and a friendly peck on the cheek, then asked, "Anybody hungry?"

I looked at the clock, was shocked to see it was almost seven o' clock. Gail shrugged without commitment. Sheila decided she, Gail, and Marie should hop in Jean's pickup, get pizza for everyone, and we could call it a bridal shower. By the time they returned they were best friends. A joint was passed around and I hesitated when I turned to pass it to Gail. She took it without flinching, and the party was on. There were plenty of teary moments, but they were mixed with laughter. Gail became an instant celebrity when she told us she was arrested for demonstrating, and by the time she gathered her stuff to leave she was invited to the wedding. She gave me her card and said, "We still have to talk, Lenny. I'm in the city for a few days using an associate's office. The number's on the card. It has to be tomorrow or the next day because I'm going back to Boston." Then she was gone, along with the monkey on my back.

CHAPTER TWENTY-FOUR

STEVEN AND GAIL
1970

·· STEVEN, VIETNAM ··

Steven had to know if he could walk or crawl to safety. Unable to lift his head enough to see, he inched his hands bit by bit toward the pain. When he reached his thighs, he felt dampness. The deepening twilight added urgency. What if his legs were useless, or gone? There was no way he would survive overnight. He could hear his pounding pulse, could picture each spasm pumping his blood onto the jungle floor. Panic crept in, the pounding grew louder and louder, the pain engulfed him, and he began to lose consciousness.

Then Steven sorted out the sounds and realized the pounding came from helicopter blades. The chopper would not come back after nightfall. If he was unconscious, they might think he was dead, might pass him by for someone obviously savable. He screamed but had no idea if he could be heard above the chopper noise. Pushing the pain to yet another level by shifting onto his left hip, he raised his right arm and forced himself to keep it elevated for a count of ten before letting it collapse to the ground. He raised his arm again for a count of ten, and then again. He resolved to continue raising his arm and counting to ten until someone noticed or his life expired. The fading light suddenly disappeared, and Steven thought he was gone. Then he felt a touch, heard voices, and the light returned. Their shadows had momentarily blocked the sun. They cut his uniform, stabbed him with a needle.

His stay at the MASH unit was a morphine-induced blur. There were a few images he vowed to keep crisp and clear for future motivation. The medics explaining how lucky he was, how ligaments and tendons ripped from their anchors became natural tourniquets, wrapping themselves around mangled muscle and fragmented bones, slowing the loss of blood just enough to allow him to survive. And later, the clueless Chaplain suggesting he seek guidance from above to help him through his anger and depression.

By the time he was transferred to a hospital in Germany, Steven already had his depression under control. It was in a box labeled "whole life fucked up by land mine" and pushed into the back of his brain with a few other items that might otherwise get in the way of reality. And reality was what Steven was concerned with, not "guidance from above," "lucky tendons and ligaments," nor the pie-in-the-sky bullshit spewing forth from the goddamn fucking lesbo therapist while she dug the heels of her hands into his muscles and lifted his goddamn fucking stumps. The anger was clearly going to be tougher to manage than the depression.

"It's possible you could walk with two prosthetics. They're making wonderful progress with new lightweight materials from the space program. Never say never!"

Steven pictured himself teetering on two peg legs, lurching forward one crutch at a time. Never. Maybe if he lost just one leg. A limp was acceptable, could be used to his advantage. People liked their leaders to have human frailties.

"FDR did a damn good job of running the country from a wheelchair," Pop used to say whenever Steven whined about a minor injury. He was just going to have to figure out how to run his neighborhood from one. They used to call him "the next Joe DiMaggio." Now he'd have to settle for "the next FDR."

They were on their way to Germany right now, Mom, Pop, and Aunt Angela, to accompany him on his trip home. Mom needed her sister's support to help her cope. Pop normally required no help with coping, but Steven was unsure what to expect given what he learned from Mom on the way to Fort Bragg. Steven tried to picture them on the plane, Aunt Angela and Mom holding hands on their shared armrest, engaging in family small talk. Would Pop be his usual pillar of strength, or would Steven need to convince Pop this wasn't going to derail the ambitious Masciarelli plans? He worked hard to prepare for the meeting and felt like he was approaching the proper frame of mind. Don't dwell on the negatives, keep pushing the positive. No legs below the knees? Get a wheelchair. Physical advantage on the street gone? Develop the mental advantage to its fullest. The future blown up along with your legs? Just a little speed bump on the highway of life.

Steven suspected something might be up when Aunt Angela came into his room by herself. She rushed over and hugged him. When she stepped back her eyes went to the foot of the bed.

"They're gone, Aunt Angela."

"I know, honey, I know," her eyes got teary, voice a little hushed, "but you're still you. I can see in your eyes you're still my sweet little Stevie."

"Sure am, Aunt Angela, that'll never change." Another hug, followed by an awkward silence. Steven looked toward the door. "Where's Mom and Pop?"

"Oh, they're taking care of some paperwork with the hospital. They'll be right up."

"Is there a problem?"

"Oh no, they're, um, just making sure everything's taken care of. Are you in a lot of pain?"

"Okay Aunt Angela, what's up?" There was another pause while they stared at each other.

"You could always tell when I was bluffing, even when you were little. Remember when I tried..."

"Aunt Angela?"

She was silent again, eyes re-tearing, lips a little quivery, composing what she had to say. "Mom needs a few more minutes with your father. He's not sure you'll want to see him; he thinks what happened is his fault. They're in a room at the end of the hallway. Your mom is trying to calm, uh, talk to him. He took this very hard, Steven. You mean so much to him. He feels responsible, thinks you probably hate, uh, don't want to see him."

Steven had psyched himself up so intently for this meeting he was experiencing the "fight or flight" syndrome, adrenalin and testosterone building rapidly then not having any way to be expended. He pounded the nurse's call button repeatedly with his fist.

"Stop it, please, Stevie, I made such a mess of this! I thought I could...seeing you was..." Aunt Angela was struggling to get her breath and composure back, "I'll get them. Just try to, to control yourself." Heeding her own advice, Aunt Angela squared her shoulders, marched toward the door. She opened it and Steven's parents appeared, holding hands, and smiling bravely.

Steven was stunned. Pop looked ten years older, not ten months. Mom let go of Pop's hand, put hers lightly on his elbow and urged him forward. That subtle but tender gesture touched Steven to the core. He stretched out his arms, palms up, and gave the "come here" motion with his fingers, like Pop used to whenever Steven looked lost and in need of some love. The hug was tentative, Steven cautious because of how frail Pop looked. The men separated and the four of them exchanged small talk about the long flight. Pops's tolerance of idle chatter was never great and, like his son, his mind was focused elsewhere. Unable to contain himself any longer, he interrupted Mom and Aunt Angela's story about the flight attendant's rude behavior. "So, you don't hold me responsible for this," pointing toward the bottom half of the bed, framing it as a question. The two women stopped their conversation mid-sentence, held their breath, and stared at Steven.

"Did you plant the land mine?"

"I sent you there."

"That's quite a stretch, Pop. It never occurred to me to blame anybody but the Vietcong."

"You know," Mom jumped in, "this may be a discussion we need to continue, but not after two hours sleep in the last 24, cramped in a seat for 10 hours, no shower..."

"Once again my little sister's right," said Aunt Angela. "We'll be back after we've regrouped."

"Well, I sure as hell ain't goin' anywhere!" Steven's attempt at humor drew relieved laughter, and a knowing smile from Pop. He always appreciated good diplomacy, especially from his protege.

"Where'd that chair come from, Angela?"

"The next room, Gino." Pop took the chair, with Aunt Angela following. They came back, took their turns saying goodbye, and Steven motioned for Mom to come closer.

"Is he sick?"

"Not physically," she whispered against Steven's cheek, "We need to talk, again."

The next morning Mom greeted him with, "Gail wanted to come, but the military only allows family members." Mom liked Gail, and always hoped their relationship would blossom into something permanent. "She'll try meeting us at the airbase. If not, at the hospital."

"Great." Steven's response was flat, neither excited nor sarcastic. Everything concerning Gail was complicated. Their relationship had been through so many phases Steven named them, like Picasso's Blue, Cubist, and Rose. There was Teen Infatuation, Bronx Separation, Long Island Exile, Brooklyn Reunion, Just Friends, and College Romance. They were currently in The War Years. Their last time together did not end well, and their ensuing long-distance correspondence did little to smooth the ruffled feathers. The loss of his legs would add major complications. He knew his noncommittal response was not what Mom wanted to hear, but what occupied his mind now were questions.

Steven had finished three semesters of law school before he was called to service, while involving himself more and more in Pop's visionary plans. Was he supposed to pick up where he left off? How long would he be hospitalized? Would he ever be self-sufficient? Was Pop going to be himself again, or relive Grandpa's guilt-ridden demise? How strong could the team of Steven and Gino Masciarelli be now? Once again, Gail would have to take a back seat to his family.

· · GAIL · ·

Gail couldn't make it to the airport, but she was at the hospital, sitting by the nurses' station with a briefcase by her feet and some papers in her hand. She looked at her watch, then back to the papers. Then she looked down the hall and saw him.

All Steven could manage was a self-deprecating expression, hands pointing to the empty footrests as if to say "Look what I did to myself."

"I'm still up here," she said, left index finger pointing to her temple.

332

Then pointing her right index finger at Steven's forehead, "You still up there?"

"I never left."

"Then we're good to go." She leaned in, kissed him on the cheek, noticed his eyes moistening and felt hers doing the same. She backed away, hand lingering for a second on his shoulder, and stayed on the periphery as nurses guided Steven's bed and his family to his room.

Steven's aunt said, "I'm going to call Uncle Eddie and let him know we're here."

His mother followed with, "We're gonna' find out when the doctors will be in to see you," and took his father's hand, leaving her alone with Steven in what was suddenly a very large room.

"How are you dealing," she asked.

"It's hard. I think I'm doing okay."

"Do you have a plan?"

Steven laughed, amused as always at her systematic approach to solving problems. "I've got a ton of plans, Gail. I'm just a little hazy on how to make 'em all happen."

Gail pulled her chair closer, took his hand. "Any of them include me?"

Steven didn't reply. The silence was telling, and Gail's grip on his hand slackened, her shoulders slumped, the smile in her eyes hung by a thread. Finally, he answered, "You've been in my plans since seventh grade. Given some of the things you said in our last conversation, the question should be am I in *yours*?"

Gail added her free hand to their grip. "Look Steven, whatever the current state of our relationship, the depth of my love for you has never changed, never will. We've been platonic, romantic..." Steven freed his hands from hers, repeated the "Look what I did to myself" wave over his lap, this time with an exaggerated, suggestive leer. Gail didn't miss a beat. "You said they amputated everything *below* your knees!" The spark returned to her eyes, the *repartee* and shared laughter lightening the mood. Gail continued, a mix of levity and sincerity in her voice. "Ever since that dorky kid took me under his wing and nursed me back to health you've been there for me. I want to be here for you, now, in any way you'll let me. Oh, and it was *eighth* grade, not seventh."

"Not for me. You were so cool it took me a whole year to find the courage to talk to you."

They heard familiar voices approaching. "We'll discuss this later, Mr. Masciarelli."

Steven laughed, her tone and visage a perfect parody of the fourth-grade teacher directing "Miss Bernstein" to escort "Mr. Masciarelli" to the principal's office. He realized he laughed three times during their brief conversation, more than he had since his injury.

· · STEVEN · ·

Steven's rehab got off to a rocky start. The facilities in Bethesda were overloaded with injured vets, and the department dealing with amputees was understaffed and overwhelmed. Most of Steven's day was spent doing nothing. The persona he painstakingly constructed while growing up was badly damaged by the land mine, and his inability to do anything about it threatened to complete the demolition. After a few days he was at the end of his coping skills.

Mom was a constant source of comfort and patience, though Steven could tell his frequent meltdowns were exacerbating the situation. He completely lost it a few times, most recently when Pop suggested using their connections to get Steven's case "moved up the ladder."

"What happens to the people I leapfrog?"

"That's not my concern right now. My concern is you."

"What if it turns out to be one of my men?"

"I can't take care of everybody, son. I can only take care of you."

"What if it's one of the medics who risked their lives to save mine?"

"Would you rather do nothing and just go crazy?"

"No, I'd rather leave going crazy to you and Grandpa!"

Pop turned and left. Mom stared right through Steven, got up slowly and followed Pop.

Stephen immediately started planning how he would challenge Pop's lack of concern for the plight of others when his parents came back. He speculated about Pop's responses, relieved to focus on something sure to happen tomorrow. But the nurse greeted him the next morning with "Your parents aren't going to be able to make it in today."

Steven was momentarily flummoxed, then thought, *"It's a ploy! Pop's playing me!"* Steven renewed his focus on the anticipated showdown with Pop, like when he geared up for Pop's arrival at the hospital in Germany. Pop looked tired when they arrived the next morning. *"Good, he's been consumed with this encounter also!"*

"I've been thinking," Pop said in his normal, untroubled manner, "of a plan that might satisfy everybody. There's a hospital in Manhattan affiliated with NYU called the Rusk Rehabilitation Hospital." Pop paused, pulled a pad out of his shirt pocket, and continued. "It was founded after World War II to treat serious injuries, has a great reputation, and specializes in amputations and prosthetics."

Steven was speechless.

"I've been working on the logistics, and there are a ton of details, but the bottom line is we should be able to get you out of here and into Rusk in a couple days. Your rehab there would start immediately, and you'd be opening up a spot *here* for whoever is next in line. I thought you'd appreciate that." Another pause, another smile, a flip of the page on his pad. Steven was still too stunned to speak. "And, here's something else I thought you'd like," Pop continued, reading from the pad, "Rusk is especially noted for its style of treatment. They were the first to treat the whole patient, and not just concentrate on the specific injury. They assemble a team to address all of the patient's needs, to get the patient back to being self-sufficient." Pop looked up. "And finally, of course, it's convenient to our home."

Steven didn't know what to say. "Uh, so, what do we, um, how..."

Mom helped him out. "I know it's a big move. Your father's been going nonstop for the last two days working out the details, and it's a little scary for all of us."

Steven broke down, started to cry. Mom and Pop quickly came over and hugged him. Steven tried to remember the last time he cried and couldn't. He was aware his parents were throwing him a life preserver, and if he didn't grab on, he might go under. "I'm sorry. It's just, it's just, something I never expected."

"I know, Stevie, I know," said Mom. "And we threw it at you so suddenly..."

"No, no, Mom, it's great, it really is. Pop, thank you. And I'm ready. I'm ready to go *this minute!*"

Pop laughed at his enthusiasm, relief and hope moistening his eyes, and smiles and tears became unanimous. "Well, aren't we the happy trio," said Pop.

There was an immediate change in activity in Steven's room. Medical staff and military personnel appeared continuously. Steven wasn't merely being transferred to another hospital, he was being discharged from the military. Pop's estimate was optimistic, but in a week Steven was a civilian with an honorable discharge and on a train to New York City. This wasn't just a change of venue. For the first time in over a year Steven was on his own.

They stopped at their apartment to pick up some clothes for Steven. Uncle Eddie had installed a temporary ramp over the front steps in advance of Pop's more permanent renovation plans. The wheelchair fit easily through the front door, but the vestibule wasn't large enough to allow Steven to turn and open the door to the hallway. The three of them struggled, got through, navigated the hallway, elevator, and the door to their apartment, and were home.

Steven instantly recognized the unique smell and inhaled deeply. Mom put stuff away and filled a small suitcase with Steven's clothes. Pop stood by the credenza in the hallway, his traditional spot to look at the mail, sorting through a neat stack left by Uncle Eddie. He handed over a small pile addressed to Steven, a letter from Dartmouth, the usual junk mail, some solicitations from magazines. There were a couple of letters from the Department of Defense, the USMC, and one from a Boston law firm with an unfamiliar name. Steven's name and address were typed, but the zip code was handwritten. Each of the five numerals was a different color. Steven put the letter from the law firm on top of a small pile of pertinent mail, gave it to Mom to put in the suitcase. She hesitated, figured it out, and was happy for Steven.

Gail, almost through her coursework at Harvard Law, was interning with a high-profile Boston law firm. She managed to stay in the DC area for a week after Steven's arrival because the firm assigned her to take notes at Senate anti-mob hearings. The irony was not lost on Steven. But the meeting at the hospital in Bethesda was a positive experience in a dismal setting. Gail's hospital visits were upbeat, as if she sensed his core beliefs were altered by what he experienced in Vietnam. Or maybe she was willing to compromise her hardline positions.

And now he was propped up in bed at the Rusk Rehabilitation Hospital with her letter in his hands. *"Don't get ahead of yourself,"* he told himself, *"The reason she was in DC was to attend hearings on anti-mob legislation."* Hoping for a turning point, Steven opened the letter.

Dear Steven;

I've wrestled with this issue day and night for a week. Against my better judgement and contrary to professional ethics, I decided I could not keep this information from you. A file was put on my desk concerning an arson in Westchester. A post-it note on the folder said it might impact the anti-mob legislation I'm currently working on. There was a suspicious fire in an apartment house in the town of Mueller. There were only minor injuries to the residents, but a vehicle caught fire and exploded, killing the occupant. There is a suspect, and the footnotes cite investigations linking the family name, Catrone, to organized crime. One of the cross references is Masciarelli. The charge is expected to be changed from arson to murder. I couldn't leave you unaware. Our history runs way too deep. My entire career now depends on that history meaning as much to you as it does to me. Please tear up this letter and the envelope and burn it, or chew it up and swallow it, or whatever spies do, and pretend it never existed.
As always,
Love, Gail

Steven, also as always, reread the letter a few times, carefully refolded it, slipped it back into the envelope and put it in a manilla folder with Pop's drawings of the apartment remodel.

CHAPTER TWENTY-FIVE

LENNY AND JEAN

1971, Mueller NY and Darren NH

· · LENNY · ·

I called the number Gail gave me the night of the impromptu bridal shower and made an appointment for the following afternoon. I organized my closet and picked out khaki chinos and a white and brown tattersall shirt with a button-down collar. Gail stopped pretending she was concerned about my insurance.

"Wait. Were you really arrested for demonstrating?" I could handle her deceiving a freak in his underwear who hid the truth from his friends, but not the trusting souls of the commune. She was welcomed into our group largely because of her gallant exploit.

"Absolutely." She grabbed a framed photograph and pointed to a defiant young woman being shoved into a paddy wagon. "That's me."

"Not a great advertisement for a lawyer."

"It is if you fight for truth, justice, and the American way.

"Your law firm doesn't mind?"

"On the contrary. They have bigger fish to fry and believe I can help."

"Yeah, that's another question. Am I one of those fish?"

"It's up to you. You were a victim of arson, not a perpetrator. Your theory that Catrone was threatening you is circumstantial. It would do no good to call you as a witness."

"So how is it up to me?"

"Catrone's connections already got murder reduced to manslaughter, the whole thing could be reduced to a slap on the wrist. We want to use this as an avenue into the bigger picture of organized crime, in which case your testimony about falsified tax returns would be pertinent."

"You mean I'd have to testify against Vinny?" I felt my feet teetering on the edge of another abyss.

She flashed that half smile of hers, the eyes showing compassion, the mouth not joining in. "That's why it's up to you. You wanna' join the fight for truth, justice, and the American way?"

I couldn't decide if I liked her or not. She was quite attractive. I mulled over whether that should be a factor in my decision and came to the conclusion that it should. That half smile was kind of sexy. Wow - I hadn't had a sexy thought in weeks. My rehab's complete!

"So, Lenny, have you always had trouble staying focused, or just since the fire?"

"I'd like a little time before trying on a pair of concrete shoes for a dip in the East River."

"Do you have your checkbook?"

"Huh?"

"The legal profession is based on billable hours. I was given a few days here on the company's dime because I'm working on a case for them. For me to stay longer, I'd need an actual paying client. And possibly William."

"William! What does he have to do with this?"

"Not a thing. He asked me if insurance law was my specialty because that was the premise I used to get you to talk to me. It seems his wife's parents have hired a lawyer."

"That would be 'deceased' wife."

"He doesn't want to get into a fight with her parents, but their lawyer keeps hounding him with questions and issues he knows nothing about. William's not sure what to do. He needs a lawyer that represents *him*. One of our partners in the New York office specializes in insurance disputes, and he can bulldog it with the best. The two lawyers will hassle it out between themselves, allowing William to deal with his loss and his baby's health. Those are the important issues. Petty squabbles should be left to professionals, not someone as sincere, trusting, and loving as William."

So, the sarcastic hard-ass changes her colors, gets replaced by Ms. Geniality, and delivers an impassioned plea from the bottom of her heart. She's a chameleon, believable in any skin. I always thought chameleons were sexy, in an icy kind of way.

"Le-e-nn-y."

"Right, sorry. I didn't bring my checkbook. My parents live in town, I can get a check and come right back. How much do you charge?"

"I'll need a thousand-dollar retainer."

"Really? You mean the kind an orthodontist puts in your mouth?"

"My teeth are perfectly straight, thank you. The money goes into an escrow account. All I'm going to do is advise you on your options so I don't think we'll dip too deeply into the account, but I'll need the retainer to convince the home office I have a client. Do you think you could drag William down here? Another potential client would help sway them because insurance cases are very profitable. You could drop your check off then."

I flashed back to my failed negotiations with Beverly McClary on the sale price of the house. Two years at Team Sports, Inc. hadn't taught me a thing. The business major was a neophyte when it came to the real rat race. This wasn't even a negotiation; she was just bitch-slapping me into submission. Maybe she's a dominatrix...

"You know your money would last a lot longer if you could avoid these space-outs."

"Right. Will you be here tomorrow?"

"Between 10:30 and 3:00."

"I'll be here around 11:00, and I'll bring the check."

"Don't forget William. If he can come, make it 12:00 and we can have a working lunch."

She had a snappy answer for every clumsy question. I told myself it was because I wasn't quite out of my funk, and I'd be sharper tomorrow. "I'll see what I can do. I gotta' go before the meter runs out and my car gets towed."

She trumped that with her first full blown smile and a cheery "See ya' tomorrow!"

We met on the first floor of the office building at a place called Arnold's Lunch. Despite its name it was a grocery store, not a restaurant. There weren't many supermarkets in Manhattan, and most residents shopped in local stores like this one. Arnold's had a deli counter and four or five hightops without chairs justifying the 'Lunch' in its name. Two Greeks wearing torn t-shirts were squeezed behind the counter moving at warp speed. Whenever they passed each other, they had to turn sideways. One would frequently hustle into a back room and reemerge on the public side of the counter with an extension grabber to reach a box of cereal or pasta for a customer. I had roast beef and melted feta cheese on seeded rye with horseradish mayonnaise and washed it down with two bottles of Dr. Brown's Cream Soda. My appetite was returning along with my libido.

Gail's plan was to introduce William to her associate over lunch, after which they'd go to their respective offices with their respective clients. Her associate's name was Hal, and he was an overbearing speed freak. I thought William was going to bow out before taking a bite, but they bonded over their shared addiction to the New York Mets. Hal was a few years older than Gail and responsible for her being hired. He was building his resume and bank account in preparation for starting his own practice representing baseball players. He knew every trivial fact about every Met, which was not hard because they had only been in existence for ten years. They left before Gail and I finished, Hal's arm on William's shoulder, his other hand jabbing a finger at him.

I was quiet in the elevator, wondering if all of Gail's plans worked out as perfectly as this. Could she be as brilliant as Julie was beautiful, or as sexy as Sheila? When I gave Gail the check, she held it up and asked, "Is this a hardship for you?"

"I thought it was necessary."

"It was."

"Was?"

"Catrone's lawyers have filed for a continuance. They're asking for a change of venue."

"Why?"

"Apparently Mr. Catrone has moved to Rhode Island."

"Can they do that? The fire was in Westchester."

"They can try. I don't think they'll be successful, but you never know. Either way, it could be months before the court decides, even longer before you'll need my lawyerly skills."

I was stunned. "I can't believe he just up and left. Your other investigation is still going on, right? You'll still need me to testify?"

"Of course. He's still in the United States, and tax evasion is a federal offense. But my firm's gonna' wait to see how the arson case plays out, and that could take a while."

The check was still dangling between her thumb and forefinger. If I took it back there might be no reason for us to see each other again, and I didn't want that to happen. "But then I'd just have to give you another check."

"Right, but if you give me this one it's going to be cashed immediately and deposited in an escrow account. Your checking account will have 1,000 fewer dollars."

"I can live with that. I'm not sure, am I still your, I mean what should I tell, uh…"

"Look, Lenny, you did absolutely nothing wrong. You couldn't foresee what happened. People like Catrone often think their reputation is enough to stop people from crossing them. He certainly could have assumed that was the case, given his history with you. Until I showed up and mentioned his name you didn't know he was connected to the fire."

"I knew."

"Oh yeah? How about before the fire? Did you look behind every door when you entered a room, check your car every time you got in it for a punctured tire or a cut brake line?" She put the check down firmly on the desk in front of me. "Your friends are a special group Lenny, and you're an integral part of that group. Whose side do you think they'd take if the shit hit the fan, yours or some dirtbag criminal's? This is not free advice. I'm gonna' charge you for my time. I'm gonna' be available if you need me tonight, tomorrow, next month or next year. Put the check in your wallet. You can bring it back when you need me."

I looked in her eyes, smiled, gently pushed the check back and said, "Take the retainer. I don't want to jeopardize the high opinion your firm has of your ability. We all need you to keep fighting for truth, justice, and the American way."

Our eyes locked for a few seconds, she smiled that smile I was really beginning to like, and said, "We'll fight together."

· · **JEAN** · ·

The New York crowd drifted into Darren prior to the wedding day, either pitching a tent behind the barn or picking a stall to call their own for a few days. Giroux Plumbing & Heating Inc.'s offices had been moved to what used to be Lee's apartment. Lee now lived in the Stinson farmhouse in exchange for taking care of that property, and Uncle Guy wanted to be sure he didn't move back when the Stinson property sold.

The two stars of the show were Darren Elby Lipson and the Giroux homestead. The perfectly maintained barn housed two dozen chickens, the garden was filled with neat rows of vegetables, and a mammoth sow nursed five piglets in a fenced area alongside the barn. The hayfields were mowed a month previously and were growing back awaiting a second cutting in the fall. The New Yorkers frolicked in the fields and took walks through the surrounding forest.

Jean was nervous about how the New Yorkers would be received. Mom had handled the last-minute change in venue well, and the timing, as Jean suspected, was a huge relief for her and the kids. Darren Elby Lipson took care of the rest. He was now a few weeks past his original due date. As soon as that day passed, he went from surviving to thriving. He was a beautiful healthy baby, the perfect ambassador between the commune and the local friends and family of Jean and Marie. He was cooed to and admired by all. At the first hint of a cry he was snatched by an experienced mother or grandmother, hoisted against their shoulder, and either walked briskly while his back was patted or had a bottle put in his mouth. He was, like his dad William, a unifying force.

The focus shifted to Jean and Marie on the wedding day. The ceremony was sincere and homegrown, steeped in the simplicity of true love. It was the perfect antidote to the angst and grief of the preceding month. At dinner, William asked if he could say something.

"I sensed, during the past month, a hesitancy to show joy in my presence. It's as if you all feel it would increase my personal pain to see you happy, or be disrespectful to Bobbi if you laughed, had fun, showed your love in front of me. Nothing could be further from the truth. I am so grateful Jean and Marie were willing to share their love. We all need to revel in each other's joys, or all we'll have are the sorrows.

"A month ago, I lost the most wonderful thing in my life. These past few days reminded me that I didn't lose everything. This wedding, this place, all of you, are wonderful things I still have. It is my responsibility to myself and my son to focus on the wonders surrounding us. So, Jean and Marie, I thank you, and Darren Elby Lipson thanks you, from the bottom of our connected hearts. May all of us enjoy the beauty of your love forever."

Jean never bought into the male hugging fad, but this called for one, and he and William embraced. Marie was beaming through tears, which was the theme for everyone the entire weekend. But it was the following afternoon after most of the guests had gone when William uttered the rhetorical question that changed everything.

Four of the New Yorkers were sharing a goodbye doob with Jean and Marie at the back of the barn. The door was open all the way, framing the fields and forest. The barn sat on land that sloped down over the sixty-foot length of the building, so the front door was ground level and the back door was about ten feet off the ground. The six friends sat, legs dangling over the edge as they took in the scene, then William asked, "How could Mendocino be any nicer than this?"

It was a galvanizing moment. Sheila sat bolt upright and grabbed William's arm. Lenny and Gail spun their heads and gaped at one another. Jean squeezed Marie's hand. The newlyweds had long ago ruled out joining the exodus to Mendocino. Intrigued by the first two-thirds of the "Turn on, Tune in, Drop out" mantra, they had no interest in dropping out. If the commune settled here, they wouldn't have to.

CHAPTER TWENTY-SIX

STEVEN

1971, Rusk Rehab, Manhattan

There had been no contact with Gail since her letter about the fire. Periods of separation were the backdrop to their relationship, and Steven had no way of knowing if this was more of the same or the end. He did know he faced a formidable road ahead requiring all his focus.

His rehab at Rusk was grueling. He employed the strategy he shared with Gail on the path behind Uncle Murray's house, but the goals he allowed a few days to accomplish took weeks. It was not for lack of effort. His athletic ability and unwavering will awed the therapists, and his results drew astonished praise. Even so, it was weeks before he mastered getting from one place to another using specially designed crutches, and that was just to prepare for the next arduous step, a prosthetic lower leg.

Law school presented a different set of problems. New York City's well-intentioned solutions for the handicapped created as many issues as they fixed. Getting to and from classes was a logistical nightmare, and the wasted time and energy was anathema to someone with Steven's obsessive nature. He arranged to take correspondence courses through Dartmouth Law School. The internet was not yet viable, so the process was slow, but Steven managed to complete one semester during his rehab. Even if he was able to attend classes after the prosthetic was fitted, he was looking at another year or two. Becoming a lawyer was a small light at the end of a long tunnel.

The implementation of Pop's vision of an east coast gambling casino required thousands of hours delicately recruiting supporters in local and state government, some of whom might welcome bribes, some of whom might deem it criminal, and none of whom could be counted upon to get reelected. It required hundreds of thousands of dollars spent purchasing land suitable for development with no guarantee the land would be useful. They needed to set up legal protections and accounting procedures to avoid detection of money laundering. They had to publicly promote the economic benefits while downplaying the fear of organized crime. And there were the two wild cards, Vito and Vinny.

After Steven settled in at Rusk, Pop asked the floor manager for a room to hold a business meeting. "We're expanding our real estate business and I'd like Steven to be part of the meeting. He wants to join our company when he graduates from law school, and I think it would do him a world of good to feel like that's still possible."

"I couldn't agree more. Having a plan for the future has a huge effect on the success of rehab. You can use our staff meeting room."

A few days later, Steven was wheeled in and joined Uncle Eddie, Vito, and Pop. He was the only member of his generation present. Vinny had been arrested and charged with arson and manslaughter. He was out on bail, but it was deemed unwise for him to attend the meeting. Uncle Eddie's goal was to distance his family from the business, so Steven's other cousins were not involved. Pop got the meeting underway.

"I looked the room over thoroughly. I stressed the need for privacy to the floor manager, who made the room off limits to her staff for an hour. We should be able to speak freely here."

"Which we coulda' done at a thousand other places." Vito saw no reason for Steven's presence other than to stack the numbers against him.

Steven, in a ploy planned by Pop, set him straight. "I received information from a contact at the law firm prosecuting Vinny. They found a connection between our families."

Uncle Eddie said, "Wait! When you say 'families,' who are you talking about?" He was excluded from their ruse so his surprise would be sincere.

"As far as I know, Uncle Eddie, it's just the Catrones and the Masciarellis."

Vito was immediately suspicious. "Who the fuck are you to be getting inside information from the Feds? You're not a lawyer, you're a nobody."

"Some classmates who didn't go to 'Nam are lawyers now and keep in touch with me. One in particular feels bad about the price I paid for going, and he calls me frequently." Steven changed the gender and the circumstances, playing on Vito's pride in serving during World War II and his disdain for those who dodged the draft. It slowed Vito's attack, but just momentarily.

"Why did this draft dodger think you'd be interested? He's just baiting you for more info."

Pop jumped in and pretended to take Vito's side. "I'm with Vito on this one, son. It takes a lot of experience to know when you're being played. Did he give any reason why he thought you'd be interested?"

"He's investigating corruption in the NYPD and came across an old case involving Vito and Louise. Our name was in the record, and it's an uncommon name."

"He's just fishing," Vito said. But he was less combative. The Louise affair was a costly mistake. Vito didn't like thinking about it, let alone talking about it.

"You're probably right Vito," Pop said, "but if it's for real it could derail the progress we've made. You and Vinny lined up some great parcels of land in the Catskills, Eddie's got a shitload of politicians who owe him in Jersey, and we've got some leads in New Hampshire. We're getting close to the big payoff."

The four men sat quietly for a bit, Uncle Eddie and Vito thinking about what they just heard, Steven and Pop being patient. Finally, Pop said, "How about we make a plan just in case he's *not* fishing. If he is, great, we don't do anything. But if it's real, if an investigation is going to target us, we gotta' be ready to take action before it's too late."

"It may already be too late for the Catskills," Uncle Eddie said.

"Possibly," Pop responded. "We'd certainly have to remove Vinny immediately."

Vito leaped to his feet. "Are you putting out a hit on my son?"

"Of course not, Vito. He just can't be involved in the project in this state."

"I say we drop the Catskills entirely." Uncle Eddie was always in favor of damage control.

Vito was still standing, stalking menacingly around the room. "You're jumpin' ship as soon you can anyway. I don't give a flying fuck what you say."

Steven said, "We have a real estate company in Providence to oversee land acquisition and possible construction of a New Hampshire resort. If we can get Vinny out of New York it would be helpful to have one of us up there."

The value of relocation was something Vito understood, and he stopped pacing. Pop asked him, "Are you still connected up there?" Vito nodded, trying to figure out how best to proceed. Pop did it for him. "Let's say we drop the Catskills and concentrate on New Hampshire and Atlantic City. Vito, you work on getting Vinny, and probably yourself, situated in Providence. You two can control the real estate and construction businesses. Eddie stays in Jersey, Steven and I concentrate on New Hampshire, you and Vinny are ready to develop and build at whichever one comes through first."

"I like it," said Uncle Eddie. There was a hint of a smile on his face, and Steven thought, *"He just realized we staged this."*

Vito stopped pacing and said, "Look at my partners. A wimp who thinks he shits white, a guy whose father went to the loony bin and whose mother fucked a gun until she died, and whose son has no legs. I can't believe I'm still hooked up with you assholes."

Pop calmly said, "I suggest each of us use our contacts to check Steven's information. We'll meet here again in a week. Based on what we find, we'll either keep the status quo or implement the reorganization of the casino project."

"This place gives me the heebie-jeebies. I'm gonna' *need* a goddamned week before I come back." Vito grabbed his briefcase, which he never opened, and stormed out. The three men sat in silence, giving Vito time to get on the elevator.

Uncle Eddie stood up, smiled, and said, "Vito won't spend one second verifying your story. See you guys in a week."

CHAPTER TWENTY-SEVEN

TWO THUGS ON A THREE-DAY TRIP

Day 2, 1972, Darren NH

"Take it easy Fred," Joe said as he walked back upstairs, "C'mon up and tell us what the problem is."

Fred began pacing the room. "They've already got the papers they need, and there's enough stuff in them to kill the deal."

"We know that, Fred. That's why we're here, so the papers won't arrive at the meeting."

"You don't understand. They must have had some lawyer research every party in the contract. There's connections to the Mafia, records of bribes, records of ME bribing state reps. Some people were killed! I crossed the line for this deal. It's so big...it goes all the way to the state house, to the Governor's office. I'll be ruined, go to jail...we could all go to jail!"

Fred was no longer the smooth negotiator, no longer the confident, influential man who knew how everything worked. He was like every two-bit loser they dealt with in Brooklyn who realized he was in over his head and suddenly needed Joe and Moe to find a way out.

"Actually Fred, me and Joe won't go to jail, 'cause we didn't commit any crime." Moe's condescending tone was back. "Let's go over exactly where each of us stands. Joe and me, we're here to make sure the meeting happens without those papers, right?"

"Yes but..."

"So, all we need to concentrate on is the kid with the papers."

"But he's not gonna' drive to the high school anymore. They have a new plan."

"Do you know what the new plan is?" This time it was Joe, no condescension.

"Where's that map I gave you?" Fred was getting himself under control. He still faced a major problem, but now the three of them were looking for a solution together. Moe tossed the uneaten pizza and grinders in the trash and uncovered the map, and Fred continued, "See back here behind the athletic fields, there's a road." Fred's finger was behind the school.

"No there ain't," said Joe. "We drove up and down the side streets lookin' for one."

"It's not a public road, it's an old logging road, and it starts right here." Fred's finger was directly behind the high school, touching the edge of the forest.

"What the fuck is a logging road? And if it's there, why ain't it on the map?" Moe wasn't buying it.

Fred explained what a logging road is, then said as he moved his finger through the forest to the top of the map, "This one continues up, off this map onto another map, then goes right behind the commune."

Moe still wasn't buying it. "But you said you can't drive on it."

"Right, but you can snowshoe or cross-country ski on it."

Joe asked, "How far would it be from the commune to the high school along the logging road?"

"It's just a guess without the other maps, but I'd say five miles, maybe more."

"You're tellin' me some kid's gonna' wake up before dawn and slosh more than five miles through snow up to his asshole and get to the high school in time for the meeting?" Moe's skepticism was evident.

Fred was staring at the map, a faraway look on his face. "One of the kids living on the commune was the high school cross-country state champion two years in a row."

"So how long would it take *him* to get from the commune to the school?" Joe needed to know if their new plan was viable.

"More than two hours for most people, less for him. It's supposed to be clear tonight, and the moon's gonna' be half full. He could start before daybreak."

Joe leaned over the map and put his finger behind the high school where Fred first indicated the presence of a logging road. "And he has to come out here, right Fred?"

Fred raised his eyes to Joe's and said softly, "He's my nephew. I mean, he's not technically my nephew, but he calls me 'Uncle Fred' and everything. My wife's sister married his uncle, the one who came to the sports show with me."

"Does he have to come out here, Fred?"

"I've kept all this from her. I've lied to her...

"Listen to me, Fred. You've been dealing with Steven, right?" Fred nodded. "Call him now, tell him we're here with you. Tell him his plan to stage an accident is no longer possible because they're not driving to the high school anymore, then explain the logging road thing in detail, just like you told me and Moe."

"I know that path well, we can figure something out."

"We don't work for you, Fred. We only do what the person who hires us tells us to do." Fred did as he was told, then held the phone out. "Steven wants to talk to one of you."

Joe took the phone and Steven said, "You're gonna' have to surprise the kid before the end of the logging road. You have snowshoes in the gear we sent with you. They look like tennis rackets. They have straps that go around the boots to hold them on."

"You walk on the tennis rackets?"

"Yes. It's easier than it sounds. They help you get around in deep snow. Fred can show you how to use them. He sounds nervous. Can you trust him?"

Joe hesitated for a few seconds before answering. "We can handle it."

"Okay. I'm going to call Barry and tell him not to go up there. Keep in touch, even use the bag phone if you need to." Steven didn't like Joe's hesitation. He called Pop first.

"I don't like it either, son."

"They could just be nervous because of Vinny. You know they always avoid taking a job when he's involved."

"Or, Vito could be using them to set us up. Remember, they're his men, not ours." They discussed strategy, then Steven called Barry with a new set of instructions.

CHAPTER TWENTY-EIGHT

LENNY AND JEAN

1971, Darren NH and Mueller

· · LENNY · ·

There was a lively discussion at the back door of the barn after William's suggestion about trying the commune in Darren.

"We can do it!"

"Here?"

"Hell, yeah!"

"Wow!"

"How?"

Marie said, "We need to talk to Nancy, David, and Julie. They've seen Mendocino, and their hearts are set on going there."

We discussed all sorts of strategies before we left, the six of us bandying about the possibilities. I was amazed at how connected Gail was with the group after attending just one of our house parties (a muted one, given the circumstances) and the wedding weekend. I volunteered to drop her off on my way back to New York, bumping Sheila out of the Fiat and into Ricky and Marlene's Daily News truck. They drove it to the wedding so they could present the newlyweds with about a thousand linear feet of prime barn board.

The ride to Gail's apartment in Cambridge alternated between thoughtful silences and animated exchanges. "What a merry band of rascals you belong to Lenny. After all you guys have been through you still wanna' walk the walk. You were so cranked up about doing the commune at Jean and Marie's I almost wanted to join you."

"Your suggestions in the barn sounded like you already did."

"I'd love to visit, but that's all. My career consumes most of my time and energy."

"I hope we can pull it off," I said. "We came up with more potential problems than solutions. And Nancy and Nick, David and Julie, that's gonna' be a hard sell."

We were silent for a few miles, replaying some of the scenarios laid out in the barn. Gail thought we would be able to get the insurance company to replace the bus, and Jean had proposed we use it as a permanent comfort station so people would just need to build a place to sleep without kitchens or bathrooms. Marie said we could have a roadside stand selling all-natural veggies, eggs, and raw milk. Sheila wanted an arts and crafts section named "Bobbi's Hobbies."

Gail asked, "Do you think the communal gatherings will keep happening at your house in Mueller or shift to New Hampshire?"

"I don't know. Maybe both if the NH5 get on board and this becomes a reality."

"Well, Jean and Marie are in, William's inspirational, and Sheila could sell a steak to a vegetarian." Another stretch of silence, more private contemplations, then a surprise. "You and Sheila seem like more than just friends."

"We have been. It's kinda' off and on."

"Yeah, I've got one of those too. Where's yours at now?"

"Hard to say. What about you?"

"Not sure. Mine has legal complications. That's your exit up ahead, Sullivan Square."

She directed me to a brownstone on a side street, where the only spot to park was at a hydrant. I started past it thinking she might ask me in, but she said, "This is fine, you're just dropping me. Stay in touch. I hope to see you soon, up here or in Mueller."

I thought there was a bit of awkwardness in her voice, which I chose to interpret as disappointment. I wasn't disappointed, I was crushed, and spent the next four hours alone in my small Italian sports car trying to figure out why.

· · **JEAN** · ·

Relocating the commune to Darren met with considerable resistance. As Marie predicted, Nancy, David, and Julie had seen Mendocino and knew exactly what their dream looked like. Nick's objection centered around marijuana. Mendocino and nearby Humboldt County were the epicenter of marijuana's popularity. Many of the locals grew their own, it was widely accepted, some strains becoming national favorites. The climate, environmentally and culturally, was way more conducive to the communal lifestyle than northern New Hampshire. Opposing factions developed, and the divide threatened to undermine the communal spirit. The feel-good vibes from the wedding weekend were losing steam.

In the weeks following the wedding, Jean detected a difference in Sheila. She seemed to exhibit a more measured approach. Jean attributed some of the change to the tragedy of Bobbi's death. He knew first-hand how that forced a person to grow up quickly, and increased maturity was one way to describe the change in Sheila. She was also spending a lot of time with William, offering support and encouragement. They were together more often each time Jean saw them. When the two of them entered a room pushing Darren in a stroller they resembled a family unit. Bobbi's leadership role was increasingly being filled by Sheila, and Jean reluctantly had to admit she was doing a fine job. But the group was stuck in a stalemate.

William and Jean formulated a compromise solution and decided a change of scenery was in order. The next meeting should be a weekend party at Lenny's to try and recapture some of the magic and momentum. They would propose their plan then. Sheila agreed a party was just what everyone needed and set the ball in motion.

Since William and Sheila were viewed as leaders of the relocate-to -New-Hampshire faction, Jean was selected to present the plan. After the customary warm-up period, the energy started to build and Jean announced he had something to say to everyone. He sat in William's traditional chair at the cosmic formica table, and everyone gathered around.

"We all know we're having a hard time deciding where we should go from here. I have an idea that might resolve some of the differences. Gail confirmed the insurance company will pay Lenny for the bus, which will allow us to buy another one."

"A Greyhound," interrupted an excited Ricky. "There are six brand spanking new Greyhound buses that were submerged for three days last month when a river in West Virginia flooded the dealership's lot. The engines and electrical systems are fried, and the insurance company just declared them totaled. You can have one at no cost if you get it off their lot before the end of the month."

Lenny asked, "Are they worth anything?"

"No, but one will be as soon as I get it running."

Jean didn't mind the interruption. The bus was not a bone of contention, and fit both plans. Everybody laughed at Ricky's exuberance, and cheered when he jumped back up and added that the Greyhounds had a bathroom and AC. It brought back a bit of the euphoria from the test drive the night before the fire. "Okay," Jean continued, "either way, we'll have one. My understanding of the original plan was that some of you would take the bus to Mendocino, spend the summer checking it out, and if it was as good as you hoped, the rest of the crew would follow.

"There's a spot at the edge of the woods behind the hayfield that my dad and Uncle Guy cleared for our Cub Scout den to have campfires. When we were older, our Boy Scout troop leveled spots inside the woods for tents so we could do sleepovers. I'm thinking we could park Ricky's super deluxe Greyhound bus where the campfire site was, renovate it into a kitchen with bathrooms, and use the tent sites for small cabins to sleep in."

Jean took a breath and looked around. Everybody seemed tuned in, though Nancy had a skeptical tilt to her stance. *'Keep going,'* he told himself, *'don't give her a chance to object.'* "But we gotta' get started now. There's still some time before winter to get ready for spring. By this time next summer, you'll either give up on the idea of a commune or have a year of successfully living on one under your belt and be ready to take the highway west to Mendocino. The only difference is the trial period will be here."

Jean looked around. There was a lot of head nodding, a few people exchanging positive remarks. But Nancy was unmoved.

"I don't need a trial period. I've seen Mendocino, and it's fucking awesome. I'm ready to go right now."

Taken aback by the blunt rebuttal, Jean gathered his thoughts and said, "I understand, Nancy. But isn't that exactly how you felt when you first came back from Mendocino?"

"Yeah, so?"

"So, you understood for some of us it'd be a huge leap of faith to uproot our lives and go to a place we've never even seen. You were considerate enough to alter your plans."

"So, you want me to be considerate for another year?"

"If you feel you need to go now, I understand. But if we decide the best thing for this group is to try a year in New Hampshire, we stand a much better chance of succeeding with you contributing. If it wasn't for the fire, you'd all be in Mendocino now, thanks mostly to you."

Nancy was still sullen but disarmed by Jean's flattery. "It may be the best plan for the group, but not for me." She managed a small smile. "I need to think on it a bit."

Sheila said, "We love you, Nancy, we're a hundred percent behind you whatever you do."

Marie fired up a joint and said, "Here's to love, Cuz!"

The love continued through the weekend. Some New Hampshire friends were intrigued enough at the wedding to make the journey to Lenny's. They were a bit overwhelmed by the New Yorkers at full strength on their own turf, but a good time was had by all, and a few said they were considering joining the experiment. Some of Lenny and Sheila's peripheral friends also talked about going from part timers to full timers. Jean and Marie both thought Nancy was starting to lean toward staying, their hunch reinforced when Ricky and Nick left early on Sunday, drove to West Virginia, rented a mammoth tow truck, and brought the Greyhound back to Nancy's. Jean considered the weekend a huge success, another in his string of personal victories.

During autumn and winter, things continued to fall into place. William, Sheila, and Darren, now definitely a family unit, moved into the farmhouse. Marie got William on the list for substitute teachers in her district, and Sheila hooked up with an improv comedy troop that performed at Lake Region resorts in the summer, and ski areas and New England colleges during the school year.

Lenny rented out his home in Mueller, took a room at the farm-house, and Jean got him a Graduate Assistant position at Plymouth State so he could take courses for free while studying for the CPA exam. He and Gail seemed to be an item as well, though Marie said that whenever she asked Gail about it she'd say her previous relationship was long, complicated, and intense, and she wasn't ready for another one. Whenever she broached the subject to Lenny he came up with some clever joke and changed the subject, but his tacit acceptance of the Sheila-William link was telling.

Weekends were packed, as New Yorkers showed up and joined in the effort to beat the onset of winter. They built a woodshed near the site where the bus would park, then started filling it with firewood. They built small enclosures on the tent sites, just big enough for a bed, some shelves, and a wood stove. The bus, once roadworthy, was driven to the spot behind the barn. The two stalls that were the old office in the barn were already insulated and heated and were converted for overflow sleeping during the winter.

New fences were added to pen more farm animals, and a section was set up for a milk cow under the back of the barn. Because of the slope of the land, it was at ground level. Jean purchased a pregnant cow through the Weekly Market Bulletin, a newsletter published by the New Hampshire Department of Agriculture listing items wanted and for sale, such as tools, farm animals, feeders, and waterers. She was half Jersey, a breed known for rich milk, and half Black Angus, known for beef. Her calf was due in the spring, could be raised for beef, and she would provide enough milk and dairy products for the commune with some left over for the envisioned farm stand. Sheila named her Sexy Sadie and went down to the barn to sing that little-known Beatles' song to her a few times each day.

Giroux Plumbing and Heating continued its growth. Nick was now a full-time plumber and would often take an apprentice or two to a job without Jean or Uncle Guy. Nancy had her own desk in the addition that used to be Lee's apartment, and Jean and Uncle Guy were considering hiring an assistant secretary.

The experimental commune was going so well there was talk about not bothering with Mendocino at all and making this the commune's permanent home. Jean and Marie thought about starting a family, and Marie scheduled an appointment with Dr. K. to discuss getting off birth control pills. Then one Saturday morning in late winter, the hammer came down.

Jean was in the barn putting together a brooder box. Marie ordered three dozen day-old chicks from the local feed store to be delivered in early spring, and the brooder box had to be ready. He assembled four 2 x 8's into a square and set a tin washtub with a hole cut in its bottom upside down on four bricks in the middle of the square. The hole was for an electric cord so a lightbulb could hang inside. The chicks could huddle under the tub, the lightbulb providing warmth for the first few days. The bricks kept the washtub rim a few inches off the floor, allowing space for the chicks to go under or away from the tub, regulating the heat as needed. Jean was just securing the bulb when Uncle Guy walked in.

"Hey, Jean. Got some day-olds coming?"

"Yeah, maybe in a week or so. Marie just ordered 'em."

"I got some news from Fred. The buyers are exercising their option to purchase."

Jean stood up. "The Stinson property?"

"And ours."

"I don't want to sell ours. They can have the Stinson's."

"They need it all. We agreed…"

"I never agreed."

"Yes, you did. The option's on both because they need the road through our property."

"I don't give a shit what they need. I never agreed to sell our property."

"It's in there, Jean. Maybe you didn't read every word of the small print."

"Then we need a lawyer."

"I don't. You may not agree now, but in the long run it's the best…"

"Show me the contract."

"I don't have it. Fred does."

Jean brushed past Uncle Guy, out of the barn and over to his house. He stormed into the kitchen where Marie, William, and Lenny were having breakfast. "Did Gail show up last night?"

"No," Lenny answered, "she had to work late. She should be here any time now."

Marie could tell something was up. "What's wrong?"

"Uncle Guy just told me the people who have an option on Stinson's place want to buy it now, and the contract I signed includes our back parcel."

William said, "Did he show you the contract?"

"He doesn't have it, Uncle Fred does. I'm gonna' go get it so Gail can look at it."

"I'll get it," said Marie. Jean was clearly agitated, and Marie wanted to avoid a confrontation between the two men.

"I can handle it," snapped Jean.

"I know you can, Smooch. But I'm just sweet little Marie, and I can handle it easier. You fill Gail in on the background if she shows up before I get back."

By the time Marie returned with the contract, Gail and Sheila were taking turns playing peek-a-boo with Darren. Gail took out a variety of markers, put on her glasses and scanned the first few pages before looking up at her anxious audience. "Okay, so this is a boiler-plate contract, meaning it's non-specific enough to be used for a variety of agreements. It is binding, but I don't believe it came from a law firm, most likely the realtor. Somebody just hit a button on a copier and this popped out. It is already sloppy enough to be challenged, but unless I can find something in the amendments specific to this particular deal, all that'll do is buy some time."

"To do what?" Jean was agitated. What if he had inadvertently signed away the land?

"Postpone the closing, make it so annoying and expensive the buyer looks for another property." Gail had resumed scanning, was making occasional checks with different colored markers, when suddenly her face went white, and she sat back in her chair. "I, I can't...shit. I'm not gonna' be able to help, I..." She stood up, now fully crying, and sobbed, "I'm sorry," then rushed outside.

Everyone looked at Lenny, who turned his palms up and shook his head slowly in bewilderment. Sheila looked at William, who had a "don't ask me" expression on his face. She stood up and said, "Men! You guys are pathetic." She stormed out after Gail. Marie quietly got up and followed. They were gone for about thirty minutes, which seemed like hours to the three men. They sat in silence, reminding Jean of when Aunt Yvette tried to stir the four Girouxs back to life in this very kitchen the morning after his father died.

When the three women returned Gail's eyes were red and a weak smile was barely hanging on. "Sorry about that. I saw a name in the contract that threw me. I need to straighten something out, something that's been hanging over my head for a few years. My two best friends here convinced me I need to face it head on and deal with the consequences. I'm okay now, I just needed a little psychological counseling."

"We're a psychological counseling *team*, sister," said Sheila, "I'm the psycho, you're the logical, and Marie's the counselor!"

CHAPTER TWENTY-NINE

STEVEN

1971, *Brooklyn NY*

Vito and Vinny were doing everything possible to drive Steven crazy. The arson was bad enough, but within three months of moving to Rhode Island they were accused of bribery and extortion. They ran into a snag getting approvals for a property in New Hampshire and bribed a town official to push it through. Fortunately for Vinny, out on bail for arson, the charges were never pursued. When Pop and Steven visited Massachusetts Rehabilitation Hospital in Boston to look at prosthetics they met with Vito and Vinny in Providence on their way back.

"The two of you know," Pop said, "how important it is to keep your noses clean."

Vito was dismissive. "That prick was lower than an alderman in Flatbush, and he thinks he's the President of the United fucking States. He's a nobody."

"Nothin' happened," was Vinny's attempt at defending himself. "No charges, no nothin'."

Steven tried again. "What we're getting at is everybody knows everyone else's business up there, and now *our* business has a black mark. Those people don't forget. It's imperative that we stay squeaky clean from here on out, or we'll be down to just New Jersey."

It wasn't long before Steven's words proved prophetic. Vinny and Vito managed to get the contract for a high-profile project in the

White Mountains to reestablish their reputation. But the project managers heard about the issues on the previous job and fired them. Pop was getting nervous about letting Vinny and Vito handle New Hampshire, and arranged for Steven's final fitting for the first prosthetic to coincide with a sporting goods show in Boston. Vito was overseas working on a smuggling deal, so Steven, Pop, and Vinny met with a realtor and his brother-in-law, a plumber who had worked on the high-profile project before Vito's man was fired. The realtor, Fred, was well connected on many levels. It was a perfect match, the meeting was progressing smoothly, then Vinny acted like a stooge in a bad gangster movie and scared the two men away.

Steven was seething on the way home, but Pop was pragmatic. "We'll wait a couple weeks, then you'll give the plumber a call. He liked you, even knew about your baseball career at Dartmouth. We'll play good cop-bad cop, and you'll explain away Vinny's aggressive behavior. It's not a bad thing if they're afraid of us." Steven's anger subsided, and he began planning his call to explain Vinny's behavior. Pop instinctively knew what Steven was thinking. "Not yet. We'll know when the time is right."

Steven was reminded of Mom saying she'd know when it was the right time to call and arrange another visit to Long Island. Where did this parental wisdom come from? Steven was beginning to doubt he would ever have the opportunity to find out. This was the longest time he and Gail went without any contact. Was this the end? Would he ever find someone willing to take on the complicated package that was Steven Masciarelli? It felt like the person who spent that idyllic summer visiting Martha's Vineyard was somebody else. The tour of duty in Vietnam was transformative, losing his legs a catastrophic exclamation point. The pace only quickened when he returned to civilian life. The gambling casino project was in the crucial stages, and Vito and Vinny weren't making it any easier.

Steven *was* able to placate the plumber and Fred, assuring them they would be dealing exclusively with him, not Vinny, and there would be no physical harm inflicted on anybody. Masciarelli Properties prepared preliminary drawings of a stately New England resort featuring outdoor recreational opportunities in the White Mountains, with unusually large lobbies and ballrooms which could easily be converted to casinos. Only Fred knew about the conversion plan. Meanwhile, he was rounding up contacts in the state legislature to push legalized gambling.

Fred knew of a property that wasn't officially for sale but was promising. They were able to secure the property, leasing it with an option to buy. They enticed Fred's state and local contacts to prepare a bill legalizing gambling in New Hampshire, and initiated a lobbying plan to enact it before the option ran out. Running that campaign was a job Pop wouldn't trust to anyone else, so he and Steven added it to their already full plates.

Las Vegas conjures images of glitz, glamor, gambling, and sexy showgirls. New Hampshire conjures red and black checked flannel, John Deere hats with earflaps, and white church spires rising above colorful fall foliage. The two locations couldn't be more different. But New Hampshirites possess a stubborn streak of independence, a willingness to swim against the tide if that's the direction they want to go, dating back to colonial days. When Steven discovered all thirteen colonies relied on government sponsored lotteries to help fund their needs, he thought it would be clever to use that fact in their pitch to legalize gambling. Further research revealed it became a rallying cry in 1769 when a very unpopular decision by the king rescinded the colonies' right to hold those lotteries.

A new source of state funds was the main reason New Hampshire was now considering legalized gambling. But even the staunchest traditionalists harbor a soft spot for glitz, glamor, gambling, and sexy showgirls. Cloaking all of the above in a centuries-old tradition of government-sponsored gambling, plus sticking it to the erstwhile evil King of England, made it a much easier sell. The support was growing steadily. It was still backroom talk, but the train to glory was gathering speed. Their next step was to get the resort approved *without* the casino conversion, and they were on the docket for an upcoming meeting of the Darren Planning Board. Then Steven got a phone call from Fred.

"We have a problem, Steven. A lot of townspeople are going to show up at the Planning Board meeting to try and block approval of the sale of the property."

"Why?"

"The eventual purpose of the resort leaked out."

"How?" Steven didn't really care. He was neither surprised nor angry with Fred. What Steven wanted to know was if Fred was still all in, and how he planned to handle the glitch.

"I guess it was inevitable," Fred answered. "As more people came on board, things were said to certain people that shouldn't have been said."

"Do you know any of those 'certain people'?"

"Of course."

"How about the locals who plan on blocking the sale?"

"I know them, too."

"What's your opinion?"

"That depends. Are you ready to go public with your casino plans?"

"Not yet." Steven wanted the state to enable casinos first, then

Masciarelli Properties would compete fairly for the right to build one. He didn't think there was a plan as ready as his. "Is anybody else doing what we are?"

"No."

"Would you know if they were?"

"Absolutely." There was no hesitation from Fred.

"I've been to a few of these types of meetings, Fred, and found board members are not fond of New York lawyers showing up to bully their project through. I'd rather not get into a pissing contest with the board. Are all our ducks in a row?"

"Yes."

"Then just make sure the yeses are solid."

"They are, but I'll check and make sure."

Steven was reassured by Fred's decisive, positive answer, which he relayed to Pop when they discussed the phone call. Nevertheless, Pop decided to have a couple of Vito's men go to New Hampshire in case they were needed. Then an unforeseen storm, an unlikely coincidence, and Vinny's ego threw the whole plan out of whack.

When Vito's men reached New Hampshire they ran into a snow squall and went off the road. They called Fred and said they wouldn't be able to make it. Fred called Steven for advice but both he and Pop were out of the office, so Fred left a message with the answering service, stressing it was urgent. The operator forwarded the call to Vinny, who returned Fred's call himself. Vinny took the opportunity to reestablish his importance by implying *he* was the one sending two guys up there, and *he* would make sure they got their asses to Fred's house *or else*.

The next phone call from New Hampshire came from Vito's men, who put Fred on the phone because the hippies changed their plan. So now Steven was dealing with a skittish Fred who was clearly shaken by the last-minute change of plans, and Vito's men had sounded hesitant when pressed if Fred could be trusted. They had a long history of dependability, but Pop's mistrust of Vito cast doubt on them. Also, they usually managed to avoid any job involving Vinny, but now had no choice. Steven and Pop thought that might tighten the screws on them enough to influence their judgement if an obstacle arose.

"One of us has to be there," Pop said. "I'll send you with a driver and a couple of our guys."

"Barry Longo's already there. If Marco's the driver, I won't need anybody else. I don't want to cause a scene if it isn't necessary."

"Good idea. What were Longo's instructions?"

"I gave him a new set after that last phone call. He's willing to go the extra mile."

"He should be. You saved his skin plenty of times. I'll call Marco, you start packing," said Pop. "You're gonna' have to drive through the night."

CHAPTER THIRTY

THREE-DAY TRIP FOR TWO THUGS

Day 2, 1972, Darren NH

Moe and Joe went into town after the phone call with Steven and purchased a spool of wire at a hardware store, then a linesman's pliers, a hammer, and fencing staples at a different hardware store to avoid suspicion. That afternoon they tried out the snowshoes in Fred's backyard. Moe slipped out of one immediately, his foot sinking hip deep into the snow. After a half hour of practice, they managed to tromp around effectively.

They packed their stuff and laid out the winter gear, no longer skeptical of its usefulness. They tested the pay phone in the Cumberland Farms parking lot where they would call Steven tomorrow on their way out of town and got a dial tone. They were not about to try the soggy pizza or soft grinders again, so they did a drive-thru at McDonalds, went past the high school and timed the trip from there to Fred's. They laid out the map, and with Fred's help picked a spot about a half mile up the logging road from the high school. They needed enough time to snowshoe up in the dark, set the wire across the logging road at knee height, and await the skier. It was also important to minimize the amount of time sitting in snow in freezing temperatures, so they worked backward and decided on a 4:00 am departure for a 6:00 am ambush.

Fred was sitting near a window in the hallway outside his bedroom. He was certain this was his last day on Earth. The only question was whether he would be forgiven for his sins and granted a chance to leave Purgatory. His wife left earlier, leaving him alone except for Moe and Joe, who were in his office over the garage. He strained to hear the sound of the door at the bottom of the office stairs open and shut, signaling the departure of the two men.

Earlier that evening he had told his wife everything. All the blood drained from her face and she slapped her hands over her chest. She was a physically strong woman, but the news was so staggering her knees buckled and she struggled to stay upright, collapsing into an armchair. Fred thought she was having a heart attack, but her anger overcame her shock, and she bolted upright and started pacing. She talked but wouldn't look at him.

"So, they're going to ambush Jean, take the papers, leave him to die on the logging road."

"They assured me they wouldn't kill him."

His wife heard him but kept on talking, needing to figure things out by herself. "They can't let Jean go if he can identify them. Once they have the papers they'll kill Jean, then get away."

"No, they're going to jump him from behind, make it look like a skiing accident, take the papers and leave. By the time he comes to and gets into town the meeting will be over and they'll have no papers." Fred was repeating what Moe and Joe told him after the phone call with Steven. He needed to believe them, so he did. His wife had no such delusions. She ignored Fred again, just kept telling herself the facts to make sure she had them right.

"This is because Jean doesn't want to sell his farm and has papers with information that would kill the deal." She stopped and asked, "Does my brother Lee know all this?"

Fred nodded.

"And Guy?"

"He doesn't know."

She was pacing and talking again. "The two of you were willing to do this to get the money. You and Lee are in this together, against Jean."

"Not anymore. Listen to me, we can stop them. Lee knew about the commune having incriminating papers because he's friends with them and told me about it because he wants the deal to go through. Guy doesn't know about this part of it. He and Jean haven't said a word to each other since Jean found out about the sale. Guy just thinks the board will uphold the contract and the sale will go through." His wife stopped pacing and looked at Fred as if she'd never seen him before. She nodded slowly to herself, and sadness overcame Fred. "It's all me, honey. I'm the devil. Lee's at fault too, but only because I used him. When he found out the buyers were Mafia and people would get hurt, he couldn't go through with it."

She backed away from Fred, felt behind her for the chair, and fell back into it. Her breathing was shallow and rapid. Fred stepped toward her, she put up her hand, and he stopped. She said, "I'm leaving." Fred came closer, she put her hand up again. "No. I'm leaving now and going to Yvette's. We'll have a family meeting; me, Yvette and Guy, Jean and Marie, she's part of the family now. And Lee, even if I have to drag him there myself."

"And me."

She stood back up. "No. I can't bear them looking at you like you're a criminal. You stay here. We'll come up with a plan."

"I am a criminal. I bribed town and state representatives, broke every real estate regulation. But I can help. I know all about…"

"No. I'll call you from Yvette's. Stay by the phone."

Fred didn't know what to do once he was alone. He paced, looked at his watch, sat, looked at his watch, got up and paced again. He wanted to go to his office, but Moe and Joe were there. He loved the office, loved sitting in the chair by his desk. He often went there even when he had no work to do. He visualized it now, imagined himself looking at the crucifix and the Popes, trying to extract some long-distance comfort. They hadn't offered much lately, and this evening was no exception. He looked at his watch. She had been gone eleven minutes. He walked to the phone, willing it to ring. It was almost two hours before it did.

"Are the killers still there?" There was no greeting from his wife.

"Yes."

"The minute they leave call the Stinson's. We have a plan. Don't fall asleep."

"Okay. Should I bring anything?" She was no longer there. She hung up before he said 'Okay.' Fred slid a chair over to the hallway window so he would hear the door, turned off the light so he couldn't be seen, and waited for them to leave.

· · STEVEN · ·

Steven loved Marco. A freshman on the varsity during Steven's senior year, Marco was a huge defensive lineman who ate opposing quarterbacks for lunch every Saturday afternoon. He was the main reason James Madison won another championship before Steven graduated. He also took everything literally. Pop told him he was going to New Hampshire, so he showed up in front of their apartment just before midnight wearing overalls and a sweater, a black baseball cap with "Stihl Chainsaws" in orange across the front, and knee-high fishing boots. Steven imagined Barry Longo, already in Darren, New Hampshire, probably wearing an iridescent purple shirt, tight pants, and shiny black boots with a zipper on the side. He smiled as he realized these were his soldiers. He was leading his men into possible combat, like in Vietnam. He had complete faith in two of them but, because of Vito and Vinny, a tad less in the other two.

They cruised quickly out of the city, six hours of dark empty road ahead. Steven's bag phone was charged and ready. He imagined the possible scenarios. They'd call his bag phone, thinking Steven was still in Brooklyn, and say they ambushed the hippie and have the papers. He would ask for details and decide whether he could take them at face value, had to see for himself to verify or, worst case, intervene. Barry was there with two sets of instructions, depending on how it played out. If physicality was required, he had Barry and Marco.

There was one nagging detail. After Vinny was indicted for arson, he and Pop considered replacing Masciarelli Properties with a dummy corporation to obscure their relationship. They kept watching for a sign that the investigation of Vinny had expanded into organized crime, as Gail's letter suggested, but that never happened. Why not? Pop thought it was because she was afraid her letter to Steven could be used to cause a mistrial and possible disbarment, and "Masciarelli Properties" on the Stinson contract would deter Gail from pursuing further litigation. Steven wasn't so sure Gail would be scared away.

· · UNCLE FRED · ·

Fred dozed through the opening and closing of the door but was awakened by their car starting and looked at his watch. It was 4:04 am.

He called the Stinson house and his wife picked up before the end of the first ring.

"Are they gone?"

"Yes."

"Put your cross-country ski stuff in the back of the pickup and come to the Stinson house as fast as you can."

Fred thought he was going to have a chance to redeem himself, to save the day, go out in a blaze of glory. When he arrived at the Stinson's he pictured the assemblage inside, fearful of the reception he was about to receive. He steeled himself and entered a large multi-purpose room that was common in many partially modernized farmhouses. Except for Marie, all the people his wife mentioned were standing around a long narrow wooden table with a few mismatched chairs and a stool. Fred was startled by the resemblance to The Last Supper. He was Judas, prepared for accusations, hoping for a chance at redemption.

In addition to the family members there were some kids from the commune. The young man who lost his wife and gave the emotional speech at the wedding was there. He had seen another, the guy in the University of Michigan hat, around town a few times. He didn't recognize the woman standing next to him, who was clearly in charge of the proceedings.

· · GAIL · ·

"I'm Gail," she said. "We're waiting for Marie to return with the copies." Gail was dressed in ski clothes, jacket unzipped, cross-country boots on her feet.

Fred reflexively tried casual conversation. "So you cross-country ski?"

"I learned in Vermont. It's how I train for the Boston Marathon."

"Really? I didn't think women could run that far."

"Yeah, well, neither did the Boston Athletic Association."

Marie burst through the door with packets of paper in her hand and gave them to Gail like a soldier reporting to her commanding officer. "Sorry. The copy machine kept jamming. I called Nancy and she talked me through it. Here's the original contract between the Giroux family and Masciarelli Properties, a list of complaints and criminal charges against officers of Masciarelli Properties including a fatal arson, a list of state legislators and town officials offered bribes, the petition to vote "No" signed by 10% of registered voters, and two copies of each."

"Are we going to overpower Moe and Joe?" Fred needed an opportunity to prove himself.

"No," said Gail. "They're professionals, we'd have no chance. We're gonna' make them think they succeeded, and hope they'll be outa' town with the bogus copy by the time one of us presents the Planning Board with the real one."

Fred was going to have to be happy with a supporting part in the plan. He and Guy, Yvette, and Gail were going to ski behind Lee at a safe distance. Yvette, the emergency room nurse, stuffed as many medical supplies as she could into her backpack. Guy and Fred shared the pieces of a Ski Patrol stretcher kit. Lee, given the starring role as the decoy since he looked the most like a hippie, would let himself be ambushed. He took one set of the copies, pushed them into his pocket leaving an obvious bulge. Gail zipped the real documents into an inside pocket of her ski jacket and gave Jean the other copy. He would drive it to the high school as originally planned. If the worst happened on the trail, Jean could validate the copy. As soon as the hitmen left the ambush site, Gail would race to the high school with the original documents. She had skied the road a couple of times with Jean, who added a last-minute suggestion.

"The final mile is crisscrossed by snowmobile trails. Once you pass the ambush site, take any of them to the left. They all lead to the high school, so you'll be able to avoid the hitmen."

"Once I pass Lee, any left. Got it. Everybody ready?" Unanimous nods. "Let's rock and roll."

· · STEVEN · ·

It was ten minutes before seven, but the school lot was already filling up and people were standing around the entrance despite the early morning cold and some flurries. Steven got the call just as Marco was pulling into the parking lot.

"I see Mr. Longo's car," said Marco.

"Make sure he sees us, then swing around and park back by the entrance," said Steven as he answered the phone.

"We got the papers," said Moe, "no way the hippie's getting outa' these woods alive. We're ditching stuff and getting the fuck out of this piece of shit town."

"Aren't you going to stop back at the contact's home to make sure it's clean?"

"We did that before we left this morning."

Steven needed them to be between Fred's and the high school in case he had to use his contingency plan. "It was dark, you may have missed something. They'll all be at the meeting. Check again."

There were a couple seconds of silence before Moe said, "Okay."

It's the Vinny factor, thought Steven, *making them anxious to be done with this job. Too anxious. I'll have to make sure myself.* Steven pretended not to notice the hesitation. He said, "Great. Nice job. See ya' when you get back to Brooklyn," and hung up.

"Everything okay?" Marco could tell it wasn't.

"I'm not sure." Gazing out to the athletic fields, Steven noticed something. "I need to check something out. Go a little closer to the school."

As they got closer, he made out the object that had caught his eye. It was a pair of skis leaning against the side of the school next to a set of blue doors. Steven pieced together a very disturbing scenario. He had spent his high school years going between locker rooms and athletic fields and was certain those blue doors led into the locker room, and from there to the gym where the meeting was being held. In Brooklyn they were always locked, openable only from the inside by pushing down on a bar. But people were less concerned with security in New Hampshire. He looked past the school to the forest behind it, trying to see if there were tracks, but couldn't see through the snow. He focused again on the skis, then recognized them. They were his Hanukah present to Gail when they took their first trip to Burke Mountain.

Steven told Marco to stop and called Pop. He filled him in, and Pop said, "That's it. The gloves are off, and Vito just threw the first punch. Give Longo the signal."

Steven turned to Marco. "I need to go inside. Be prepared for anything Marco, we're playing on their home field." When Steven walked past Longo's car he slowed, dropped a crutch, picked it up and continued. Barry Longo started his car.

· · TWO THUGS, DAY 3 · ·

Moe and Joe went back to Fred's house. They did a twenty-minute cursory recheck and left. It was starting to snow, and they didn't want to get stuck again. They both knew the only reason they went back at all was so neither of them would have something over the other if they didn't. They were partners, but when push comes to shove the only one you can trust is yourself.

They were glad to be going down Mountain Road for the last time. They were pleased with themselves for overcoming so many obstacles and getting the job done. The folks in Brooklyn were pleased, and they would be handsomely rewarded.

As they approached a curve, Moe put his foot on the brake and it went all the way to the floor. A large sedan raced alongside and forced them off the road. The Jeep went over the snowbank and into the forest where it pin-balled off three large trees before landing on its roof.

The sedan, with only minor damage along one side, continued to the next driveway and pulled over. Barry Longo got out and hustled to the crash site, scrambled over the snowbank, and approached the Jeep cautiously. He could see the driver's head, bent at an impossible angle at the neck. The windshield was gone, as was the passenger. Longo pulled his gun out of his jacket pocket, scanned the area, saw an arm reaching out of the snow. Approaching cautiously, he checked the body, felt no pulse, searched the pockets and took the packet of papers, then went back to the Jeep to look at the exposed underside. The cut in the brake line was visible. He grabbed a large branch and wedged it into the line, roughing up the cut and making it appear as if the branch broke the line. He reached through the broken window in the rear door and carefully extricated the bag phone, then jogged back to the sedan and headed to Cumberland Farms.

· · **STEVEN** · ·

Steven hobbled into the school on crutches and his one prosthetic as briskly as possible and stood by the open doors to the gym. He heard a loud cheer followed by enthusiastic applause, saw Gail shoot her arms over her head and meet a guy doing the same as he bounced down the bleachers, and recognized his face from the employee's handbook of Team Sports, Inc. He was the one Vinny tried to scare with the fire. They clasped hands and jumped up and down, then hugged, then kissed. Turning to other people, their backs to Steven, arms around each other's waist, Gail's hand slipped down to his butt and gave it a squeeze, then returned to rest on his hip.

As they left the parking lot, Marco pointed to the woods behind the school. Emergency vehicles were there, and people were scurrying around, two carrying what looked like a stretcher. Moe's report ran through Steven's head, "... *no way the hippie's getting outa' these woods alive*" and his blood turned cold. The same could have been said about him when he was lying on the jungle floor with his legs half gone. The only difference was instead of a helicopter it was an ambulance and two police cars. Steven felt sure the result would be the same.

He stopped at the Cumberland Farms and Marco checked the phone booth. There was a folded paper in the change receptacle, which he gave to Steven. "*Buenos dios mi amigo, no mas hombres.*"

Back on the highway Steven gave Pop the bad news from the hearing and Longo's confirmation of his deadly deed.

"It's on," Pop said. "The only way this will work is without Vito and Vinny. Put on your helmet and tighten the chin strap."

This is how it happens, Steven thought. No blazing Tommy guns, no brave shootout to protect a *Don*. It was just a business decision, damage control in a deal gone bad, and now blood was on his hands. He was on to New Jersey, where there would be more.

EPILOGUE

STEVEN

Spring 2003, Brooklyn NY

Marco helped Mom into the limo while Steven hopped around to the other side. He had stopped using the second prosthetic a few years ago, preferring the three-point support provided by the crutches and one leg. He was still athletic enough to stay balanced as he moved about, his posture was straighter and taller, and his pace actually quicker.

Marco slowly steered the limo through the winding streets of Green-Wood Cemetery while Steven and Mom sat quietly in the back. Steven wondered if this would be the last of these commemorative events. It was the fifth anniversary of Pop's death, and the number of visitors had dwindled dramatically. Uncle Eddie and Aunt Angela were there and brought one of Steven's cousins with them. Vito attended the funeral and the first anniversary, after which he publicly exclaimed "Cemeteries gimme' the heebie-jeebies" and never came back. Vinny finally pushed the wrong person too far and was killed in a parking lot shootout eight years ago. There would be no Vincenzo Catrone IV.

A handful of the old-timers paid their respects to Gino because they still used the Masciarelli money laundering schemes, but most had moved on after the Atlantic City casino closed. He and Pop used the money from the good years to invest in real estate and were able to survive the economic downturn in good financial condition. Steven and a few trusted employees manage the properties.

When Marco made it out to the city streets, Steven watched his old Brooklyn neighborhood go by until they got on the Belt Parkway and headed for their Long Island home. He took out his briefcase to check his afternoon schedule. As he sorted through some papers his eyes briefly focused on a see-through pocket with an envelope in it, then moved on. The envelope was from a Boston law firm, addressed to him, and the five-digit zip code was hand-written, each number with a different colored marker. Mom, who always notices everything her son does, put her hand on Steven's and gave it a gentle squeeze.

· · LENNY · ·

Spring 2003, Darren NH

The group on our deck included about a dozen twenty-somethings keeping a casual eye on their children as they chased each other (and our two dogs) around the large backyard. William, Sheila, Darren, and his wife were up from New York for the weekend, and Jean and Marie were hoping to join us later for hotdogs and hamburgers. I was basking in the congenial vibes, and for some reason my gaze settled on our dogs. One was a magnificent 65-pound pure-bred Standard Poodle named Fenway. Lester was the other, a mix of so many unrelated breeds that William described him as "half dog, and half dog." Fenway was showing his age, but Lester was not. And then it happened, my first new Rule to Live a Better Life in decades. But this was not a suggestion or a theory, this was a *mandate*, the Mandate of the Mutts.

Mutts live longer, healthier, and happier lives than pure-breds. They are not susceptible to hip dysplasia due to breeding for an arbitrary ideal body shape. They do not have trouble breathing through noses that have been genetically reshaped to match the acceptable profile. They are not emotional basket cases from being shrunk to a tenth of their breed's original size. They are more successful because they *inter* breed, instead of *intra* breed. They are showing the human race the key to the survival of our species, an example we have summarily ignored. We still have time, but it is fleeting. The Mandate of the Mutts can no longer be ignored.

There are some encouraging signs. The demographic that increased the most in the last census was multi-ethnic families. Here I sit, watching three generations cavort happily in the middle of one of America's whitest states, and my generation is the only one that's all white. The dozen or so members of our kids' generation include two Asians, Darren Elby Lipson's wife is African-American, and she's sporting a small baby bump, so that'll be another multi-ethnic family. The human race has a chance!

"That's your phone, Dad."

"It's on the small table behind you. Toss it here Son."

"You don't throw an iPhone," admonished my disapproving daughter. But he did, a nice soft lob over everyone's heads into my cupped hands.

"Hello? Hello? Shit, it was Mom, I think I disconnected her."

"Press the phone icon, bottom left, hit 'recents' then touch her number." The instructions came from my daughter, along with an exaggerated eye roll and giggles from her friends.

"You know if you keep doing that with your eyes they'll get stuck in that position." This was a variation of what I used to tell her when she was in kindergarten and loved to cross her eyes. That was twenty years ago, but in recognition and repudiation she crossed them now and added a stuck-out tongue. I followed her instructions and got my wife. "Sorry dear, I must have hit the wrong button. What's up?"

"I just bumped into Jean and Marie at the market, and they can make it for dinner. Do we have enough meat?"

"We'll be fine with the hot dogs, maybe a little light with the burgers. What market are you at?"

"Demoula's."

"Great. Go to the meat counter and ask for Jay."

"I'm at the meat counter and I'm staring at Jay."

"Wow. It's a bird, it's a plane, it's...Gallant Gail!"

"Oh no, Lenny, were you telling the story again?"

"Some of their friends wanted to hear how we met."

"R-i-ght. What do we need?"

"Tell Jay I'm making Lenny Burgers. He'll take some chopped meat in the back and add the ends of other meats he's got laying around. I'll probably need another pound to be sure we have enough."

"They're bringing the kids."

"Make it two pounds."

I heard her give Jay the order and then she asked, "anything else we need?"

"I don't think so. Maybe a few more ears of corn..."

"I already got that."

"Of course you did. You're Gallant Gail."

"Seriously? I hope you told the abridged version."

"Oh no! It was the full Monty, the uncut version from the original album with all the extra guitar riffs and the juicy details. They hung on every word."

"I bet they did. I'm embarrassed already." There was a hint of a giggle mixed in with her exaggerated exasperation.

"Hurry home, Dear."

Most of our kids' friends were feeling out their own relationships with significant others, and one took note of my tone during the phone conversation.

"You guys work together, don't you? Wait—are you the PALS?"

"We are. The People's Accounting and Legal Services."

"Oh my God! My parents use you. They said you were wicked awesome!"

"We enjoy it. It can get dicey when the same client tries to use both of our services. You know, there's a really funny story about the first time that happened to us…"

JESS SHAPIRO

I was born in Brooklyn in 1947 and raised on Long Island. My wife and I graduated from Penn State in 1969 and got married in 1970. After two years we quit our teaching jobs and "Turned On/Tuned In/Dropped Out" to a commune in Oregon. When we returned east we bought an old farmhouse in New Hampshire and, no longer willing to work for "The Man," started our own school. The assimilation of a couple of liberal city kids into a conservative small town was eye-opening, and an idea for a novel began to percolate. After we retired to Martha's Vineyard I got serious and finished *The Theory of the Sofa* in 2025.